ROCHESTER

By J. L. Niemann

Order this book online at www.trafford.com
or email orders@trafford.com

Most Trafford titles are also available at major online book retailers.

© Copyright 2009 J. L. Niemann.

All rights reserved. No part of this publication may be reproduced, stored in a retrieval system, or transmitted, in any form or by any means, electronic, mechanical, photocopying, recording, or otherwise, without the written prior permission of the author.

Printed in Victoria, BC, Canada.

ISBN: 978-1-4269-1639-7 (sc)
ISBN: 978-1-4269-1640-3 (dj)

Library of Congress Control Number: 2009935847

Our mission is to efficiently provide the world's finest, most comprehensive book publishing service, enabling every author to experience success. To find out how to publish your book, your way, and have it available worldwide, visit us online at www.trafford.com

Trafford rev. 12/10/2009

Trafford PUBLISHING® www.trafford.com

North America & international
toll-free: 1 888 232 4444 (USA & Canada)
phone: 250 383 6864 ♦ fax: 812 355 4082

For the men who inspired me:

*One who forced me to write,
one who supported me,
another who made me laugh,
and for the one who gives me hope.*

Foreword

IN 2006, AN excellent BBC adaptation of Charlotte Brontë's 1847 classic romance novel *Jane Eyre* starring Ruth Wilson and Toby Stephens was offered to lovers of romantic classic fiction. Following the programme's broadcast, Stephens' definitive performance led to the creation of a website celebrating his acting career and specifically his remarkable portrayal of 'Rochester'. Many already loved the gothic imagery of Brontë's tale of forbidden love, but Stephens' interpretation breathed new passion, fire and dimension into the character of 'Rochester', adding mystery and allure to one of literature's most complex and best loved leading men.

Inspired by Stephens' portrayal, a small but significant variety of fictional writing based on the characters of 'Rochester' and 'Jane' emerged on the website, some of which progressed at length, building a considerable readership following. This *Rochester* started life as one of these writings. At once in a league of its own, *Rochester* quickly gained a large and enthusiastic readership literally the world over, all who waited with bated breath, and not always patiently, for every successive chapter that flowed forth for over a year.

Divided into three parts, the first is here now in published form, honed and refined thanks to the commitment and creativity of its writer and the encouragement of many fans who wished fervently for *Rochester* to culminate in just such a published version.

This is a passionate story written for the discerning reader of romantic fiction who wants more! So often a book will offer the story of a relationship, will hint at its depths, but rarely executes the risk of taking us further. *Rochester* has taken that risk and gives to us a richly rewarding exploration of compulsive love as well as the passion of a meaningful relationship-with nothing held back.

Do not attempt to read this story as Edward Fairfax Rochester's viewpoint of the original *Jane Eyre*. For all the classic work's greatness and intensity, Brontë wrote during an inhibited era and in a fashion akin to all that was gracious, albeit close to the boundaries of acceptability for its time. This version of his story not only diverts from the original storyline in that coincidental turns of fate are discarded and true human desires are permitted, but it is written with unapologetic honesty for a modern, sexually mature audience of the 21st century, and is done so with love and emotional intelligence.

Only read this book if you are interested in a version of the classic story written from a powerful male perspective, one that explores the fullness of love in all its details; passion and desire, beauty and ugliness, frailty and strength, chaos and redemption.

It is an honour and a joy to be asked to write this foreword. Enjoy…

Debbie 'Debs' Moran
York, England   2009

Acknowledgements

Thanks to:
My family, for their endless patience.
'Tobettes' one and all for believing in me, staying with me, loving this Rochester and keeping after me through 62 posted chapters to continue telling them what he was telling me.

The 2006 BBC production of *Jane Eyre* directed by Susanna White, written by Sandy Welch, and starring Toby Stephens and Ruth Wilson for providing so much incredible inspiration.

Toby Stephens for bringing Edward's image to life.

Charlotte Brontë. Every time I read your *Jane Eyre*, something new is to be discovered, and I relearn just how powerful imagination and writing can be.

Jean Rhys for her haunting 1966 *Jane Eyre* prequel, *Wide Sargasso Sea*.

Sarah McLachlan's 1997 album *Surfacing* for serving as my imaginative soundtrack.

And to Pastors Bill Roman and Peter Rose-Kamprath of Hope Lutheran Church, Toledo, OH for giving life to *Rochester*'s 'Peter Wood'. Thank you both for all that you gave. I will never forget you.

JLN / 'Windblownrose'

Chapter 1

THERE WAS A time, a bleak and seemingly interminable time, when pleasant reflection was rather an oddity for me. Still I cannot fathom the grounds for my stint in purgatory, but nevertheless so it was. Rarely did I revisit the bygone then as I do now, finding little enjoyment in contemplating details, conversations, thoughts, actions, people. Most were closely entwined with some regrettable recollection or bound to incidents too painful to exhume, all best kept relentlessly hushed. In those days I lived only for the present. What came before, and what was yet to come, held nothing for me.

That said, amongst the few pleasing and most vivid of my earliest recollections is that of nestling upon my mother's lap, wrapped with her inside a voluminous shawl of moss green Kashmir, together watching a heavy snowfall whirl beyond a lofty window. In her south tower *atelier*, as Father named her private workspace, we sat surrounded by paintings and artists' accoutrements, quietly talking in the early hours of that New Year's morning. As yet we remained in our bedclothes having risen before Father, Rowland or any of the servants. Mother gently rocked us in her chair and warmed my chilled feet in her hands, speaking to me in the way she always did. As an equal and not as a simple-minded little dolt which was rather my other parent's wont.

"Edward darling," she dreamily murmured into my hair. "As you grow, take little interest in things that are past for they are imperfect. Permit expired time to bury its own dead. Whenever you find that the time has come to begin a new book of blank pages, take it up with pleasure. Write and draw and dream in it of hope."

I was five years old.

Wind and snow gusted beyond the glass, blending with our pensive mood that morning to create a haunting remembrance I've carried all my life. Perhaps this is owing to my losing her less than a year later, yet her words became a poignant melody repeated within myself time and again as years passed, when tides of despondency rolled in and threatened to dash my capacity for hope to matchwood. Still, I often revisit those moments, the safety of the hour's calm and my innocent surety of her permanence. How pure life was then.

For years afterward I listened to men and women talk their nonsense of refreshing optimism encountered with each January One, something akin to throwing shut windows wide to the first sign of spring. With one's slate cleared of bygone misfortune and resolved mistakes, as they would inform my jaundiced view, any heart with reason to hope might look ahead for its best days to come. I could feel their joy and be pleased for them but ever with the acrid flavour of envy.

Such was my inauspicious spiritual state on the eve of 1840, more than fourteen years into my time of affliction. Minutes ticked toward the commencement of a new decade, finding me reclined into my practiced state of melancholy as I smoked the night's final cigarette, threw back an unnumbered dose of Armagnac and cynically reflected that New Year's optimism was a fanciful heap of shit that certainly had no business with me. Though I was yet a young man (or 'young-ish' as the current dictum prescribed) and a wealthy one at that, with both vast experience collected behind and a lifetime remaining ahead, the prospect of ever knowing happiness was indelibly reduced to hollow fantasy.

Long ago I learned to accept my fate and shut away the most exalted of man's passions designed to keep us from sinking into despair: Hope. My ever-present flow of tears went dry and I carved for myself an existence that provided a measure of relief. Thereafter, from year to year nothing changed. Roaming the world, engaging in the odd superficial acquaintanceship, spending... always spending... money, time, life... such were the comforts I could obtain.

And so as the hands of my pocket watch approached midnight, sending 1839 to die away into obscurity, I extinguished my candle, listlessly lay back in bed and asked again for fate to revisit my sentence of despair.

"Hear me," I asked with a palm pressed to my heart. "Lord, if you can and will listen for my voice, then please, hear a prayer. Let this be the year."

My words were whispered into the darkness where I lay, surrounded for miles by no one and nothing but isolation, wind and sea. My hand felt the vacancy of bedclothes beside me, and I whispered into my loneliness, "I must find you, my love."

For greater than a fortnight afterward I remained there at the French seaside villa, habituated to the disappointment of unanswered prayers. Then a letter arrived and because of its summoning contents I sent my travel boxes on and soon departed myself.

Through the following days I rode northward, leaving behind my Mediterranean retreat set beneath a sky of balmy sunshine to advance deep into bitter English winter. Upon each nightfall my lodgings were made at a different roadside inn where beside my cold traveller's bed I sank down to kneeling upon floorboards and prayed in my own way.

"I do not wish to go there. Grant me strength so that I may continue. Permit me a reason to believe. This must be the year, Lord, or surely it will be my last."

Empty and despairing, I turned down the coarse sheets of an inevitably creaky bed and shivered with draughty cold, unaware that I was in fact heard and the time for my redemption chosen.

Chapter 2

Late afternoon in mid January found my journey at long last near its end. With first light I continued on the same frozen northward road, into the same biting wind as yesterday and the day before. Somnolent with the droning tramp of my horse's gallop, the unremitting cold and a dull sky above, my thoughts remained fixed upon the single bilious point sharpening odiously as I neared my destination.

Five miles from journey's end, I stopped to rest in the quiet Yorkshire town of Millcote. Leaving horse and dog sheltered against a south-facing wall, I entered The Black Swan, finding the establishment dark and deserted save for the ancient proprietor. Thoroughly numbed, I replied brusquely to his enthusiastic "Welcome home to you, Sir!" and went directly to the tavern lounge where I collapsed into a chair by the fire. Huddling before the glowing hearth I awaited my requested coffee whilst determinedly working to quell generalised discomfort.

But a few miles remained. Why did I choose to delay? And why had I already lingered so long? Departure from this area, so I reflected, was always accomplished far more expeditiously than the return to it.

'Keeping the inevitable at bay, Rochester?' suggested my oft-loquacious inner voice. Possibly the proprietor heard my muttered reply of "Belt the livid hell up", but surely I was the last to care. Thankfully he set my cup and plate down and then left me to adopt a more agreeable humour unassisted.

Half-frozen hands and feet thawed painfully as I glowered into the leaping flames. Presently I shut my eyes and concentrated on spontaneously presented images of Yorkshire, my home, in summer. Green fields backed by a blazing sun, tall grass swaying in a gentle breeze, songbirds calling. Returning to northern England was always far more bearable in warmer months than in the dead of winter, but on this occasion it could not be helped.

My daydreams wandered on, bringing images of a French Riviera eventide, all golden and crimson as the sun's fiery orb descended into the sea. Five days ago I enjoyed such a scene whilst standing alone on the porch of **Les Plages de Paradis**, a white-washed villa nestled all alone into windswept dunes; a stone's throw from the water and a world away from this place. Alone as I was for weeks and painfully lonely at times, I could feel at peace there. On the veranda I would stand with fists thrust deep into pockets, passing pensive hours listening to lapping waves and watching distant boats sail away, dreamily taking pleasure in the warm breeze on my bare neck and arms.

Despite my peaceful existence there, a hypnosis of dread came to fill my senses. As each evening beyond the turn of the year lowered sun into sea, I became ever more certain that I would soon be in England, crossing the threshold of my ancestral estate, Thornfield Hall. And once again, I would be wracked with every malevolent association thereof. A single, pithy letter from my agent brought the premonition to pass.

So here in Millcote, my journey had all but come to a close. The Black Swan's cheerful old innkeeper, brave enough to make a second attempt despite my black mood, provided added warmth in diverting my thoughts toward the particulars of local gossip. With half a century's experience attending to weary travellers, the man knew his business.

My chilled spirit thawed as I heard Millcote's inconsequential news since last I was here - whom had married whom, land bought and sold, those recently deceased, which wayward son found himself tearfully supplicating before the magistrate, and which unwed daughter's expanding belly girth afforded her sudden exile to parts unknown.

Listening absently to his lisping prattle I took coffee and fresh bread. After a time I requested to be left undisturbed and turning again to the hearth, meditatively rallied strength, warmed my body well and began to heed my own cautions to soon depart. The tavern's leaded windows were dimming to twilight gray. I stood, paid the bill and once more threw about my shoulders the black wool cloak. The innkeeper wished for me a most pleasant homecoming. I met his rheumy eyes directly and replied, "Not bloody likely," earning myself a strained smile and sinewy pat of my hand.

At the door, I fastened the cloak's steel clasp, placed hat and gloves, took the whip in hand and moved out into the street.

Winter in northern England and all about was a subdued gray or brown, bleak and silent. Naked trees quivered in the icy breeze and an overcast, steely sky hung low and oppressive. My black Arabian stallion, Mesrour, stamped restlessly on the cobbled street whilst Pilot, my Newfoundland dog, sat watchful and ready in the protection of a tailor shop awning. Once in the saddle, I wrapped the cloak closely about and took up Mesrour's reins. His ears pricked back, awaiting my signal. Pilot came to stand nearby, looking up at me expectantly.

All arrangements were made to deliver my belongings home to Thornfield and so there was no further cause for delay. I must proceed. Home unfortunately was a loathed place and the epicentre of all the shame, despair and hate that had driven me to the far reaches of Europe and back again for the past eleven years; of all the associations that led me to commit acts which now caused me to detest myself as well as their accomplices and source.

Months had passed since I last saw the Hall, since I brought young Adele to live there under the shadow of my protection and then left her. 'Hopefully,' I thought as I pulled frigid air deep within my lungs, 'within a fortnight I will escape once again.'

Mesrour stamped and shifted his weight in the icy wind blowing along the deserted street. I drew another deep breath and exhaled frozen vapour. 'Must go, Edward, must go.'

With a touch of the whip, my horse reared and we were off on the five miles homeward. Galloping over time worn roads, leaping frozen patches here and there, I glanced about at the familiar scenery. I was a boy here. Light-hearted and carefree, I roamed amongst these fields; the stone walls, stiles and trees as my companions. They comforted me now as well known objects do. My mind's eye recalled days of long ago; of playing and running through golden fields in summer, lingering in honeysuckle perfumed lanes until after sunset, searching for butterflies and other insects, and marvelling at the world's beauty.

My brother, Rowland, four years my senior and now deceased these past nine years, stole into my reverie. Ever haughty and superior, even as a child, Rowland would not condescend himself to play with me. This came as no disappointment since he did not share in my reverence for natural beauty. He took no pleasure in such cherished items as turning leaves, cloud formations or birds in flight. It was universally understood that my brother was the cherished one, the pre-ordained firstborn and heir to all things Rochester. Rowland was selfish as a child and became a cruel-hearted youth, relishing the act of killing my avian and insect treasures either to prove his superiority or simply see me cry. I quickly learned to hide precious things from Rowland as well as the grief he inflicted.

Suppression of grief. Yes. Of that I had become a master.

A misty rain began to fall as Mesrour galloped on with Pilot keeping pace behind. I turned my face to the sky and felt the fine rain wet my cheeks and lips. Blank nothingness filled all above.

"God in your heaven," I murmured. "Why hast thou forsaken me?"

An amused chuckle sounded inside my head. 'Why in the bloody hell should He not forsake you?' Conscience promptly replied. 'When you have for so long forsaken yourself?'

This was true enough. Only of late had I begun to sincerely long for a purer life than I previously knew; since the age of twenty-three when everything changed and I gave myself up for lost. The ensuing years rendered me heart weary and soul withered, and the sinful society in which I indulged throughout my purposeless roaming existence became a cankering reminder of how miserably I had failed myself. How though privileged as I was, there were some things I could never have.

I thought of Adele and the act of lifting that thin and neglected child out of destitution in Paris, an abandoned tot forsaken by her mother. Perhaps I managed to redeem myself slightly by committing this one charitable measure. Thoughts veered to Adele's mother, Celine, my former mistress. Certain as I was that Adele was not my daughter, the child would always represent irrefutable evidence of Celine's betrayal of my devotion.

Celine. The French opera dancer who charmed the gold out of my British breeches pocket and intoxicated me with her beauty and skilled lovemaking. She would expound endlessly on my male beauty, my athletic physique and the glory of my raven hair falling in waves and curls (her words, not mine.) Resignedly aware that I was not handsome by conventional definition, I eagerly consumed every drop of the sweet poison she fed me. Other men amongst our society complied far better with the popular conception of masculine beauty, and in their presence I was acutely aware of the marked differences; they with their blond hair, pale skin, thin shoulders, and soft, dainty hands and feet.

I, you see, am dark, broad shouldered and muscular. Celine assured me of her preference, whispering hotly at my ear *'mon bel ange, Edouard'*, and hungry for admiration I was easily ensnared. But it was not long before doubt, jealousy and insecurity added hints of sour to mingle with sugar-sweet. I was not entirely ignorant of the fact that my lover's true adoration was for my money. Anything she wanted I gave, whether they were jewels, gowns, and a splendid suite of rooms in a luxurious Parisian hotel, or horses and carriage at her disposal. Her caprice was evident, but I was a willing sacrifice. My pride swelled with her compliments, but there was more. With Celine I could slake my thirst for passion and take all I needed, as lust was an ever present vice I could not rein in.

At the start of our liaison I was a gentle, considerate lover, but before long I ceased to delude myself and became cognisant of her calculated lies and avariciousness. So late in the night, candles burning low, my French inamorata and I writhing amongst sensuous linens in her perfumed boudoir, I would become violent in my selfish pursuit of gratification. Caring nothing for her, I thrust wildly, ferociously, my fists full of her flaxen hair… wanting to punish her for using me. Later as we lay breathless, she would gaze into my eyes and tell me she adored me; that she would never love another. But soon the truth was laid bare. Celine was not only an accomplished dancer. She was also a supremely talented actress.

Thus I mused as my horse galloped on. I cast my eyes to the earth as shame and remorse crept into my core along with the icy wind. Surveying the desolate landscape and lulled by Mesrour's droning canter, I ceased to think in sentences, only words. Betrayal, hurt, fear, loneliness, Bertha, anger, despair, guilt. God. I want.

'You want?' Conscience sneered. 'You want what?'

My reply came without a moment's hesitation. "Love," I said aloud. "I want to love. And I want to be loved."

No reply.

Since I well knew that such a gift would forever be denied me, I placed the word amongst the others that fell hopeless upon my stone cold heart.

Upon clearing a rise, I perceived through the misty distance a first glimpse of Thornfield Hall. The old, massive stone battlements and towers rose up against the barren, sodden sky. This was my house.

'I own that damnable pile of rubble,' I thought. 'I own its secrets as well as its hateful inhabitant. Nothing short of a miracle that the entire Goddamned place has not yet burned to the ground.'

Grace Poole's last letter spoke of her charge's increasing preoccupation with fire and with all things that could burn. Now I must add pyromania to my prize's impressive list of aberrations.

The rise declined into dell and there I diverted off the carriage road, entering onto the less-frequented river path. Fog hung thick in the valley where to my right the river ran high and rapid with rain and melting snow. Noise of turbulent water rushed in my ears along with the more distant bleating of sheep grazing dead grass on the hillsides. Mist and rain bleared my eyes.

'Soon,' I told myself, 'Soon I will be warm and dry.'

Mesrour's pace slowed. His hesitation increased as visibility in this damned whiteout fog became practically nil. I refused to relent, irritated and impatient more with my thoughts than with the horse, but I whipped him mercilessly nevertheless. A bright fire and a glass of port were comforts I could obtain. Pilot was ahead now, invisible to me and barking with energy. The sheep. Yes, must be.

Quite suddenly a human form appeared out of the dense fog to stand directly in my path. It stood silent, still as death and shockingly ethereal in this microcosm of white. I started and gasped. The spell shattered as I saw the girl, for a girl it was, look up at me. She, too, was startled and stepped back defensively. No wraith would react so. Surely.

But Mesrour was skidding and rearing back, far back. We toppled. Down I went onto the coarse gravel path leaving my left leg pinned beneath the horse's weight and my ankle wedged between stone and stirrup. Searing pain shot through me, straight to my brain, sending a howl of agony reverberating through the valley. I gasped, cursing and swearing with vehemence. The horse righted himself quickly enough, and I did too, not wishing to remain prostrate on the wet ground. Upon attempting to bear weight on my left foot, another bolt of pain shot up my frame. I swore even more colourfully and leant down to feel my booted ankle. Only a sprain. Pilot was bounding about me now, barking and baying until the hills echoed.

The girl stepped out of the misty white, coming close to me. "Are you hurt, Sir?" she asked over the noise. Her voice was smooth and soft, full of genuine concern.

"Down, Pilot!" I roared whereupon silence immediately fell. I wanted to swear at this girl but checked myself, as I thought, admirably. "Witch! What are you about, lingering in the fog, scheming to fell the horse of an unwary traveller? Get off away with you!"

She stood firm. "I've as much right to this path as yourself, Sir. What's more, brusque words shall not drive me away. Seeing as your foot is injured, I should prefer to see you safely mount your horse before continuing upon my own purpose."

I looked at her then. Small and slight in build. No more than twenty years old. Her grey-green eyes were levelled directly upon mine. She was attired quaintly in plain grey with a tartan shawl, winter bonnet and leather gloves. Her face was pale but for cheeks and lips faintly rose tinted with cold. She showed no fear of me, no consternation at the situation or my rough tone. She clearly meant to help me whether I sought her help or not.

"Curious time of evening for a young miss to traipse along a secluded bridleway," I tetchily observed.

Her shoulders squared. "It is yet afternoon, Sir, and this route, to my knowledge, is generally regarded as a footpath."

The dignified yet respectful tone of her delivery stirred curiosity in me. To what house did this person belong? I foresaw no consequence in asking and so I said, "Shall I find confidence in the assumption that the objective of this twilight trek of yours, young lady, is to arrive at your place of residence? And if so, where would that be?"

"My home is Thornfield Hall, Sir, " she answered and turned to point into the thick fog. "It is only a short way along the river. I would be pleased to fetch help should you require it."

Silently I questioned whether I was dreaming and cast my eyes over her attire for a longer moment. Not a servant. Her dress and speech were certainly not that of a servant. Well what then?

She read my quizzical expression and helped me. "I am the governess."

Recollection dawned. "Bless me, of course! The governess."

The girl looked at me quizzically. Mrs. Fairfax sought through a letter some months ago for my permission to employ a governess for Adele. I replied to Thornfield's housekeeper with a terse affirmative then promptly forgot the whole business. And here she was. Would this be the manner best suited to introduce myself as her employer? I thought not. Additionally, my return to Thornfield, never announced beforehand, bespoke of an adolescent delight in flustering my employees with their master's sudden reappearance. Why should the governess be any different? I turned toward Mesrour, standing some distance away in the fog.

"Try leading him to me," I said, and then remembering civilities added, "Please. If you would be so kind."

She was clearly disarmed with the task but set her slender shoulders and walked cautiously to the stallion. Mesrour towered over her, and I smiled with amused anticipation of the forthcoming scene. She made several attempts at grasping the reins but spirited as he was, Mesrour would not permit her near his head. He reared, snorted and stamped but the girl, although frightened, persevered. 'A rare one,' I thought, surveying her posterior form.

Some moments later, I relented and called, "Come here." She turned to look at me. "Come!" I repeated. She left the agitated Mesrour and came to where I stood. "A thousand pardons," I said to her as I placed an arm about her slight shoulders. "Necessity requires me to make you useful." With that

I leaned my weight heavily upon her frame. Gentle arms went around my waist and together we moved along the gravel path toward the horse. Thus supported, I looked down on her as we progressed forward. Medium brown hair was arranged plainly, modestly. Her warmth rose and could be felt upon my cheek. I inhaled of her deeply, finding that she smelled of nothing but soap and pure water. Delicious.

The women of my privileged society delighted in liberal applications of perfume and musk, would smile coquettishly, fan themselves flirtatiously, wear elaborate gowns of expensive fabrics and adorn themselves with jewels. This girl was none of that. I found myself dazzled.

Surely I was dreaming. Yes, here in this swirling fog, I was in a most pleasant embrace, utilitarian as it was, with this most fascinating creature. She wanted nothing from me. In fact she desired only to give her assistance. A chilling thought entered my mind. Had I ceased to live somewhere along the journey home? Had I died and this little form so close to me now was an angel taking me to the hereafter?

'Steady on, Rochester. She is the governess. Your governess.'

We approached Mesrour and I grasped the reins, mastering him directly. With regret I took my arm from around the warm shoulders so pleasurably leant upon and sprang up into the saddle, wrenching my ankle painfully in the process. I drew a deep breath and looked down at the girl. Her face was turned up to mine. I surveyed her look steadily. Creamy white skin. Full lips. Those grey-green eyes continued to meet mine directly. Conventional opinion would label this girl plain. Not displeasing, but plain. I thought her lovely, standing there looking up at me in the misty rain. I wanted to touch her soft skin and feel its warm smoothness underneath my fingertips. My whole being wanted her close to me again as she had been a few moments since.

"Thank you, Miss...?"

"Jane Eyre, Sir," she replied clearly.

Jane Eyre. I nodded, looking about our murky and bleak surroundings. I did not like leaving her here in this solitary river valley with dusk descending by the minute and considered for a moment ordering her to step upon my boot-toe to mount the horse with me. I would take her home. The prospect of having her in close proximity again appealed strongly. I would open my cloak and wrap her inside with me, riding with my arm about her waist, sharing warmth and breathing her in, perhaps walking Mesrour slowly the remainder of the way to Thornfield. Where was she going anyway?

But I discarded the impulse, reminding myself that I was her employer and professional decorum must be observed outwardly, never mind what longings burned within.

I looked down on her as she patiently awaited leave and said, "The afternoon grows dark and the river runs high. You should not be out. Return to Thornfield directly."

Miss Eyre levelled her cool, steady gaze at me and replied, "Once I've been to Hay and have seen my letter posted, I shall do exactly that."

Independent, this one. And self-reliant. Her expression said more. It said, 'And who are you, Sir, to tell me what to do?' I found her countenance as easy to read as a favourite page of poetry. It was all right there. So open and so completely without deception. I also read curiosity there and some annoyance. Our chance meeting had, after all, interrupted her progress as well. And now the rain was turning to sleet.

So she was going into Hay to post a letter. She had a good forty-minute's brisk walk there and back, returning along this path well after dark. Fresh, new sentiments welled up inside... protectiveness, for one, but jealousy lurked there too. To whom was she sending a letter? Who existed in her life that was so important she might traverse bitter weather in sending correspondence?

'Well, I must not detain her,' I thought. 'Let her go.'

With my hat secured in place, I took the whip in hand and said down to her, "Make haste with your errand, Miss Jane Eyre. You must hurry home without delay."

Her inquisitive face remained turned up to mine as Mesrour bounded forward. I whipped the horse into a gallop. "Jane. Jane," I said aloud and delighted in the thrill of mingling her name with the word 'home'. Looking back I saw nothing but thick fog, and that intensifying protectiveness constricted my heart all the more.

'She will get back very well,' I told myself. 'Do not fear for her.'

Before long, the river path was left behind, a burbling causeway crossed and Thornfield's drive entered. The gates were closed and so I let myself in. No longer wracked with deep foreboding, I noticed a smile playing on my lips. Thornfield appeared, as I stood surveying it in the freezing rain, genial... actually. I wanted to be here, wanted to move about its environs and resume my post as Master of the Hall. Upon dismounting my horse and with Thornfield's familiar cobbles beneath my feet, I smiled and felt hope. I felt anticipation and comfort in knowing that Jane Eyre would soon be coming back. Leaving Mesrour in the stable, I managed with only moderate difficulty to cross the courtyard and entered the Hall through the front door.

Chapter 3

THE ENTRANCE HALL was silent, save for the soft ticking of an antique clock down the corridor. Candlelight flickered from ironwork sconces on the stone walls. 'Cold in here,' I thought, 'but dry at least.' I regretted walking from the stable unassisted. Painful as the effort had been I did manage, but searing pain was now accompanied by an undeniable swelling constricted by my boot.

I made my way into the musty and darkened study, the air smelling of damp ashes. Glancing at my desk it appeared in the gloom to remain precisely as I left it, strewn with maps, papers, books and artefacts of my preoccupations with entomology and ornithology, the mounted insects and preserved birds wearing a thin coating of dust. I moved to the hearth; its grate cold and neglected. No cheerful fire had warmed this room for months. With my sodden riding cloak thrown off, I fell back on the unyielding bottle-green leather sofa, rested my head back and sighed as my foot throbbed incessantly. My riding breeches were rain soaked and I longed for a hot bath. Fatigued and thoroughly chilled, my previously buoyant spirits again sank like a dead weight.

Presently I awakened from my gloom to the rustling of dress skirts and footsteps in the hall. Leah, Thornfield's cook/housemaid, peered through the doorway and took the knob as if to shut the door, unaware that I watched her from the darkness. This I could not resist.

"Leah!" I barked.

She gasped, hands to mouth and eyes round. "Oh! My goodness! Sir, you've come back!"

"Well yes, apparently so. Go find John and bring him here. And pour for me a glass of port. And tell John that Mesrour requires tending but have him come here first. And light a fire and some candles in this damnable cold room."

Leah rang for help then flitted about the room, lighting candelabra and arranging kindling with coal. Meanwhile I gingerly lifted my leg onto the sofa. My sofa, dammit, if I wanted to put my boots on it.

"The port, Leah, the port!"

She hurried to pour my wine and set the sherry glass on a nearby end table with a trembling hand. I took a deep swallow then slammed the glass down, surprising myself that it did not shatter. Port gave nowhere near the punch required for this upcoming ordeal.

"To hell with these dainty doses! Bring a tumbler of whisky, Leah, and be quick!"

She halted her bustling and looked at me strangely, then left the room to fulfil the task, returning presently with a crystal tumbler containing no less than six ounces of amber liquid. Was she trying to kill me? Well, fine actually, just the dose I required. I put the glass to my lips and threw back the contents in two bolts, relishing the inferno in my chest as it went down. Soon, both pain and perception were pleasingly dulled. As a good fire leapt and crackled in the grate, I absorbed its heat with much pleasure.

Minutes later, John entered the study and regarded me with a phlegmatic, "Sir." A taciturn fellow of advanced years, John was never much for effusions of welcome or farewell which was fine with me because nor was I.

"John, come here and pull this boot off of me," I beckoned. "And careful going, my ankle is sprained."

He smirked a gap-toothed grin and took rough hold of my boot. After several excruciating attempts it was off, and I lay gripping the sofa and heaving deeply. Leah spoke the words I could not; for John to summon Dr. Carter immediately. With a nod he departed.

Left alone once Leah went to fetch Mrs. Fairfax and my supper, I effectively returned fully to my customary foul temper as master of Thornfield Hall and lay back on the sofa, subduing my pain and scowling at the fire. Would it be better to meet with Grace tonight or wait until daylight? 'To hell with it,' I thought. 'Wait until daylight.' The whisky, not my preferred poison but efficacious nonetheless, left me placidly numb and without vitality enough to endure a north tower visit tonight. As the fire crackled and leapt, I returned to the single pleasant glimmer buoying my soul. Grey-green eyes.

Soft, smooth skin. Full and enticing lips. She was like a shimmering star on an otherwise black night. 'Jane... Come home, Jane.'

The clock in the hall struck seven. I looked to the diamond paned casement windows now dark with freezing rain falling fast and tapping the glass. I should have brought her home with me. My eyes shut and I envisioned riding with her in the saddle; my arm firmly about her waist, the cloak enclosing us both, and her slight shoulders against my broad chest. Breathing at her ear. She, offering her neck. Damn all professional decorum! Damn that letter!

A knock at the study door shattered my pleasant dream and announced the housekeeper's entrance. Mrs. Alice Fairfax was a distant relation by marriage who this year would celebrate her twenty-seventh year in the Rochester employ. An admirable and punctilious stewardess, Mrs. Fairfax managed my sprawling estate most satisfactorily in my absence. As a spry sexagenarian, more buxomly stout than ever and bearing a florid complexion grown downright crimson upon my unexpected return, she bustled into the study and launched into her effusive airy chatter. Welcoming me warmly, pacing about, gesticulating and fretting on the weather, the dreariness of winter, the outrageous price of coal etc., she called to mind a corpulent goose attempting to take flight and honking for all it was worth. I turned away, unable to suppress a smile.

Mrs. Fairfax positioned a table before me and set my supper down, all the while continuing her rapid talk; tsk-tsking my long journey and the treacherously frozen roads as affronts of consequence to almost supersede my injury. Stopping my ears with the heels of my hands might appear ruder than even I dared, but the impulse presented itself nonetheless. Instead I fixed my stare on the fire and launched into consumption of my repast, absently nodding to her questions and ignoring those that sought verbal response. Thankfully she soon lost interest and went to fetch her knitting basket.

Once fed and of a more agreeable mind, I posed inquiries for her beginning with, "All has been well here I trust, Mrs. Fairfax?"

"Oh yes, Sir," she said, looking up from her stocking or under-drawers or whatever it was she knitted. "Nothing but a quiet, wearisome winter. No incidents to speak of."

I nodded. "And Adele?"

"Oh! Mr. Rochester! That child has been the heart and soul of this house. Such a perfect joy she is," the housekeeper gushed. "Sophie has already put her to bed. Would you wish for me to wake her?"

"No, no. Leave her," I said and fixed my eyes again on the fire. "And ah, what of the governess mentioned in your most recent letter? You had found someone if I recall correctly. You spoke highly of an appropriate person's qualifications and references."

"Miss Eyre! So fortunate I was to find that young lady, I assure you, Sir. Such an excellent teacher for Miss Adele she is and an invaluable companion for me on these long winter evenings."

I looked at the old lady. Perhaps this was the reason Miss Eyre wished to go walking at this time of evening and in such inclement weather. "Where is our new governess at present?" I asked. "I wish to interview her myself. Fetch her."

"Sir, I am terribly sorry. She volunteered to go into Hay to post a letter for me. I said she should not go. The walk is so far and the weather really is not..."

But I ceased to hear her, occupied as I was in enjoying the evaporation of jealousy. Still, there could be a man in Jane's life. Perhaps she was promised to someone; the son of a family acquaintance? Also, I considered, it was not unheard of for a woman her age to be widowed. I would uncover all answers at first opportunity but not tonight. I was weary and morose. No need to drag Miss Eyre's spirits down along with mine.

Dr. Carter arrived soon thereafter, proceeded to wrap my ankle and assured me of no broken bones. Then after providing instructions for rest and elevation as well as leaving with Mrs. Fairfax an analgesic elixir, he departed. John helped me up the stairs to my chamber where a fire burned merrily in the hearth, and my bed, lain with fresh linens, awaited. I dismissed John and undressed, peeling away the wet breeches, unbuttoning my pullover linen shirt and discarding all in a sodden heap by the door. At the fire I knelt before the heat and warmed my dampened skin, rubbing bare thighs and arms free of cramping stiffness. How incredibly pleasurable this was after so many hours tensed with chill. Dreamily my eyes opened and shut, envisioning her.

The river path. My arm around a young woman and hers around me. Oh, I could smell her sweet freshness and feel her slight form beneath my weight. Her shape captivated me as did the touch of her slender, delicate, feminine hands. My palms met black, curled hair over my chest and followed its central line down and down.

'Touch me. Jane. Do not be afraid. Soft, creamy cheeks. Lush lips. Caress me.'

Opening my eyes, the emptiness of life alone quite engulfed me. Although the urge was strong to do so, I did not cry. Not tonight when instead I could anticipate her return. I wrapped myself in a dressing gown, went to the window and waited for her there. Downstairs, the entryway clock struck eight.

An hour passed. 'Why does she not come?' My eyes strained, searching for a little form battling through wind and rain. I hoped Mrs. Fairfax would have the good sense to prepare a hot bath for her or a pot of tea at the very least. Presently I did see a slender, feminine form enter the courtyard below, lightening my heart considerably with relief. She did not hurry nor seem dejected in posture. My glimpse of her was brief, and so once Jane disappeared from my view, I removed my dressing gown and slipped into downy bedclothes.

Warm, flickering firelight cast deep shadows as the steady patter of rain on glass lulled and consoled me. Too weary for anxious musings, I shut my eyes and welcomed sleep where I could meet a particular young lady alone in recollection, her face turned up to mine in the misty rain.

There, in the murky river valley once more, I did not let slip the opportunity to fully kiss her upon those inviting lips. In my fantasy, her resistance, strong at first, gradually wavered and soon she was kissing me in return, her face turned up to the freezing rain now glistening upon her lovely soft cheeks, hungrily tasting my mouth.

Thus content, I slept.

In the night I woke to wind howling and shrieking in the courtyard and around my casement. Sleet mixed with dense snow to scour the windowpanes upon each forceful winter gust. In the hearth a low fire and glowing embers burned, the room thus fallen cold and dim. I lay in bed and listened. Whether the shrieking came from outside or above, I could not be certain, but the sound changed in pitch and timbre, high and hysterical one moment then low and sobbing the next. I shuddered, eyes scanning the bedchamber's shadiest corners, imagining the possibilities. Soon, I drifted back into sleep where fitful and bizarre dreams ebbed like tides in and out of my sleeping consciousness, bringing unsettling dreams filled with foreboding images.

I woke again as the clock struck three and felt a breeze cross my face. My breath was held. Was I not alone? I waited, listening, nerves coming unstrung, looked about and waited still.

Nothing. Only the wind.

But sleep did not come again until dawn when first light permeated the room and I fell into a deeper sleep where a far differing dream awaited me.

In it I walked over an expansive field at sunset surrounded by warm golden light and waving timothy grass all about me. My fingers were entwined with those of an angel dressed in filmy sheer white, and I led her deep into the fields. Finally coming to a stop, I there lay her down in the grass. Her grey-green eyes fastened upon mine; her firm, slender body beneath me. I caressed her cheek with gentle fingertips and brought my mouth to hers. She held me, wanted me and drew in my quickening breaths. She kissed me the way a woman in love kisses a man. I needed to look upon her, and our lips parted. She sighed and breathed 'My Edward. My love.'

Sleep took me away.

Chapter 4

THE SUDDEN TWITTER of squabbling starlings upon my casement sill announced the arrival of morning in a singularly pestilential fashion. As if their incessant noise was not irksome enough for one so averse to early rising as I, glaring daylight flooded my chamber between drapes I had forgotten to close. Both might have been ignorable but for the triple annoyance of a tentative knocking at my chamber door followed by a gravelly masculine "Sir?" John had come to wake me and build a fire in the darkened chamber hearth.

I sighed and testily called, "Come!"

My lone male servant shuffled into the bedchamber and regarded me with a perfunctory nod, then set silently about his morning duties. The room was so bitterly cold that I waited in my warm bed with the quilted coverlet pulled up high to preserve both warmth and the residual exhilaration of early morning dreams.

Eventually I deemed it necessary to consider what lay ahead for the day. A meeting with my agent, Philip Bennett, could be expected in which we would review the books, rent receipts, current and expired mortgages, etc. I could also anticipate the arrival of my land broker, Alex Gilger, to discuss the acquisition of a large and desirable parcel situated nearby. And possibly the local vicar, Peter Wood, might pay his respects since awareness of my presence always proved to travel with disarming rapidity. Additionally, there was the arrangement made last night through Mrs. Fairfax to meet with

Grace Poole late in the afternoon. Then, this evening, once all tedium was behind me, I would summon Jane Eyre and her pupil to my presence.

Within a quarter of an hour, I was out of bed, unwrapping my foot of Dr. Carter's handiwork and preparing to soak in the bath. In the tub I sank down, groaning as hot water eased and loosened aching muscles, then shaved and afterward took care to dress formally.

An accurate word to further describe that sedulously productive day would be 'tedious'. By early afternoon, a cracking temporal headache had driven me into a malignant mood and I returned to my chamber, leaving the door ajar and curtains drawn to shut out aggravating light. In the semi-darkness I lay across the bed with an arm over my eyes and attempted to doze, but the voices of a woman and child approaching along the gallery woke me. My heart leapt, recognising the speakers immediately. She was near my chamber door now. Silently I repositioned myself to watch her movements unseen.

Jane and Adele, wearied of the schoolroom, had come upstairs for the gallery windows' snowy view over Thornfield's far-reaching grounds. There they lingered for a time, talking in mixed English and French on the wintry landscape and lapsing into impromptu instruction on local geography and cardinal directions. Adele soon tired of her lessons and fidgeted and whinged as Jane patiently persevered. But as the clock downstairs struck the hour, teacher permitted student to scamper off in search of her nurse. Jane remained at the gallery windows, leaning with palms on the marble sill and making pictures in condensation on the glass.

Silently I turned over on my bed and propped on elbows to better see her, to study her shape, slender shoulders and petite waist. Without a bonnet, her hair no longer appeared medium brown but instead, in the light of the gallery windows, the colour was a rich chestnut brown, parted along the centre and plaited and coiled in a thick knot at her nape. I wanted to see it unbound and spilling over her shoulders, down her back, brushed smooth, prepared for bed. She sighed and paced the matting, smiling to herself occasionally with thoughts, I fancied, upon some pleasant dream or remembrance. I was anxious for the evening when pointed questions might be asked and, under the guise of an inquisitive employer, she could be drawn out.

I wanted to know her, to discover her character, tease away each layer of who she was and establish the essence of her core. Why? I did not with good reason know why, except that as a man I was attracted to her. She fascinated me, as yet without definition or reason. Fleeting grounds for such keen interest to be sure.

Mrs. Fairfax called to Jane from downstairs whereupon she turned and abruptly left my view. I listened to her rapidly receding step, then turned onto my back and gazed at the bed hangings above, angry with her for leaving my sight. Darker suggestions wove their way into my thoughts, ones reminding me that I knew nothing of this girl. Her background and parentage were mysteries to me, as were her ambitions for the present and future. No actual conversation had yet transpired to give substance to her appeal. She well could bear despicable flaws of personality, might be shallow, base and unoriginal. Or worse! What if after shown due regard, she blushed and flirted with me, fawning coquettishly as both unwed and wed ladies seemed reflexively to do in my presence? Would she admire all I said and did, complementing my dress, my home and my person in response to the most tentative like regard? Would she see in me, as did scores of others, opportunity? I had yet to be intimate with a woman who did not cherish a deeper love for my money than for me, and so sincerity in that tender sentiment was a foreign concept for me. Perhaps this Jane was no better than all the rest; no more genuine, no more innocent and no more capable of meshing with my heart or mind.

Ruminating on these possibilities, my surly capacity for reason decided that I had given this stranger governess far too much undue credit. Young Miss Eyre was my employee and nothing more. At the time of our meeting on the river path yesterday eve, I was mired in a dreadful state of despondency, loathing a return home, permitting myself a rare rehash of painful memories, ruminating on my longing for love, when she stepped into my path as if in response to my wretched thoughts. Surely it was mere happenstance that she did. How foolish of me to give myself over to favour not remotely earned!

Yet, since meeting this Jane Eyre, she occupied my thoughts constantly. I could scarcely concentrate upon a single thought otherwise, and regardless of effort, I returned continually to daydreams of loving her, being loved by her and, to my self-condemnation, of bedding her.

I recalled the scene by the river yesterday. Any other young miss of her station would have blushed and stammered in my presence, shown fear and given whispered apologies before hurrying away. But Miss Eyre proved herself something extraordinary. The concern in her voice. Her willingness to help a man whom she had never before seen and might never see again. A man who spoke to her most churlishly, as I since regretted. Her independence and poise, her loveliness; none could be erased from my mind.

This seemed an alarming lack of control over my own consciousness. I counselled myself that the stress of returning home to Thornfield was enough to trigger any variety of fond fantasies in a habitually battered nature and so had nothing at all to do with Miss Eyre as a person. She, like all common hirelings, must earn every scrap of regard I bestowed upon her. Interest in her beyond the duties of a governess must be quieted immediately.

I moved from bed to sofa and sat scowling at the fire, vexed with myself for such weakness and angrier with Jane Eyre for capturing the potential to disappoint me.

She *could* disappoint me. This evening might prove yet again how completely poor a judge of character I could be. She lured me, quite unintentionally to be sure, but still I resented her for it and was now left feeling utterly foolish. Where females were concerned, I consistently found myself intimately associated with the most mercenary and integrity flawed of the entire crew, without exception.

A governess! Half my age at least! Bah! And yet my defences were effortlessly thrown down to lay prostrate at her feet.

Watching flames leap within the hearth, I cracked my knuckles, crushing back benevolent feelings like discarded matter beneath my boot-heel. A malignant smirk crossed my face. I knew the way to behave with her now.

Chapter 5

THIS VIRULENT STATE of mind did not improve as the afternoon progressed. A brief conference with Grace Poole in the north tower clinched that. I dined alone and as evening approached moved into the library where I took my place in a high-backed Rococo armchair near the fireplace fender and commenced with smoking and drinking as if tomorrow might never come. I half hoped it would not.

A low seat was precisely placed on the carpet in bright firelight, a short distance from mine. Resentment of past, present and future wrongs now seized me absolutely. Disappointment was my inevitability, and although excitement pinged every nerve, I planned to meet its source with defences held high.

The library was chill on that January night despite a bright fire burning in the hearth. No candles lit the room's recesses leaving deep shadows to enclose my carefully constructed setting of intimate conversation. The clock ticked and the fire crackled. Thornfield was otherwise silent. As the seven o'clock hour approached, Leah came quietly to refill my port without a word exchanged. My wrapped ankle I propped on an ottoman, and one hand adjusted my tie and collar while I continued to sip, wondering as I had done for hours how Jane would be with me. Brought low by doubt and thus mired in a murk of surliness, I rallied my guard and prepared to see eagerness quenched by anticlimax. I was determined to either move beyond uncertainty and appreciate a fresh association, or be done with the girl and block her out. Whatever the ruling by evening's end, proper conduct prescribed playing the stern, exacting master throughout. In spite of my best effort to appear and to *be* indifferent, feelings fluctuated more wildly with each anticipatory minute.

Impatiently I sighed and fidgeted, wanting only to commence my performance. I glowered into the fire and chided my nerves as they leapt with each noise in the corridor and beyond. This would never do. An indelible boundary must be lain down, one in which I would never be tempted to cross.

Adele arrived first, bringing Pilot with her. "*Bonsoir*, Monsieur Rochester!" she sang out in her piping voice.

"Sit down, child," I grumbled.

She sidled to my chair's arm and said in a honeyed tone, "*Tu m'as tant manque.*"

"Hah! You missed me you say, little Varens. Of course you did," I mocked. "True to the fibre of your French nature, Adele, with your very existence hinging upon the receipt of gifts, the only *grand désir* sweetening your wee heart is that of claiming a present."

She hopped about, clapping her hands. "*Oh! Un cadeau pour moi?*"

"In English, Adele! When you are in this country you will speak the native language. Have you learned nothing in my absence these past months?"

"Quite the contrary," she saucily replied in thick accent. "My English is very good. I have an excellent teacher."

"Yes, so Mrs. Fairfax informs me. What in blazes has become of your teacher tonight? She is late and keeps me waiting."

The child wagged a finger at me. "No, she is not late since it is not yet seven. Ah! You are cross and have been drinking port, Monsieur. You must not frighten my Miss Eyre."

I promptly banished the child to a shady corner, charging her to quietly amuse herself there until such time I deemed her behaviour worthy of my attention, much less a present. She obeyed with a smirk, knowing from experience that I would not disappoint.

More minutes ticked by. I mulled and sipped. Child prattled to dog. Finally, the clock began to chime. Upon the seventh tone, the faint sweep of a dress could be heard in the doorway behind. Then came Adele's beckoning gestures and whispers confirming Jane's arrival.

"Miss Eyre!" I called out.

"Yes. Good evening, Mr. Rochester," came her voice from some distance behind.

"Must you linger there in the shadows where I cannot see you?" I asked without turning. "Come forward! Sit by me."

Seconds ticked before she moved, apparently gathering her mettle to enter into the firelight and my observance. I sighed, testily tapping fingers on the chair's arm. She advanced, met my eyes and nodded, then primly took the seat offered, perching there with a back straight and hands folded.

Boldened with drink, I looked her over for a long moment before speaking. Again attired in nondescript grey, Jane appeared in the same modest fashion as earlier that day. The flickering light accented her skin. I found myself studying the softness of it, the warmth and youth of her face, all with fully concealed but wilful enjoyment. Her dark lashed eyes meanwhile roamed over the shelved books, mantle piece, paintings on wood and canvas, down to her scuffed boot-toes, which upon my notice were quickly retracted beneath her skirts. I smiled at that.

"From where do you come to us, Miss Eyre?"

She lifted her chin and met my eyes again. "Lowood Institution, Sir."

The name struck a faint chord of memory and I spent a moment in thought, placing it until a vague but surely infelicitous connotation was formed. "Charity school," I recalled. "Religious academy for orphaned and impoverished girls. Not so?"

"Yes, Sir."

"Right. I read of it some years ago. Overseen by a parson. His name was.... Brock... Brocking..."

"Brocklehurst," she tonelessly confirmed. "You are correct on all counts."

"Hm. And your parents?"

She smoothed her skirts. "I have none."

Her frankness further piqued me. "I see. No family at all?"

"No one, Sir."

"Then where is your home?"

She exhaled sharply and almost smiled. "But for here, Thornfield Hall, I have no home."

I looked at her and let those points absorb. "Surely you were placed into the guardianship of such a school under the attentiveness of some... person?"

She nodded. "Yes, Sir, I was. My uncle's wife. Her consent was required upon my departure from Lowood to strike out on my own as it were, but there is no remaining familial connection. I have not seen nor exchanged a letter with her for more than eight years."

"Eight years. At which time you were sent to school."

"That is correct."

"What age were you then?"

"About ten."

"And so you are now eighteen," I wryly concluded. "Mathematics, you see, is useful in a variety of situations."

Quietly she replied, "Yes, Sir. Indeed."

The Lowood name once held the infamous reputation of lamentable living conditions for its young pupils. Newspapers across northern England ran regular feature pieces nearly a decade ago on a typhus epidemic resulting in death for more than half the student population. Editorial debate on accountability and a public outcry for the school's appointment of a more financially responsible and benevolent committee was fierce. Betterment did come about over time, but shortly thereafter I abandoned England for the Continent and read nothing more of it.

I looked Jane over again and gauged her size small, build slim and skin pale. No doubt her history was one of fairly severe hardship. Details on what life dealt her before entering that abhorrent institution I did not ask, knowing that some memories are too personal and painful to revisit.

'Perhaps one day,' I thought, 'I will earn her confidence and she will tell me all.'

Jane looked to me more openly now, and I wondered what she saw as her eyes rose and fell over my face.

"You have friends, surely," I suggested. "Fellow pupils? Teachers?"

She shrugged ever so slightly. "Yes, there were acquaintances in associate teachers at the same school. The local postmistress was also very pleasant to me upon our few meetings." She searched her thoughts for other possibilities but had nothing more. "Interaction outside of the school was nearly non-existent, Sir. I had one close friend, her name was Helen, but she died at school a number of years ago."

In watching her face I could not determine whether she blushed or if nearness to the hearth was what warmed her complexion. I decided her high colour was due to the fire. She showed no evidence of shame or discomfiture otherwise.

In response to her equanimity, I charged into the remainder of the topic. "So you would have the world believe you've no husband, no intended, no parents, no one outside of Thornfield's environs to call your own?"

A flicker of amusement brightened her. "Does this disturb you, Sir? Mrs. Fairfax is in possession of my antecedents and character references should you wish me to fetch them for you."

Grinning, I sipped my port and replied, "I've seen them. And no, I am not concerned for the veracity of your story."

In my partially benumbed state, I fell to mulling pleasantly; comfortable in sharing silence with my unassuming companion. It seemed she existed in an identically lonely circumstance as I, something that intensified my fascination thousands-fold. Previously quashed sentiments of protectiveness sprang to life. With no one outside of Thornfield by way of kindred, I found an unexpected pleasure in substituting my house for her home. Thus far I was impressed but would not yet permit surliness to be checked.

My gaze moved lingeringly over her ivory skin and full lips. Abruptly I asked, "Do you think me handsome, Jane?"

"No, Sir!" was her startled, ready reply to which I gave an acerbic laugh. Although I did not expect her to say 'yes', it did wound for her to answer so rapidly in the negative.

"Why in heaven's name not?" I pressed, leaning forward. "I suppose I posses all the features of any other man. Tell me, what is it you find so offensive?"

She shook her head and blushed in deep discomfiture. "Mr. Rochester, I am terribly sorry. I spoke too quickly. It was a blunder…"

"One for which you will be answerable. Does my brow not please? My jaw, nose or eyes are not right with you? Or is it my frame with which you find fault?"

Her gaze followed where I led, then finally she did meet my eyes. "Please Sir, allow me to disown my original reply. I was too abrupt. I should rather have said 'beauty is of little consequence' or 'one's character within is what makes a person.'"

"What crocks of nonsense!" I laughed. "Certainly no other of your feminine ilk would quest for such depth over beauty. And I see you only give such ready reply upon cross-questioning."

"Begging your pardon, Sir," she said vehemently, "I've never equated beauty with virtue or graciousness, and wealth certainly is no barometer for goodness either."

"Oh? Is that right, Miss Eyre?" I pushed as my interest became piqued almost to impropriety. Clearly she was far from the likes of fawning females checkering my past, but I meant to challenge her sincerity nevertheless. "If you were to learn that I am worth upwards of sixty thousand pounds, young lady, surely your low opinion of my physiognomy would improve exponentially. You might even think me the most handsome man you'd ever seen."

She looked at me steadily; pink rising again to her cheeks. "I have happened upon very few men in my life, Mr. Rochester, and can therefore count myself a poor judge of masculine beauty. But I should think that any man who might draw my eye will do so with nothing but inner allure, and only upon its certain evidence will he be beautiful to me."

That silenced me.

Her eyes swept over my brow, hair and skin, then conspicuously studied my eyes, building her own impression of the man inside. I watched as she unabashedly surveyed me. My gaze was the first averted for I feared what her sagacious observation might find. Remorse, shame and sinfulness were there in force. A damaged person was the core she would find, for inside myself, that was all there was.

On my guard, I lifted my eyes to hers once again and formed a perception of my own. Jane wore a presence about her; a profundity of spirit and intelligence combined with a subtle, untapped sensuality. She drew me in, and my fright of that magnetism fascinated me all the more.

Jane arose abruptly from her seat and turned to address the child playing quietly in the firelight's periphery. "The time grows late, Adele," she cautioned.

"I unnerve you, Miss Eyre," I said, "because I talk candidly. The hour is not so late, and I have not yet finished with questioning you. Let Sophie take Adele up to bed."

Jane turned in surprise to see Sophie in the shadowy doorway behind, having not heard her approach. Nurse whispered to child, "**Enfant! Il est temps de dormir**," and Jane watched with a shade of discomfiture as Adele bade me goodnight and attempted to kiss my cheek, then hurried away to her nurse.

I robustly ordered, "Yes, child! Upstairs to bed with you!"

From the doorway Adele all but wailed in her melodramatic best, "Monsieur! But what of my gift? I've waited patiently and been so quiet! Did you not think of me while you were away? Have you nothing for me?"

"Oh for God's sake, yes! Yes! You may find your **boite** atop the piano over there. Spare me the particulars of your rapture as you take it away."

The child shrieked with delight, then stopped to nibble a finger before saying, "You brought nothing for Miss Eyre?"

"Out!" I commanded menacingly.

Adele took her box and Sophie's hand, quitting the room. Her piping voice could be heard extolling the virtues of fine gifts all the way up to the nursery.

Jane and I were left alone. The young governess remained standing and turned to me in profile, examining a painting above the mantel and clearly unaware of the vantage point presented for any man's appreciative eye. I took full advantage of it. Delicate shoulders, narrow waist, rounded bottom. I swallowed down port and licked my lips.

"Did you expect a present, Miss Eyre?" I asked her. "Are you fond of presents?"

"I have little experience of them, Sir, and no cause to think myself entitled to one now."

"You fall back on over-modesty. Adele, though not bright nor particularly talented, has in a short time made significant improvement."

Jane again caught herself in a remote smile. "You have given me my *cadeau*, Mr. Rochester. Please be assured that your thoughtful consideration is met with my gratitude. There is no finer reward for a teacher than praise of her pupil's progress, and so I thank you." Her undertone of irony was more playful than impudent. She did not fear me, nor my almost insolent manner of questioning, but in fact seemed enlivened by it.

Jane looked from the painting to me. "You are an admirer of Pieter Brueghel's works, Mr. Rochester."

Again she surprised me. "Selected pieces," I agreed. "That one above the mantel I claimed at auction in Brussels. My competitors yielded with little fight, I was so openly covetous of it. A Moroccan shipping magnate outbid me for the Brueghel piece I wanted most; *Haymaking*. Bah! What did he know of haymaking?"

She studied the painting further. "This one is called *The Harvesters* if I recall correctly. It was originally was done in oil on wood." Then she looked more closely and added sceptically, "This isn't...?"

"Good God, no!" I laughed. "I may be well-off, Miss Eyre, but the purchase of a 1565 original Brueghel is categorically beyond my means. What you see there is a copy completed by his son."

"Gracious," she mused while studying it on tiptoes. Accustomed mainly to the jaded society of the over-privileged, I found her awe most pleasing.

"Such an impressive work, Sir. I do find that the son's copies place greater emphasis on landscapes and less so on the humanity of his father's peasant subjects."

I nodded, surprised by her acumen. "Similar perspectives have been widely argued for two and half centuries, Miss Eyre. Tell me, what renders a convent school-girl so well versed in the science and skill of visual arts?"

"I pored for hours over volumes of this dynasty and other Reformation artists throughout my childhood, Sir. Not whilst at Lowood to be sure since fine pictorial books could certainly never pass a school board censorship referendum. Mrs. Reed on the other hand had not the least care what I spent my time looking through."

"Mrs. Reed."

"My uncle's wife."

"Ah. So you were studying artists' technique before the age of ten," I sardonically summarised. "Heavy handed material for a little girl. That would be akin to Adele taking an interest in the works found scattered about this stone fortress. You may have perused them by now. My father harboured a penchant for the elder Brueghel's more disturbing depictions of social commentary."

Jane turned and said over her shoulder. "Adele and Sophie are frightened of them, Sir. Particularly *Battle of Carnival and Lent* hanging near the north tower entrance. They avoid that piece at all costs despite my having explained its intended meaning."

We went on to discuss the painting and its multitude of depictions encompassing a ritual of eating, drinking and carousing before the forty days of Lent. Her interpretations were analytic, philosophical and exceedingly well articulated. I found myself completely disarmed and could not recall ever having had such a conversation with a woman in my life. Her mind was a rich, fertile landscape, clearly suited for far greater than her narrow lot afforded. My guardedness of uncovering a disingenuous nature in her was washing away. The initial impression formed upon our first meeting, of a true and genuine character, was quite correct. Still, I strove to maintain a stony exterior and when she suddenly, moments later, seemed to remember her subordinate place in my house and followed it with motions to excuse herself for the night, I protested with greater vehemence than intended. Worse, I grasped her wrist and forcibly drew her back down into the low seat.

"Sir!" came her surprised exclamation.

"Young lady, tonight you will remain with me for as long as I keep you. The fire is not sufficient company to divert my repellent thoughts, nor is Pilot, nor is simple dame Fairfax, not a prattling brat, nor Thornfield's servants. I do not want a book and I do not want to watch the silence of falling snow. The burden of my melancholy rests with you." I eased and released her wrist. "Talk to me for a little while longer."

Her eyes widened. "What more would you like me to talk about?"

"Anything of your choosing."

She fell silent, setting her mouth to a grim line.

After a full minute I asked, "Well? You choose to be dumb?"

She looked at me, uncommonly annoyed.

"Miss Eyre, I shall dust off a word I rarely employ for the sole sake of avoiding another evening spent in harsh recollection: 'Please.' Tell me anything you like. Do this old bachelor the honour of admission into a mind unpolluted by wrong or remorse." I was in danger of saying far too much and checked my monologue with one further word. "Stay."

She considered, lacing her fingers together and openly puzzling my request, the time, our unchaperoned circumstance and me.

"Another hour. At most," I quietly urged. Lord, how I wished to fully read her apprehension.

Finally she conceded. By the close of that evening, I was well acquainted with Jane's formal, respectful, intelligent and well-spoken character. I could read her expressions at times, and once or twice she brought me to smile at myself as she did the same with me. I admired her, enjoyed her, could not take my eyes from her and wanted this hasty hour to stretch out to eternity. Eighteen years old, alone, educated to the very best her rank provided, courageous and self sufficient, this young woman was earning her way in a situation she was well qualified to occupy. After twenty years of slipping and falling on my own icy disdain for whinging, pampered debutantes, I came to respect this Jane's natural perseverance immensely.

If she felt an attraction to me, it was well concealed, or perhaps her coolness was merely a result of being unused to the society of men. Had she smiled and giggled with familiarity, I would have been displeased, but she was reserved throughout, and as I realised later, she never actually smiled at all. She sat calmly where I had placed her, very collected, listening and conversing with ease.

As the ten o'clock hour approached and the time to dismiss her neared, I requested she play the library's piano; Adele having informed me earlier that her teacher played quite well. I found this to be true. Jane played a pretty and leisurely lullaby not recognised by me and did so more than competently.

"Name the composer," I called to her.

She ceased to play. "Myself, Mr. Rochester. The only pieces I am able to play without looking at music are my own. Piano is a nurtured talent for me, not a natural one I am afraid."

I might have argued otherwise but opted to hold my praise. Indulging her in my good favour would be an imprudent extravagance sure to result in spoiling the appeal earned thus far.

Whilst listening to her play and frustratedly musing my own interests, I looked through her portfolio of artwork. Her drawings and paintings showed talent, but I was more impressed with the subject matter. They were, if not dark, sombre. Introspective. One would expect a girl of her age to paint frivolous, romantic images, but Jane's choice of subject revealed a deeper, more meditative mind. Happiness and pleasure were rare emotions indeed for Jane. I did not keep her much longer and replied to her soft "good night, Sir" with a tepid nod.

After another hour and a freshened glass of port, I repaired to my own chamber and settled before the fire, ruminating on all that was said tonight. My disquietude of this afternoon was silenced. Wrung out from a mentally and emotionally trying day I knew that I should go to bed, but excitement of body and mind disallowed any such design. I felt desperate, as if I needed to *act* upon something. And, though I was hesitant to admit to it with any distinction, my heart reached on some otherworldly plane for Jane's.

We both were alone. I had no family, my own parents and sibling long since dead, and although there were many acquaintances, few were true friends. I looked at her silently and steadily upon learning tonight of her disconsolate life, yet conceived in my soul was a longing that consumed me. How I desired to console and protect her, to discover together what it is to be held and kissed and comforted in love. We were the same, this girl and I. And I was convinced that when our eyes met, we both knew it.

Alone in my room now, I was so taken with her I could scarcely breathe. She was in her own bedchamber, likely removing pins from her hair and shaking out its length to be brushed, releasing her constricting day attire in favour of a loose nightgown or turning back bedclothes to lie down. A wild desire to take her in my arms drove me, and oh, how I worked to fight it back. I could not allow my passion to run unbridled, as I knew it was quite apt to do, but instead must be patient and discover her over time. I must draw her to me and win her love. Losing her to doubt, to inopportune timing, my past, interference, another man, any adversary or impediment would be unendurable.

I lay down on the bed, my heart racing, and crossed arms on my forehead. Conscience spoke up, clear and harsh. 'You cannot have her, Edward.'

Knowing this to be true, I stifled a frustrated cry and turned my face into the pillow.

Chapter 6

As winter drew to a close and spring fast approached, I remained in residence at Thornfield Hall. With no desire for self-imposed exile to the continent, I instead preferred to settle into comfortable routine at home, conducting business during the day, taking a solitary supper in the evening, and summoning Jane to my study for companionship as evening drew toward night.

Most days I would meet with my agent or solicitor or banker, sometimes with tenants, venturing on occasional visits with nearby gentry, but I always looked forward to coming home to quiet, pleasant hours by the fireside with Adele's young governess. Frequently I would have her read to me as we sat in facing chairs before the fire. As she read, I would settle back and stare at the leaping flames and glowing embers, listening peaceably.

Jane was an excellent narrator, her pitch rising and falling with the tempo of the story, then resting occasionally for a sip of tea or discussion of what was read. During this time I discovered in her an interest in science and took much pleasure in imparting the knowledge I had hitherto accumulated. She proved a most attentive student, absorbed all I had to share, and soon we were conversing on topics of entomology, ornithology and animal behaviour. Occasionally, I would invite her into the library where she would play the pianoforte for me, or I for her. Her tunes were lovely ballads with numerous selections composed by her. Such surprising cleverness, curiosity and talent existed in this sheltered young lady.

Throughout those winter weeks, her general demeanour remained respectful always and serious much, but light-hearted I was sure, just beneath. During the day, if I passed the schoolroom, I might listen briefly at the door. Adele, whose obstinacy could previously try the patience of St. Francis de Sales, became in time docile and teachable under Miss Eyre's guidance. As a governess Jane was patient yet firm, and the child responded by fully applying her efforts with desire to please.

February turned to March, and there remained intervals when my mood degenerated to sombre and often brooding introspection. I could not change this because the root cause of my melancholy was ever-present. If I per chance met with Jane in the gallery or gardens, I might sometimes nod curtly in acknowledgement or other times not at all. She accepted my ill humour and left me to myself until called to the study in the evening when her pleasing conversation would skilfully distract me out my wretched state and have me discussing topics of mutual interest for hours.

Jane in time became progressively more relaxed and natural with me. She smiled the most pleasing and artless of smiles so that I often had much ado to resist reaching out to touch her. On one particularly balmy evening as we took our places before the fire, she lifted the monthly periodical *Nature*, but I took it from her and covered her graceful little hand with mine.

"Come, Jane. Fetch your shawl," I said. "Let us walk in the gardens tonight. Today I noticed the snowdrops and crocuses emerging, and I see that a lovely half moon is rising to light our path. It seems a shame to remain indoors."

She hesitated for a moment before smiling gently and said, "As you wish, Sir."

We strolled that evening over damp grass as a light breeze wafted amongst budding trees. To set her at ease as we walked alone together save for Pilot, I told her tales of my travels to cities all over the world. She listened attentively but spoke little, fiddling with her fingers somewhat nervously. This would never do. I wanted her conversation. Hoping to elicit a less guarded reaction, I recounted the story of my attempt at speaking Greek upon arrival at an Athens hotel.

"I stepped to the reception desk of this most lavish establishment," I told her, suppressing a smile. "You must imagine the hotel, Jane. Beautifully furnished in Chippendale and Rococo, gleaming floors opulently adorned with woven rugs from Persia and the Orient, crystal chandeliers, black marble desks and tables. Upon ringing the bell, a pristinely attired clerk came to bid me welcome and take down my particulars. As this young fellow handed across the room key, I enquired, '*ParakalO, Ekh'i banAnes to dhomAtio?*' or 'Please, does the room have a bath?'"

Jane grinned as she listened.

"The clerk took a step back, glared at me quite strangely and replied, '*Den Katalaveno*' or 'I do not understand.' I rethought the words, and finding no fault with them, posed my query again. More forcefully this time. The poor chap stammered and blushed like mad."

Jane smiled more broadly.

"Then an elegantly robed matron who'd been fanning herself in the corner and apparently listening to this exchange approached, took my elbow and whispered in Queen's English, 'Young man, you have been adamantly enquiring whether your room is equipped with… bananas.'"

Jane dissolved into laughter. It really was the most glorious sound I think I have ever heard. Her laugh was infectious and soon she had me beaming with smiles and laughing as well.

I could not remember when I last felt so light-hearted. I watched her, reflecting that in no other company could I find such enjoyment or serenity. How I wished to take her hand as we continued walking but remained at a suitable distance of course. She turned to me, mirthfully describing a similarly mortifying blunder she made during French recitation at Lowood. Her shawl-wrapped shoulders became less tense as our conversation flowed easily, and I believe she actually skipped once or twice.

At the foot of Thornfield's candlelit staircase that night, we lingered quietly in one another's company until the entryway clock struck ten times. My heart raced as she faced me. Her skin lured my touch but I restrained.

Jane's voice was a whisper. "Good night, Mr. Rochester." Oh, her lips. Plush and delicious.

I discreetly wet mine and replied, "Good night, Miss Eyre. Sleep well."

The following morning, as I left my bedchamber, Pilot's barking drew my attention to a gallery window. From there, I watched Adele and the dog play as Jane wandered nearby, gathering crocuses for a bouquet. Slipping into my jacket, I immediately went downstairs and out into the grounds where I approached the little group walking along the shallow, stony river that meandered through Thornfield's lower gardens.

"Miss Eyre," I called to her. "Will you walk with me?"

Her cheeks were rosy with the fresh morning air as she looked up from a bed of crocus blooms. "I should be pleased, Sir."

As I wandered away, she fell in step beside me. At a fallen tree, I asked her to sit with me awhile, leaving the trailing Adele to play with Pilot nearby.

There by the water I looked nervously to Jane as she waited, holding a yellow and violet bouquet in her lap of gray muslin. I wanted her to know Adele's origins, but furthermore was compelled to confess myself to her. The recollection of Adele's mother, Celine, continued to haunt me, and I needed to share that burden. Too much was kept locked away inside.

Quietly glancing to me, Jane was angelic as she sat waiting with attentiveness devoid of misgivings. She was the only person to whom I had ever wished to impart all of the shameful truth of my history. So much weighed upon my mind that, as I spoke to her, the pleasure of confession was unexpectedly intense. I told her of Celine's betrayal with a young and handsome officer, how she brought him to the hotel suite provided for her by me, and how I caught them as they undressed to make love. Never before did I admit aloud that it was my wealth Celine desired and not myself as a man at all. Jane listened, her grey-green eyes searching my face with faith and concern I scarcely deserved.

"Adele's mother was an opera dancer and an actress," I told her, leaning intimately forward for a moment. "She was very beautiful and most eloquent in her flattery. Why that in itself did not serve as prophecy for her faithlessness, I shall never be able to say."

Jane lifted her face, her eyes smiling to mine, and I was certain she did not find displeasure in what she saw now.

I asked, "Do you know what it is to be devastated in love, Jane? Romantic love is of what I speak."

She shook her head. "I do not, Sir."

"No. No, of course not. You do not know what it is to love."

Her eyes flicked pointedly to mine. "Do you?" she asked.

Oh, such a spell this little witch could cast upon me. I nodded and answered, "Yes, I do know. But you, Jane, you have never felt a lover's heart beating within his breast. Have you?"

She, the object of my desires, knew nothing of such a tender and simple intimacy. She studied my face, my eyes, then shook her head. "I have not, Sir," she admitted.

I looked seriously at Jane and those sweet lips, never kissed. The time was coming to awaken the woman sleeping quietly within, and it would be I who brought her forward.

Some mornings later, upon vacating my chamber I proceeded along the gallery to the staircase, passing Jane's chamber. The door was left slightly ajar and there I paused. She was gone to the schoolroom with Adele by now, and all about was empty and hushed. I reached to the door to gently push it open, finding the chamber vacant. Diffused morning light and silence filled the room.

I glanced about, noticing the orderliness of Jane's belongings. The bed's green coverlet was smooth and straight. A white nightgown lay neatly folded upon the pillow. An intense impulse overtook me to lift her nightgown in both my hands and bring it to my face, breathing in her warm, sleepy, soap and water scent. But I left it untouched, instead walking about her chamber, noting a tiny pair of black boots under the desk, hairbrush and comb placed neatly on the dressing table, an easel, paint box and brushes set aside in a corner.

Intending to leave I turned toward the door, but my step arrested at the bed. Gazing at it for some seconds, an inner vision replaced conscious thought. There, I beheld Jane asleep, curled on her side, rich chestnut brown hair splayed over the white pillow as she breathed the slow even breaths of deep and untroubled sleep. I stepped closer to the bed and shut my eyes, seeing myself there with her, spooned to her back with my bare arm holding her slender body close to mine. Too blissful to sleep, I lay the softest of kisses to her exposed shoulder, neck and along her downy nape, ever careful not to wake her.

As I stood at the bedside, I began to sway and reached out for the bedpost to steady myself. Upon opening my eyes, the sensual, serene daydream evaporated. Withdrawing from the room, I left the door slightly ajar and went quickly downstairs, my pulse racing and throat dry. I avoided the schoolroom knowing that I could not face Jane calmly just now.

Going to the kitchen, I rapidly consumed a black coffee and sent John to the stable to saddle Mesrour whereupon I quit the premises and rode off in the direction of Millcote.

In my study that evening, as I warmed my hands at the fire, nervous anticipation caused them to tremble. Imagine! A man of my age, station and worldliness trembling with want for a woman like Jane. An eighteen-year-old governess! How absurd this seemed to me, yet all day I was unable to think for any length of a single subject other than her, just as yesterday and the day before. Worse yet, I was in danger of telling her so; of roundly accusing her of bewitching me as she had once done my horse, and if saying so might bring about her spontaneous, mocking smile, then I absolutely was at risk!

Conversation together no longer came easily for me. Each evening we took our customary places before the fire whereby she read to me from scientific periodicals or books of poetry whilst I strove in avoidance of continually gazing upon her as she spoke, shifting uncomfortably as unsolicited images stole into my imagination.

Last evening I had made quite a fool of myself, surely. As she read to me from a recent publication on snowy egret migratory patterns, my mind again wandered to more stirring territories. Her gentle voice suddenly stole through my visions.

"Sir? Mr. Rochester?"

I snapped back to looking at her. "Hm?"

Jane's unchecked grin sent a powder-blast thrill through me. "I asked, Sir, if you've ever been to Cyprus, since this species of egret typically migrates from England directly there."

"Ah, Cyprus." I cleared my throat and straightened in my chair, covering my lap with folded hands. "Um, yes, actually I have…"

"You were not listening to me read," she said, shutting the periodical. "Perhaps I should leave you to your thoughts tonight."

"No! Ah, what I mean, Miss Eyre, is please continue. You have my attention. Please. Read on."

That was only last evening. Tonight I paced before the fire, furious with myself for becoming so uncontrollably affected. A brandy was poured, swirled energetically, studied in lamplight and sipped. Fingers tapped madly on the mantle. Setting the glass down, I arranged my cravat, collar and jacket lapels. With the remaining brandy thrown back in a single shot, I rang for Jane to join me in the study, then chose a nonchalant attitude at the chess table, leaning upon the edge as brandy-induced calm gradually washed anxiety away. She came along quietly, entering the room as I openly watched and took her place before the fire, straightening and smoothing her gray skirt.

"I trust you enjoyed your time in Millcote today, Mr. Rochester," she said amiably. She knew that I had spent the day in town for pleasure, not business, intending to replenish my wardrobe amongst other personal pursuits.

"Thank you, yes, Miss Eyre. I trust you enjoyed your school day," I replied in like tone. Approaching the fire, I handed to her a book of poetry; one purchased in town that afternoon. She touched the gold embossed letters and handsome leather binding.

"A lovely little volume," she offered and met my eyes for an extended moment.

I could no longer simply look at her. My vision absorbed her wilfully. My fingers, lips, cheeks, and all my body, straight to my toes, longed to feel her warmth.

"Will you read to me?" I hoarsely asked.

A single nod was given in reply. She opened the book to where a marker was left and read, "Christopher Marlowe. *The Passionate Shepherd to His Love.*" Glancing to me, a playful smile came across her lips. She began:

> *Come live with me and be my love,*
> *And we will all the pleasures prove,*
> *That hills and valleys, dales and fields,*
> *And all the craggy mountains yields.*
>
> *There we will sit upon the rocks,*
> *And see the shepherds feed their flocks,*
> *By shallow rivers to whose falls*
> *Melodious birds sing madrigals.*
>
> *And I will make thee beds of roses*
> *With a thousand fragrant posies,*
> *A cap of flowers, and a kirtle*
> *Embroidered all with leaves of myrtle;*

Here, Jane paused, and lifted her chin but not her eyes. She pulled in a deep breath then continued.

> *A gown made of the finest wool*
> *Which from our pretty lambs we pull;*
> *Fair lined slippers for the cold,*
> *With buckles of the purest gold;*
>
> *A belt of straw and ivy buds,*
> *With coral clasps and amber studs:*
> *And if these pleasures may thee move,*
> *Come live with me and be my love.*
>
> *The shepherd's swain shall dance and sing*
> *For thy delight each May morning:*
> *If these delights thy mind may move,*
> *Then live with me and be my love.*

At the close of the passage, she lowered the book to her lap. Large, clear eyes rose directly to mine as silence filled the flickering, crackling firelight.

It was done. The poem revealed me as an ardent man inviting this woman to be my lover. There was no retracting my feelings now. I had unalterably stepped beyond propriety. My breathing was held.

There were times during the preceding weeks when whilst together I caught her eyes upon me. She would instantly avert them upon discovery. But now she met them steadily as the silence between us drew out. Presently her gaze left mine and wandered about my face, over my hair and finally settled upon my lips. I watched her, motionless. Her breathing quickened. She wet her lips, and just as I wished them to do, they parted.

"Jane," I whispered.

Suddenly, as if pulled by cords out of herself, she sprang from her chair. Her eyes were cast anywhere but on me and cheeks flushed deeply in the firelight. She abruptly thrust the book at me.

"Forgive me, Mr. Rochester. I find myself rather tired and unwell this evening. Permit me to return to my chamber."

Reaching for her hand, I said, "Jane! Do not go!"

She dodged me. "Please accept my apologies, Sir. I must bid you a good night." And with that, she flew from my study.

Chapter 7

THE DARKENED STUDY was now oppressive in silence. I remained by the fire for some time longer with eyes fixed on the flames, pensively considering Jane's reaction to the poem. It may have been imperceptible, subtle at most to anyone else, but knowing her as I did in all her control and reserve, the poem's effect was nothing short of dramatic. Recalling the entire scene, a blaze burned within me rivalling the fire my eyes beheld without.

I left the hearth and moved toward the study's windows, opening the casements wide. A chilly, freshening breeze meandered in, doing little to cool my fervour, so I removed jacket and vest, throwing them onto the leather sofa.

A soft tapping came at the door followed by Leah peering in. "Do you require anything, Sir?" she asked softly from the doorway. Looking about, she saw that I was alone.

"Brandy," I muttered.

Leah returned momentarily to place a snifter on the end table and then took her leave. With glass in hand, I walked about the shadowy room, listening to night sounds entering from the open windows. A mockingbird called in the distant orchard. I sipped slowly. It would be a long evening spent alone.

I approached the antique chess table purchased many years ago by Father in Barcelona. Recently I taught Jane to play; I being black and she white, of course. She listened closely to instruction, memorising the rules directly, and in our first match she very nearly trounced me. During subsequent evenings, we played chess in our comfortable silence, occasionally punctuated by a snarl or burst of raucous laughter when a particularly shrewd move was made. I accused her of having played before.

"Certainly not, Sir!" Jane had indignantly replied. "Mr. Brocklehurst's hidebound committee would have fits if asked to consider such sport in Lowood's curriculum, despite the analytically stimulating benefits. A whispered game of cribbage or bezique between dormitory beds was the extent of our competitive leisure.'"

"Incorrigible rebel," I accused.

"Oh yes, 'rebel' is me all over, Sir."

"Well, at any rate," I conceded peevishly, "competitiveness courses thick through your veins alongside your witchery."

She answered that with a devious smile and took my bishop.

Not for the first time did I mentally note that this young lady was exceptionally clever. More than a few men of my acquaintance found intelligence in a woman undesirable and intimidating, but as I watched Jane survey the board for her next move, I found her acumen potently alluring.

Conversation was not always necessary for us, and we would read separately in domesticated peace for hours. I longed to take her hand and touch her slight fingers as we read independently or to stand at the close of the evening, extend my hand to her and ask, 'Mrs. Rochester, shall we adjourn to bed?' But instead, Jane would rise as the hour became late, tranquilly bid me a good night, sometimes touch my shoulder as she passed, and seek her own room. I wondered how much longer I could continue this chaste masquerade.

Circling the deserted chess table slowly and running my fingers over the squares, I sipped brandy thoughtfully as the Marlowe poem came to mind again. It spoke everything I wanted to say to Jane: 'Come away with me. We will live together far from this place and for only one another.' I knew that she enjoyed my company and even suspected an attraction as daily it became more evident that our psyches fit together like pieces of an intricate puzzle, but did she feel love for me? Did she want me as a lover and life partner? I simply did not know. Now, after witnessing her reaction to my own confirmed feelings, I felt that the fine layers of Jane's reserved blockade were rent apart, permitting a breathtaking glimpse of promised requital.

Lifting the poetry volume from the end table, I leafed through the pages and recalled the scene of finding it in the bookshop. Whilst perusing the poetry section, a locality to where I rarely ventured upon visits there, a familiar voice addressed me from behind.

"Rochester!" he enthused in whispered tones "How on earth are you?"

This was Arthur Eshton, a long-time friend and resident of the neighbourhood, and a man with whom I had always enjoyed much in common. We were about the same age, both lifetime students of science and nature, and of very similar senses of humour. We also had in common being second sons of wealthy parentage.

"Eshton, " I said, clasping his hand heartily. "What have you been doing with yourself, you old rascal?"

"Only just back from the Netherlands, doing some research at Leiden University and working toward a doctorate. The quest for enlightened thought marches on despite nightly attempts to douse the flame. Yourself, Edward?"

"I've been back from the continent nearly three months. Could never resist a British winter, you know."

"Hah! Or a British woman perhaps?" He nodded to the shelves of poetry before us. "Taken up a new interest, have you?"

"You might say that."

"Uh huh. Anyone I know?" Arthur asked, perceptive as always.

I grinned but shook my head in the negative.

"Come, let us find a quiet corner," he suggested. "I've an onerous proposal in need of your consideration. But not here."

We wandered through the narrow aisles, past shelves crammed floor to ceiling with dusty books, deep into the International Philosophy and Religion section where we paused and spoke in hushed tones.

"Have you heard from Blanche since you've been back?" he asked with his impish smile.

"Good God, no. Can I expect to?"

"With certainty. The Ingrams will host a house party beginning next week. Invitations are going out. You know they will insist upon your attendance."

I chuckled softly. "Blanche has frightened off every eligible bachelor within a fifty mile radius. How old must she be now? Twenty-five? Her gorgon of a mother is growing desperate."

"Yes. Desperate, receptive to most any interested party, and in danger of insolvency. Word has it that Blanche's shopping excursions are the stuff of *beau monde* legend. London, Paris, Milan. Word has it she was in St. Petersburg last spring! The Lord and Lady need a husband for her. Badly. Their manhunt has scoured Britain from Hadrian's Wall to Tower Hill, and not one contender has leapt forth to take up the gauntlet." He elbowed my ribs, adding, "And right here, in her own back garden, both the Rochester name and estate are eligible to the last degree!"

"Bloody hell," I snorted. "I could not afford Blanche, even if she were worth the effort. Do they know I've returned to England unattached?"

"Of course they do! Mummy keeps close watch upon one Mr. E.F. Rochester, don't you know?" He laughed. "Imagine having Lady Ingram as your mother-in-law!"

I could not share in his mirth, being the target of that woman's designs. "Heaven protect all men from such a fate. Imagine having Blanche as a bed partner."

"I do," he smiled. "What man has not?"

"Beauty is that young lady's sole redeeming quality," I cautioned him. "Regret would come even before the wedding night commenced. But a good Bordeaux might help *you* through it, young Mr. Eshton."

"Penniless me! It never would happen, Edward. 'Tis you the Ingrams ask after, and so you must make an appearance at this party regardless of your history with Blanche. You are absent from Thornfield so frequently, you must not think of begging off this time."

"I will await an invitation and give it no further thought until then. Are you going?"

"Yes. I have an interest of my own to pursue," Arthur said, the mischievous grin returning.

"Who?" I asked, not at all surprised. Arthur frequently escorted a comely young lady on his arm at such gatherings, but never was the pairing seen twice.

"Louisa Dent."

"Louisa? Hang on, did you not escort her to Lord and Lady Wallingford's Midsummer Night's Ball a year or two hence? Oh ho, this must be serious!"

"No, that was Millicent, the elder sister. Nice eyes, bad teeth, horsey laugh."

"Ah. Yes. Now I know the girls you mean."

"Girl. Singular."

"But Louisa is a twin, is she not? An identical twin?"

His grin turned to a leer.

"I never can tell them apart," I reflected. "What is her sister's name? Amy is it?"

"Yes, Amy, and I can tell them apart. Louisa kisses better," he smirked as I turned my eyes briefly heavenward. "Look, Edward, come to Stoneleigh Park tomorrow. We need to catch up. Come early."

"Will do," I promised, laughing still at his incessant naughtiness. "See you then."

Upon returning to the poetry section, I flipped through the pages of a number of books, rejecting and replacing each. Then I happened upon a beautiful little volume bound in black leather entitled *A Selection of English Poetry*. It contained a verse recalled from college days some eighteen years ago. Being the crass youth I was at the time, it spoke nothing to me beyond insignificant romantic drivel. Standing in the bookshop, I read it through once, then twice. Maturity allowed me to see it with new eyes. Tender inclination had me feel it with a new heart. I took it home.

Alone in my study now, Jane having read the poem and deserted me an hour since, I lay the book down and reflected that the life I knew for the past eleven years would be unbearable to resume. The prospect of each evening spent alone struck cold to my heart. I would welcome travelling the world again, but this time with Jane, opening her fertile, young mind to new experiences, places and philosophies.

With each day of Jane's presence in my home, I fairly vibrated with the life, hope, goodness and comfort she brought to me. To lose her would be a prostrating blow indeed.

'It is all right,' I reflected. 'She has only gone upstairs to her chamber. Let her contemplate what happened here tonight. Let her simmer in newfound desire. Hell, I've been living with it for weeks.'

Still... I ached.

I lighted candles at my desk and took my place in the antiquated chair, gazing through the open window at the night sky. Hundreds of stars were shining clear and bright in the blackness. A whip-poor-will's call came on the breeze, lilting and sweet from the wooded glen to the east. How pleasant it would be to stroll the grounds with her just now. I knew that if she stayed much longer looking at me with desire in her eyes as she did, I would have taken her by the hand and led her out into this glorious night. I would have brought her into the shadowy starlit orchard and there, amongst the fragrant trees and falling dew, would have brought her arms around me and enveloped her in mine. With a gentle hand to her creamy white cheek, my gaze devouring those entrancing eyes, I would have kissed her mouth, long, sweet and searching. Yes, I would have kissed her, tasting her lips, softly licking them until we were both breathless. And unless she resisted me, I would not have restrained myself.

But would she have resisted me? Again, I simply did not know.

Turning from the window, I wrenched my attention back to the here and now, and glanced at some letters deposited on my desk earlier by Mrs. Fairfax. In the flickering candlelight, I read through the bank documents, investment statements, and yes, as predicted by Eshton, an engraved card from Ingram Park. Detecting a floral scent, I brought the card close to my face. Orange blossom and iris. She had perfumed the damned thing, the silly cow.

I turned it over, broke the ridiculously ornate seal, opened and read her florid script:

> *My Dearest Edward,*
> *Have the goodness to attend a house party at Ingram Park starting 4th April week. Too much time has passed since we last were together. Our party would be dreadfully dull if I could not expect the pleasure of your presence.*
> *Yours ever, Blanche*

I leant back in my chair, tossed the invitation onto the cluttered desk and groaningly ran fingers through my hair. Desperation was plain in Blanche's words. I smiled, softly singing, "I'd rather be dead than be married to you..." when there was a soft knock at the door. "Come!" I called.

Mrs. Fairfax bustled in, directly approaching the desk. "Sir, your presence in the north tower tonight is requested by Grace. She has been asking for you, and seeing as you are alone..."

This was the last damned thing I wanted to contend with tonight, but as I was lacking a reasonable excuse, I interrupted with, "Yes, yes, of course. Tell Grace I will be up later."

"Very well, Sir," the old lady said, then upon retreating to the door added, "Do exercise care with her, Sir."

I looked up at her from the bank statement I was now opening and replied, "Shut the door, Mrs. Fairfax."

For another hour I dithered about, perusing the letters' contents and worked on my brandy slowly. When it was finished, there was no other reason to delay the task ahead. With a candle in hand I went out of the study and ascended the stairway to the second story. In the gallery I halted at Jane's door, noting the glow of candlelight beneath it. I stepped closer and lay a hand on the oak panel.

If I tapped, would she open the door? I wanted to be in this room with her so much more than where I was going; to the woman awaiting upstairs.

"Jane, open the door," I scarcely whispered. "Take my hand and pull me inside."

She was moving about her chamber. There was the creaking of the wardrobe door followed by the shifting of material. She was removing her dress perhaps. With lips nearly to the door I breathed, "Hold me close to your sweet young body. Give me your strength. Tell me you love me because... because I feel that you do."

Silence fell within.

Such foolishness. I took my hand from the door and continued along the gallery. Proceeding past the nursery, Mrs. Fairfax's rooms and my chamber, I turned down another corridor, then again, and came to an ancient oak beamed door set in a barren stone wall. From the frame above I brought down an equally ancient skeleton key. Three dead-bolt locks I opened, passed through the doorway and carefully bolted the door behind me, then tucked the key into my pocket. The spiral stone staircase before me was eerily blue-hued with starlight glowing from beyond the few narrow panes. I arrived at the topmost step where another ancient oak door stood locked. Using the skeleton key once again, I opened it and entered into a richly appointed bedchamber housing magnificent antique furnishings including a regal four-poster bed with crimson hangings. A Turkish tapestry adorned the length of one wall. I lifted and draped it across a hook revealing yet another formidable door upon which I now softly knocked.

The sound of rattling keys and locks being shot back, three in all, broke the north tower's weighty silence. The door opened allowing light to pour into the crimson chamber, and there, casting her stout shadow was Grace Poole, a formidably built woman of about fifty years whose profession and personal excesses aged her another fifteen. Expecting little exchange with this laconic personage, I began with dry salutations.

"Good evening, Grace. How do you do?"

She shrugged and half curtseyed simultaneously. "Getting on, Sir."

"And your charge? How is she behaving tonight?"

"Oh, fair tolerable I daresay."

"I am told you wish that I should visit tonight. Is anything the matter?"

Grace's emotionless features took on a trace of buoyancy. "Your last visit was months ago, Sir, and so I thought of having you see her changes for yourself. Of late she is improved in the night hours. I believe you may be interested in seeing the difference."

I was led into the inner chamber, a sizable stone walled cell with a low hearth, sturdy fender fronting a low fire, barred windows, narrow bed and worn rug. A cleared table occupied the centre, flanked by two plain wooden chairs. Occupying one was Bertha, this dungeon's tenant for the past eleven years. Dressed in a dense linen shift that may once have been white, she sat quietly, palms down on the table. Long, coarse black hair obscured her profile. I went to the table cautiously and took the chair opposite her.

"Bertha? How are you?" I asked.

She raised her face to look at me. Eyes that had long been vacant, like a doll's eyes even early in her psychosis, tonight were clear and astute, much as they had been fifteen years ago on our wedding day.

"Hello, Edward. You came to visit me. How nice."

"Yes," I said carefully, more than a little startled. I was on my guard, knowing she could spring at any moment. "Grace says you are feeling better in the evenings."

"I am, thank you. She takes me walking on the roof at night. Did she tell you?"

I shook my head 'no'. "Does she then? I will talk with Grace now."

"Yes, Edward. I do like your sapphire cufflinks," Bertha said, and then lowered her head again.

Grace and I stood near the door, our eyes on the table's occupant, talking in hushed tones.

"You see, Sir? I can actually maintain conversation with her some evenings."

I cleared my throat and asked, "For how long has she been exhibiting these episodes, Grace?"

"Oh, for two or three weeks now, Sir. When the weather is favourable, I take her up to the roof at night. She must have fresh air and exercise, and she no longer attempts the tricks she once did when I unlock this door. Still, I do not dare take her through the house to the grounds, but on the roof I can watch her and let her walk. It seems to have done her some good." We both looked at the quiet Bertha, and Grace added, "She is not quite as combative as she once was."

"Has she been lighting fires as mentioned in your most recent letter?"

"She tried about a fortnight ago," she said, straightening to her full height and breadth. "I put a stop to that."

I nodded, keeping my eyes on the motionless figure at the table. Bertha had not moved a limb. She scarcely seemed to breathe.

"Grace, I know that I needn't tell you, but... be on your guard. I will accompany you when you take her to the roof if you wish."

She shrugged. "I can manage her, Sir. Have done so for a long time."

"Yes. Of course you can," I conceded, not wanting to spend a single unnecessary moment in the presence of either woman. "Good night, Grace," I said, turning to quit the room and glanced at Bertha. Her face was now lifted in my direction; eyes upon me and her lips curled slightly sending an icy shiver prickling over my scalp.

Exiting hastily I shut the door and listened for locks to slide into place. I secured both the crimson bedchamber and north tower doors, replacing the key on the frame, and sought my own chamber.

Chapter 8

"A VERY GOOD MORNING, Sir!" Mrs. Fairfax cheerfully sang as she met me at the staircase foot the next morning. "You slept well I trust?" By seven I was bathed, shaved and dressed although a restless night had freshened me little.

"No, Madam, I slept very poorly indeed."

"Oh. I am dreadfully sorry to…"

"I will be out much of the day. Expect my return after dark."

"Of course, Sir. Your breakfast will be lain shortly in the dining room."

I looked up to see Jane lingering at the top of the staircase, adjusting her sleeves and diligently ignoring the entryway below. Surely she was tarrying there in hopes of my departure before descending herself. I delayed, watching her, not caring what Mrs. Fairfax thought of this behaviour. Jane finally looked up from her sleeve. Our eyes met and I gave the slightest of nods, then turned my back and went to the dining room.

The day was passed as planned, at Eshton's family estate of Stoneleigh Park. We enjoyed gorgeous weather though it was rather windy, and we rode about his father's landholdings, talking of mutual interests and recounting tales of our travels. Late in the afternoon we returned to the house for billiards, a generous aperitif, and then following a sumptuous meal of broiled venison, we industriously sampled liqueurs carried home from his extensive travels. Late in the evening, I bid my friend a good night and started off in deepening twilight, glad that Mesrour knew the journey ahead. I relished my sublime mood; such being a rare state of mind for me. My horse galloped along in the light of a full moon, a stiff breeze at my back, past shady emerald fields dotted dimly with grazing sheep.

Thornfield, I pondered as I rode, now held for me the realisation of polar opposites. Hope and despair, pleasure and pain, love and hate. The root of my problem was that the latter half of this juxtaposition was bound to me like the shackles of durance vile whilst the former were mere gossamer apparitions. I could deny truth if I wished. I could overleap obstacles of custom both social and religious, entwining my soul with what I knew to be my salvation, but in doing so would risk discovery and loss. For the sake of self-preservation, was I not justified to live by my own law and deny that which was universally inflexible? As each day passed, I became more certain that I was. Conscience remained mercifully mute.

Arriving to Thornfield's courtyard, I left Mesrour tethered in the stable and entered through the front hall. The time was near ten. I wandered into my study where a good fire burned in anticipation of my arrival home, removed my riding cloak and jacket and tossed them onto the sofa, then collapsed into my chair beside the fire.

Some minutes later, Leah looked in. "Sir, might I bring you something to eat? Or a glass of port?" she asked taking the cloak to hang up.

I considered a brandy but thought better of it. "Tea, Leah. And would you tell Miss Eyre that I have returned?" It would be pleasant to have Jane's company whilst savouring recollections of a day replete with good companionship and fine weather. Perhaps I would take her into the drawing room and teach her to play billiards. Why not? She should share my ebullient mood. Moreover, it was high time we faced one another after the episode of Marlowe's poem.

Soon Leah returned with a tea tray. "Sir, Miss Eyre has gone out. Mrs. Fairfax says she went over to Hay."

"She what?" I leapt up, outraged. "To Hay? In the dark? What on earth for?"

"Ah, for a walk I suppose? Or possibly to post a letter? Sir, I do not know," she said, setting out cup and saucer. "She set off nearly an hour ago."

I checked my pocket watch. "At nine o'clock? And you permitted this?"

Leah looked at me in puzzlement. "As a servant, I have no right to question the governess, Sir. May I ask, has something happened that you must speak with Miss Eyre so urgently? Perhaps I can help."

I was no longer listening but rather searching for reasonable action. 'If I go back to the stable for Mesrour, he may yet be saddled and I could go after her.' Then, a few moments later, a calmer course stepped in. 'No. No. Do not go after her. Wait.'

Over my shoulder, I dismissed Leah with a curt, "That will be all." Well sobered now and my mood having plummeted, I swore mild oaths peppered with Jane Eyre's name. I went to the table and poured tea, returning with it to my place by the fire and resigning myself to a homecoming spent alone. Irritated and perplexed, I sank back into my chair and gazed at the empty one beside me; the chair customarily occupied by Jane. Her timing of departure made plain a deliberate scheme to avoid me.

And so I passed the ten o'clock hour occupied with reading a recently published novel, listening to the wind howl down the chimney and adopting a generally fractious mood. Meanwhile, I awaited footsteps in the entryway and her soft tapping at the door. Nothing came.

Finally, as the hour struck eleven, I set my book aside and went up to my chamber. Passing Jane's door, I noticed the light of a burning candle from beneath the threshold and heard a brief rustling of paper within. 'So she's back. And not a word to be said to me. That is simply perfect, Jane.'

In my room, the curtains were drawn and a subdued fireplace glow danced about as I removed boots but did not undress. After washing hands and face at the china basin, I took a candle to the writing table. With paper and pencil before me, I absently busied myself sketching fanciful images of boats and sunsets and scribbled attempts at poetry in French, Italian and German. In doing so, I reminisced on journeys to foreign destinations and people come and gone in my life. Dispassionately I recalled bygone mistresses and other, more transient liaisons. College days came to mind as well as the young ladies I had known and courted in those days. Whimsical flowers and grasses appeared on my paper before I chided myself for such nonsense, then folded the paper and tossed it into the desk drawer. Returning to the fire, I put my feet up on the sofa and mused broodingly.

'Why would Jane avoid me?' I puzzled. The seconds following Marlowe's poem were apparently the pivotal point. In those instants she became conscious of something frightening in those ardent words, something she felt compelled to evade.

I tried to envision her perception of the situation and to see myself through her eyes. How many men could she have known in her life? Had she ever felt attraction until now? **Was** she attracted to me, master of this great estate, a man of wealth and worldliness, of fine tastes and talents? Nearly twice her age? Unmarried? Such a man takes an interest in her, calls her to his presence each evening, they find much in common, a natural sympathy, compassion, attraction, desire. These sentiments were new and likely terrifying to a girl of eighteen making her way alone in the world.

She had found a family in the inhabitants of my house, and so it was plausible that Jane was recipient of Mrs. Fairfax's cautionary, motherly interference. Possibly she had been advised to distance herself from me. I of course cared nothing for what the housekeeper and servants thought, but this did not mean there were no whisperings amongst themselves, and to Jane. The companionship she and I created was unusual and likely suspicious to the observant eye. How many masters behaved as I did, striking up friendship with their young governesses? Maybe not infrequently, I considered smiling, but that was lasciviousness, not…

The word 'love' made its introduction at that moment.

I could not use the word, even in my mind. But I used it with Jane without thinking twice. 'Come live with me and be my love.' And I had frightened her.

As I sat pondering before the fire upon my chamber's sofa, a distant door unclosed then clicked shut again. Who could be creeping about at this time of night? I went to my own door, soundlessly opened it and looked out into the chill gallery to find a flickering candle receding toward the staircase. My curiosity was piqued and I followed, closing my door and stepping silently in stocking feet along the matting. Standing at the top of the staircase, I could see by the candle's dim light a young, agile form dressed in a shawl and white nightgown advancing through the entryway. Her hair was long and loose over her shoulders and down her back. Her step made no sound.

I followed just as soundlessly, along the stone walled corridor, past the dining room, study and drawing room, finally seeing her arrive to the library. She went in and shut the door. There was another entrance to the library, around the back of the drawing room. In the darkness I went there and approached. Stone steps descended into the library and here I remained, unseen in deep shadow. Her candle was set atop the piano as she quietly built a fire in the hearth. Once it blazed well, she stood watching the flames from the aged Oriental rug, and I studied her in profile. Rich chestnut hair fell to her waist, smooth and brushed in preparation for bed. The same tartan shawl I had seen upon our first meeting was gathered close about her shoulders. Her long sleeved white nightgown fell to floor length where bare toes peeked from beneath.

Watching her in the flickering glow, I drank in her solitary, understated, ethereal beauty, so natural while at the same time completely enchanting. Dignified and polished, she rivalled any of the grand ladies of my social circles. Better. Truer. Her loveliness lured me, yet I sat down on the cold stone steps, my arms pulled in close for warmth and enjoyed the comfort of simply being near her again. My soul was at ease in her presence.

She went to the piano. Now I watched her from behind, her long hair covering her back. After brief exercises, she began to play. The first was a ballad played for me once before, one she had composed herself and I thought exquisite. Then came snippets of a tune I had never before heard. She played and stopped and made notations as if constructing a new piece. After a time she rose from the piano, took her papers and returned to the fire, settling into the enormous wingback chair habitually occupied by me when in the library. She extended her bare feet to the warmth of the blaze and tapped her pencil thoughtfully against her nose. I smiled from my shady vantage point. She made some notations on a page, contemplated and wrote again. Then, much to my astonishment, she sang. Her lovely alto voice filled the room.

Every sense in my body was transfixed. The loveliness of her voice was surpassed only by her words, speaking of a hopeless longing for the love of a forbidden man. She sang with passionate longing to give this man all of herself, to comfort him and to bring balm to his pain. She was singing to me. I knew it, felt it, and the certainty reverberated through me like an earthquake. I never imagined that this girl, so reserved and controlled, a novice who had scarcely entered womanhood, could harbour emotion so bare. In astonishment I watched her rise from the chair and return to the piano. She continued to work out the music, her voice entering occasionally with the words of love and longing. Listening, I leaned forward and placed my face in my hands. Had I been a man of a more fortuitous fate, I would have marked myself blessed indeed. But my fate was brutal and wretched. Though I hungered for the love of a woman as much as any other man, I was cursed to be denied it. As I listened, my affection for Jane was changing with each word and note. Before this, I had been interested, passionate and pursuant, but now I was all hesitance and contrition. And passionate still, to be entirely honest, but now I was cognisant that I could hurt her. I could damage and devastate her. If I charged forth, wanting her and obtaining her, I could and would drive her to the ground and destroy her, even if that was the very last thing on earth I wanted. Listening to her sweet voice, I knew it was beyond my control and merely a matter of time. Whatever action taken with her and with this love I helped to create, Jane would eventually grieve. Her soul was awake and it was destined for pain.

She finished the last notes on the piano, returned to the fire and nestled into the chair with her bare feet beneath her. A wan smile and thousand-yard stare played about her face. I saw a new and entirely different person there; no longer my platonic companion or acquaintance, but my life partner and lover. Yet, the ominous fact remained that since her emotion now matched mine, danger, fear and loss had entered and taken centre stage. And I would never intentionally hurt her, ever. I would rather suffer in my own private hell until my final day.

I shivered in the dark and cold, then stood from the step, sighing. I turned and went into the drawing room, intending to silently steal back to my chamber to be alone with my misery, but Jane had heard my sigh and come after me. She placed a hand on my arm before I could go.

"Sir?" she asked in the darkness.

I turned and took her hand from my arm, intending to release it and leave her here.

She persevered. "Sir, return with me to the library."

I sighed. "If I go with you, Jane, your pain will only come sooner."

She took my hand, her warm fingers encircling mine, and drew me towards her. I obeyed. Starved of her companionship these past two days and for physical affection for an age, I could not resist her. We went together to the fire and I knelt in the bright warmth on the rug.

'I don't care,' my lonely heart said. 'Come what may tonight, I simply do not care.'

Reaching up to her hand, I opened my arms to her and drew her into my lap. My embrace enclosed her body while she wrapped her arms about my shoulders. I succumbed to the heaven of holding her and buried my face in the warmth of her neck and hair.

"Jane," I breathed. "Jane, if I could die now, it would be the happiest death imaginable."

Her warm and clean scent, her strength as she held me; all were intoxicating. Her body was as sweet and touch as pure as I remembered from the evening she helped me by the river. My palms lay spread upon her back, and I struggled to check my need to explore. Beneath her nightgown was only her; no corsets, petticoats or other nonsense. Oh, her body in my arms felt magnificent. Before long I could restrain myself no longer and ran hands down her back, my fingers over each individual rib, down her spine, along her hips. 'Please,' I prayed silently with all my might. 'Let me have her.' We remained in front of the fire, clinging to one another like lost souls, and I suppose that is what we were. When we spoke, words came in whispers; not for fear of being overheard, but for fear of shattering our fragile intimacy.

"How long were you there, Mr. Rochester?" she asked. Her lips brushed my brow as she said it, and I held her tighter.

"I followed you here."

"Why did you?"

"Jane." Her lips moving over my brow drew my upturned face compellingly. "Do you not know? Could you not feel how deeply I missed you?"

Her arms tightened around my shoulders. She brushed my black, loose curls away from my face. I could feel her heart steadily beating. She took a deep breath and its pace quickened. "The song I was writing," she said softly, "is for you."

I lifted my face to kiss her neck, but only once. More and restraint would have been lost. "I know," I whispered.

We were silent for some minutes. She stroked my hair. I breathed her in.

"Do I frighten you, Jane?" I asked.

She thought for a long moment. "No, Sir," she said softly. "My love for you frightens me."

I looked at her and she at me. It was done. Confirmed.

We were fearful for very different reasons. Hers were monumental in her eyes but nothing to me. Custom, differences in social class and age. All meaningless factors. Insignificant as dust or smoke. Were it only so simple, I would have had her down on the floor, kissing her, drawing from her promises to marry me. My fears were more tangible and therefore more crushing. Everything I wanted was here, except for the freedom to make her mine.

Then I thought, 'I could lie. I could deceive her.' But the bitingly cold voice of Conscience, or was it Reason? Or was it God? came forth and galvanized my agony with one word, 'Enough! Edward, enough!'

I buried my face again in Jane's neck as tears blurred my vision. We all cry at times. Our tears arise from frustration and hopelessness for the most part. I was rife with both. Jane laid soft kisses to my forehead, both comforting and tormenting me in turns, holding me with all she was. Soon, burgeoning passion versus hopelessness was too much for me to manage. Releasing her, I removed her arms from around me, then lifted her to the chair, set her down and backed away. She watched me, her expression filled with confusion and the hurt of rejection. My vision swam. As she opened her lips to speak, I turned and was gone.

Returning to my chamber, I shut the door and stood before it, willing to hear approaching footsteps and her little hand knock. How long had it been since a woman held me and kissed my face lovingly? Had one ever genuinely done so? It felt so good that as yet I was spellbound with it. I growled and whimpered through stinging tears of frustration. 'Jane! Come! The night is ours. No one will know. Oh, God! How I need you!'

Part of me, albeit a miniscule part, hoped she would stay away. If she came to my chamber, she would be in danger she could scarce anticipate. I was ravenous for her love and would employ every method in my considerable arsenal of seduction to obtain all of it. Minutes passed and she did not come. I went to the desk and again took paper and pen in hand, opened the ink well and began to write.

My dearest Jane, I penned, but then thought, 'No. No.' I could not attach her name to the horror I was about to acknowledge on paper. The page was crumpled and tossed aside. On the second sheet I wrote:

> *My Love,*
> *I am married. I have a wife. In March 1825 I was wed to Bertha Antoinetta Mason in Spanish Town, Jamaica. My wife is insane. A maniac. She is imprisoned in the north tower of Thornfield Hall. I hate my wife. She is my prisoner and I am hers.*

Here, I reread the words, twice, thrice, then folded the page unevenly and locked it in the desk drawer. Confessing these dreadful facts on paper gave no satisfaction. I craved to confess to Jane, have her know all of my secrets and look at me without judgment. I needed her to accept the terrible reality of my life and love me regardless of it. She may love me, but she would never stay with me. Knowing her, I knew that.

Once undressed, I slipped into my cold bed. The clock downstairs struck once. I wanted to sleep, to escape, and I thoroughly lacked the will to live. Wind continued to howl beyond my casement.

'Save your sweet Jane, Edward. Your best act of love would be to sacrifice yourself and so save her.'

Fantasy is harmless and comforting normally, though as dreams brought Jane into my bed, I felt driven nearly mad with wanting her. My long-deprived hands grasped and caressed bedding; bare legs writhed to enwrap hers. Tears came and went. As sleep finally enveloped me, a nearby door unclosed and shut again.

'Jane, come sleep with me. I hurt you tonight and am sorry. Let me say so.'

Chapter 9

IN THE FOLLOWING days I occupied myself with conducting business either at the Hall or at the residences of my agent or solicitor. An ever present premonition of eminent change hovered about me; a feeling that I must prepare. All dealings previously suspended must now be solidified. The constant diversion of work served to free my mind of personal conflict during waking hours, but discord of heart and mind never failed to visit during the silent night hours after I had gone to bed. It would then come upon me like a deluge from above, and insomnia was the result.

Temptation was painfully near during those lonely hours. No longer did I call Jane to my presence in the evenings, nor did she seek me. During days at home, I circumvented the schoolroom and spent my time sequestered in the study. My sole visitors, other than business associates, were Mrs. Fairfax and Leah who brought food and drink unbidden, for I never had appetite or felt thirst. All sensibility was obscured by a desperate need to remain occupied so to keep inner longings at bay.

Early one morning, I unexpectedly met Jane in the gallery as I left my chamber. In passing we acknowledged one another with a small nod, and she offered a faint, "Good morning, Sir." But I could not permit her to proceed away from me and came to a dead stop, grasping her hand. Our eyes met. She stood controlled as ever; head up and features steady, cautious and correct. Despite her propriety, our moments of embrace in the library came straight back, requiring much effort on my part to keep from clasping her close once again. Instead I squeezed her hand lightly, released it and went on. As I descended the staircase, I chided myself for trembling so.

The afternoon was spent at the dining room table with my solicitor, Alistair Blakely. We had finished firming the details of a neighbourhood land parcel acquisition and were now enjoying our tea. Blakely was Father's and Rowland's legal counsellor as well and over many years proved himself an individual to be trusted. He was an elderly gent with humour dry to desiccation, but still I found him immensely likable. In my youth, he immediately endeared himself to me with an impressive talent for birdcalls.

"Edward," he began, lifting his cup and saucer, "whilst I am here, allow me to broach a topic you have laboriously dodged for a number of years."

"My will, no doubt," I impassively guessed.

"My boy," he sighed, "I feel I must state the obvious. You are the sole possessor of a considerable estate with multiple landholdings, properties, investments... the list continues on. And you have no will. This is foolhardy and I do not mind telling you so!"

"This is not a matter I wish to go into."

"That is too damned bad!" he snapped in the fatherly tone he occasionally employed with me. "You know that I hold none but your best interests, and I tell you that this matter is imperative. Your brother died a young man. What is to say that you would not meet a similar fate?"

'If only it were so,' I thought, but instead said aloud, "Rowland's penchant for excess far surpassed mine."

The solicitor hoisted a bushy white eyebrow aloft and muttered, "Marginally, if rumour is to be believed, Edward. But no matter. Your personal amusements are of little interest to me other than your bent toward spending your life gambolling the world over."

"You seem to take umbrage with that, Alistair!"

"Only because you have no heir, Edward! Ships sink, pestilence befouls, political uprisings escalate, *dispensed lovers avenge*."

I snorted a laugh at that one.

"We must discuss what is to become of your estate should you die," he affirmed.

Both fell silent for some minutes. My avoidance of this conversation lay in the simple fact that eventually Bertha must enter the topic. Two persons in England knew what she was to me; Grace Poole and Dr. Carter. Grace I told on her date of hire since her charge's ranting would surely document our marital history directly. And Dr. Carter because of his medical expertise, which in this case proved useless. Looking at this shrewd solicitor whom for the past three decades held intimate acquaintance with the Rochester fortune, I was sure he also knew.

I was married less than one season before my wife's insanity became apparent. Her father and brother were well aware of madness coursing through the family bloodline, as I later discovered. Jamaican gossip claimed her own mother was mad, and while the daughter was yet a child, was found drowned in the sea under mysterious circumstances.

Bertha's infamous acts and unchaste behaviour were my humiliation whilst sharing our marital home in Jamaica. Upon certainty of her illness, I wrote to Father, imploring him not to tell anyone in England of the marriage, and upon learning the tawdry and despicable details, he agreed to remain silent. But two months had already passed. He must have told someone. His solicitor for instance.

With a glance about to be certain we were alone, I said, "Alistair, let us be candid with one another. You know, don't you? Father must have told you."

"Of your marriage to the Mason woman?" he unabashedly replied. "Yes, Edward. I have always known. Your father was most pleased with himself for securing such a profitable union for you. And then upon learning of your wife's unfortunate mental decline, he came to me asking if the marriage could be dissolved. I shall say to you precisely what I said to Ian in response. The law does not permit a husband to abandon his marriage due to or in the presence of his wife's mental illness, as you well know."

"Yes," I bitterly acknowledged.

"What I do not know, Edward, is her current location. Does she live still?"

I tossed my head toward the north end of the house. "She is upstairs, locked away with an attendant looking after her."

He shook his head and gave a tsk-tsk. "I see. A most regrettable circumstance."

Regret? The understatement brought a sardonic smirk to my face. "So," I said. "The Rochester fortune shall, should I die, fall into the hands of a mad woman. Or rather into the hands of the next of kin, her brother, Richard Mason, the gentleman who helped devise that swindle wedding for his rapidly declining sister."

Blakely sighed. "So it seems. Your father provided me with a précis of the Mason kinsfolk. Father Jeremiah, now deceased, fell primary beneficiary after Ian and yourself. Now, upon your death, son Richard does become claimant."

"All most unscrupulous, would you not agree?"

"Without a doubt, young man," Blakely readily assented. "Yet a disagreeable history does not negate the claim, which, as it stands, is entirely permissible. You may bequeath what you wish to whom you wish, Edward, but without an heir, the bulk of your estate must be proffered to your legally recognised wife. After all, a not insignificant portion of your net worth was obtained through your wife's dowry. Twenty thousand, was it?"

"Yes."

He nodded and regarded me seriously. "You must also be aware that if the estate's legatee, Mr. Mason as it were, should find your allotments to others overly generous, it is his rightful prerogative to contest your will."

I sighed petulantly, looking about the splendidly furnished dining room. Never before did I care what happened to Thornfield Hall or to my wealth should I die. Why should I care? I would be dead. But now I did care. The thought of being separated from home, loyal staff, and, yes, from Jane, by sudden death, leaving all dependents without home or security and with no more than the remains of a meagre salary, left me uneasy indeed. And there was Adele to consider now that I had assumed responsibility for the child. Mrs. Fairfax, Leah and John were trusted persons employed with the Rochester family for many years, and so I could not be so negligent as to leave them without provision. 'The Rochester family indeed,' I thought. 'Look at what is left of it.'

Sipping my tea, I leaned back and reflected. If I could have my life as I wished, I would take Jane as my wife and all of this would be hers as well as mine. We would have children, and there really would be a Rochester family again. Heirs would abound, that was certain, I thought smiling. Our fortune would be equally divided between our children unlike Father's ideas for Rowland and myself. I considered this bittersweet image whilst gazing at the rich window hangings filtering bright afternoon light, at the ornately painted ceiling, rows of silverware, etc. then looked back at my legal counsellor. If the most I could do was ensure that the futures of my home's inhabitants were well provided, then I would let Blakely draw up the appropriate papers.

"Fine, Alistair, you win."

"Good man, Edward," he replied, taking a brandy snap from the sweets tray. "We shall begin immediately."

Late that evening, I retired to my study and closed myself in. A fire burned merrily in the grate as all was otherwise shrouded in quiet. The diamond-glassed casements were shut, the night being far too windy to leave them open. I wandered the room slowly, aimlessly.

Evening hours once so anticipated and pleasing now tormented me. The silence, deep shadows and boredom were burdensome enough, but worse was the ache in my heart for Jane; for her warm, affable conversation. I longed for her sudden arch smiles that could send my heart's rhythm askew, for comfortable mutual understanding, stimulating competition at times and the pleasing society of one so good and gifted. What had become of us? I searched my mind for a way this might have been avoided, but concluded that we inevitably stepped past our platonic, professional regard and found we desired to be together as man and wife. And in doing that, we both perceived impossibility. So we came apart.

Alone these evenings, I would distractedly revisit that night in the library by the fire and remember her song written for me with its sheerness of longing conveyed within. Somewhere in this massive house, at this moment, Jane also was tormented. I could feel it. Sometimes I would rise and go to the door, my heart commanding me to go to her, to say all that I was bursting to tell her, to kiss her, to wrap my arms about her slender body and to love her. 'No. That would be wrong,' or so Conscience and Reason would reprove. And I must agree. Already I had endangered her.

Tonight, I roamed about my study, lost in memory since there seemed nothing malevolent in drawing pleasure from past events. There, I could again feel her arms about my shoulders holding me close and feel her soft lips touch my face. Alone, I would once again suppress desire; the same that coursed through me on the night in the library as in so many more. I wished with all my soul that I had tasted her lips then. She was so close in my arms. But now the moment was gone, and soon, I would be too.

"Sir?"

I was jolted back to the present. Mrs. Fairfax had come in. "Yes, what is it?" I testily asked.

"I am sorry to have disturbed you, Mr. Rochester," she said. "I knocked at the door."

"What do you want, Mrs. Fairfax?"

"Grace asked that you go up tonight. Late she said. If you will."

Likely to walk the roof with Bertha. Yes, I must do my bit. I had long felt guilty for leaving Grace to manage alone every hour of the day and night. Though she was well compensated for her work, respite was also deserved. And now to keep Bertha under control on the roof as well, it was too much to expect of any individual, even one as stalwart as Grace.

Wearily I answered, "Yes, tell her to expect me later tonight."

"Very well," she said and turning to leave asked, "May I bring a brandy in for you, Sir? Or a glass of port?"

"Brandy would do well, thank you," I replied. Anything to deaden the pain.

Later that night, I shut myself into my chamber and removed formal evening attire of jacket, waistcoat and trousers. After pulling on a pair of canvas breeches, I lay down on the bed's coverlet. My head swam and ached. The first brandy was replicated with another, then a third. All were consumed rather quickly, and having had no supper, the effects were surprisingly strong. Feeling hot and feverish, I unbuttoned my shirt and flung it wide. The bedchamber's fireplace was ablaze with light and heat, and I thanked John for his attempt to kill me by hyperthermia.

I did intend to go to the north tower tonight, in about an hour. A brief rest before going would serve me well. With my head on the pillow, I turned toward the casement window but had no energy to rise and open it. My hand reached out but missed it by a considerable distance, then dropped onto the bed.

'In a few minutes. I shall get up in an hour.'

Sleep evaded me every night for the past week, but now it came and carried me swiftly away. I slept deeply, and when the dream returned of trees rustling on a breeze and of walking in fields, I sank deeper. Calm blanketed me. I recognized the field, the sunset and waving timothy grass. Far away across the field stood my angel in white. I went towards her, walking, then running, but could not reach her. She began walking away. The waves of grass became water and the sunset turned to fire. My footing was now upon a boat surrounded by a rough, rolling sea of grey-green. Now the boat was ablaze! My angel appeared on the far side of the flames where I could not reach her. Fear and desperation gripped me.

Then, a voice broke through the boat's roaring fire: "...Sir! ...Heaven's sake!... Sir ... wake up!"

Cold and wet came down on me as waves surged hugely over the bow. Startled by icy water and a woman's panicked voice, I bolted awake.

Fire! In my bedchamber!

I leapt up and onto the floor, spinning about to see the inferno of my bed. I was not alone. Someone... who? Is that? Yes! Jane! She was in my chamber, attacking the flames with a coverlet. The hangings all around my bed were alight, and now the bedclothes had caught. I pulled hangings down and threw them to the floor, smothering them with the scorched coverlet before leaping to the far side of the bed to stamp out flames. Jane found more water in vases, threw their cut blooms to the floor and doused the burning bedclothes. Finally, with the fire extinguished and bedclothes smouldering, we stood back to breathlessly survey the ruin of my bed.

"Are you hurt?" I asked, my fully intact attachment to her tightly interwoven with protectiveness.

She stood beside me, gasping from exertion and panic, looking to me with grave concern. "No, I am not, Sir. But you were nearly burnt to death in your bed!"

"What did you see, Jane? What happened here?" I asked, knowing full bloody well what happened. How much had Jane seen and heard?

She shook her head and said, "I do not know. I heard a noise outside my chamber, and someone attempted my door. I was frightened and called out. Then came a laugh, Sir. I waited some moments before coming into the gallery and found it smoke filled. I followed the smoke to your door."

Nodding and working to appear calm, fury rose up in me like boiling flood waters. She meant to attack Jane first.

The room was now cold, dark and hazy. How long had I been sleeping? The fire in the hearth burned low and dim, but by the brilliant light of a high and full moon I could clearly see all. Small and pale, Jane shivered in her nightgown and sought to warm her bare feet, one atop the other. I looked about for a dry and undamaged blanket but found none. My dressing gown was left draped over the sofa. I took it up and threw its weight about her shoulders, closing the lapels around her and warming her arms. Suddenly I was aware that my unbuttoned shirt gaped widely, and at the same time Jane's eyes fell from mine to sweep over my chest. A faint, involuntary gasp escaped her lips. Her eyes widened and darted to the fire. Smiling softly, I took her cool hand in mine and brought her around the sofa to the warmth of the hearth. There I seated her and pulled the dressing gown about her, then added coal and kindling to the fire, building it up well.

"Better now?" I asked.

Her long, loose hair shimmered in the firelight and skin blushed warmly. She pulled the thick material closely about her, extending her bare toes to the fire. "Yes, Sir, I am warm. Thank you."

I lifted her chilled hands and warmed them in mine. "I must see to the servants," I gently said and released her to pull on my boots. "Do not leave until I return. Will you wait here for me, Jane?"

Her eyes fixed on the fire, and I remembered my bare chest, smiled and buttoned my shirt. She considered my request, then nodded. "I will wait, Sir. If you wish."

Taking a candle, I went to the door, my mind racing with anticipation of what might lay ahead. Fury, fear and excitement all crept deeper into my core by the second. "Jane, I am going to lock this door. Do not open it for any reason. Do you understand?"

She looked to the door then back to me. "Yes, Sir. You will not be in any danger, will you?"

"I shall return when all is secure." It was the most I could give.

I stepped out and locked the bedchamber door. Alone in the blackened gallery I found myself in a murderous frame of mind. My wife had attempted to burn me to death, stood over me as I slept, setting fire to my bed, and at that very moment was walking freely about the house. The safety of my dependents was jeopardised. I shook with wrath and held the candle aloft but its light only cast deeper shadows down the gallery and into corners. She could be anywhere. My ears strained for the sound of her coming up behind me.

In the nursery, Adele slept soundly in her bed, and in another corner of the room, her nurse, Sophie, too slept on. I left them and shut the door, moving on to Mrs. Fairfax's rooms. Locked. Clever old bird. Moving along the gallery I passed my chamber door, approaching the north tower. Long festering grievances of my father's betrayal welled up inside me and fused with wrath as I took tentative step after step.

Aloud I whispered, "Are you pleased with yourself, Father? Is this what you wanted for your son? For your Goddamned flesh and blood? The bride *you* chose is stalking me in the dark, inside your precious mausoleum of a Hall." I whipped around, then to each side holding the candle high. "No, you have not won yet, old man. You cannot break me. Merciful God has sent me hope and comfort so that I yet may live."

Corners were turned slowly, carefully; my nerves tensed to the shattering point. The clock downstairs suddenly struck and I leapt, my heart pounding. It was two o'clock. Blood rushed in my ears as I breathed deeply and continued on. Bertha may have gone downstairs or back up into the north tower. Or she could be out in the grounds, running away. God help the little village of Hay and its darkened farmhouses along the way.

Silence and blackness surrounded me. I reached the ancient oak panelled door leading into the north tower and found it left widely open. At the gaping doorway, I reached up to the frame, feeling for the key, but it was not there. As I lowered my arm, a low laugh came almost at my ear. Much shaken, I collected myself, stood back and placed the candle in my non-dominant hand, then slowly shut the door. There she stood, looking at me eye to eye for she was quite tall, with a wild smile splitting her once pretty face as she triumphantly held up the key for me to see.

"You are looking for this, Edward?" she asked in her low Creole tone.

"Give the key here, Bertha," I said, barely concealing my fury.

She pouted. "No. You want to lock me in that room upstairs. You hate me, I know! You want me to die there."

"Bertha...," I warned, moving toward her carefully.

"You no longer love me," she said with exaggerated pathos.

"Give the key to me."

"How long it has been since last we bedded, my darling. But I remember how you like it. Shall we? Right here will do." With another hideous smile she slid the shift from her shoulder.

Wrath overtook me. Grabbing the key from her hand I pocketed it, seized her arm and flung the door to the north tower open again. She wrenched herself free of my grip and with both hands lunged for my throat. I threw the candle down and all light was gone. Now in complete darkness, with disgust and fury driving my actions, I shoved my attacker away but she gave a savage scream and charged again. My hand tightened into a fist, and aiming by sound alone, I settled her with one well-planted blow to the face. She collapsed into a heap on the floor.

In the blackness I stood over her and rocked myself, my hands clasped over my mouth, suppressing the howls of agony rising from deep within. Never had I struck a woman in my life, and I was horrified. I should have restrained her! Should have held her arms back. Not even in Jamaica, where I attended her in our airy clapboard marital home on a remote hilltop, oftentimes alone, did I resort to such a method of restraining her. How much the years of hopelessness had changed me! Was there no end to the misery this marriage would bring?

With the key in my pocket, I lifted my wife's slackened body over my shoulder and carried her up the winding north tower steps, through the crimson bedchamber to her stone prison. Grace Poole was asleep at the table, her head down on folded arms and a stoneware mug set before her. I deposited Bertha onto her narrow bed, went to Grace and stood looking down on the snoring attendant. I lifted the mug and smelled the contents. Rum. With a SLAM! the mug came down on the table, waking Grace with a start.

"Mr. Rochester!"

"Good evening, Grace."

"What...? Where is...?" Then turning to see her unconscious, bloody-faced charge, she leapt up. "Oh! Mr. Rochester, Sir. I am so terribly sorry. Please. You must forgive...'

But I had taken a candle and was out of the room, closing the door and locking it. The remaining deadbolts were secured, and with the key in hand

I returned downstairs to my chamber. Weary and teeming with self-loathing, I unlocked my door and entered. The fire had been built up again, but I did not see Jane.

'She has returned to her own room,' I thought, and searing disappointment added to my miserable spirits. As I advanced toward the fire and around the sofa, my heart leapt. Jane was there, curled asleep on the sofa, wrapped in my black woollen dressing gown. Her long hair lay against the quilted silken collar, its length fallen to the floor making a lovely cascade. I knelt on the rug before her and silently thanked God for the one gift of her presence. All was so abysmal in my life. Simply being near Jane offered an oasis of comfort, and I watched her sleep for a long time for if she woke, she might leave, and I could not bear that.

I lifted her long chestnut hair and ran it through my fingers, around my face and neck. I studied her eyelashes, nose and the curve of her lips. Fingers were lured to her skin. My touch ran across a velvety soft cheekbone and the backs of my fingers down her cheek. It suddenly occurred to me that my hand ached from the strike I delivered in the gallery, and my breath caught as I imagined bringing a fist to this face. 'Never, oh never. Nothing but soft caresses.' I tried to suppress tears but again could not. I looked away and let the tears spill over, wiping them away with my sleeve. Jane was waking, opening her eyes. Seeing me, she quickly sat up and pulled the dressing gown close about her.

"I am very sorry, Sir. I fell asleep," she said. Then, "Everything is all right I hope?"

I stood and left the sofa, trying still to control my tears. I cleared my throat. "It is as I thought, Jane."

"Oh? How, Sir?"

"You say you saw a person in the gallery?"

"No, I did not see anyone, but I did hear a person outside my door. And that person made a strange sort of laugh."

"You've heard that laugh before or something like it?" I asked.

"Once before, Sir. There is a woman who sews here, in the north tower. Her name is Grace Poole. I've heard her in her rooms, laughing in that way. She is a singular sort of person."

Just the explanation. "Yes, you've guessed it, Jane. Grace is, as you say, singular. We shall think no more about it." I was quick to end the subject. Quick to end my lying.

Jane was clearly doubtful but said nothing. She looked tired, dejected, and she did not meet my eyes. I needed to send her away to her chamber. Conscience and sensibility ruled that I must place her away from me where

I could not bring her harm or shame, but since watching her sleep, touching her face and hair, my stifled yearning for her was gaining strength and threatened to conquer. My mind was not right, and I did not trust myself.

"Go back to your own room now, Jane. In a few hours the servants will be up."

She paused and looked at me for a long moment. I could feel the hurt inside of her, present this past week. Present since the night she said, 'My love for you frightens me.' Since the night we held one another in the firelight and I kissed her neck, then left her. Jane rose from the sofa, leaving my dressing gown lain over the back. She passed me silently and went to the door. But watching her leave, my heart and soul mutinied against fact and fate.

"And you will go?" My brain searched for pretence and found one. "Jane, you saved my life," I told her and indicated to the scorched bed. "Come. Let us at least shake hands."

She hesitated at the door. For a moment I thought she would continue away, leaving me without another word, but she turned, quietly and watchfully coming forward to take my proffered hand. All of my resolve disappeared in those instants. To hell with reason. To hell with the future and past. Life is brutal and we must obtain our comfort where and when it is offered. I could not send her away nor allow her to leave me. Looking at her in the glow of the fire, at those grey-green eyes in which I had become lost so many times, I knew it and could not deny it. I loved her.

Standing here, holding her hand in mine, her touch mastered me. She owned me. I took her hand in both of mine, swallowed hard and said in a quavering voice, "I must tell you, Jane, that I knew from the time we met, on that rainy evening by the river, what you would become to me. From the instant I beheld you, something pure and fresh stole into my heart and has held me fast ever since." There. It was out. I breathed deeply and looked above, then back to her. "I knew you would do me good, Jane. You saved me tonight! How pleased I am to find myself in your debt."

She had been watching my eyes, my face. Her expression was yet apprehensive, and I felt the slight tension of her hand pulling away from mine. "There is no debt or obligation in the matter, Sir. I am only glad I happened to be awake."

I laughed softly and stepped closer. "You saved me from an excruciating death. You think it no more than a minute service do you?"

Jane again attempted to extricate her hand, but I would not release her. I could not permit her to leave this room and abandon me to another night of wretched thoughts and insomnia. Her sleeping soul was on the verge of awakening, and I wanted, I needed, to be the recipient of that glory. 'Wake, Jane' my eyes begged hers. Nothing reproving spoke to me. This moment was natural, right and good.

"Sir, I am cold," she said, drawing away.

"Ah. Yes. Cold. Right then." I lifted my dressing gown from the sofa and threw it about her shoulders as she stood looking up at me with surprise. My hands on her now was the last decorum could withstand, and in one swift motion I took hold of the lapels, drawing her forcefully close. Her hands went up against my ribs, restraining me. My intention was to press her body to mine and kiss her, but her sharp gasp and wide eyes stopped me. I waited, my lips so close to hers that I could feel her rapid, warm breaths.

She looked from my eyes to my lips. It seemed a wordless eternity passed. Presently Jane's apprehension receded, shoulders loosened and she regained herself. The feel of her rhythmic hot breath on my lips tantalised unbearably, and my body fully responded to her near proximity. She gently pushed me away. I let her but would not release my grip on the weighty dressing gown lapels. She lifted her face, searched my eyes, wet her lips. Then, she shocked me absolutely by raising a hand to my shirt collar and followed it down to the first button where, never taking her eyes from mine, she unbuttoned one, then another. My heart raced, thumping so that I could hear it. She continued to unbutton, ceasing at mid abdomen. I did not dare move. 'Touch me' my mind begged her.

Fingers slipped beneath the shirt's opened fabric where warm, tentative touch met my bare chest. My body convulsed. Her hand moved left, exploring through dark, curled hair, and a soft palm caressed the rise of muscle, slowly wandering over curves. This hand came flat to my chest, and she paused and smiled, feeling the beat of my heart. The pleasure of her gentle, feminine touch was indescribable. Continuing to explore, her fingers found nipple, and I convulsed yet again in response. Fingertips circled and teased, my head fell back and I stared dreamily at the ceiling, my breaths coming in short gasps, fists gripping fabric, trembling violently. 'Do not think, Edward,' my mind said. 'Just feel.'

And I did. Time and consciousness swam and melted away. I breathed through it, the pleasure so intense, so exquisite, it neared pain. 'If she brings her mouth and tongue to me,' I thought, 'I will not be able to stop myself.' She did not. After a time, I looked back to her, to her face flushed with desire, eyes questioningly on mine. I released the dressing gown to place my hand over hers, pressing her palm to my chest.

"My cherished preserver," I whispered. With gentle fingertips, I traced her jaw line, her cheek and brow. So velvety soft and smooth. With a hand against her cheek and fingers into her hair, I pulled her close, needing the intimacy of our kiss. 'Control, Edward. Her first kiss.' Yes. Oh, yes. I brought my mouth slowly to hers, our breath interlacing. My lips brushed hers gently, and I lay soft, loving kisses along both. She responded, parting her lips under mine and kissing in return. I savoured the sensation of her kiss; of her lips tentatively catching mine to taste and suck gently, feeling delicious vibrations in her throat. Innately passionate was my Jane. Our breathing came laboured, our hearts pounding. Her hand slipped around to my back and beneath my shirttail, pulling me closer, but with this I restrained her. As aroused as I have ever been in my life, I feared my excitement would frighten her. But she pulled me closer; no uneasiness between us.

We were borne away on a wave of passion, standing there, our mouths exploring, hands drinking in sensation, locked together. Perhaps I could have seduced her, could have taken her down to the carpet before the fire and claimed her as my own. She was out of herself and with further skilled stimulus, I doubt she would have stopped me, and if I loved her less, I would have. But I had no wish to take. In the past, my own pleasure was all I considered and I took it greedily. But for Jane, I only wanted to give, and there must be no shame or regret left behind.

So I took her hand and brought her to the sofa where I drew her down alongside me, laying together. Our kissing was fervent, her quivering uncontrollable, and I steadied her in my tight embrace. Softly, I stroked her cheek and neck. Her slender arms pulled me close, her fingers in my hair. My caress swept over her chest and down; down to the row of buttons closing her nightgown, and I opened one. With this she gasped and pulled away fearfully, her eyes searching mine.

I shook my head slowly. "I shall not hurt you, Jane. You are in my hands and are safe. Permit yourself to feel my touch."

Resistance lessened. My fingers unbuttoned again, and her hand flew to my arm at the bicep, gripping it. I smiled and softly kissed her lips, slipping a hand inside her nightgown. Her gasp was sharp and back arched. I lay quietly at her side as fingertips ran along lovely skin, between her breasts where I felt the intense thumping of her heart, exploring rise and curve of firm, young delicate softness. "Beautiful," I assured her. My touch kneaded until her body was quite permissive, whereupon rigid nipple was enclosed between my fingers. Her body tensed, now for quite a different reason, eyes closed, breathing coming in gasps and shudders. Gently I kissed her face as my fingers worked, whispering her loveliness. I wanted so much to use mouth, tongue, and lips but did not, wondering whether I could bring her along this way alone.

Gently and rhythmically, I squeezed and rolled her nipple. My knee fell between hers, restraining her increasing writhing, and her bare ankles wrapped around my booted leg. Every muscle tensed and she became rigid from head to toe. Her breaths through parted lips lessened to barely perceptible gasps. "Breathe," I whispered to her, working her nipple continuously. Watching her, I was fascinated. She gripped my arm tightly and shook with rigid tension. Suddenly, tremors shook her frame throughout. Again and again she gasped heavily and cried out once. Her release went on, and I joyously continued her pleasure until the last tremor left her. She lay quietly in the firelight, her breathing slowing, swallowing occasionally. I watched her, propped on an elbow and softly smiling down on her.

Jane opened her eyes and looked at me. "Mr. Rochester," she began, and I laughed. She was not going to call me Mr. Rochester in private moments, not after tonight, was she?

She smiled and said, "What... umm... what was...?"

I laughed softly again. "That, my love, was a climax. Your first, I take it."

She nodded, embarrassed.

I smiled and kissed her, a low laugh rumbling in my throat, then shifted so that I lay on my back and pulled her onto me, covering us with the weight of my dressing gown. My hands wandered along her back, feeling each individual vertebra and caressing her hair. She laid her fingers to my bare chest.

"Did you like what I did?" she asked slipping her hand under my shirt, a saucy smile over her lips.

I smiled at her insecure, sweet innocence; my heart quickening with the thought of those first moments tonight. "Loved it," I whispered.

She smiled with me. "I loved watching you."

"It gets even better, Jane." My hand came to her face and drew her mouth to mine. We shared a long, deep, searching kiss. Then, thinking of how the scene began, I said in an accusatory tone, "You started this. Your spells... Did I not say you are a witch?"

"I am no witch, Sir. I only wanted to feel the beat of your heart. You piqued my interest with that suggestion."

"Ah yes! Our conversation by the river. You remembered that, did you?"

"I remember everything you tell me," she said, and I believed that to be quite true.

"Jane," I said softly, gazing up at her. "I've missed you terribly these past evenings without your companionship. Words can not express how much."

She stroked my face, my lips. "I am glad I stayed tonight," she murmured. "There has been such pain in my heart. It is gone now."

"Mine too."

The fire cast a warm flickering glow as she settled into me, her hands beneath my shoulders and cheek resting on my chest. Life, even for me, proved to have its treasures. I silently prayed that Jane and I would not be separated for very long, but I knew the time was approaching for me to go. 'Not yet, I thought. Let me have now. Time, go slowly.'

I was exhausted. Tonight I experienced both agony and ecstasy, nearly died and was saved, and had given without taking. All that was good in my life was here in my arms but not for much longer. Downstairs, the clock struck four. Jane slept in my arms and I savoured the rise and fall of each breath. Her weight was a delicious burden. My hands caressed her back as I looked to the fire and burning embers. 'Do not think, Edward. Feel.'

Chapter 10

WHEN MY EYES opened again, grey light of dawn was gleaming between the chamber's heavy velour drapes. 'Not yet' I thought, looking away to the dying fire. 'This must not end yet.' In defence of our fading moment, I clasped Jane close to my heart. Tonight, tomorrow, next week – all of this would have been a dream and with daylight would come change. For the past week, since the night I followed Jane to the library and come away knowing she loved me, I resolutely built a fortress around my heart so that this day, this coming act, would be painless. And last night I willingly, wantonly tore it all down. Now we both would bear wounds that would soon gape and bleed. 'You are selfish to the nth degree, Edward,' Conscience chided. 'Did you not consider her?' I supposed I did not.

Reluctantly I acknowledged that the time of our parting had come. Gently I rose from the sofa and shifted Jane in my arms. She groaned, clutched my shirt and slowly opened her eyes, all sleepy peacefulness. With a serene smile, she embraced me and raised her lips to mine. She kissed me full and soulful. I went weak, thinking, 'What would I not give to keep this woman with me every minute of the night and day?' Nothing. There was nothing I would not give. But I would not hurt her to make it so. No matter what torment it caused me, I must protect her to the last. 'Save your lovely Jane, Edward,' Conscience agreed. 'Save her.'

Kissing, hands caressing and exploring, our passion escalated swiftly and we trembled in one another's arms. I had to put a stop to this and somehow rein in the tremendous force driving us. I must leave her today, and certainly

I was not growing any closer to doing so. All resolve was required to pull away from her. Her face was flushed with desire, her hair long and loose, breathing deeply, unbound curves beneath her unbuttoned nightgown plainly discernible. I whispered a haphazard prayer and might even have whimpered.

"Come, Jane, we must stop," I said to her, breathless.

Seeing my serious expression, she sat up and moved away from me on the sofa. "You are correct, Sir. I must go to my own room."

I nodded and we stood. With our parting eminent, I lifted her in my arms, wanting to pretend if only for a minute that I was carrying her to bed. To our bed. She read my thoughts and gave a knowing smile. With her head on my shoulder and arms about my neck, I carried her out of my chamber and along the faintly lit gallery, into her own bedchamber. Gently I pushed the door shut and lay her down.

I sat at the bedside, looking down on her. Taking her hands in mine, I ran them over my rough, blue-black, morning-shadow beard. We laughed, and I kissed her fingertips. This was a strange mix of desire and sadness for we both knew that daylight had brought an end to our dream-like first passion and a world of uncertainty awaited us. As she lay there in her bed with her hair all about her, she was nearly impossible to resist. I touched her face and moved long strands away from her forehead, imprinting the sensations into my brain to sustain me in future.

"You will go today," she said, studying my face. How did she know so easily what I thought and felt?

I looked away to the dim grey light beyond the window. "Yes, Jane. I must."

She slipped her hand into my shirt and over my heart. "I wish you would tell me what it is that troubles you. Why do you run from Thornfield Hall?"

"Jane," I said, "I run because I have painful thoughts, and the Hall is a constant reminder of their source."

"But why do you run from me? I am here. Have I not brought you happier thoughts since you've again been in residence?"

With a quavering laugh, I replied, "I am not running from you! Oh Jane, you've no idea what twenty years has done to me. Time can bring much damage. I must go because you deserve better than me."

She brought her hand to my cheek and searched my eyes. "There is no such thing."

I brought my head down and hid my eyes in her nightgown. 'Oh God, Jane, I do love you.' But I could not speak it. She was so honest and true. She truly believed that. She lifted my face and we kissed as if drawn together by some otherworldly force; soft, deep and slow. Oh, I loved it. Nothing else, no one else, had ever been like this. Jane touched my soul when she kissed me.

Inevitably passion flared, and as before I rallied my strength to pull away from her. Onto my feet, I forced myself to walk across the floor, and not looking back, opened the door and left her. I returned to my chamber with a dizzying blend of heartbreak and sexual excitement skewing all perception. There, drapes were opened wide and strengthening daylight illuminated the room shattering the warm, intimate setting of the night before. I surveyed the bed; a scorched, dampened mess of destroyed hangings and bedclothes. 'Jane, my angel in white, you saved me.'

It was early yet. The sun was not quite above the horizon, but a clear sky of periwinkle blue promised a fine day. Meadowlarks, finches and mourning doves chirped and called in the orchards and grounds. I was terribly tired and wondered how long had it been since I slept a full night. Closing the drapes I went to the fire and built it up again, then removed my boots and lay back on the sofa cushions. Arms over my head, I stretched languidly and thought.

I thought of the tempting answer to my dilemma. It wove its way into my consciousness during this past week and like the biblical serpent, toyed with me during my most vulnerable hours, leaving me more than smitten. The answer simply consisted of this: feign a wedding. Marriage to Jane would be of my heart if not sanctioned in the eyes of God or man's law. Never should I tell her of my previous marriage or of Bertha Mason's existence. I was married in Jamaica and therefore no records existed of the union here in England. If done quietly, Carter was not likely to ever hear of Jane or our wedding. And Grace would not breathe a word of it - her ample salary depended upon a promise of discretion. Besides, she was now in my debt owing to her drunken lapse of last evening. Not another soul in England knew my history. Others such as Mrs. Fairfax, Leah and John were of course aware that a lunatic was kept in the north tower, but they believed her to be the Master's bastard half sister; a clever bit of improvisation on my part and an admittedly spiteful posthumous slight upon my father's memory. Yes, it was an odiously juvenile act, I know, but deservedly so. Furthermore, Jane had no family to interfere or make enquiries concerning me.

So, I would propose to her, take her to church and there would be a wedding ceremony. Afterward I would whisk her away from Thornfield to travel the world. Our home would be a villa in the south of France on the Mediterranean near Narbonne, and there, secluded and alone, we would love our days and nights away. All matters of postal correspondence would be screened by me before meeting her hands. Life alone together would be blissfully under my control because, you see, no shortage of endurance existed in me, and I could run forever if necessary.

But as temptation toyed with me, Conscience and Reason would slip in a word. Why was I harassed continually by my conscience? I knew men who philandered without an inkling of guilt. Not only did they co-exist with a wife and children, but they kept mistresses all about town and dallied with the parlour maid as well. They considered it their right and due. Not I. Conscience was ever at the ready.

'Edward,' its calm voice pointed out, 'Truth always comes to light. Do you wish to spend the remainder of your life evading truth, fearful that Jane may learn of Bertha's existence? What would Jane do, even years from now, if she discovered herself deliberately lured into a feigned union with a defrauded wretch such as yourself? All trust and confidence would be destroyed. She would despise you.'

One other crucial point bespoke. 'Given your passion for this young, healthy miss, it is probable she would become pregnant before the close of your first season together. And then you would have children to consider. Illegitimate children. How would she react upon finding one day that they were conceived out of wedlock and raised amongst a web of lies? When the time of your death arrives, Thornfield and your amassed wealth will not be the entitlement of your children and their mother. Your loved ones would be labelled by the law as your bastards and mistress.'

This was where my temptation stopped in its tracks; with the thought of Jane despising me, our children labelled illegitimate, all living destitute and despising me as well. The potential of this coming to fruition is what strengthened me to leave Jane.

'I will go,' I replied to Conscience. 'I will distance myself from Thornfield Hall, from the location of both angel and demon, and from the site of temptation to commit a heinous crime against the woman I love.' I needed to think clearly and not make rash decisions that would ultimately seal the fate of two people. Probably more. Definitely more.

Having mulled these ideas for the umpteenth time, the same command spoke to me now as had done every day and night for a week: 'Leave Thornfield. Go to Ingram Park. Those persons, who are after all your social peers and neighbours, expect you there. Afterwards go to France and there remain on that quiet porch of your white washed villa and find peace enough to make the most important decision of your life. You can not think rationally here.'

All sorts of suggestions would interject, the most worrisome being: What if Jane is gone when I return? I could not expect her to wait for me, not for an indefinite period of time. Counting all the reasons I loved her and of the qualities I valued in her, I thought also of the reasons I could not keep my eyes and hands away from her. Would those qualities be lost on all other men? Certainly not. She may find someone else in the meantime. Suddenly, lying on the sofa, a fresh and sharp possessiveness gripped me. If I did not marry her, someone else would. Another man would have her, would receive her kiss and would retain her promise of everlasting love and devotion. On their wedding night, he would take what is mine. She would give herself without her full heart because her heart was with me!

Base motivations invaded me throughout. 'It is me she wants!' Agonising over this, I arose and stalked about the room. A starburst of white-hot jealous aggression seared my brain. I thought of Jane married, pregnant with another man's child and felt as if I had been punched in the gut.

A crisp vertical line of bright light now shone through a gap between the curtains. The time was growing late. I undressed thoroughly, throwing breeches and linen shirt over the back of the sofa as my jealous mind chanted 'She is mine! Mine! Mine!' I reached for my dressing gown. In throwing it around my shoulders, a wave of her scent surrounded me, breaking through my bilious meditations. I could smell her and myself mingled together. I breathed her in, again dizzied.

'Tired. I am so tired.'

I went to the sofa intending to lie down but was too agitated to do so. Possessive masculine instincts continued to course through me. I breathed deeply, trying to relax. At the same time I became aware of a fine tremor in my shoulders and back, first ignited last night when Jane unbuttoned my shirt and touched, sending thrills of exquisite pleasure through me. Pleasure that brought me to gasp and tremble violently. I went to the fireplace and leaned a forearm against the mantle, staring into the low, crackling flames.

Last night was unlike any encounter I had ever experienced with a woman. No woman's passion had ever been in such complete accordance with mine. None before, not wife nor mistresses, was ever an acceptable fit, not sexually nor emotionally. Always it was the Rochester name, my wealth, social status or some other *objective* that they lusted after, and none had ever loved me as she did. That was certain.

Last night and this morning... the memory of it all grasped me by my vitals and held me helpless. Jane's hunger for me was painted all over her face and body. She glowed with it, emitted it, radiated it. It was primal and my culpability matched hers. Her kisses breathed love into me, caressing my soul and I drank it up greedily. She responded to me so absolutely. Our fervent kissing sent her quite out of herself, and then my touch of her breast, of her rigid nipple, built and carried her through a powerful climax. Leaning against the mantel, I placed forehead onto wrist. Closing my eyes, I thought again of Jane's kiss, her soft lips and hot breath. I opened my dressing gown.

Her hand on my chest, teasing me, driving me mad.

My hand slipped down to my own excitement.

Her mouth on mine, gently sucking my lip.

Rock hard, painfully desperate for release.

Love you, marry you, my bride, take you to bed. Yes, to my bed...

Pleasure building in the core of me.

Oh, love me. Yes, you are ready for me. I will break you, take all of you, make you mine, make you cry out...

Pleasure mounting, then exploding.

Yes! Oh, now! Now! Together, flood you, make you my wife ...

I unleashed a cry from deep within as my seed incinerated with faint hisses in the flames. Once drained, I fell back onto the sofa, heaving with relief.

Presently I glanced about the silent room and asked of no one in particular, "How long am I to live this way? Alone?"

The pleasure of post climactic release should be savoured in bed with my wife, touching, talking, laughing... loving. Why was it so wrong for me to want what all other men had? Since I was twenty-three years old, I was forbidden to love any woman. It was not my fault, Goddammit! I was the dutiful son. I did what Father expected of me without question. I permitted him to banish me from my home and exile me to a foreign land where I was handed down a life sentence of loneliness. And why? What sin had I committed? This unjust result was not of my doing. I had been but a naïve dupe.

Looking to the morning light glaring between the drapes, I recalled Genesis. *And the Lord God said, it is not good that man should be alone. I will make a helpmeet for him.*

'Could that please apply to me, Lord? Would that be all right?' I closed my eyes in prayer. And finally slept.

From deep sleep, far away, there was a knock at my chamber door. I vaguely heard it in my dreams but it meant nothing. Louder knock. Then another. The sound drew me from the world of tranquil sleep back into my empty bedchamber and awake. This was a sleep deprivation conspiracy. Must be.

"Sir? You there, Sir?" came John's voice.

Covering myself with the dressing gown I called, "Oh for the love of God, come!"

The door opened and he peered in. "Sir, it's gone eight o'clock. Thought I should wake you. Good heavens, Sir! What's happened to your bed?"

I yawned and smoothly lied, "Left a candle burning on the bedside table. The hangings caught fire as I slept. It was brought under control before too much damage was done."

"Lord save us! Right, then. I shall inform Mrs. Fairfax. Bath and shave, Sir?"

"Yes. I will be departing for a house party as soon as I am ready. Expect me to be gone for a fortnight or more. You must prepare my clothes, John."

"Yes, Sir. Directly. The bath is being drawn for you."

"Be sure to pack my dressing gown. This one."

"Uh, yes, of course, Sir."

I hauled myself up and began preparation for my bath. "John, is everyone up now?" I asked.

Busying himself at my wardrobe, he replied, "No, Mr. Rochester. The governess has not yet appeared this morning either."

"Well, leave her then, John. She has looked tired to me. Let her sleep." Was there no end to my fabrications?

Soon I was soaking in a hot bath and shaving by the mirror set across the tub. Whilst carefully scraping my jaw with a straight razor, I decided that Thornfield would be missed. Indefinite separation from Jane was too wrenching a prospect as of yet, and so that became a component resolutely blocked from the equation. Instead I reflected that I had been in residence for nearly four months and since then became settled into a pleasant routine almost as if it were my home. I tried to think of Thornfield as home, but could not. It was my father's possession. Ian Rochester's foreboding pile of stone as it had always been. And only by default did I become possessor and tenant.

Sinking down beneath the water, I wetted my hair and soaping it thoroughly. Time to play the role of Master of the Estate. I hoped to heaven that Eshton would be there at Ingram Park, and even better if some of the other men of my generation were present as well. Lord and Lady Ingram were infamous for hosting house parties that were in actuality thinly disguised matchmaking symposiums. I doubted sincerely that I could stomach such an ordeal, so hopefully their liquor supply would be plentiful. Yes, that would do well. A brandy in the evenings. Brandy, as in my study by the fire with Jane… conversing… kissing.

'Edward. Back on track now, all right?'

My concentration shifted again to the Ingram family. The widely respected Lord and Lady were parents of debutante daughter Mary, who, although innocuous enough in my opinion, bore a terminal case of the giggles kept effervescing by her most insipid wit. This was doubly unfortunate in revealing far too often her remarkably wonky teeth and a laugh that universally called to mind a mare in season.

Son Andrew was an amusing study himself. A braggadocio youth with an effete brand of masculinity affording him the reputation of a very successful lothario indeed, he may choose to be present at this gathering or he may not, depending what else was on offer.

The Lord had been a good friend of Father's many years ago and was a hearty fellow whom I generally liked. Lady Ingram was something else altogether; a haughty, opinionated, condescending, overbearing crone who seemed inexplicably convinced that I was the perfect match for her darling eldest daughter, Blanche.

The said Blanche Ingram was quite the belle of the county upon her societal debut nearly a decade ago. Undeniably beautiful, tall, blonde, blue eyed, with flawless skin and a fine figure, Blanche possessed command of several languages and an array of accomplishments including piano and voice. But she was quick to temper, cruel to those of a lesser station, hollow of soul and spirit, and possibly the most self-obsessed woman I had ever known. Heavenly on the outside yet a cesspool within.

Shortly after Blanche's eighteenth birthday, Lady Ingram launched endeavours to make a match of us. When my presence was requested at a ball, cotillion, hunt, outing or house party, I masterfully portrayed the image of Blanche's suitor, mostly because I found the daughter's ineffectual attempts at beguiling me so entirely entertaining. But also because I enjoyed, at any opportunity, taking Blanche to a vacant room or out into secluded grounds for an intimate tête-à-tête that normally disintegrated into a thorough groping of her curvaceous body. Blanche was pleasing to the eyes and hands but otherwise vapid and useless, and so I rapaciously took my fill. She would tolerate only so much before pushing me away, the picture of a scandalised innocent, and would upbraid me as a 'cur' or an 'animal.' *Hilarious!* Particularly so since I happened to know that she had been fondled by men of gentry the county over, which made her feigned modesty doubly assault-worthy. But the prospect of claiming my name and fortune would briskly whittle away Blanche's indignation incurred by my taking liberties. Then the scene would repeat. And that was the sum total of my romance with Blanche Ingram.

Now, after bathing and building the image of high societal presentability, I looked myself over in the mirror, acutely aware that I would not be meeting Blanche with my customary lustful sportsmanship. Desire to so much as kiss her hand was lacking let alone take her to a secluded location for a meaningless dalliance. 'Before arriving,' I thought, 'I must contrive a means of avoiding her sole company. Perhaps she will not be interested in me.' Then I recalled the simpering tone of her invitation. This may be a very brief visit to Ingram Park indeed.

Dressed in white ruffled shirt and cravat, royal blue waistcoat, charcoal jacket and trousers, diamond stickpin and cuff links, I arranged my black wavy/curly hair and inspected myself in the wardrobe mirror. And found no cause for objection.

There was one untidy end requiring my attention before departing, so taking the north tower key, I went through the second story corridors to the ancient oak door, made my way through locked doors and up the staircase to the ornate boudoir until I came to the final locked portal. I knocked. Locks shot back and Grace Poole stood before me.

"Sir," she said with an abridged curtsey, her eyes fixed laterally on a window.

"Grace, I trust that whilst I am away, you shall maintain your post with your faculties fully intact."

She thrust her chin and kept her eyes elsewhere. "I shall, Sir."

"Perhaps you are not aware that she attempted to burn me to death in my bed last night? Or that upon being discovered, she attempted to strangle me?"

Grace flushed crimson. "No, Sir. You do have my deepest apologies for the incident." And then looking directly at me, she added, "I did notice your effective manner of subduing her. Missus' nose will likely have righted itself by month's end if that is of any concern to you."

Her cheeky imputation galled me. "She is not to cause trouble in my absence. Is that quite understood, Mrs. Poole?"

"It is, Mr. Rochester. And, Sir, if I may suggest, perhaps it is time you considered relocating her to Ferndean Manor?"

"Perhaps, Grace, it is time for you to sever your dependency upon rum and remember your place!"

We glared at each other. I was as dependent on Grace Poole as she was on me; an unsettling thought to say the least. With nothing more to say, I turned on my heel and vacated the north tower.

Upon returning to my chamber, I found Mrs. Fairfax and Leah scurrying about, stripping the bed and setting the place to rights. I deposited the north tower key in a dresser drawer.

"Good heavens, Sir!" exclaimed Mrs. Fairfax, "It is a mercy you were not killed last night! Please do try to be more careful with your candle."

"I am leaving," was my brusque response. "Expect my letter in a fortnight or more when I better know my plans to return to Thornfield or to the continent. Grace has her instructions."

"Yes. Very well, Sir," said Mrs. Fairfax. "Have a most pleasant journey."

"Thank you," I curtly replied and left the room.

In the gallery, my purposeful pace ceased at Jane's door where a strong desire held me to knock. I started away, then again arrested my step.

'Go, Edward. Leave her!'

No! I could not! I must see her again before miles of land, and perhaps of water, came broad between us. I looked about, and finding no one in view, went to her door and entered, closing it softly behind me. The room was dim, curtains drawn, the atmosphere hushed. Jane lay in her bed, curled upon her side and sleeping deeply, much in the way I envisioned her once in a daydream. I stepped to the bed and knelt upon the rug.

How on earth was I to do this? To leave Jane when I was so in love with her and wanted only to be with her? I felt my throat and chest tighten as I cursed my fate again and again. Meanwhile my hand lightly touched her cheek. So lovely. She inhaled deeply and exhaled, murmuring softly. I should go and let her sleep. But she rubbed her face on the pillow and her eyes slowly opened. Awake, she looked at my face, hair and clothes. She shut her eyes and smiled.

"Come, Miss Eyre," I said softly. "You have something to say?"

She opened her eyes again, a smile still on her lips. "You are so beautiful," she said.

I smiled. "You know, I was thinking the same of you."

"I am glad you think so," she said, stretching with arms above her head.

"I do."

Then she asked, "Will you kiss me?"

"With great pleasure," I replied, and I did, soft and lingering. Minutes passed like seconds.

"I thought you were going," she finally murmured, smiling.

"Having a bit of trouble with that," I said and smiled though my heart was heavy. "Tell me how to leave you Jane. I cannot do it on my own. Help me."

"Edward," she said, and I thrilled at the sound of her voice speaking my name for this was the first time she said it. "You must do what feels right in here," she said, placing a hand on my heart. "I know you would not hurt me. Whatever it is that troubles you, go and set it right. You know where I shall be."

I took her hands and, closing my eyes, kissed her fingers. Held them to my face. Genesis. Bone of my bones, flesh of my flesh. He created woman from man's rib. Our passion, Jane, began last night with your hand on my ribs.

And before the tears came, I pushed back from the bed intending to stand, but she caught my arm and pulled me close. She lifted up to me, her palm to my cheek and kissed me, pulling me down to her.

She took me where she wished, mouths feeling, thrilling, and searching. Tears came and I let them.

Chapter 11

I EXITED JANE'S BEDCHAMBER in a state of delirium, half blinded with self-doubt and heartbreak. In the vacant gallery I gazed at the sharp demarcations of morning light on the matting and listened to distant voices of servants in my chamber.

"Jane, I am so in love with you," I whispered at her door. "Sometimes it is more than I can bear." In vain I attempted to focus bleared vision, brought the heels of my hands to my eyes and stomped my boot on the matting. 'Do it, Edward. Selfish bastard, go!' I spun around and forced myself to descend the stairs.

In the deserted kitchen, coffee remained warm on the stove and a plate of tea scones had been left on the table. Taking the scones to the sideboard, I absently slathered them with marmalade and consumed all quickly. Possibly the generous tots of brandy last night were to blame or it may have been my reluctance to depart, but nothing held flavour; all tasting much like sawdust. A twenty-mile journey lay ahead and time for a proper meal would not come until late tonight, but still, appetite failed me.

'Cannot eat and do not sleep. You are in fighting form, Rochester! Well done!'

As I moved about the kitchen and refilled my coffee, John entered. He poured himself a cup and rhetorically asked, "Off now, Sir?"

I nodded. "Nearly. Mesrour is readied?"

"He is. In the courtyard. Your trunk shall arrive at Ingram Park on the morrow. Would you care for a proper breakfast before you go, Mr. Rochester?

Leah is upstairs ironing new bed hangings for your chamber, but I'd get some bacon and eggs on for you."

"No. I must be going. You added a change of clothes to the saddle bags?"

"Aye, Sir, and your shaving kit. Ah, wait one moment! Leah said you must take this." He handed to me a paper parcel. "Madeira cake for the journey, I believe."

"Very thoughtful of her. And John," I said, turning at the door, "take care of the house and the ladies while I am gone."

"We always manage very well, Sir," he replied with his gap-toothed grin.

Leaving a houseful of women and a child in the guardianship of one old codger man-servant did not sit well with me although I had, of course, been away from Thornfield many times before without a moment of trepidation. This time was different. Bertha was semi-lucid at night and had proven herself quite cunning. She was given to bouts of pyromania, and with Grace not entirely trustworthy, I was uneasy leaving the women to fend for themselves, particularly Jane who seemed to be the primary object of Bertha's interest. Protectiveness and my love for her made this departure indeed difficult. Furthermore, there was little Adele's safety to consider.

"John, I want all chamber doors locked from the inside each night," I ordered. "The nursery, Mrs. Fairfax's rooms, the governess's chamber… tell them to lock themselves in. It is my wish."

John stared at me in puzzlement for a moment, but nodded assent. "We shall do as you say, Sir."

Leaving my half finished cup on the table, I went out to the courtyard where my horse awaited, snorting upon seeing me and stamping the cobbles impatiently. Pilot stood nearby, wagging with excitement. I climbed the mounting step, settled into the saddle and galloped Mesrour down the drive and through the gates.

Masses of spring flowers, tulips and hyacinths brightened Thornfield's grounds, and fruit trees in their fullest bloom waved in the morning breeze. I scarcely noticed them. My mind held a singular purpose and that was to create distance between the Hall and myself.

Riding away from Thornfield, I returned to questioning the necessity of this departure. What difference did it make whether my problems were mulled at Thornfield, Ingram Park, at a Mediterranean villa or on the moon? Facts would not change with my geographic location. Nothing had changed over fifteen years! Already I had spent countless hours in innumerable locations futilely contriving a way to extricate myself from such a snare, but like a maddening riddle, there was no discernible answer. I was bound to an impossible marriage.

However, if Bertha suddenly ceased to exist, my life then would resemble what it had in my youth; when I was happy and free. Admittedly I was no innocent. Dark considerations shadowed my thoughts on many an occasion. More a fantasy than an actual plan, scenarios of Bertha's demise played out in my desperate imagination more times than I cared to acknowledge, but wishing, or worse, praying, for another person's quietus is nearly as sinful as committing the act itself. This was the impetus for her transfer from Jamaica to England, for at Thornfield I could have her safely confined and adequately attended by another whilst I exiled myself to the continent. If we had remained in co-existence, alone in that West Indies hilltop bungalow, she surely would have met her end at my hand. And according to Jamaica's notoriously draconian legal system, my sentence as a convicted murderer would have been worse.

Another, more subtle manner of relieving myself of her burden was at my disposal in the form of a house I owned, Ferndean Manor. Much smaller than Thornfield, this once stately fieldstone edifice was located deep in a wooded glen about thirty miles south of Hay. Cloaked in ivy and set far back from an overgrown, nearly forgotten road, Ferndean was a dank and rundown house, neglected these many years. Last I saw the place, it was rife with mouldly walls and translucent air that hovered balefully inside and out. Even as a child I was fearful of Ferndean Manor; a weakness exploited by Rowland who would torment me with tales of malignant spectres haunting the foreboding corridors and chambers.

To incarcerate my insane wife at this location would have been, to me, uncommonly inhumane, though on occasion I admittedly considered disposing of her there. As yet, I could not bring myself to act upon the temptation.

Riding now along high hedged, sweet smelling lanes, I recalled that far back in the mists of time, I once stood before vicar and altar, and promised God, Antoinetta (as she was known to me then, for I could not bring myself to use her given name of Bertha) and myself, that I would love and honour her all the days of my life. Well, I never actually loved her to begin with, but I wanted to and tried to. I did even *like* my wife for a short time, which proved the tenderest emotion she could summon in me. We lived together, talked, laughed, and bedded often and passionately, if not lovingly. The best of intentions were in place for a lifetime as man and wife. Then her already frail sanity disintegrated with alarming rapidity before the eyes of our servants, neighbours and myself. All appeal was replaced with horror and desperation as I helplessly watched the human woman I wed quit her being and leave a soulless wretch behind.

To discard her now to existence in a domicile I myself would loathe to inhabit would be an act of contempt beyond the pale. The deleterious atmosphere and total isolation with none but Grace Poole would bring about her certain demise, and that was too calculated an act for me to execute; as criminal an assassination as by any other method.

Yet, since last night's attempt on my life, the idea of sequestering Bertha away at Ferndean seemed more appealing that ever it had before. Today, Grace unexpectedly suggested it. I was sure she considered Ferndean the perfect measure for her own future. How long, I wondered, had she been considering broaching the suggestion?

I pitied Grace really, locked in that stone cell with her lunatic charge day after day for fifteen years. Surely this was damaging to her sanity as well. No amount of salary could buy back time, freedom and mental stability. If she consoled herself with drink, who was I to cast blame? Certainly I consoled myself with drink often enough. Yet, if I transferred Bertha and Grace to Ferndean, Grace would become free to regularly intoxicate herself without the slightest monitoring to keep her in check, whereupon Bertha may escape and run wild. Grace might then 'correct' her all too often and vehemently. Bertha and Grace alone at Ferndean? No, that would never do.

And so my mental flirtations with Bertha's demise never advanced further than the dark recesses of my labyrinth mind for I could not allow myself to be guilty in the death of another person, no matter how hated that person was to me.

This morning, once alone in my chamber, I thought that there was nothing I would not give to have Jane, but this was not entirely true. There was one thing. I would not exchange the burden of a lunatic wife for that of a guilty conscience. You see, to the casual observer I may appear hewn of flint and with a heart carved of iron, but in actuality, I am all trifle and cream. Generously laced with sherry.

Around mid afternoon, I brought Mesrour to a halt at the crest of a ridge. A glorious view of patchwork farm fields and tiny houses, grazing livestock and low stonewalls was laid out before me in the valley below. A beck of crystal water meandered down the hillside, burbling pleasantly under the declining sun, and there beneath a copse of willows my horse grazed as I unpacked the Madeira cake. In the shade of a rocky crag, I settled down and marvelled at the beauty of God's green earth. Billowy white clouds sailed across the azure sky above, and I wished up to them that Jane were here with me. All pleasant things should be shared with her, and so I dreamed of holding her in my arms, close to my heart whilst sitting atop the world as now.

"Jane," I said to her from miles away, "What can I give to you? I love you so completely, but all I can give...," and I cast my eyes again to heaven, "... is me."

Would that be enough for her? Would she accept that I could not give her marriage? I knew the answer to that as well as I knew my own name. Hours were spent with Jane, learning her character, gathering the seeds of her personality shaped by strict religious upbringing at that hypocritically dogmatic boarding school, all convinced me of early-instilled prejudice. She would never consent to be my mistress. Independent and stubborn, she could live alone if self-respect required it. As much as Jane wanted me hours ago and held fast to my kiss and touch, I knew she could shut all of that off at will. No reckless slave to passion was my Jane. Control and reserve were the stone and mortar of her spirit, and they could be in every respect impenetrable if she wanted them to be.

Having consumed sufficient, I collected my horse and climbed back into the saddle, calling to Pilot who was far off chasing rabbits. With a long look to the view before me, I gave thanks for such an extraordinary day thus far. Passion in the early hours, waking later with Jane in my arms, kissing, touching, talking... tears... and now I was far from home in this beautiful location. What other uncommon events would this day bring?

"My Lord," I prayed aloud, "My intentions are good. Please lend me your wisdom." And with that I set off once again, now with the sun lowering before me.

My arrival to Ingram Park came just after seven o'clock. I entered the grounds through the gates, went round the back and came to the stables.

"Edward!" an approaching voice called. Andrew Ingram. "Edward Rochester. So very glad you could make it!" He came forward with a hearty handshake.

"Hello, Andy. How very good to see you again. I see the ladies permitted you some time at home with your family."

"Yes, I do tear myself away on occasion," he said with a mischievous smile. "My parents and sisters will be so pleased you decided to join us."

"And how are your parents?" I asked, giving the reins to an awaiting stable hand.

"Both are quite well, thank you. Antithetical as ever, but it works for them. Come into the house and see everyone. They will be delighted to see you."

I faced him fully. "Whom can I expect to see?"

"Oh, it is a small party, Edward. Other than the Colonel and Mrs. Dent and Lady Lynn, it is mainly the younger set. Amy and Louisa Dent, Arthur Eshton, Henry and Frederick Lynn. They are taking tea in the conservatory along with both my sisters."

"Delightful."

My next few hours were spent in polite if dull conversation with the elder attendants of the Ingram house party over a splendid late supper of roast pheasant. A fine postprandial coffee with choice of whiskies rendered all moods sublime. As the hour grew late and want of entertainment inspired restlessness amongst "the younger set", each eventually wandered through the drawing room's French doors into the gardens. Ingram Park did have lovely gardens but they were far too formally designed for my taste with their stilted topiaries and imposing Roman columns consistently spaced amongst beds of perfectly confined geometric proportions. The wilder layout of Thornfield Hall was more to my taste with rambling orchards, sunken fences draped by antique roses, chaotic perennial gardens and far reaching hills of waving grass.

Carrying glasses of burgundy, Arthur Eshton and I strolled through Ingram Park's prize-winning rose garden.

"So, Edward," he ventured with an impish smirk. "How do things progress with your new found interest in poetry?"

I hid my smile behind a sip of wine. "Far more stimulating than one might ever anticipate, my friend."

"Ah. Perhaps I shall spend time in the poetry section myself."

"You well could find something there for your lovely Louisa," was my leading retort.

He sniggered. "Or for myself. Or for my Auntie Beatrice's eightieth birthday gift."

I caught his caustic tone. "You are still seeing Louisa, are you not? I noticed little conversation exchanged between the two of you at dinner tonight."

"Oh yes, we see one another. It is casual for me, but she wants a proposal and is becoming more overt about it by the day. I don't know, Edward. Committing myself to one woman simply is not in me. I like my life as it is."

"Then Louisa is not the one for you," I said, taking a seat beneath a rose entangled arbour and enjoying a protracted swallow of wine.

He looked at me for a long moment. "Edward, is everything all right with you?"

"'Course. Why?"

"Such a statement is peculiar for you. I hope you do not mind my saying so, and I only make this observation because you are my long time friend, but you are looking rather preoccupied. More than that, you are looking a bit rough."

"Rough?"

"As if you've not slept in ages. What's more, you've lost weight since you last came out to Stoneleigh Park. Something troubles you I daresay."

I blew out a deep breath while gazing up to the starry sky. "Poetry, Eshton old boy. Beware poetry. It all begins with poetry."

"All right then," he said, taking the bench opposite mine. "You do not eat and you do not sleep. You've taken up a new interest in romantic poetry. Do you want to know my diagnosis?" he asked with a sly smile. "Come on then, ask."

"Enlighten me."

"I'd say that you, my friend, are in the mortal clutches of love."

I grinned. "And I'd say you are damned right as usual, Eshton."

He gave me his broad, boyish smile. "Well then! You must tell me about her! Who is she?"

"Arthur, you do not know her. She is not amongst the regulars of our circles. She is," and I shook my head and sighed, "different." The moon shone brightly, and we could see one another plainly.

"And you love her, Edward."

"Yes," I said promptly and decisively. "I do."

"Then you will ask her to marry you," he pushed, more a statement than a question.

"No, I cannot," I said with a rueful smile. "That would be impossible. Extenuating circumstances make it impossible for me to marry her."

He quietly asked, "She is already married?"

"No," I laughed and added, "I am." But I said it too softly to be heard.

He turned up hands in bewilderment. "Does she not love you?" he suggested.

"She does love me."

"And so where is the problem? It sounds perfect."

"It is. And is not," I said and produced a cigarette case from my inside breast pocket. I offered one and we paused our talk whilst lighting. Then I leaned back and continued, "She is so true and pure, Arthur. It has nothing to do with my wealth. It is entirely *us*. This may seem completely foolish to you, but I shall say it nevertheless. Knowing her makes me a better man; less selfish and more feeling. This... I cannot say what it is... this *need* for her," I told him, "is so entirely different than anything I have ever known."

He was looking seriously at me across the path.

I asked him, "Do you never long for a wife, a home, children? You are my age, Arthur. Do you see yourself alone all your life?"

He shrugged and said, "Honestly I have never given it thought. I have never known a woman who could make me want those things."

"I do," I said, my gaze back on the night sky, linking stars into constellations. "I want all of those things." We smoked in silence for some moments.

"Well I do say, Edward," he eventually burst out, "that if loving a woman would make me as sickly and miserable as you, then I say no thank you. Ah! Here is my lovely Louisa now, and just look at who is with her!"

I came forward to see Louisa and Blanche turning a corner and strolling toward us.

"Christ almighty," I said under my breath. "Eshton, you cannot leave me with Blanche!"

"Louisa, my sweet!" he greeted her, standing and shooting a sidewise glance at me. "Shall we enjoy the moon and stars together?"

"Oh Arthur, that would be simply heavenly!" she giggled.

A wave of nausea swept over me and I tossed my cigarette like a dart over the opposing bench as I watched Eshton and Louisa wander off in the direction of the woodland garden. Damn him.

Blanche slowly came sidling forward. Her elaborately arranged flaxen hair was up off her long, graceful neck which was dressed with a choker of tiny diamonds that flashed in the moonlight. Her gown's sweetheart neckline revealed just enough cleavage to capture one's attention. She smoothed her voluminous white dress, looking salaciously at me as if I were a choice confection.

"Edward, you are looking well," she said in her purring tone. Leave it to her to either not notice my physical deterioration or not care enough to comment.

"And you are lovely as always, Blanche," I returned.

"Yes. Mother, Mary and I have recently been to London for a divine shopping excursion at all the best boutiques. This gown amongst them," she said smoothing yards of silk. "Do you like it?"

Looking at her across the path and surveying her entire picture, I concluded that I could not possibly have cared any less. "Very nice," I said and sipped my wine, watching her thoughtfully.

Blanche was beautiful. If only she would keep her mouth shut and develop a semblance of depth, she might be able to snare herself a husband. She advanced along the path toward me, paused looking expectant, so I slid along the bench, making room for her to join me. She fluffed her ridiculously capacious skirts and settled next to me.

"I am really so glad you came, Edward," she cooed. "I think of you often enough. We must spend more time together." With a forefinger she began to trace curly designs on my thigh.

There was a time when I would have responded to such conduct by taking her into the woodland garden and behaving in a most ungentlemanly fashion, but tonight I only looked at her.

She came in close, cool fingers to my cheek, warm breath on my neck, then took my earlobe in her mouth and nibbled. I held my breath, awaiting my body's usual reactionary interest, but... nothing. I felt absolutely nothing. This may as well have been Mrs. Fairfax attempting to seduce me.

Having achieved no response, Blanche apparently decided to employ more provocative expedients and slid a hand down into my inner thigh.

I inhaled sharply. "Blanche...," I started as her hand wedged into trouser crease. This was simply too much. Abruptly I stood. "Blanche, I've had a long journey today. If you will be so kind, please allow me to excuse myself from your company. I wish to retire now."

She rose from the bench and stood directly before me, a hungry gleam in her glacial blue eyes. "Now, Edward, do be nice," she purred. Her hands upon my chest slid upwards, around my neck, touching my hair. She stepped closer, her body tight against mine, bulging cleavage pressed to my waistcoat. In protest, I raised my hands but found them on her waist.

'This is not happening,' I thought. 'I cannot do this. And more importantly, I do not *want* to do this!'

She came in close again and kissed me. Hers, as ever, was a cold, mechanical, constrained excuse for a kiss. As her lips moved ever so slightly over mine, I found myself detaching from the present and returning to a sensual scene of firelight and passion. My checked longing for Jane sharpened into striking focus. 'Jane, my love. Your deep, soulful, erotic kisses were felt right down to my fingertips and toes.' They filled me up, made me want her so much.

Suddenly I realised what I was doing, turned away and began to laugh, gently pushing Blanche from under the thorny arbour onto the garden path. The absurdity of allowing her to kiss me whilst fantasising about Jane overtook me, and I stood there under the rose arbour laughing most hysterically. Blanche watched me, far from amused, glaring at me with hands on hips.

"Edward," she huffed, "you really are *the* most impossible man!"

"I am going into the house now, Blanche and will now wish you a pleasant evening." I turned down the path, making my escape and laughing still.

"Hah!" she cackled after me. "Oh, that is rich, Edward! Always so insatiable for me in the past, now you cannot be bothered? Is there *a problem*? Feeling your age are you?"

Stopping, I turned to look her over and thought how exhaustively I disliked her. "Good night, Blanche," I said and continued toward the house.

Having secured another dram of the drawing room's burgundy supply, I extended end-of-day pleasantries all around, found my bedchamber with the assistance of a valet and thankfully closed myself in. The lavish boudoir was comfortable and quiet as a cheerful low fire gave a subdued, flickering glow. I locked the door in view of Blanche's brazen advances this evening as it would not do to wake in the night to find her climbing into my bed. Problems abounded for me as it was.

I moved about the room, swirling my wine glass and noticing such objects as the change of clothes lain out and pressed for the morning. No trunk had arrived as of yet but would sometime on the morrow. I wished to have my dressing gown now, wanting to bring it to my face and breathe Jane's sensual sleepiness mingled with both our passion scents. I went to the bed and lay down, stretching out.

"Damn it all," I murmured staring up at the high ceiling. "What in the hell am I doing here?"

Was it really necessary to travel here, to Ingram Park of all places, in search of resolution and clarity? Was I so desperate to solve the riddles of my life that I bolted from my own home and ran twenty miles into the arms of Blanche Ingram? Was this a rational act? Perhaps my own sanity was coming apart.

At this late hour, alone in this unfamiliar room, I longed for home, for Thornfield. I wanted to be there where Jane was and wondered what she was doing. At this late hour, likely she was asleep, or perhaps she was in the library at the pianoforte, or in my chair by the fire reading a book. I wondered if she might be thinking of me now. My hand rested over thumping heart. Her heart was beating at the same time, and that comforted me.

All I came away to accomplish was already done. The issue was reduced to a simple question: Who was more important to me, Jane or myself? I fancied myself righteous by saying that I would never hurt her and that I must save her while sacrificing myself, but had I done so thus far? If I were the conscientious man I wished to be, I would have found her a new situation and sent her far from me before our love overtook us. But I did not, because I was selfish. Last night I permitted my resolve to crumble; was strong until pushed by dread of her leaving me to traumatic aftermath spent alone, and then heart and soul prevailed, claiming victory. My privileged upbringing clearly failed to teach self-denial.

Whatever the case, I must learn self-denial now. A cursed, damaged, aging wretch as I had no right to one so innocent, lovely, good and gifted as she. As I said to her this morning, she deserved better than I, but I could not bear to imagine her with that other, better man. So my inventory of facts were as follows:

I could not make her my mistress.

I could not marry her.

I could not return to Thornfield and live with her platonically.

I could not go on deceiving her and thus build a life with her based upon a lie.

My course of action was repellent but plain. I would convert my loving heart to one of stone, and upon return to Thornfield, must send Jane away. I would find new employment for her somewhere safe and comfortable. No doubt she would despise me for a time but eventually she would forget me; surely before I ever forgot her. Her heart would recover. Mine? I was not so sure.

Lying there, silently conferring with myself, this new course of action sounded so correct, so stinking pious, in theory, however my bid for canonisation was hooked on one point. Last night, when I shook Jane's hand and found my resolve crumbling, I acknowledged that she mastered me, she owned me, and I loved her. Powerful convictions indeed. To send her out into the world, away from me and alone, would require superhuman strength, and I, master of Thornfield Hall, world traveller and experienced man of means, was but a man in love. Not a lionhearted warrior.

I undressed and slid into bed. "To hell with it," I muttered aloud. "No more heavy rumination for tonight." Instead, I finished my wine and allowed myself to relive all of my favourite scenes of last night and early this morning. They were all favourites. I settled down, closed my eyes and smiled, looking into her grey green eyes gazing back at me with love and desire. I felt her mouth come to mine, her hands pulling me close. Again I softly licked those exquisite, full lips. I listened to her gasp and heard her cry out, then felt her tremors of release. She looked at me once more, all pure honesty in her faithful heart as she said, "You are so beautiful."

As sleep came closer and I fell deeper, her voice echoed, "My love for you frightens me."

I murmured in reply, "Do not be frightened, Jane. Just love me."

And sleep finally took me.

Chapter 12

Sleep tethered me like an opiate. After a week of restless nights or outright insomnia, I fell hard and fast into a world of deep dreams. On this night my dreams began immediately upon drifting off, where the clearest, most startling visions took place in the same expansive field of waving grass. This was the second such consecutive night.

Alone in the warm, golden sunset I walked. A blood-streaked auburn orb hovered half descended into the horizon and waves of fine grass shimmered all around me. Leaves of distant trees rustled. I wore a white shirt and black trousers, my feet were bare, and beneath them was the distinct feel of bent blades of grass. The sun's blazing glare dazzled my eyes. All was so vivid. Then I was not alone. My angel in white was there but very far away. I watched from a distance as her long chestnut hair blew about in the breeze, her white robes fluttering. I did not go to her. Nor did I turn away. I remained motionless, quietly mourning the distance between us.

As the night drew on, the field returned. Now my angel was near. I walked through the grass to approach her. Her white robes were a nightgown and her feet were bare like mine. She was weeping; hands to her face whilst shoulders were wracked with quiet sobs. I knelt in the grass and drew her down into my lap. Hot tears came down to wet my face and my hands, and I held her tightly, pained and helpless to ease her anguish. I lay her down in the grass, kissing her wet cheeks. Lay on her, close; her bare legs rising up around me.

"Do not cry," I whispered. "My love, I'll not leave you."

Her tears slid down to the grass. "You will," she said, her gaze leaving mine and fixing past me on the sky, golden light reflected in her eyes. "You already have."

The following day, I roamed about my wealthy, worthless existence in benumbed distraction. Absently I observed the party's hosts and guests displaying their finery, making every effort to impress with talent and conversation as I meanwhile occupied a state of despondency; my habitual locale if truth is to be known. Today, my melancholy was derived from last night's dreams as they stayed with me and troubled me deeply. My spirit hungered for Jane, and the only place I could find her was in sleep. When I found her there, she was distant. She had lost faith in me and was inconsolable. I took this as a clear harbinger of the future; our wounds of separation gaping and bleeding.

After dinner, Amy Eshton sang for the gathering *un'aria Italiana* as her sister accompanied on pianoforte. I occupied a distant sofa, my perception hazy as thoughts remained inward, wishing for weeks past and a time when I would call a young lady to my presence in the evenings. She would greet me with a soft, pleasing smile, genuinely contented to be near me. Hushed conversations by the fireside, discussing books, people, places, times, science, nature, she kept pace with me point for point, and I forgot that there were twenty years difference in our ages. We shared complete accordance. I was drawn to her every word, every thought and idea. Something extraordinary evolved between Jane and I during that time. As our eyes met for spans of hours, I could dive into hers and wrap my soul around her soul. Talking to me, her voice low and articulate with eyes fixed on mine, I found my true self mastered and enveloped by her. There had never been a remotely similar human interaction for my comparison.

The memory of it diverted me from the superficiality now before me. The finery and materialism displayed in this room, as well as their artistry, were all flimsy and colourless compared to the intuitive spiritual intensity I found in Jane. Then, physical discovery was added. I continued to reel from the passion ignited between us that night. All conscious thought was thrown aside and the world around us ceased to exist. As nothing more than man and woman, we found ourselves starved for one another, searching and feeling as if our lives depended upon it. I was awed at the time, and here, twenty miles from her, I painfully longed for more.

Andrew Ingram took a seat beside me. "Edward, how about leaving the ladies while we gents go off to enjoy a ride?"

The women were gliding about the room, all flowing gowns and feathers, tinkling laughter and theatrical expressions. A small cluster gossiped animatedly in one corner. A pair was seated at the piano. And then there was their queen. Blanche stood near the gossiping flock, disengaged precisely enough to invite the conversation of another, her haughty, peripheral glance cast in my direction. To disregard such an invitation by my hostess would be ill-mannered and unwise.

"Excellent suggestion, Andy. Please allow me some moments to speak with your lovely sister. I will meet you on the drive."

"We will wait for you," he said, looking from Blanche to me with a grin.

I joined Miss Ingram standing at the fireplace mantel. "Blanche," I offered with a nod.

"Well Edward, are you now quite recovered from your journey?" she asked with thinly veiled sarcasm.

"I am," I replied, then ventured, "'Tis a splendid party. Your parents do enjoy entertaining a crowd."

Closer and more intimate she said, "As do I. Perhaps I will have the opportunity in the foreseeable future."

"Quite possibly," I said, levelling a cool, steady gaze at her. "You've no deficit of suitors if rumour is to be believed."

She waved that away. "I think you know where my interests lie. You and I have such…history together, do we not?" The hungry gleam had returned to her eyes.

"We have enjoyed our time together, to be certain."

She faced me, close and imperious. "And we will again. Do not disappoint me tonight, Edward."

"We shall see," I said, then turned and left for the stables.

The afternoon changed from bright to bleak in the span of an hour. Heavy clouds scudded across the sky, and a chilling wind lifted and swirled our cloaks as we rode. Andrew Ingram, the cousins Henry and Frederick Lynn, Arthur Eshton and myself cantered southward across open fields of grazing sheep as the sky grew progressively more sombre. We must have appeared an ominous band; five men in black cloaks and hats on horseback riding through farm fields and traversing solitary lanes. All were relieved to be away from polite company for a time. Freedom exhilarated one and all, and coarse conversation began almost immediately upon bringing our horses to a walk.

Andrew and the two Lynns, all of whom were a good ten years younger than Eshton and I, centred their conversation around young ladies; conquests won and those still sought. Eshton and I exchanged knowing glances.

Though we no longer indulged in such swagger, our penchant for sharing ribald tales having died away with the advent of our thirties, we listened with amusement but did not participate. I wondered, as always, how much of their boasting was wishful thinking. The younger men lacked detail of their encounters, adding to my suspicion of improbability, but I also noticed that they focused only on their own satisfaction, attributing no importance to that of their lovers. 'Amateurs,' I thought.

Listening to these brainless youths, I was struck by their lack of consideration for the young ladies involved. Some were identified by name, and I came away with a very clear image of who had been doing what with whom. It was a sickening betrayal of trust really. I briefly imagined myself leaping into this conversation with details of my night with a virginal governess and found that I was ill with simply contemplating it. No, never would I do that. Those hours were as sacred to me as a divine epiphany, to be guarded close inside and never sullied. 'These fools have no idea what it is to love,' I silently observed.

We came to a shallow river and dismounted, allowing our horses to drink and graze. I strolled upstream and was soon joined by Eshton. "Believe any of that?" he asked.

"Not much. The girls they spoke of should rethink their selection in suitors."

"Yes," he said smiling. Then we were quiet for a time. He presently spoke again. "You had little to say at the house today."

"Thinking. That's all."

He looked sideways at me with his characteristic smirk. "Did you enjoy your time with Blanche last evening?"

"I might have, deserter who calls himself 'friend'! And did you enjoy your time with Louisa? No proposal I see, from her exaggerated pout and your continued grin."

"Definitely not! We had a lovely time until she went on about our future once again. Nothing dampens my ardour faster than that."

"You do not love her, Arthur. What are you going to do? Play with her indefinitely then end it when you've tired of toying with her? Have her hate you?"

"No! Oh, I do not know what to do about her. She is beautiful and nice, but that is all there is! Like a croquembouche pastry, a man simply cannot live on such trifling piffle. I am waiting for something."

"Oh? What would that be?" I asked noticing his wistful smile.

He sighed. "Edward, you are one of the few persons with whom I can discuss my studies. No one else seems to find them interesting; not my family and not Louisa." He then paused.

"Go on."

"Well, when I was at Leiden University, I studied some very interesting theories about bonding. Humans are capable of extremely profound attachments, the most awe-inspiring seen in identical twins, but this has been known to occur between unrelated persons as well. The two individuals are connected in some inexplicable way, experiencing physical cravings for one another that haunt them when apart, much like a chemical addiction. Sometimes they are telepathic with one another. Does that sound unbelievable to you?"

We approached a fallen tree. A cold chill had gone up my spine and I wanted to sit down. "No, Arthur. I believe it," I said, now noticing a fine tremor in my hands.

He sat beside me and continued. "These persons feel that their bond is not the product of intentional effort but rather of divine grace. They have found the one person who owns the key to fit their locks, so to speak. Their truest selves can step out and honestly, completely be who they are. Somewhat like you said last night about your young lady, you believe she has unveiled the best part of who you are."

I nodded, speechless.

"Perhaps she holds the keys to your locks, Edward. And I do not love Louisa. We have no bond. But the possibility of finding that exists, so should I wait to find my other half? Or should I assume it will never happen and marry someone I can only just tolerate?"

My voice was hoarse, "No, do not marry for convenience, Arthur. Marry for love. Believe me about this. I know of what I speak."

"It is interesting how the bonding theories mesh with factual biology and animal behaviour. You've been a student of both sciences. Let us tests some postulations, Edward. I will make suppositions about your lady love and you tell me if I am right."

"Oh, this should be good," I said, the cold chill beginning to quit my body.

"Right then," he said. "I guess that she is still fairly young. Late twenties?"

"No. Try again."

"Younger?"

"Yes."

"How old?"

"Eighteen," I said quietly, smiling.

"Eighteen? Good Christ, Edward!" and he looked at me with bright, admiring eyes. "Now I know you see this as clearly as I do. She is very young, healthy, nice body?"

"All true."

"And knowing you, I will wager that she is a very bright young lady. Exceptionally bright."

"Right again."

"And you said last night that you want a home, wife and children ..."

"Stop there, I know what you are getting at, Eshton. You think I have a subliminal attraction to her based on reproductive urge. Get the young, healthy female and secure the continuation of my genes. I cannot deny that there may be a subconscious component of that, but I assure you there is far more to it."

"I know that, Edward, which brings me back to the bonding theory. The groundwork is there, meaning the selection of an appropriate woman. Then built upon that you have love, and a very profound love from what I have heard thus far," he said. "She is quite a lot like you I should think. Introspective, serious, stubborn. And alone, is she not?"

"You are too damned astute for your own good, Arthur," I said as the wind whipped up. We drew our cloaks in closely.

He looked at the ground and quietly asked, "What is it like to love a woman so much? And to couple it with a perfect subconscious fit?"

I turned my face up to the steely, grey sky. "Sometimes it feels like drowning, Arthur. And sometimes my inner pleasure is similar to that of an approaching climax, but a pleasure felt in my heart and mind. It is a very physical response."

He looked at me, and I could see that he understood. "Anything like telepathy between you?"

"No," I laughed, then reconsidered. "Actually, I often have vivid dreams of an angel visiting me in a windswept field under a blazing sky. It is her, surely, as if she comes to me while I sleep, to be with me and calm my anxieties."

He nodded. "And you say the situation is impossible. You cannot marry her."

"No," I said with sullen finality. "I cannot."

"Edward, there must be a way. You cannot lose hope. Without hope, we die."

There were times lately when all I could manage was to close my eyes and breathe myself into the next minute. Any more than that and existence was simply too much. Now was one of those times.

Frederick Lynn was calling from downstream. Our riding companions were gathering their horses, preparing to start our ride back to the house.

"We will talk more, Edward," Eshton said as we stood and started back downstream.

"When do you plan to leave the party, Arthur?"

He shrugged. "I have no pressing engagements for another six or eight weeks, so I am in no hurry for departure."

"Good. When the Ingram party breaks up, you must consider coming to Thornfield for a while. Unless, of course, you relish the prospect of biding your time at Stoneleigh in the company of your loving kindred."

"No! No, thank you. An extended visit to Thornfield is a fine idea, my friend. Very good of you to ask."

"Well, the offer holds but only if you agree not to abandon me to Blanche's sole company once again. What an unconscionable act to perpetrate upon your fellow man."

He laughed. "Sorry to have done that to you, Edward, but she was such a beast in the days before you arrived, fretting that you would not appear at all. I knew she would not take kindly to any attempt on my part to protect your virtue."

I scoffed at that. "My virtue is a distant memory. And never mind Blanche. I shall see to her."

All the company dined that evening upon a marvellous roast leg of lamb with mint. Hosts and guests, resplendently attired in opulent regalia, sat round the lengthy table chatting animatedly. Despite the blustery change of weather, we'd had a fine day of camaraderie, and everyone now looked forward to an evening of party games and displays of musical talent. Frederick Lynn challenged me to a game of chess for later that evening to which I heartily accepted. As our final course came to completion, Lady Ingram's sharp features surveyed her guests and she tapped a glass gently with a fork. Conversation hushed.

"Our dear friends," the Lady said, "Mrs. Dent has informed me that in another week, she and her husband," with a nod to the Colonel, "will return to their home in Warwickshire so that he may take the county seat as magistrate." A brief pause for congratulations and applause, then, "I am afraid at that time our festivities here at Ingram Park must come to a close. A dreadful spell of renovations shall be undertaken you see. Our time together, we are sure, will be enjoyed to the fullest until we must part."

Everyone chatted with dining neighbours on the grand plans for Ingram Park's improvement, yet I remained pensive as a glimmer of an idea, a scheme really, entered my mind. I looked around the table at the guests, their showy raiment, habits and the haughty pride of most. My eyes settled upon Blanche who tonight was regally attired in vermilion silk, her blonde curls swept back from her fine-featured face to cascade behind her shoulders. A single diamond pendant flashed at her throat. The arrogant manner in which she surveyed others, lips curled with some inner duplicity, was classic Blanche Ingram.

Yes, this would do very well. I turned my attention to my hostess seated across the table. "Madam," I addressed Lady Ingram in full voice, "Upon the conclusion of our time here at Ingram Park, may I extend an invitation to you, to Lord Ingram, to your children and guests, of joining me at Thornfield Hall as a means of extending our delightful companionship?"

Faces brightened and a rousing chorus of "Oh, yes!" and "Let's do!" burbled about the table; young ladies clapping hands and men nodding in agreement. 'Good,' I thought. 'This is just the expedient to accomplish what I must.' But if I were to do this, I must embrace it entirely. I could not dabble. And glancing at Blanche, whose eyes studied me with pompous satisfaction, I added, 'And you, dear heart, are going to help me to do it.'

After dinner, our group moved off into the drawing room, and as I chatted with the Dent twins in the doorway, Lord Ingram placed a hand on my arm to detain my attention.

"Edward," he began, producing a key from his waistcoat pocket, "Be a good lad and select the wine for the evening. You've seen my cellar, have you not?"

"I have not, Sir."

"Then Solomon here shall show you," he said and raised fingers to call forward a passing footman. "I do not leave the selection of wine nor the key to the servants, young Rochester, not even to our senior butler. He partook the remains of two bottles of my best muscatel during Christmas last's festivities, but he is getting on in years after all. Please forgive this imposition."

"No imposition at all, Sir," I said, taking the key. "I would be pleased to do so."

Solomon presently returned with two lanterns and led me through a maze of darkened corridors until we came to a stout door at the far end of a passage.

"You will find your way back all right, Sir?" he asked, handing a lantern to me.

"No trouble," I assured him and unlocked the door.

Wooden steps led down into darkness. I descended them into the chilly, silent cellar with a lantern held aloft, finding floor to ceiling racks, entirely filled with bottles, dividing the majority of the cellar into darkened aisles. I entered one, traversed the length and stood dusting and reading wine labels arranged by country of origin. Many were French or German, Italian, some Spanish or Portuguese and found that Lord Ingram had even added a number of Oriental and South American varieties. I roamed between the racks, suitably impressed with his collection.

The door to the wine cellar unclosed. No footman called but instead came the light step of a woman and swish of crinoline skirts. This came as no surprise, knowing that she would not waste such an opportunity. I raised the lantern and caught sight of a vermilion silk dress descending the stairs, sighed heavily and came forward holding the lantern at my side. She sauntered casually across the plank floor and stepped close to me, blue eyes ever cold and calculating. Her orange blossom perfume obliterated the smell of cedar and dust, and was admittedly stirring. Again, her choice in attire revealed just the right amount of cleavage to ensnare the attention. It did.

I met her icy eyes and spoke first. "Why do you pursue me, Blanche?"

"For the simple reason that you are the man I want, Edward," she said, all thoughtless self-assurance. "I am perfectly aware of how, shall we say, *difficult* I can be. I need a man who is as strong and indomitable as I. As you pointed out last evening, I do have many suitors but none match you. They are weak, spineless, gutless excuses for manhood. You, Edward," she said slipping a hand inside my jacket, "are precisely what I need in a mate. Formidable. Lusty..."

"And wealthy," I added, hating her absolutely. I set the lantern down on the floor.

Her hand moved across my back. "We must merge our fortunes, Edward. The Rochester name will be the grandest of all gentry in these surrounding counties," she said, her other hand stealing inside my jacket and around me. Her fingernails ran down my back and came to my buttocks, pulling me close. If I were going to engage in the charade I envisioned, my role must begin without delay. Besides, I am not carved of stone, and as she kissed my neck I allowed myself to respond, but my feelings for Blanche were acrid, caustic and selfish. No gentle caress motivated my fingertips. I restrained myself for as long as I could. Her hand slowly moved around my hip approaching the front.

I snapped...attacked her like one possessed, grasped her blonde hair and brought my mouth roughly to hers, kissing her hard. My hands went around her waist and clutched her tightly to me as I harshly kissed her neck, breathing heavily, wanting to bite her but having no wish to leave telltale marks. Now a hand went to her breasts and forced its way down the front of her gown, squeezing a generous handful and twisting nipple. She responded like a ragdoll in my arms, limp and emotionless. I found myself angered by her deficient response, lifted and took her to the dark, far end of a wine aisle and brought her roughly up against the plank wall. Her response, I do not recall. It did not matter. Taking handfuls of silk, I frantically pulled the hem of her dress up until my hands were on her thighs. Roughly I raised her leg around my hip. Fingers touched stocking tops, soft inner thigh and undergarments. I took a handful of her blonde hair in one hand and pulled her head back, watching her clear blue eyes as I slipped fingers into warm, soft wetness.

That was enough for her. Her hands came up and she shoved at my shoulders, eyes flashing with anger and indignation. "You are an animal, Edward! Why do you treat me like a filthy whore?" she demanded.

I released her. "This is what I am, Blanche. Take it or don't. It gets no better. Not with you."

She stomped her foot, looking genuinely for a moment as if she might cry but then composed herself. She readjusted the front of her dress, her hair and the hem of her skirts, then went to the stairs and ascended. The door shut with a bang, and I went back to the plank wall at the end of the aisle, far from the flickering lantern light. My excitement was gone as quickly as it came. I leaned against the wall, considering what had happened. The difference between my response here tonight and that with Jane a few nights since was diametrically opposite. Blanche was right. Part of me was animal, as with all of us, but with Blanche, there was no love, no bond to temper my base drives. Marriage to her would be empty, like taking a whore for a wife. Senseless.

Standing against that wall, amongst racks of wine, my longing for Jane grew searingly painful. In losing her, I would resign myself to a life of similar, insensitive interludes with whatever woman would have me. I doubled over, hands on knees and released a sob. 'No one will ever replace you, my Jane. I want no one else. How can I live this way once you are gone?' Taking a deep breath, I answered myself softly. "I will wake each morning and breathe all day. Then the next day, I shall do it again."

I straightened and went to the lantern, dashed away the odd tear, and proceeded to choose an eclectic array of wines including a Bordeaux, a Verdicchio, Cabernet Franc and a Marsanne. I ascended the stairs, closing and locking the cellar door behind me, found my way back to the drawing room and set the bottles on the sideboard where a footman came to uncork and pour. I took a generous glass of Bordeaux to the chess table.

"Ready, Edward?" Frederick Dent asked, approaching.

I took a walnut armchair and said, "Let's get started. You will be black, Dent." I could not bear to set the chess pieces as I had done in my study for Jane and myself; she as white and myself black, only to look up and see a callous youth for an opponent instead. It would be blasphemy, and already I had betrayed her enough.

That night, after slipping under the covers of my bed, sleep again took me quickly and completely. Somewhere in the early hours of morning, deep in my dreams, the field appeared before me again. This was the third consecutive night. Same golden sky, same virulent sun. My angel was near. No white robes, but instead she wore a nightgown. She took my hand and led me far into the waving grass. Soon she paused and stood before me.

This time it was I who cried. Dreamlike sentiments of longing, fear, remorse and hopelessness bound me tightly, and she smiled softly, told me I belonged to her, and she would never let me go. I was pleased and comforted. She laid a hand on my chest, over my heart.

"Do you love me?" she asked.

"With all that I am," I tearfully answered.

Our actions were slow and deliberate in my dream. She drew me down into the grass. Her white nightgown parted revealing lovely breasts, and the hem was brought up to bare thighs. She straddled me and with eyes fixed on mine, took me into herself. My back arched. The golden sky blurred.

She moved purposefully, slowly and rhythmically. Total pleasure engulfed my every nerve and cell. Our palms pressed together. Fingers interlaced. 'Must not release before she. Please her as long as she wishes. Live to be her man.' She cried out, gripping and releasing me. My own intensity was now permitted to peak. Golden skies sparkled above. A roar from the heart to the heavens vibrated in my chest as part of me was torn out and left inside of her. I held her tightly.

'Come. Kiss me, my love. Keep me deep within you, where I can flourish... and be free.'

Chapter 13

I AWOKE GROGGILY THE next morning to bright, broad daylight and the unshakable impression that the night was spent in a waking existence of some other place or time. I sat up in bed and looked around my guest chamber. The dream was real and powerfully stirring. It was so clear in my mind upon waking that I recalled every detail, each sensation, touch and sound. It had actually happened, I was sure. Somehow, she spent the night with me. Loving me.

Noticing I was a bit sticky, I laughed at myself but also because of the dream itself. It was not so much the thought of having dreamed of lovemaking, which is always pleasant enough, but it was the culmination that amused me. Sexual dreams were no rarity for me, but the final part, the… insemination… (dare I even think it?) was always absent as if something to be feared and omitted in physical pleasure. The notion of having released a part of myself to become a separate entity, well… it startled me. Perhaps Eshton was correct in that I did harbour a subconscious desire to be a father. Maybe his interpretation was correct; that I had found my perfect fit, the one woman I deemed worthy to be my wife and mother of my children.

"I am surely losing my mind," I whispered smiling at myself and laid back in the white sheets to stretch luxuriously. I reclined with arms overhead and looked up at the corniced white ceiling, revisiting the dream's stirring details. God, it had felt good. I tingled from head to toe even now. Much time had passed since last I made love to a woman. More precisely, nearly one year was gone since I ended a three-month affair with an Italian *signora*, the hot-tempered Giacinta.

Gia, as I called her, was an enthusiastic lover, that being all I required in choosing a mistress at the time, but her jealousy knew no limits. I recalled the scene at an opera in Venice on the final night of our liaison when my mistress and I, both elegantly attired, mingled during intermission in the balcony with other gentrified attendants. A young lady, the comely sister of an acquaintance and chaperoned tonight by her own parents, approached through the crowd for the exchange of pleasantries. I greeted her warmly, kissed her hand and turned to Gia with intention for introductions but found her glaring at me with an inferno behind her dark eyes. In effort to diffuse jealousy I smiled and started, "Giacinta, please meet Miss Caroline..." whereupon Gia slapped my face. Hard. I forced myself to recover quickly. With apologies to Caroline, I left Gia behind at the opera amidst a barrage of amused smirks and whispers, returned to the suite of rooms we shared in a Venice hotel, and after gathering all of my belongings, vacated the premises instanter. Never did I seek Giacinta again.

Nearly every romantic interaction stored in my memory was awash with such distasteful images; all but the most recent, and although that one was a source of constant pleasure, I was about to alter it in the very near future. The prospect of devastating Jane crushed me agonisingly. 'This is not my fault,' I told myself. 'I did not seek this fate! It sought me. I am helpless.' But the one thing I could do for Jane was shelter her from wrong and ruin. And when she was far from Thornfield and her love extinguished, I could console myself with that. 'Sure you can, Rochester.'

I lolled in bed and tousled my hair, finally deciding it was time to rise. My dressing gown lay at the foot of the bed, and before placing it about myself, I brought it close to my chest and face, joyfully inhaling her. So familiar it was, as if I held her close and breathed her scent only seconds ago. I wrapped the dressing gown around myself and rang for a servant whereupon a footman appeared to arrange shaving materials and a bath. Soon, I was soaking my body and scraping my jaw carefully, studying my reflection in the mirror. Dark hair, pale green eyes, strong features. Not classically handsome by society's standards, but I was secure enough in my looks. More important were Jane's observation. 'So beautiful,' she told me, all sweet honesty in her heart. God love her.

Once attired with my customary sartorial elegance, I quitted my chamber, seeking the Ingram dining room. After breakfasting with other late-risers, I asked Andrew to secure for me pen, ink and paper. He readily led me to his study, provided me with the proper materials and left me in privacy. I took the chair at his desk and penned a letter to Mrs. Fairfax, informing her of my intentions to return to Thornfield in one week with a dozen or so houseguests. She would easily manage the arrangements without requiring detailed instructions from me and would of course know to prepare a number of bed chambers, hire more servants from Millcote, formulate menus and see the Hall sparkle from attic to cellar. I smiled imagining her bustling state of agitation upon reading my letter, then waxed the closure and stamped it with my sedately decorative 'R'.

With that accomplished, I leaned back in Andrew's chair and mulled all potentials about the business. No doubt Mrs. Fairfax would inform Jane of the coming assembly and describe them to her with all the illustrative power she possessed. Mrs. Fairfax had seen the Ingram family at Thornfield once before, at a Christmas party some years ago, and would likely impart an accurate description of Blanche's beauty. I wondered at Jane's possible reaction to it or if she would be affected at all. Her reserve and control made imagining jealousy difficult. Such pettifogging was beneath her, surely.

Jane had absolutely no reason to be jealous since it was my firm opinion that Blanche had nothing over Jane, not even beauty. Jane was the epitome of youthful female loveliness in my eyes; far more alluring than Blanche's brassy pretentiousness. I twirled the pen in my fingers, thinking of Jane's words in reference to physical beauty, 'It is the character inside that determines beauty.' In that case, Jane was a Venus diMilo and Blanche a hideous troll.

To play upon insecurities Jane might harbour deep within served no purpose but to bolster my own self-esteem whilst minimising hers, but who does not crave repeated evidence of another's love and devotion? I certainly did. I missed Jane acutely, and the thought of returning to Thornfield where I could see, even heighten, evidence of her love for me was tempting indeed. I would not know until I saw her and observed her reaction whether she could be jealous. Besides, if I were to accomplish what I felt I must, then a reaction from Jane was essential.

Taking the letter in hand, I vacated Andrew's study and went in search of Blanche. I found her in the conservatory, reading a novel in the morning sunlight amongst a plethora of hanging greenery and other potted plants. She was regally attired as always, today wearing a gown of violet silk with black tulle overlay. Her hair lay down over her shoulders in carefully arranged ringlets. She looked up as I entered. The bright sun reflected strongly in her blue eyes making them appear decidedly unnatural. She placed her book in her lap and waited for me to speak.

"Blanche," I said, taking the low ottoman opposite her. "Please, accept my apologies. My behaviour of last night was unforgivable, and I hope you will find in your generous heart a pardon for my actions." Yes, I actually said it with a straight face.

She lifted her chin and glanced about with half lowered lids, seemingly considering my words.

Time to go for broke. "Your beauty brings out such behaviour in me, Blanche," I said in a deep, rumbling tone. "You are so lovely. Simply ravishing," and I let my eyes sweep over her hair, face, bosom. "I can scarcely constrain myself when you are near, and particularly when you touch me as you did." Yes, shift the blame a little…

I waited, hoping my words would appeal to her immense vanity.

She moistened her rosebud lips. "You must endeavour to be more gentle with me, Edward. Just look at my neck!" she scolded, drawing her blonde ringlets back. Her ivory skin bore faint bruises, and there were reddened areas where my evening-growth beard excoriated her tender flesh.

Leaning forward I lifted her hand and caressed fingers with exceptional gentleness, looking intently into her eyes. "I am sorry," I whispered.

Satisfied, she resumed her haughty, self-assured posture. "We shall try again later," she said, surveying me up and down. "And you must give some thought to my words of last evening. Of merging our fortunes."

I nodded but offered nothing.

"It is time, Edward. You must take a wife, and your wife must be me. All around us know this to be true. Thornfield needs a lady's influence and you need me, whether you realise it now or not."

I let my gaze drop to the flagstone floor, suppressing a smile. "So you will come to Thornfield with me?" I asked. "You must show me where my home and I can benefit most from your influence."

"I think that would be wise."

Furthering my role of suitor, I took her chill, slender hand fully in mine. This masquerade required convincing Blanche of my gentleness. I shut my eyes and brought forth in memory the morning Jane and I were last together, in her bedchamber, her hand in mine. I brought the hand to my face, kissed palm, swept it slowly over my face, finally kissing each fingertip with all the sensuality that came so naturally with Jane. For a few moments I lost myself. When I reopened my eyes, Blanche was gazing at me with a look of combined desire and disbelief.

I returned her gaze and thought, 'You've no idea just how tender I can be in my passion. And you never will.'

"Blanche, I am going into town," I said in the same intimate tone while lowering her hand into her lap. "I've a letter to post to Thornfield informing the staff of our arrival plans and date."

She was still looking at me. Silent. She nodded faintly in response.

"Expect me back soon," I said and left the conservatory. A self-satisfied smile spread across my face. That was simply too easy.

Soon, I was off in a northward direction toward town with Mesrour galloping along the carriage road. I was glad to be alone for a time. Too much socialising always set me feeling claustrophobic, and this was too lovely a day to miss, with a fresh, bright blue sky above and sparse clouds moving west on a cool breeze. May was and remains my favourite month of the year. Everything in bloom, the world green and revived is surely nature's bathing of the soul.

I slowed my horse, listening for birds calling and identifying each species. 'I must teach Jane to distinguish birdcalls when I get back to Thornfield,' I thought. 'She possesses an excellent memory and will be able to identify the sounds directly. I will take her for walks in the meadows, bring my field guide and telescope, and we shall...' Then, I remembered. No, there will be none of that. None. And the day did not seem quite so lovely anymore.

Upon arriving into town I dropped my letter in the post and left Mesrour secured on the main road. I wandered about some shops, having no desire to return to Ingram Park just yet, and went into a textile warehouse where I browsed the fabrics, my mind always returning to Jane. She needed dresses. Since I first met her, Jane owned none but the same three grey cotton frocks that likely were her teaching standard from Lowood. My fingers touched silks, brocades, calicos, and poplins, imagining her in dresses of soft pastels or rich blues and reds, smiling at the mental image of her winsomeness. I wondered if she would allow me to send her into Millcote to have dresses made for her. A departing gift, I would call it. It would hardly do to send her on to her next situation without helping to improve her wardrobe, now would it? This was the least I could do for her. She had performed her duties admirably and deserved a reward beyond her meagre salary.

I drifted along an aisle of silks in shades of white and noticed the yards of lace veiling. My heart swelled imagining her in a wedding dress, adorned for me in white silk with a delicate veil down her back. If only it could be. She would be a most beautiful bride, and I would be the happiest, proudest bridegroom on earth. A wan smile remained on my lips as I departed the warehouse.

An adjoining shop displayed jewellery, and there I perused the cases of gold, silver, diamonds, other precious gems and pearls. Much was garish and ridiculously ostentatious in my opinion, but as I rambled slowly along the glass cases, my eyes settled upon a dainty necklace of pearls strung in graduating sizes. Very elegant, understated and lovely. Very Jane. 'I must have it,' I thought with no idea of what I would do with it once purchased, but buy it I did. The necklace was placed in a little rectangular box on a bed of red velvet.

"For your wife?" asked the elderly shopkeeper as she wrapped it carefully in paper.

"No, madam," I replied, smiling faintly. "For my sweetheart."

Smiling eyes met mine. "A fortunate young lady, Sir," she said.

"It is I who am fortunate, Madam," I returned, but my smile faded. Fortune, overall, had yet to be kind.

Taking my purchase, I left the shop and tucked the box into my inside jacket pocket. The sun was high in the azure sky, and I deemed it time to return to Ingram Park for midday gatherings. I strode back along the street where Mesrour awaited, thinking of the necklace and the fact that Jane had no jewellery to my knowledge besides a cameo brooch given to her by a favourite teacher upon departure from Lowood. Jane deserved so much more. She deserved fine things beyond jewels and dresses. She deserved a home, safety and the love of a family. She had nothing and no one. It wrenched my heart to know that a woman as insensitive and callous as Blanche Ingram meanwhile had everything. Fate could be most unjust.

That night, alone in my chamber, I took the little box from my jacket, and by candlelight fingered the fine, smooth pearls, trying to fathom Jane's reaction upon receiving it. How in God's name would I hand this gift to her and then send her away? I wrapped the string of pearls around my left wrist twice and fastened it, admiring their perfection against my skin. So lovely. Like her. I then unbuttoned my cuff and tucked the pearl string into the sleeve, refastening buttons after it. I would wear it until the time came to give it to her, leaving it to absorb my heat and live with me each day. In some way, she would be taking part of me with her, and that thought brought back last night's dream of making love with her in the field.

'Yes,' I thought smiling. 'Sort of like that.'

The following days were spent engaged in typical leisurely pursuits of the gentrified class. The gentlemen hunted or went riding or in inclement weather stayed indoors to read or play cards. Party games and displays of talents in music, voice or recitation filled the afternoons and evenings. The time wasted slowly away as I anticipated the return to Thornfield. I remained in general company as much as possible, having no desire to be approached by Blanche whilst alone. She did manage to find me traversing darkened, solitary passages on two occasions, both in which her amorous advances irritatingly presumed an identical romantic interest. I managed to oblige and kissed her dispassionately, conscious to avoid the degeneration of these interludes into further lusty assaults. Not a difficult trick if I determinedly thought of someone else; Lady Ingram, the jewellery shopkeeper, Grace Poole, Queen Victoria. I blocked Jane resolutely from my thoughts. Thinking of her whilst touching Blanche was a sacrilege. Besides, if I thought of Jane, I may begin to return Blanche's frigid kiss with genuine, sensual fervour, and it certainly would not do to have that.

The day of return to Thornfield finally arrived. I awoke early but remained in my chamber busily packing my trunk unassisted, my heart troubled. A number of nights had passed since my angel visited me in my dreams, and I woke each morning disappointed that she had again stayed away. I would go to sleep wearing the string of pearls about my wrist, hoping to meet her sometime during the night in the grassy field at sunset. No field, sunset or angel appeared after the night we made love in the grass. So I began taking my dressing gown to bed. A thirty-eight year old man sleeping with a dressing gown bearing the scent of a woman he loved but could not have? Pathetic. This morning as I prepared to leave Ingram Park, I extricated the dressing gown from amongst the bedclothes, folded it carefully and packed it in the trunk, shaking my head at my own absurdity.

Following a banquet breakfast that morning, the gentrified party began to withdraw from Ingram Park. Lord and Lady Ingram, Blanche, and Mary occupied one carriage, Louisa and Amy Dent and Lady Lynn took another, a group of ladies maids and valets occupied a third and fourth laden heavily with trunks and boxes, and on horseback were the Lynn cousins, Andrew Ingram, Arthur Eshton and myself. Our party took the eastward road on this cloudless, fine day, anticipating arrival at Thornfield for supper at eight.

For much of the day I rode ahead of the group, glad to have time to contemplate without disturbance before arriving to Thornfield. My decision had been made and the events to achieve its end set in motion. It could not be stopped now. As the distance to Thornfield shortened, I found myself becoming increasingly anxious. Doubt of my decision weighed heavily upon me.

Admittedly, I was not a good Christian, did not attend service regularly and lived a rather decadent, sinful existence until the recent past. But on occasion, I did stop for a one-to-one with my God. Today, as my anxiety increased with each passing mile, I spoke to God inside my mind.

'Lord, I believe that what I am doing is right but I do not know. If I am wrong, please intervene to stop me before she is hurt irreparably. You know that I love her. Please, give her comfort and lead her to safety.'

Eshton rode a short distance behind but now advanced to my side. Perceptive to the last, he caught my eye and gave me an encouraging grin, clearly aware of my troubled thoughts. He did not speak, allowing me the consideration of mental seclusion. 'Someday, I will tell him of Bertha,' I considered. Never had I talked to anyone about my nightmare marriage and its continuing aftermath. Never. I kept it all inside and let it singe and decay me like a pitiless corrosive. There was no point discussing it. No one could help me.

As planned, we arrived at Thornfield whilst the sun was setting. Horses and carriages, ladies and gentlemen filled the courtyard. Servants hurried to our assistance. My guests congregated on the courtyard cobbles, stretching stiffened legs and chatting animatedly. Stable hands and drivers took the horses and carriages away, and servants began to whisk trunks upstairs to the second story bedchambers. Mrs. Fairfax fluttered about bearing a florid complexion threatening acute hypertensive crisis as she oversaw all activities.

Within a half hour, Thornfield was settled to a low hum as ladies and gentlemen prepared in their dressing rooms for dinner. I wandered about my home and into the study where I flipped through a stack of letters on my desk. The room felt dejected and lifeless. No ringing tones of laughter around the chess table, no low conversation before a blazing fire, no comfortable domestication of a youngish man and a younger woman reading separately in contented harmony. And it all fell apart here with the reading of a single damned page of poetry.

Exiting the study, I came across Mrs. Fairfax flitting about in the entrance hall, remembering and forgetting tasks in a state of flustered discombobulation. I lay a hand on her plushy arm.

"Mrs. Fairfax, settle down. Now please, take a message up to the nursery. I wish for Adele and Miss Eyre to join my guests and I in the drawing room after dinner." I said it slowly, being sure she fully comprehended my request in her distraction.

"Yes, Sir. I will tell them directly. Surely Miss Adele will wish to begin dressing in her finest frock and ribbons immediately."

As she turned to ascend the staircase, I asked, "All has remained in good order during my absence, Ma'am?"

She turned. "Oh, yes, Sir. No difficulties to speak of. Your directions were followed to the letter."

"Fine." Grace too had kept her word. I nodded and left my housekeeper to continue up to the nursery.

Dinner that night was a delectable roast Herdwick lamb with thyme and onion sauce followed by coffee and pecan sponge cake. A true masterpiece of Leah and John's culinary skill, and surprisingly I did have an appetite. But perhaps this was more a wish to linger at the table, drawing out dinner indefinitely as to avoid what was sure to come.

When the clock struck the hour, guests began to rise from their places to wander toward the open doors of the brilliantly lit drawing room. My staff had truly outdone themselves, and I admired their pride in Thornfield Hall. As the last to enter the room, I stood surveying the scene from the doorway. Seemingly a hundred candles flickered brightly, illuminating the finely appointed room with a warm glow. Guests mingled about, observing paintings and other decorative items, chatting and laughing gaily together. Glancing toward the opposite end of the drawing room, I found Jane tarrying at a distance. My heart skipped. She stood with Adele, looking at a volume opened upon a table, her side turned to me. My eyes fixed upon her profile. Inner battle ensued.

Resolve cried, 'Do not look at her Edward! Turn your eyes away! Do it now!'

'No, I cannot! I must see her!'

Our last moments together were in her bedchamber, her chestnut hair splayed over a white pillow, arms pulling me closer, kissing me with incredible sensuality and the love I so desperately needed from her. Touched her, wanted her, loved her. Tormented by leaving her.

My Jane! Love you. We shall be of one flesh. Kiss me, please.'

She looked up as if hearing my voice, sought and quickly found me. Upon her eyes meeting mine, her youthful face lightened and glowed with genuine pleasure of the heart. Her love came to me across the room, caressed me and filled me up. The desire to go to her was extremely intense, and I wanted painfully to kiss her, lift her in my arms and take her upstairs where I could lay her down and love her.

'Jane, I've missed you so.' I gazed at her across the room, savouring the pleasure of being near her, just as in my dreams of grassy fields beneath a golden sky. 'You are here. Need you, love you so very much.'

A person came to stand close to me. Blanche. The scent of orange blossom and iris distracted my senses. She had come to my side and was pressing her bosom to my arm, pressing in close to whisper something at my ear. I have no recollection of what she said but distinctly recall feeling her breath on my neck, her hand moving up my shirtfront and cool fingertips resting on my cheek. My eyes never left Jane. But hers left me. She straightened up and turned to fully face my unabashed admirer.

Jane's eyes swept over Blanche; her hair, sparkling jewels, pure white gown, down to her slippered feet and back up again. Her expression altered swiftly and dramatically, becoming the same look of confusion and rejection that had come over her face late one night when I left her before the fire in the library; after she had told me that her love for me frightens her, after I kissed her neck and held her close to my heart... then left her. It was the same look multiplied by one hundred. One thousand. Jane's eyes came back to mine, and I watched as her loving visual caress was replaced with pain; the subtle, helpless anguish of love betrayed. Her mind tried and failed to accept what she was seeing. She looked away with desperation in her features. Then she looked back to me.

Suddenly she whirled around and stood turned away. Adele looked up into her face with concern, speaking to her. Jane shook her head and placed a hand on Adele's shoulder, guiding her forward out of the drawing room, out into the entrance hall.

Remorse ran me through like a finely whetted rapier, the pain far worse than I ever anticipated. 'Goddamned self-centred, blockheaded fool that I am!' I had awaited this moment with near anticipation, wanting Jane's jealousy and needing reassurance of her love. What I managed to do was lacerate her gentle, true, loving heart deeply and irreversibly.

I looked to my left, to a group of guests gathered around the shining black grand piano and found Eshton standing there. He was looking at me seriously, questioningly, then to the door from where Jane vacated the room. Eyes back on me, he mouthed the words, "That is her?" A single nod was my reply.

"You must excuse me please, Blanche," I said and went after Jane. Into the entrance hall I hurried and stood at the foot of the staircase, watching as Jane arrived to the second story. She took Adele to the nursery then went to her own room, shutting the door.

Meanwhile, my mind screamed at me, 'Stop! Do not go after her! This is what you wanted and how it must be. Let her go. She will cry but she will recover. If you go to her, you will hurt her more.' The temptation to run up that staircase to Jane's door was unbelievable. Another serpent in my Garden of Eden. The guilt overwhelmed me. I had willingly, calculatingly and callously wounded my Jane by bringing Blanche here. I wanted so much to go to her and comfort her, but that was in no way possible.

I knew precisely what my lovely Jane was feeling for I once was in that place myself. Celine Varens led me into that dungeon cell of jealousy and betrayal, and well acquainted me with the tortures inflicted in such a place on those reckless enough to love purely and honestly. I came away with a gashed heart but also far wiser. So would Jane.

'Leave her, Edward. Let her cry alone.'

So I went into my study and lit a single candle, sat down on the leather sofa and stared into the dark fireplace, touching the pearls on my left wrist through my shirt.

"I am the most abandoned, selfish son-of-a-bitch on this planet," I told myself. It only just occurred to me what I had done, and I wanted to take a pistol to shoot myself. Really.

Jane and I must part for her own safety. Understood. But there was another path I could have chosen. I could have returned to Thornfield and taken Jane somewhere private such as here into my study, could have held her hands, looked into her eyes and confessed every last detail of my marriage, of all mistresses, of every lie ever told in my pitiful, dissipated life. I could have openly confessed my love for her and told my fears of losing her, then let her make the choice. Love me or not. Stay or go.

But no. Never for a moment did I consider relinquishing control to allow Jane the decision of what would become of us. The control had to be mine. I had to say how it would be.

"You, Edward, are alone because you are a self-absorbed, inconsiderate bastard," I said to myself, leaning forward with face in hands. "You do not deserve her. Never did. You already have what you deserve."

Chapter 14

THERE CAME A tap at the study door left ajar.

"Edward?" a masculine voice softly spoke. I looked up to see Eshton through the darkness. He sought me from the doorway then advanced into the room whereby I placed my face back into my hands. He came around the sofa, taking a club chair near the darkened hearth, and regarded me silently for a time. "Edward," he finally said. "What can I do to help you?"

"Nothing," I said firmly, then rethought that. "No, actually there is something. Stay here."

I went out of the study, along the entrance hall to the kitchen, threw the door wide and strode through the clamour of dinner clean up to the pantry. With that door flung open as well, I scanned the contents. On the top shelf was the reserve liquor supply, and I took down an unopened bottle of scotch, then shut the pantry door with a bang. Again I walked past the astonished staff, all silenced whilst holding plates and serving dishes suspended in mid air. Out of the kitchen and into the dining room, I opened an enormous glass case containing a vast array of wine glasses, snifters, tumblers and so on. Taking two tumblers, I returned with my cache to the study. There I carelessly dropped the glasses onto the chess table and slammed the bottle down.

Eshton watched me, his expression apprehensive. At my desk I extracted a pouch of fine Cuban tobacco and papers, rolled a cigarette and offered to Eshton, "Smoke?" He shook his head 'no'. At a candle I lighted my cigarette and went back to the scotch, breaking the seal and pouring myself a supremely generous dose.

"Allow me to pour my own, thank you," Arthur said with a wary expression.

I gave him a 'suit yourself' shrug and flung myself heavily onto the sofa, resting one booted foot on the leather back. Then I commenced my evening pursuit: smoking and drinking myself into oblivion.

Eshton leaned forward in his chair. "What are you doing, Edward?" he said with grave concern.

I blew a smoky plume at the ceiling. "'Fraid I don't understand."

"Oh, of course you do!" he said. "You are going to drink yourself incoherent because you broke that girl's heart, and it's killing you. You love her, but that did not stop you tormenting her with Blanche, and let me tell you it was painful to watch."

"Then don't watch."

"Edward, this is Arthur! Your friend! Whatever the problem is, you cannot manage it alone. You are hurting others and yourself. It is unconscionable!"

"Arthur, *friend*, drink or be gone."

He frowned at me and then got up, poured himself a modest measure and returned with it to his seat. "Edward...," he began.

I cut him off. "I am not going to discuss this with you."

"Why not?" he said with rising ire. "Too proud to ask for help? Think you know how best to manage? Well obviously you do not! You and that girl are in love. Anyone can see it between you. It was palpable tonight for Christ's sake! And to be so vicious... I cannot understand you. I tell you this, old friend, if I ever had that with someone, you could not force me to be so cruel! For any reason."

"I did nothing vicious. And 'that girl' is a governess. Her name is Jane."

"Well yes, obviously she is employed by you. What will you do with her now? Sack her? Send her out of Thornfield?"

I considered that. "Yes. Precisely what must be done," I answered, inhaling tobacco smoke deeply.

"Do you know what I think?" he said, spite thick in his tone. "I think she is better off."

I ginned bitterly. "Arthur, I could not agree more." Then I got up and lighted more candles, knowing that soon I would be unable to do so.

Eshton watched me move about the room. "You have a houseful of guests," he quietly pointed out.

I shrugged and shook my head. "To hell with them." Refilling my glass, I went back to the sofa.

"And Blanche?" he asked. "What have you to say of her? She was asking after you and thought you might be ill."

"*She* makes me ill! Are you worried about Blanche suffering a broken heart? Ever try to crack a solid block of ice? Her only motivations are pride and greed, Arthur. To that woman, I am a means to an end and nothing more. I am sick to death of such tiresome, self serving dross from the **gentler** sex."

He looked about the room, shaking his head. "So why did you invite all of us here?" he asked. His glass remained untouched.

"If you must know, to use Blanche to break Jane's heart, thereby ending her love for me," I said with a malevolent snigger. "I succeeded admirably, wouldn't you agree? And maybe whilst Blanche is here I will finally get her into bed since that is all she is good for anyhow. 'About time these years of suffering the Ingram women paid off. What more was my purpose you may ask? To play a few good games of chess with you, to see this house resemble something more than a stone crypt…"

He looked about in attempt to rationalise my reasoning. "So you intentionally destroyed the girl you love and wish to marry, meanwhile seeking to bed another woman who wants to marry you but whom you despise."

I considered that. "Well done. Aptly put."

"That is one hell of a triangle, my friend."

"'Tis a fragmented triangle now," I said, laying my head back and enjoying the relief of pain slipping away. I sighed deeply and added with eyes closed, "Drink, Arthur."

So we settled in, occasionally regarding one another benignly and talking of guns, horses and drinking establishments. I smoked until my coordination to roll cigarettes failed, then drank until my consciousness went dark.

Later…

Hard, cold stone floor against my face. Spinning, everything. Heaving, retching violently. Two men dragging me up a flight of stairs, exclaiming in disgust, pulling my shirt away. A cold, wet cloth on my face. Cannot breathe. Wish to die. Then, nothing.

I awoke the next morning to a dimly lit room and the steady drum of rain against a window. My eyes opened slowly but immediately I thought better of it. Completely coherent but sick and weak, my head throbbed painfully. What in the hell had I done last night? Was it an attempt at suicide? I could not even get that right. I opened my eyes again to find a person pulling a chair beside my bed, and my vision focused. Eshton. He looked at me with his characteristic mischievous grin. If I could have laughed, I would have.

"Good morning, Edward! You look like death."

"I should be so fortunate," I replied, my voice rough. Then expecting the worst, asked, "Who saw me this way?"

"Oh, be of good cheer, old boy! Not to worry. Your old friend Eshton wove a tale of Rochester being called away suddenly, not expected to return tonight, such a terribly important individual that he is."

Grateful, I relaxed. "Thank you, Arthur. You are too good to me."

"You would do the same for me. In fact I think you have once or twice."

"I did. Christmas '31. And thanks to a bit of fence wire from the stable and some fortuitous gravity, your mother never did notice what you did to the tree. Now we are even. How did you get me up here?"

"With great difficulty and no help from you, thanks very much," he said. "After you fell to the floor in your study, I fetched your manservant, John is it? Together we hauled you up the stairs whilst your housekeeper wove for your guests an apologetic tale of Mr. Rochester's departure to town. You'd prefer not to hear further details, Edward. It is over."

I nodded and sat up in bed finding my shirt absent. I looked at my left wrist.

Eshton said, "I suppose you know there is a ladies' pearl necklace about your wrist."

"Yes. It is a gift for Jane. I bought it for her in Huddersfield. Lovely, is it not?" And I raised my arm to the morning light.

"Pardon me, but I am having some trouble understanding. You have intentionally broken the heart of a girl who loves you, and now you want to give her jewellery?"

"I know what I am doing," I wearily replied.

Arthur leaned in and met my eyes. "Do you?"

Soon John was summoned and a bath arranged along with my request for steaming water and a jar of salt. Ambling to the tub with shaving supplies, I threw off the remainder of my clothes and lay the necklace carefully aside. Then I sank into hot water as aching abdominal muscles eased slightly, and as I cleaned my teeth with saltwater, I reflected on my abhorrent behaviour of last night. The pain of having injured Jane was greater than expected. I could not bear to think of her wounded so, and it pained me continually to revisit the scene in my mind. The thought of her crying alone in her bedchamber where only a fortnight ago we tussled with flaring passion was more than I could endure.

'Think only of happy memories,' I advised myself. My chest tightened with remembering our night in my scorched chamber and the following morning. I could yet feel her touch; her hand gently on my cheek as she pulled my mouth to hers and kissed me deeply, the love in her eyes so unmistakable when she came away. How I hungered painfully for more. But I could not have it.

She would be forever altered, would avoid me, regard me coldly if interaction were necessary and begin efforts to find herself a new situation. Certainly, she would not stay at Thornfield much longer.

'I must help her to find new employment,' I thought. The prospect of seeing her advertise was utterly insupportable. Any range of detriment could befall a girl of eighteen employing such a stratagem.

Conscience, never far for very long, chimed in. 'Yes, Edward, you are right! You only need look at what became of her first attempt at advertising for employment.'

Hm. True enough. Vicious, unconscionable and cruel Eshton labelled my actions, but at very least I could ensure that no harm came to her next time. Something suitable and safe must be found. Inquiries must be made immediately.

I dressed slowly and carefully, hoping a hunter green waistcoat would provide an impression of freshness and vitality. We do venture to dissemble, do we not? The pearl necklace was replaced on my left wrist, inside my buttoned sleeve. Chamber doors unclosed and the voices of my guests filled the gallery. Hopefully Mrs. Fairfax would see them to the dining room since I had little interest in playing the benevolent host at the moment. Still feeling a bit queasy, my enthusiasm for breakfast was non-existent, and even after a bath and shave, I fancied myself to resemble a gussied-up street vagrant and little more. Besides, there was a chore to perform and now was an appropriate time to dispatch it.

So I took the north tower key from my dresser drawer, and once the gallery was utterly quiet, ventured out. Through the locked doors and up the winding stairs I went, into the crimson bedchamber until I came to the final portal. I knocked and waited, listening to the unbolting of locks. Grace opened the door. She did not appear any fresher than I, causing me to wonder if her night was not spent in a similar drunken stupor. Having anything in common with Mrs. Poole was not a state of affairs for which I cared to aspire, but I did find it curious that the basis of our bacchanalian behaviour rested with identical origin.

"Grace," I said shortly, unable to muster greater enthusiasm. "How is your charge today?"

"Please, Sir, come in to see her," she blankly offered.

I sighed and entered the inner room. Looking about immediately. Then I found her on the bed where she lay, on the floor, as if she had been sitting and suddenly fell over. Her eyes were blank, vacant, staring. I went carefully near and crouched down, my hands ever at the ready if she leapt. I watched for a full minute. She never blinked. She scarcely breathed.

"Grace," I asked, not taking my eyes off the catatonic woman before me. "How long has she been as this?"

"She remains this way nearly all day, Sir, in one position or another. She can hold a single posture for hours. It is a fairly new behaviour, certainly since the last time you were here."

"She does this also at night?"

"Oh no, she is altogether different at night, Sir. Very clear minded. She talks quite coherently and has lately been asking for people she knew before coming to Thornfield Hall. She says she has a brother, Richard, who knows she is here and insists that a letter be written to him so that he may come to collect her. She says she is expected by a person in Jamaica."

Now I turned to look at Grace. "She does? Who expects her?"

"She talks of a man named Kerry or Cary. And when I asked whom it is she speaks of, she said 'my husband.' What do you make of that, Sir?"

A faint flicker in the remotest depth of my brain was ignited. It had been many years since I heard such a name associated with Bertha. "I have not the slightest idea, Grace," I muttered.

"I feel quite sorry for her at times, Mr. Rochester. She has no real idea of how long she has been in this room. Time means nothing to her, nor seasons nor years."

"Has she said anything of me?" I asked, my eyes again on the immobile woman before me.

"Not often. When she does, she refers to you as 'that man who hates me.' At least I believe she is speaking of you."

"Uh huh. Do you continue to take her walking on the roof at night?"

"Yes, most every favourable night, Sir. She seems to enjoy it. She laughs and actually giggles like a little girl."

"And she will stay in this current state for how long typically?"

"Until sundown. I will try to have her eat and drink soon. She likely will take nothing until late tonight however," Grace said.

"Look, Grace," I said, standing and looking to my employee with intensity. "I have a houseful of guests at the moment. I want no antics from her at nt. You will keep all doors locked tightly and your keys well protected. Is that understood?"

"Of course," she said. "And Sir, I do wish you would come one night to talk with her. Possibly you can make some sense of her ramblings. Perhaps a walk on the roof together?"

I moved toward the door and looked back, finding Bertha completely unchanged. "Lock up, Grace," I said and exited the room. Through the bedchamber to the winding staircase I went, and there on the steps I stood thinking.

To write a letter telling Richard that his sister wishes to go home to Jamaica? Would that prospect not be ideal? To put her on a ship and see the very last of her? Such fantasies were almost too sweet to contemplate. The problem was that Richard would never resume responsibility for Bertha. He and his father disposed of her to avoid further duty and paid dearly to do so. Yet, I paid more as it turned out. Richard did write from time to time asking after his sister's welfare, but a long while had passed since his last letter. Dropping the occasional note to me was a feeble but effective method of protecting such a colossal investment. After all, he stood to claim the Rochester fortune in the event of my death; a fact surely not forgotten by him.

'In the event of my death,' I inwardly repeated. 'In the event that his sister kills me is the most likely scenario, and he knows it. Richard Mason, my dear brother-in-law.'

I descended the stairs, contemplating Grace Poole's revelation that Bertha asked after a man named Kerry or Cary, a man whom she apparently associated with Jamaica and thought of as her husband. Now that one would require diligent mental mastication, and I knew just where to begin… but later. Right now, I must appear before my guests. A coffee would be most welcomed, too.

Chapter 15

THE DETOUR TO the north tower that morning succeeded in keeping my cankering remorse at bay for a short time, but now back on the second story, recollections of last night's drawing room scene came once again into focus. Jane would be in the schoolroom by now, busying herself with teaching Adele. Perhaps I would go and listen at the door if only to hear her voice and make certain she did not sound too dejected.

So I proceeded along the gallery, and as I passed my own chamber, another nearby door unclosed. Jane's. She exited her bedchamber and, not noticing my presence immediately, walked directly toward me. She looked up. Suddenly aware, her shoulders set straight, chin up, expression cool. I was immediately gripped by an inexplicable impulse; went to her, grasped her arm, spun her in the direction from which she had come and directed her without hesitation back into her chamber, shutting the door behind us. Leaning with my back against her door, I regarded her silently and seriously, without any idea of what to say to her. She stood before me, equally silent and attired in grey with modestly fashioned hair, hands down at her sides. Her expression was unflinching, controlled and plainly uncertain of my motives. The only telltale evidence of having sustained last night's grievous injury was a slight shadowing of poor sleep beneath somewhat reddened eyes.

My hands were brought behind my back where they clasped tightly. I did not trust myself to speak or move. My eyes delved into hers deeply.

'We have a bond,' I thought as I looked at her. 'Hear me, Jane. Feel what is in my heart. Feel my love. I swear to Christ I am going to find a way to make you mine.' The words trembled on my lips as my eyes burned into hers. Her upward gaze reached into me, into my soul, and soon something about her softened. 'She understands. Thank God.'

Jane stepped forward and came close to me, eyes fixed on mine. Her hands were brought to me, touched my abdomen lightly and slid to either side of my waist. She bent forward, bringing her forehead into my chest. I would not unclasp my hands despite wanting so much to hold her. Trembling had begun the moment her hands touched me. I bent my head down, touching her hair with my lips and looked over her to the bed.

'If I were not so sick and weak I may not be able to maintain the control I've got,' I told her in thought. 'I would take you to your bed and love you as much as you would let me. Want to love you so desperately.'

She looked up into my face, my eyes. I shook my head slightly. 'Jane, do not kiss me. My resolve will go if you do. I was weak to bring you here. This is my fault. Help me be strong. I cannot do it alone.'

She stepped back from me, eyes still fastened on mine. "Say something," she said.

I looked about the room, then back to her. "You have always known what is in my heart, Jane. You read my thoughts. Have you done so now?"

She paused, then quietly said, "I think so, Sir. But I want you to say it."

I shook my head and looked down at the floor. She was quiet. I looked up again. "You are tired," I said. "You've had a bad night."

A fragment of a smile came across her lips. "Yours was worse," she said.

"You don't know the half of it," I weakly laughed. "Or as astute as you are, perhaps you do."

She stepped close to me again but did not touch me. My hunger to kiss her tormented me soundly. She searched my eyes and asked, "Do you love her?"

My hands were breaking free of one another. I grasped my wrist quickly, feeling the pearls beneath my shirt. I shook my head slowly. "No. I do not."

Jane nodded, eyes on mine. "She is very beautiful," she said, so close I could feel her warm breath.

Again, I shook my head slowly, drowning in a sea of grey green. "She is not you," I whispered and watched her take that in.

She looked from my eyes to my lips. "I believed you would never hurt me. I was wrong in that."

"Jane, I hate that you've been hurt. It tore me up. I wanted to die."

She smiled softly, looking at me straight on. "Never fear, Sir. I am tough. I could take it."

What occurred to me, as had done before, was that this young girl was in fact tough. A survivor. She must have endured a great deal of hardship and trauma in her earlier years to have grown so resilient. In no way was she defeated or victimized. I could break her heart but could never destroy her. She would simply turn away and go on with no help required of me or anyone else. No whimpering casualty was my Jane. I stood with my back to the door and gazed at her with an increasing smile on my lips. If there was ever a shadow of doubt before, then it was absolutely vanquished now. This was the woman for me.

She was not finished with her questions. "You kiss her," she said, more a statement than a question. "You and she shared a kiss at Ingram Park."

'No lies, Edward. Your lies end here. Truth hurts sometimes, but say it.'

"Yes, Jane," I confessed, and I was truly ashamed for the empty, pointless lustiness in which I indulged with Blanche Ingram. Her cold, lifeless kiss was nowhere near the stirring brilliance of Jane's deep, sensual kisses. I mentally set myself in Jane's place, imagining her with a suitor she would kiss romantically. Intolerable, maddening, heart wrenching to even envision it! Angry with myself now, somehow I succeeded in hurting her again.

Her eyes glistened. She backed away from me.

"Jane, it was nothing. Never have I felt for her, or anyone else, what I feel for you."

She disregarded that. "I will not stay here, Mr. Rochester," she said, retreating to quite the opposite end of the room. "We have made a mistake in allowing our professional association to degenerate into personal affection. No good ever arises from overstepping conventionality. I will secure a new situation as quickly as possible."

"Degenerate? Mere 'personal affection'? Jane, please..."

"May I request of you a reference, Sir?"

Misery crept into my heart's core. I was hurt. My attempt at honesty was rewarded with disdain, and self-centred as I was, I wanted to strike back at she who inflicted my wound.

"You can expect your reference in good time," I told her. "Meanwhile, you are to appear with Adele in the drawing room every evening that my guests are here. It is my wish. Do not neglect it."

She quickly crossed the room and with an ireful, determined expression came up close and fast, bringing hands to my face. Turning her head slightly she brought her lips so near to mine that they very nearly touched. She was going to kiss me, rough and forceful as is my personal wont, and my whole being thrilled. I quivered as if an earthquake rolled beneath my feet.

She held the near-kiss and looked up into my eyes. "You do not scare me," she said, and released my face, backing away as a devious smile spread across her lips; the same smile she would flash in my study when she bested me at chess.

I thought, 'Good God almighty! How I love this woman!' and watched her back slowly away. I had not moved from leaning against the door, hands behind me, but her interrupted assault left me breathless with anticipation. With deep admiration I surveyed her, standing a few yards from me, shifting her weight slightly side to side, the devious smile lingering. Formidable, like me, she was.

This eighteen year old governess with no family, friends, money or home had asserted herself toe to toe with the master of this great estate; her much older, wealthier, more connected employer (and would-be-lover), coming away victorious. I was awed by her courage and fortitude. My head fell back against the door, and I worked to control my heaving breaths. I stared at her with all the intensity that coursed through me.

'I will have you, Jane Eyre. I will marry you and I will bed you and I will fill you with my seed every day for the rest of our lives and you will love every second of it. God damnit to hell, I am going to find a way to make it happen or die trying.' Eyeing her up and down, I said aloud, "Yes, you will love it."

Comprehension was evident all over her face as she nodded, "Yes, I will."

I turned abruptly and opened the chamber door, bursting out into the gallery, amused that each time I departed that room I was in need of a good dousing with ice water. Jane walked past me to the nursery, cool and reserved as always.

'There is no one like you, my Jane. Never will I want anyone else. I love you absolutely and completely.' My grand plan of destroying our love had disregarded the crucial element holding us together, and that was our resilience. The coming weeks would not be easy.

I stood at the top of the staircase wondering if the day would come that I could say to her 'I love you.' I thought it constantly. How good it would feel to say at last. Never in my life had I said it to a woman and meant it. To Jane, though, it would pour from me and once it did, the words would never stop. I no longer wanted her to cease loving me and truly felt I could not survive without knowing she was somewhere keeping love for me in her heart, even if from hundreds of miles away.

Our future was more than uncertain; at best it was precarious. Not five minutes ago she was asking for a reference so that she could leave Thornfield and go somewhere, anywhere, else. And I as yet needed to place her away from me and that was morally certain, especially after this most recent scene in her chamber. Unchaste impulses raged through us both the entire time. How much longer could we restrain ourselves?

My remorse of earlier had ebbed somewhat, and I felt that I knew her better than ever before. The love between us was altered, regrettably, never to return to the unblighted purity we enjoyed a fortnight ago. Now there was hurt, jealousy and uncertainty in the mix; never mind impending separation. But somehow I felt that we could weather it all and, owing to our battle scars, be forged of stronger constituents. It was a rare moment of optimism for me.

Mrs. Fairfax came into the entrance hall. Looking up, she called to me, "Mr. Rochester, Sir! Just coming to fetch you. The guests are requesting your presence."

I glanced toward the nursery. 'We shall continue another time, my love.'

And I descended to breakfast.

Chapter 16

THE WEATHER THAT day was wet and miserable. Therefore my guests and I spent the day indoors, and with the sole exception of my sickly self, one and all maintained remarkable buoyancy despite the sodden conditions out-of-doors.

A fine breakfast overseen by Leah and John consisted of kedgeree, kippers and devilled kidneys. I partook scantily, nibbling dry toast and sipping a steaming mug of black coffee as I glanced round the table, observing my finer fettled companions tuck-in, all the while valiantly endeavouring to conceal my substantial infirmity. Conversation was light and thankfully did not require frequent contribution from me. Positioned at the head of the table as I was, Blanche had chosen her place opposite me. If pre-connubial bliss was the suggestion she wished to engender, then all around us seemed to receive it readily. To me, her perseverance smacked of desperation. I watched her haughty posture as she trialled the role of Thornfield's mistress, giving orders to servants and addressing guests with authoritarian confidence. All fell cold on me. Ridiculous and tiresome were my impressions of Miss Ingram so that not even her beauty could temper my increasing disdain. I knew from where my scorn arose; from the solid conviction that the woman for me was Jane and only Jane.

'You, Blanche,' I thought as my gaze extended down the table, 'have about as much chance of becoming mistress of Thornfield as I have of becoming Pope. Another, far better woman has rightful claim to the place at this table you now occupy.' I watched as Blanche summoned servants by snapping her fingers, a habit I detest. Equivalently irritating was her dismissal of them, consisting of waving the attendant away. Her contemptuousness toward those of a lesser class was unpardonable, and with each passing minute I found her, the entire woman, insufferable.

This morning she wore a powder-blue silk gown with elbow length puffed sleeves, and her hair was elaborately plaited and arranged atop her head, giving the impression of a blonde coronet. All eyes admired her it seemed, and I searched the company for another pair that could see Blanche's behaviour in a similar light as I but found none. All seemed to revere her as the evident aspirant to an imperceptible throne. Until I came to Eshton. He would glance in my direction and exchange with me subtle, amused grins, wondering at my methods, surely, but seemed interested in watching my subterfuge play out.

In the afternoon, the men repaired to the west end of the drawing room to play billiards while the ladies busied themselves with reading, playing piano or embroidering samplers. Such were the diversions of the idle rich. Now in my third week of participating in these banal pursuits, I was nearly numbed with tedium. My mind would inevitably return to more stimulating topics such as estate management, the price of tea, and of course, the scene in Jane's bedchamber this morning. Yes, she was unquestionably far more compelling than anything or anyone in this marginally haut monde society. Disinterestedly I watched my guests move about the drawing room, my mind wrapped around an inward puzzle.

Jane exhibited such refinement and elegance beyond her station; so much that I wondered if it were plausible that she was descended from gentry. Her poise may be an innate quality. Or was it owned to conscious betterment of herself? I doubted Brocklehurst's institution had anything to do with it.

'No,' I decided, 'It is of her fabric. The blood in her veins courses aristocratic. Must do. Not one in ten thousand school-girl governesses would possess the composure, grace and sophistication she does.' And no other would be capable of mastering Edward Fairfax Rochester as she so effortlessly did. Her presence, admittedly, took quite a visceral affect on me, evidenced by the fact that I quaked at her touch. Her near-kiss of earlier this morning reduced all sensation in my body to the skin beneath her hands and to my lips crying out to her in spite of myself: 'Do it, Jane, Kiss me.'

Thinking of it, I felt my knees weaken. I wandered away from the billiard table with the clicks of balls becoming hazy in my perception and continued my inward, meandering thoughts. Remembrances and revelations held me spellbound. I compared Jane with women of my past. True for all previous lovers, the single act of physicality that I desired was the final, consummating one. Quite honestly, I cared little for touch or kiss in the past since building my lover's excitement was no more than a frustrating act of false considerateness. But now I understood how delicious touch could be. How caresses were their own ultimate act. How kissing deeply and passionately could culminate in the intermingling of one soul with another, having its very own sense of offering up the most tenaciously guarded, undisclosed part of oneself.

The comparatively chaste acts of my night with Jane were unlike any other experience in my life, so in a way it was my first kiss as well. The intensity had shocked me, and I was drawn to linger in the sensuality of it like never before. Acknowledging this, I allowed my mind to wander further down the path of lovemaking, into uncharted provinces. I imagined taking Jane by the hand, she in pristine white on our wedding day, and leading her to our bed, looking into her eyes. 'Jane, my love, trust me. Tell me you love me.' Removing clothes slowly, savouring the gradual revelation of skin. Hours may pass, our bedchamber's daylight turning to dusk then darkness. Touch and discover all of her. Kiss and thrill her everywhere. Lie passively, caressing her hair, watching her discover all of me. Fingertips, wrists, lips, cheeks, breath and bodies caressing. Responding, thrilling to sensation. Playing her brilliantly, as she plays me. Giving all of myself. 'Anything for you, Jane. Make it last. We have our entire lives, my love.'

Far away, a voice. " ... um, Edward?" Snapping back to consciousness, I looked at the group of billiard playing men watching me with amusement. "Your go, old boy," Henry Lynn chuckled.

I stepped up to the table, and despite my lack of mental and physical fortitude, succeeded in caroming the nine into a side pocket. "Enough for me, gents," I said, handing the cue to Arthur.

"You are not well today, Edward," said Lord Ingram. "Why not have a rest for a while? Join us again later."

"Fine idea, Sir. Should anyone require me, I shall be in my study," I said and turned to exit the room.

Blanche noticed my intent to depart and turned from her conversation with Lady Lynn. She intercepted me; her orange blossom and iris fragrance precipitating a sudden and thankfully mild surge of nausea. "Edward, may I join you?" she more suggested than asked. There was no point hoping she would have the grace to leave me in peace.

"Blanche, I am truly unwell today and simply wish to lie quietly to enjoy a nap," I told her.

She ignored that and determinedly stated, "I will care for you," then snapped her fingers at a passing footman. "Tea service in the study, and be quick!"

There was absolutely no wonder that this woman could not acquire a marriage proposal. She sabotaged herself continually. I shook my head at her and thought, 'No amount of beauty can rectify your deficiency of brain or heart.'

"There is something you wish to say?" she asked testily, reading my expression of distaste. "Have you a problem?"

I grasped her arm and glared at her closely, gritting my teeth. "I am going into my study. Alone. You are to stay here and try your damndest to keep your foolish mouth shut. This asinine behaviour of yours *will not* present itself in my home nor will you speak in that manner to my servants!"

Lady Ingram came quickly. "Now, my dears, please let us not have a scene! All is going so well. We must not upset our guests, Rochester." She nodded to observers, laughing nervously.

Her '*our* guests' did not escape me, but we must choose our battles whilst in the heat of war, mustn't we? I relaxed my grip whereupon Blanche wrenched her arm away.

"There, now, dears," continued her mother. "You must kiss and say all is forgiven."

I held my head high and looked into Blanche's icy, unfeeling eyes with contempt. Bed her? This thoughtless, frigid mercenary would never be good for even that. With a chilly nod to Lady Ingram, I turned and vacated the drawing room. From the dining room I took a stemmed wine glass from the cabinet and poured myself a measure of claret, just to settle queasiness and mitigate fury you understand. Then I took it to the study and shut the door.

It felt marvellous to be alone. Behind my desk I opened the diamond paned windows to a steady downpour. The rain provided pleasant, blank noise, and the wet garden air smelled sweetly of fresh cut grass. I took my chair and put my feet up on the desk, sipping claret contentedly. A knock at the study door interrupted my peace. "Come!" I irritably called.

Mrs. Fairfax entered with a tea service tray. "Sir, your tea," she said and looking about added, "Is Miss Ingram not with you?"

"No, Madam. You must accept my apologies for the false request. I do not require tea. I will be in this room for a matter of hours and do not wish to be disturbed again."

"Yes, very well, Sir," she replied and retreated from the room with the tray.

Once solitude was restored, I began the task of clearing my desk. With papers set aside, books stacked and writing implements in their proper place, I opened a lower drawer and dug far back into the myriad contents until my fingers touched a steel box. With some difficulty, buried as it was, I extracted it. The key; where had I placed it? A number of locations inside the desk were tried until it was found, hidden inside a black velvet sleeve in a topmost drawer. I opened the box.

An oilskin pouch imprinted with the name of a Jamaican distillery was there amongst other clutter. I removed the pouch and emptied its contents onto the cleared desk. Foreign coins fell out along with yellowed bills, receipts and bits of paper. Two gold wedding bands dropped onto the scarred surface making a metallic *ting*. With one finger, I set the smaller of the rings aside but the larger I lifted and examined. The ring was like new; shining and unscuffed. I placed it on my left fourth digit making a perfect fit. Antoinetta had insisted that I too wear a wedding band, but I did not wear it for long. I now admired the subtle contrast of gold against my skin and enjoyed a brief fantasy of again being married, this time to the right woman. I removed the ring and set it beside its counterpart.

Next I sifted through papers and set the coins and currency aside. My attention turned to receipts and folded sheets of parchment, now brittle and cracking at the edges. Each were opened and carefully spread out on the desk. Included were: a bulletin from St. Benedictus Church, Spanish Town, Jamaica dated 18th March 1825. A smudged receipt, written by one Henri Breault, Esquire in the amount of £65. A letter from a Kingston physician that began, "Dear Mr. E.F. Rochester: Sir, it is with sincere and deepest regret that I must inform you, following diligent evaluation of your wife's condition..." I tossed that letter aside hastily.

A second letter, stained, yellowed, torn was unfolded and the scrawled handwriting scanned. " ... the English gentleman Mason is her stepfather... her own sire's name was Collier... madness through the blood, all of them! ... Mason would dispose of his wife's sad daughter not to an asylum but to marriage with an Englishman who knows nothing of her. We must meet, Mr. Rochester." The signature was a scrawled 'Darby Collier'. A Jamaican child wearing tattered clothing and jam all about his mouth handed the letter to me; a little messenger paid in roly-poly for his task. I read the letter, and having no immediate response to give, dismissed the child to scamper away down the green hillside. By now I was sickened with certainty that my fledgling marriage was further disintegrating into a nightmare with each new day.

My outward vision fully turned to memory. I was there again in that hot climate, watching an entirely different scene. Humid afternoon, my clothes stuck to my skin, rain pattering leathery flat leaves. The smell of cloves and lime trees, colours vivid. An open bedroom window. A white summer shift lies discarded on the floor, and a woman, my wife, sits at the dressing table dressed in a peach linen chemise, brushing her thick, dark hair. My eyes follow her bare, raised arms and smooth motions of the brush, and I am savage. Hard and nearly deranged with desire, I take her supple arm and pull her onto the bed. She is beneath me, across the crisp white linen sheet, and without a word I frantically pull the hem of her chemise to her waist. Unbuttoning my breeches, the drive is insurmountable. I am flush with steady consumption of rum and cannot stop myself. Her blank eyes coast across the chipped plaster ceiling, and I think abstractly of wax dolls and Parisian whores as I pull her compliant legs around me, search and spread, rapidly finding my mark to drive myself in to the hilt. So rough is the act, I shut my eyes and care for nothing but the release of my maddening ache. Battering at her, coming closer, fantasies flashing through my brain of this being any one of a dozen other, more stimulating women. Need release! Get it, yes! Get it. Emptying into her, gasping, swearing, breathless. We lay exhausted and turned away from one another on the bed, without ever speaking a word or offering a caress. Not wanting to see her, hear her, know her, feel or be near her, I shut my eyes and sleep.

My thoughts were pulled back to the study where rain continued to beat steadily beyond the open window. I looked at the wedding bands, and placing a finger in each, circled them around the desktop. After a time, I unfolded slips of paper quickly, not so carefully, looking for a list of names recorded long ago in the house I shared with my wife, at a time when my hopelessness was still a bloodied, fresh wound. More receipts... Ah, here it is! Writing in my own hand; names, dates, places, snippets of conversations. I scanned the words and fixed on a name. Kerry Collier.

"Yes," I said aloud, recalling scenes of long ago. "Kerry Collier."

Scanning my list again, I found another name, that of a servant. Amelia. She was a comely, light-skinned negro, and I now recalled her shape and pale eyes. Memory showed her leaning on the veranda railings of my Spanish Town bungalow, indifferently graceful but respectful enough, telling me unbidden of rumours circulating about town. Rumours concerning my wife.

"Master, I hear one time that Miss Antoinetta and Mr. Kerry get married, but that surely be none but foolish talk. Miss Antoinetta a white girl with money. She won't never marry no coloured man from down the wharf."

Trying now to remember what she said of him, this Kerry was a… what had he been? My memory searched and then settled upon the answer. A fisherman. Yes, a poor native fisherman living in a tiny thatched hut on the beach.

Amelia turned away from me, her hand sliding from face to neck to breast, and added with a nod to the house, "I am sorry for you, Master. She not who you think, nor *what* you think."

In response I flicked my cigarette end out into the rain and asked, "Is that right? Who is she then?"

Amelia shrugged thin, dark shoulders. "She not that Mr. Mason's girl, I know. Her mama marry him, mebbe, oh, ten year back. Lots of stories 'bout that, 'bout her real papa and his women, 'bout him bein' madder'n a March hare," and she paused to gauge my reaction.

Numbed with rum and wretchedness, I gave her total indifference.

"But you've no use for my tittle-tattles, Master." Amelia turned and gave me her back. Leaning forward over the railing, up on toes, her back arched slightly. She raised her shift's hem. "You like to see, Master? You like I show you again?"

I would. And she did.

Thunder rumbled low across the meadows of Thornfield, and I listened, sipping my claret thoughtfully. My wife was without question unchaste on our wedding day. As the years wore on, I became more certain of my suspicion that upon our first night as man and wife, this was not Bertha's sexual initiation nor anything like it. Experience taught me that.

Then I thought of the lurking presence of a man and the occasions of seeing him loitering behind the bungalow. Once Bertha's madness progressed enough to require incarceration inside the house, still she managed to escape on occasion, and each time I found her in the company of that same man, remembered for many years in the plural 'men'. But actually it was only one. She would cry upon being taken from him. When she did cry, I was startled to find she retained enough humanity to weep.

As for the rumours of a marriage, who could say? Bertha was introduced to me in Jamaican society as Richard Mason's unwed younger sister. The family patriarch, Jeremiah Mason, corroborated the relationship, and our marriage certificate named her as Bertha Antoinetta Mason. I gave a short laugh now, thinking of how I still did not know whether 'Bertha' was her first name or second, nor whether Bertha actually was the daughter of Jeremiah Mason and his reportedly deceased wife. To think otherwise was to believe unsubstantiated hearsay and the ramblings of a mischievous, jealous servant girl. I cared nothing for the opinion of my Jamaican neighbours and so internalised the rumours surrounding my misfortune as they became public knowledge. Burying them within myself, I lived quietly with their possibilities gnawing at my soul for the next fifteen years.

Out of the scattered papers I plucked a receipt, one with the name *Henri Breault, Esquire*, the Spanish Town solicitor consulted by me in attempt to dissolve my marriage, futilely. I turned the receipt over and read the address printed on the back, legible as yet but barely, copied the address down and set it aside. Then all papers were folded and contents placed again in the oilskin pouch, save for the wedding bands. Those I took in hand and examined further.

I was married, truly married, for such a short time. Weeks really. 'Someday,' I thought, touching the cool smoothness of the rings, 'I shall be married again and will wear a similar gold band. One identical to my wife's. I will be gentle and thoughtful and faithful. You will see, Jane.'

With the rings dropped into the pouch, I locked all in the metal box and buried it in the desk's bottom drawer. Then I lifted the slip of paper with the copied address, wondering whether this solicitor was in practice any longer. There was but one way to find out.

Upon finishing my glass of claret, I decided enough work was done for one day and I deserved a nap. A good one. So upstairs I went to my chamber and closed myself in, drawing the drapes. Jacket, waistcoat, shirt and boots were cast aside; my dressing gown was taken from its place in the wardrobe and brought with me to my bed. I lay down, holding it close, disappointed that Jane's scent was gone from the material, and so settled upon touching the pearls at my left wrist abstractedly. I shut my eyes.

"I must give this dressing gown to Leah for a wash one of these days," I murmured and laughed softly to myself, then drifted off into dreamless sleep.

Dinner that night was roast grouse with whisky and marmalade sauce. Whisky. 'Cute, John,' I thought. 'I must remember to thank him.' Tonight, the personage at the opposite end of the table from myself was Lord Ingram for which I was appreciative. I imagined a restrained dressing-down by Lord Ingram to wife and daughter; something to the effect of 'behave yourselves!' and possibly 'you are dashing every chance of a proposal!'

I, of course, was well aware that hopes for an engagement were the sole reason they accepted my invitation to Thornfield, and it was the event expected by everyone present. I could feel my guests' anticipation as if all were arresting their breath, staying exhalation for the grand announcement. All but Eshton, who continually held the expression of an amused spectator of a lawn tennis match.

Following dinner, the party repaired to the drawing room where all was once again brilliantly illuminated with candles. Heavy draperies were drawn over rain-spattered windows and a blazing fire crackled in the immense hearth. Uniformed footmen drifted silently about with trays bearing champagne flutes or snifters of cordial. I entered the room with Lady Ingram at my side as she tenaciously pursued a debate begun at dinner; the divine right of the rich who possessed 'good blood' as she termed fortunate birthright versus punishment with imperfection and poverty for those of 'bad blood'. Such attitudes sickened me (as if I had not been sickened enough today) and I looked about the room for my preferred companion, one with singularly more enlightened ideals than this titled ignoramus.

There was Jane, in a distant window seat with nearby candlelight aglow on her cheeks, diligently studying a book without the slightest awareness of how lovely she was to me. To avoid any guest finding my admiration apparent, I turned away to join a conversation with the Dent twins on matters of travel abroad. After some minutes, I turned back in the direction of the window seat and found Jane where my eyes had left her, but beside her now was Frederick Lynn. Their heads were turned toward one another in the flickering candlelight as she listened to him talk. Then she spoke. And smiled. Both were animated, apparently discussing the contents of her book. He turned his upper body to her, and I watched as she turned hers to him, her eyes meeting his in conversation.

Jealousy seized me with ferocity! Damn him. Damn him to hell! He was handsome, ten years younger than I, and suddenly I hated him with energy. The entire room diminished down to two people; a lovely young woman talking with a virile and handsome young man, closely and evocatively. My visual perception turned red.

"Edward," Eshton spoke as he came to my side. "You see something interesting?"

I looked at him pointedly, my agitation evident.

"It seems your lady love recovers from heartbreak quickly," he observed. "And commendably at that."

"Piss off, Arthur."

He laughed. "I believe I shall speak to her myself," he said and strolled across the room to the conversing pair in the window seat. He was apparently welcomed into the conversation, and the three engaged in light-hearted dialogue with laughter often reaching my ear. 'Damn it,' I thought, 'Where is Blanche?'

I need not search far as she was hovering nearby, awaiting my invitation into private exchange.

"Blanche," I said, turning to her with poorly concealed disinclination. "The remainder of your day was enjoyable I trust."

"Oh yes, Edward, quite," she drawled coming close and touching my lapels. "But you and I must not quarrel again. Our tiffs do upset Mother and Father so."

"Hmm. Surely they do," I dryly replied, and then looking sceptically into her ice-chip eyes asked, "What is it you really want from me, Blanche?"

She cast her glance sideways, surely attempting to formulate an answer not tailored to the ruination of her designs. I looked her up and down, my mind flicking to recollections conjured in the study earlier today; of releasing my sexual tension upon my wife all those years ago, forcibly and greedily. The notion of replicating that scene occurred to me now. Perhaps in a nearby room. Perhaps on the dining room table. Dinner was by now cleared away. 'Hm... take her in there and close the doors, lift her onto the table', commence once again the battle with petticoats and skirts...'

But no. My fantasy was more a delusion than an ambition and it lacked any real vitality. Merely a knee-jerk reaction of my former self and perhaps a feeble attempt to assuage the agony of jealousy's bite.

So I spent the evening listening passively to inane conversation humming all about me whilst determinedly keeping my hands away from the circulating platters of alcoholic libations. At one point Eshton and Frederick Lynn requested the chess table be brought into the drawing room whereupon four footmen carried the weighty antique piece from the study. The two began a game, soon observed by Jane, Adele and the Dent twins. I glanced toward their direction in time to see Eshton encourage Jane to take his place as Frederick's opponent whilst he excused himself momentarily, and she readily took the vacant seat, playing ivory to Freddie's ebony. The resulting surge of jealous resentment quite impaired me for an extended moment.

Then I thought, 'I deserve this entirely.' Cogitating on the situation, now with a glass of Riesling that miraculously appeared in my hand, I became rather amused as my jealousy turned to unmitigated admiration. Jane managed to turn my scheme around on me and executed it far better. I did not think it possible to love her more with each day, let alone each hour. But I did. Oh yes, I did. Her exceptionality made me love her madly for simply being who she was.

With the hum of conversation in the background of my thoughts, I firmly decided that tonight I would seek her out. Even if I did not touch her or speak to her, I must look into her eyes and be assured she loved me still. Looking back to her as she surveyed the chess table, I spoke to her in thought. 'I must have your love, Jane. Like air, I must have it. Or else I shall die.'

Chapter 17

THE EVENING'S REMAINDER was a haze of restless anticipation for me. The hands of every clock in Thornfield moved in conspiracy at an uncommonly slow pace whilst I stayed my fidgeting and sighing with probably one glass more of that spectacular Johannesburg Riesling than I should have partaken.

Vaguely I observed one after another of the ladies play or sing, and conversed with my guests as little as possible without seeming completely uncivil. Lady Ingram however, oblivious to others' disinterest in her small-minded opinions as was her darling Blanche, took a seat beside mine and attempted to draw me into discourse on 'hirelings' behaving in a familiar manner amongst their betters. She jutted her angular face toward the far side of the drawing room at the pair playing chess.

"Really, Rochester!" she protested, "How can you tolerate such cheeky deportment in a governess of all people? Playing at chess with the gentlemen!"

"And why should she not play, my Lady? She is very good with chess," I responded.

She looked at me in great astonishment. "Ladies do not play at gentlemen's games! And do you mean to tell me *you* engage in such recreation with her yourself? When you are alone?"

"Yes. I do."

"Shameless!" Lady Ingram said, openly glowering at Jane. "Simply shameless! The entire breed is of the same material. Ingratiating, flirtatious trollops all of them. 'Tis disgusting the way these low born girls wheedle their way into the drawing rooms of gentry hoping to snare themselves an affluent husband or, failing that, a paramour. Despicable it is! You must mind, Rochester, that she remembers her place with you."

"Miss Eyre is doing nothing wrong," I pointed out, amused at the titled matron's agitation.

"She *is* doing something wrong! Just look at the way she makes eyes at Freddie Lynn."

I did look and found Jane doing nothing of the sort. But Lynn was eagerly eyeing Jane across the table like some delectable buffet viand.

I asked, "And your invaluable recommendation in this matter, Lady Ingram?"

She snorted a laugh. "You must send the child to school immediately, Rochester. Preserve your little French poppet's innocence by removing her from the seat of such disgraceful immodesty. Come, you must make the promise that you shall."

I shook my head and laughed. Adele no doubt had witnessed some shockingly immodest behaviour in her sexually indiscriminate opera dancer mother; the variety that might even cause Lady Ingram to re-examine her definitions.

"Schools are expensive, Madam," I replied, "and Adele is receiving a fine education from an instructress whose character is irreproachable. Your argument is well taken, but I must assert that it is entirely unfounded."

She tsked and sighed petulantly before constructing her further argument. "Also to keep in mind, my dear," she said, leaning in, "is that Blanche would never have it. Neither the governess nor the child. You know my daughter well enough to see that, surely."

"I do," I replied, glancing at said daughter who was now seated alone at the piano, her demeanour haughty as ever.

"Rochester," the Lady ventured. "You must soon find for your governess new employment and your sweet little ward a school. Would you not agree?"

Unfortunately yes, I did agree. "And you have a suggestion to offer, do you not Lady Ingram? Not for the school, that is easily managed, but for the governess?"

She thought for a moment. "I do have an association with a viscountess in western Ireland who mentioned in a recent letter a well-to-do family with five daughters. 'Spirited' girls, one might say. The mother apparently cannot keep a governess for longer than a few months. Perhaps your girl there may serve the O'Gall family better than did her predecessors."

I looked at Jane. So bright, good, honest and lovely. To send her far from me and into circumstances so inhospitable would be distressing indeed, but not unfathomable. She would be safe, I would know her location and would additionally be assured that she was occupied in teaching and not canoodling with a virile young admirer. I truly am a selfish bastard. You do not have to tell me. I freely admit it.

"If you would supply me with the name and address of this family, Lady Ingram, your generous assistance would be most appreciated."

Her expression brightened immeasurably. I knew how her calculating mind was interpreting my response. "Yes, of course I will, Rochester, just as soon as I return to Ingram Park," she said, now glowing with smiles.

I nodded and listened to the Lady's continued prattling whilst glancing to Jane with an escalating wretchedness in my heart. Our separation was near.

The entryway clock struck eleven times. Sophie had taken Adele away to the nursery long ago, and the guests now began to retire one by one to their chambers. As the room cleared further, Jane stood from the chess table to bid Frederick Lynn and Arthur Eshton a good night. With a nod and curtsey across the room to me, she turned and disappeared.

Eshton came near and clapped me on the shoulder. "Splendid evening, Edward. As the hour grows late I too will wish you a good night." He leaned down and added quietly, "She really is a marvellous girl. It is no wonder you love her."

"Yes. Thank you, Arthur," I said with a laugh at his mellow candidness. "Sleep well."

For nearly another hour I remained in the drawing room. Candles burned low as I listened to a steady stream of rain against the windows, thinking and anticipating. I found my heart quickening and entire being nervous. I planned to go to Jane in her chamber tonight. There, I would kneel by her bedside and hopefully find her awake. Other than that, I did not know what to do or expect.

When the clock struck the first of twelve chimes, I went out of the drawing room, up the staircase to the gallery and arrived at Jane's shut door. I touched the panel, not yet ready to knock. What was I waiting for? Nervous, my heart raced. The air was cold in the gallery, and I began to shiver. Or tremble. Then I knocked softly and waited. No response. I knocked again. Nothing. So I turned the knob and opened the door. In flickering firelight, Jane's bed was turned down but vacant. Not here. Where ...? Then, I guessed where she had gone and retreated into the gallery, down the stairs and along cold, darkened corridors until I heard piano and voice in the library. There I stood, outside the shut library door, listening.

She was playing a ballad done for me once before, one she said had no written lyrics, but before I opened the door, her clear alto voice began. I entered the library to find Jane at the piano, dressed in her plain gray evening attire. A single candle was set nearby, illuminating her features clearly. She turned to look up at me, but I went past her to the fire and took my chair, setting my feet up on the ottoman. Meanwhile she continued playing, in no way unsettled by my presence. She hummed the tune softly while playing, and I stared off into the fire, revisiting her passion in memory. My appetite for her love was whetted razor fine.

I arose from my chair and removed jacket and waistcoat, watching my form throw her into shadow. She ceased playing and turned her head, listening, not looking at me. I stood beside her for a moment, then tapped her hip with the back of my hand; a silent request for her to move over. She slid along the piano bench, and I slid in beside her.

"You wrote lyrics for that one," I commented.

"Some."

"When did you write them?"

"Last night. Today."

"Was that song for me as well?"

She sighed deeply. "It is for how I feel now, yes. About you, me, us."

"Tell me what you mean," I said.

She was silent for some moments, hands in her lap, looking down. "I do not know who you are," she said quietly. "I feel I know nothing at times."

Her words cut me. "You know me better than anyone, Jane."

She gave a short laugh. "That is not saying much. I doubt you are, or ever have been, completely open with any person." What could I say? She was right. So I said nothing. She looked up at me, eyes searching mine. "You are going to marry her."

"Jane ...," I started.

"You do not love her, but you will marry her. Why? For her wealth? For her beauty? Is it because all of those people expect it of you?"

"Jane, you do not understand."

"I do! I understand perfectly," she said, becoming roused to something like anger. "What a lot of fun to dally with the governess, but any serious intentions ..."

"You listen to me now!" I said turning to face her, my own anger rising. "I never said that I was going to marry Miss Ingram. I never said it to her or to anyone. Where are you getting this idea?"

"Specifically? From Mrs. Fairfax. But everyone here seems to think a proposal is eminent. The servants. Adele even thinks so. Your friend Mr. Lynn is certain an engagement will be secured by week's end..."

"So you've discussed me with Frederick Lynn, have you?"

"He brought you into the conversation, not I."

"Yes, I noticed how friendly you and Frederick became tonight," I said peevishly, turning away from her.

She was silent. When I looked back at her, she wore a mischievous smile across her face. "It hurts, doesn't it?" she said, raising her eyes to mine.

Softly I admitted, "Yes."

She pushed a little further. "You were jealous to see me playing chess with Mr. Lynn?"

To say no would have been a blatant lie. I turned to her and met her eyes. "Very much so. What hurts more is this belief of yours that I 'dallied' with you for mere amusement. Is that truly the way you see it?"

"What am I to think? You tell me you kiss Miss Ingram and do not deny plans to marry her."

"Jane," I said, pained by the hopelessness in her voice. "My life is overrun with complications. Please believe me when I say my intentions are good. I want to protect you above all else."

She shook her head. "You are right. I do not understand."

I sighed and tried again. "It is my sincere hope that one day I can discuss everything of myself with you, openly and completely. Now, I cannot."

"Why?"

"Because I... I need to keep you safe from harm and wrong," was my reply, turning to look at her. I took her hand from her lap and held it in both of mine. She was so precious to me. We sat hip to hip on the bench, our arms touching, talking softly in the warm glow of hearth and candlelight. Temptations wove their way into me deeper still, and my nervousness resumed. To hell with resolve, eminent separation, conventionality and all other impediments. All that mattered was her soft skin and full lips.

"Kiss me," I whispered.

She smiled impishly. "No."

"Why not?"

"Because you kiss that Blanche Ingram!"

"Jane, it is not as you think; not as it is with us." And then, laughing, I added, "Besides, Blanche cannot kiss to save her life."

"Oh?" she grinned.

I nodded, smiling. "Stiff. Frigid. Really terrible." Then I looked at her. "You. I cannot figure what it is, Jane. You. Your kiss. I've been able to think of little else since the night we spent together - and the following morning."

"Miss Ingram's kisses are poor in comparison because she does not love you." She turned to look at me. Eyes on mine, her gaze soon fell to my lips. I knew it would not be long now.

"Jane," I said softly, deeply. "Tell me you did not enjoy your time with me the night we spent together. Tell me you do not think of it."

"I cannot say that," she said, turning her body toward mine. "I do think of it. Constantly."

I came a little closer. "Then kiss me."

She was quiet, thinking, looking at me; at my eyes, my lips. The clock ticked by as she masterfully drew it out. She must have been anticipating this scene since the morning I went away for certainly I was. Waiting for her, my trembling began, and I whispered again, "Jane. Kiss me."

She brought my hand to her lips, opened the palm and lay kisses to fingertips. With my palm to her cheek, she closed her eyes and caressed my hand against her skin. I came in close; could wait no longer. She came forward, meeting my lips absolutely. Instantly we responded to one another, passion escalating faster than anticipated. I marvelled at the immediate, potent rush it sent through me as both my hands went to her neck, her face. I pulled her to my mouth, breathlessly opening hers beneath mine. Oh, yes. Had craved this incessantly, every night and day. Deep and desperate, I needed it all, and I tasted, licked her tongue with mine. Again. Again. A deep gasping sob rumbled in her throat as her hands went into my hair, pulling me closer, returning my kiss hungrily.

I broke free of her and changed my position, now straddling the bench to face her, and pulled her slight frame into my broad chest. Turned at the waist, her arms were now tightly around me. Her hands went behind my neck and knotted into my hair as she kissed me with lustful intensity. Her hot mouth, arms around me, hands drinking up sensation; all of it was driving me quite mad. I was so very aroused. More, I needed much more. 'God, help me keep control. Will hate myself if I hurt her. Must find the strength to slow us down.' I pulled away from her suddenly, my hands restraining her at the shoulders. Her face and eyes were awash with desire, skin flushed.

"Don't stop," she protested, attempting to reach for me. "Please. Let me."

"Jane, we are moving far too fast," I said, my hands holding her arms.

She shook her head. "No. Oh, please. I want this."

So I lessened my grip on her arms and she slipped a hand around the back of my neck, pulling close again. I obeyed her pleasurably. Her mouth came to mine, now softer, more deliberate. I dropped my hands to my thighs, delighting in her sensual kiss, in being the focus of her passion, and breathed deeply as I revelled in her inherent expertise. Her hands explored me, slowly absorbing the contours of my shoulders, my arms and back.

My hands went around her slight body and moved up to her hair. I began pulling pins out and tossing them onto the floor until her hair came down, wavy after having been done up in a twisted knot. My heart racing, I spread her long hair out over her shoulders, loving the length, warmth and thickness of it. I wanted it all over me. Yes, naked, in bed, with this long, rich chestnut hair all over me. I pulled her as close to me as I could, cursing the stiff, constrictive corset beneath her dress. Suddenly, she broke from me and stood, and I watched as she grasped her skirts and threw a leg over the bench, straddling my thighs.

'Oh, yes. Yes!' And I pulled her close, drawing her pelvis right up to mine. My hands on her hips, on her open thighs, I wished our clothes would simply disappear. Fighting with layers of petticoats trimmed in lace, I growled at them for separating us. Tremors shook my hands as I caressed her calves, squeezed them gently, fingers exploring up her stockinged legs.

Jane's arms wrapped around me, her kiss soft, calm, searching. So deliberate, she caught my lower lip and, knowing I loved this, gently sucked it and teased it. Deep, guttural noises I barely recognised as my own rumbled in my throat and chest. My breathing was laboured as I held her body tightly to me, my face turned to hers, loving the sensations she triggered in me. She was amazingly adept at drawing me to the brink of my control and then gently backing me away. Again and again she proved it. Reality blurred and swam, and I cared for nothing else. My universe consisted of nothing else.

'Now,' I thought. 'I need what I came for, and I need it now.'

So I brought my hands up to the nape of her neck and found the first button of her dress. My fingers undid one, then another, a third, down to the centre of her back. My hands went to her shoulders and pulled her dress forward, exposing her neck, shoulders and upper chest. Taking a handful of her hair, I gently drew her head back. Her graceful neck before me, I placed soft kisses all around, up to her ears and back down. She shuddered and her hands clutched my shoulders. With each kiss, she gasped faintly, her chest heaving unevenly. "Ohhh," she sighed. I continued; my hot breath bathing her neck and ears, slightly licking her satiny skin. Her hands moved from my shoulders to my back, fingers digging in. "Ohhh, Edward," she breathed.

I softly worked on her neck and shoulders, loving the feel of her skin against my lips. My hands moved up her waist to the swell of breasts. She squirmed against my pelvis, and in reflexive response, I convulsed. Working to keep control, I pulled the neck of her dress down and placed kisses across her chest.

"Say it," I whispered. My hands dropped to her hips and I pulled her as tightly to me as I could, spreading her thighs widely. Her head was far back, lovely skin exposed, completely offered up to my mouth. My hands came up her body again, approaching her breasts. "Tell me, Jane," I whispered, "Say it."

A small cry escaped her lips, and her breathing was ragged. She swallowed. My mouth went to the hollow of her neck and worked slowly downward, my forearms crossed on her upper back with a hand deep in her hair.

"Tell me," I whispered deeply.

"Ohh," she breathed. "Oh, God. Edward." She breathed deeply, her fingernails drawing across my back. "Ohh. Edward, I love you. Oh, I love you. Love you." And she brought her hands up the back of my neck into my hair and kissed me deeply, breathing the words "I love you" into me. I pulled them deep inside, keeping them lost and protected within me. She released her kiss and held me tightly. And I smiled. With my heart, body and soul I smiled and was supremely happy. This is what heaven must feel like, I believed, and then felt the familiar stinging in my eyes. Jane's hands came up to either side of my face. She made me look at her. Her eyes studied mine, but she said nothing.

I said, "Do you never cry, Jane? You've seen me cry. The morning I left you." My eyes welled over and spilled. I laughed at myself. "And now."

"I cry sometimes. I cried last night...." and her voice trailed away. She looked down. "I could not bear it. Seeing you with her."

I shook my head and smiled through blurred vision. "No, Jane. There is no one, no one that could take your place," I said, burying my face in her neck, "Please, love. Have faith in me." I looked at her again. Now her eyes were shining in the candlelight. "Are you happy, Jane?"

She nodded, not looking at me. She was suddenly downcast and I could guess the reason. I wiped my tears away and softly said, "I bought something for you, a gift, while I was away."

She looked at me sceptically. "Did you?"

I unbuttoned my left shirt cuff, folded the sleeve twice and raised my wrist before her. "This," I said.

Jane's expression was incredulous. "Umm, what is that exactly? They look to be pearls, I know, but why are you wearing them on your wrist?"

I undid the clasp and took it off. Holding each end, I held it before her. "Because I wanted it close to me before I gave it to you. Take it."

She lifted a hand, and I lay the necklace across her palm. She touched the pearls and smiled. "Warm! And beautiful. You purchased this for me?"

"Jane, you deserve lovely things. Let me have the pleasure of giving something nice to you."

Closing her fist around it, she lowered the necklace onto her thigh and raised her eyes to mine. "You do. When you look at me. When you say my name," she said quietly, her voice not quite steady. "You give me something I have never known. Something that I am finding I need so much." Her eyes filled and she looked up at the ceiling, blinking tears back. I noted her determination not to cry in my presence. Once controlled, she lowered her eyes to the pearls in her hand and said, "Thank you."

I took the necklace from her hand, placed it against her neck and fastened the clasp behind. The pearls were beautiful on her bare skin, her rich hair falling over her shoulders. With my hands on her back, I placed my lips to her chest. Into her skin and into her heart, I silently mouthed the words, "I love you, Jane." And I held her tightly wishing I could speak my thought aloud.

'Someday, if ever I am a free man, I will tell you that, Jane. And my next words will be, "Marry me, please".'

I hoped with all my might that my actions, voice, kiss, caresses spoke the words for me, and that she would again read my thoughts as she had done so many times before. She stroked my cheek, her eyes searching and reading mine. Then she kissed me soulfully. It thrilled me again.

"I want to hold you," I said to her softly. "Only you. Not an armful of corset and petticoat." My fingertips traced her bare shoulders and arms. "Corsets are the most ridiculous things ever invented, are they not? I do loathe them."

"Do you?" she asked. Then she brought her leg from around me and stood beside the piano bench. Her hands went behind her back and she worked on the remaining buttons. She pulled the dress away and it dropped to the floor. My throat went dry. I stared at her fixedly. She stepped out of the dress and tossed it in a heap a short distance away, then unlaced her boots and threw them near the dress. Hands behind her back, she undid more laces and closures. The corset came free and she flung it onto the dress. She was wearing a thin eyelet camisole beneath. So thin, I could easily discern the peaks of rigid nipples beneath, the outline of breasts and her slim waist.

"Jane," I hoarsely said. "What may I ask are you doing?" But the idea of stopping her was unthinkable. I watched her, my heart racing, the trembling resuming in full force. Hands behind her back once again, she unbuttoned the closure of her petticoats, and they too dropped to the floor. She stepped out of them and tossed the white bundle onto the heap of clothes. The last to go were her black stockings, which she wrapped around her hand and threw aside. She stood before me in camisole and matching knickers of pristine white cotton. My heart felt unsteady and I momentarily was faint. Air. I needed to breathe.

Jane came back to my side and threw her leg over me again, straddling me as she had done before. In her dress it had been exciting but this was unbelievably erotic. I looked at her with pure lust over my face. My hands went to her legs, up into her knickers; thighs smooth, lovely, open wide around me. Her firm nipples were directly before me and realised I was salivating. I pulled her pelvis close, hands on her hips.

"Feel that?" I said, my voice thick with wanting her. "Feel it?"

She nodded and moved her hips against me.

"Jane, have you any idea of your peril at this moment?" I huskily asked, my restraint dissolving by the second.

Her hands came up to my face and she kissed me deeply. Continuing to move against me, she broke our kiss and said, "You asked that I have faith in you, Edward. So I will."

"Oh, good God. Oh, my...," I gasped. "Jane, please."

Her hands went to my shirt buttons. One after another, she swiftly released them, and I was devoid of strength to stop her. She controlled me completely, rhythmically moving against me, breathing deeply, very obviously obtaining much pleasure as well. She opened my shirt and pushed it back over my shoulders. Her hands swept through the dark hair covering my chest, smiling lustfully as her fingertips stroked my nipples. I trembled violently and throwing my head back, released deep sobs in time with my breaths. Jane wrapped her arms tightly about my shoulders as her feminine warmth kneaded against me. "Ohh, Edward. It is good."

I was nearly out of my mind. The pleasure that coursed through me lingered right at the peak of excitement but would not cross. I grasped her hips tightly. "Jane! My God!" And some part of me, not myself, bolted my body onto my feet and carried her to the rug before the fire. I lay her down, her legs wrapped about me. In the low firelight, her face was suffused with excitement. I was aware of myself enough to know that removing our remaining clothing and making love to her would be glorious in the short term but would later be poisoned with regret. So I kissed her face, her neck, groaning into her hair, thrusting urgently against her.

"Edward," she gasped, "Show me how to please you. Teach me. Edward. Please."

I kissed her insatiably and took her hand, placing it to my hard centre of excitement, showing her the way. She readily learned, and soon both hands went down, quickly working at the buttons of my breeches. On hands and knees, I gazed at her in lustful amazement, no longer afraid of frightening her. She pursued me ravenously, hands pushing breeches further down my hips, drawing me out. She proved to be a clever, adept student in everything I taught her. Her hands worked me, and my consciousness swam as I became overwrought with pleasure. I raised her camisole and lowered her knickers, exposing a flat, delicious belly. She drew me along, my pleasure heightening and spreading.

"Jane, oh yes, Jane, I'm going to, please, yes, now! Now! Ohh! Now!" Deep sobs broke from within me as I convulsively released torrid fluid over her smooth, soft skin. It came and came. I heaved my breathing over her, my eyes closed with the darkness sparkling before me. It seemed a long time before I was drained, then I fell beside her onto the rug and groaned deeply, gasping, coughing.

When my breathing slowed, I opened my eyes, apprehensive to meet hers, but I did finally, cautiously. She lay with an arm behind her head and eyes down at her belly, an amused smile playing on her lips. With one finger she traced lines across her skin with my semen.

"What are you doing?" I laughed.

She looked at me. "Oh, Edward, that was the most beautiful sight I can imagine." She looked at me with amazement, smiling, giddy. "You are so beautiful. I am... speechless!"

"You amaze me," I replied, smiling at her. "A novice only just out of a veritable convent school, yet you have innate qualities that simply stun me."

Continuing her pursuits on her belly, she said, "Yes. You do bring forth surprising behaviour in me."

"Shocking. Scandalous." I said. "What would Mrs. Fairfax say if she came in just now?"

"Oh," she said, glowing with smiles, "I do not care in the least."

"Stay there," I told her and got up to button my breeches. I took the low burning candle from the piano and went out to the kitchen where I found a soft dishtowel. Upon returning to the library, Jane lay where I left her on the rug before the fire, stretched out with ankles crossed and a finger swirling in my fluid.

"Stop it!" I laughed and knelt beside her to wipe her belly dry, then looked down on her, smiling. This time, post-climactic bliss would be shared with my Jane. I stroked her cheek and leaned down, kissing her softly, sweetly.

"You were the aggressor here, Jane," I accused, glancing to the piano bench. "I wanted to slow us down but you... You seduced me." My fingers played over her camisole and firm nipples beneath. "Naughty little witch."

She looked up at me and asked, "How old are you, Edward?"

I cast my eyes to the rug, feeling an honest reply would be destructive, but she deserved at least a semblance of truth. "Probably too old for you, Jane. Old enough to be your father."

"Is that why?" she asked.

"Why what?"

"Why," she started, "why you want me to leave Thornfield?"

I was startled. Just how did she know such things? I never spoke of them. But she had it muddled. "You've got it wrong, Jane."

"You see the necessity of my departure as well as I do. Come, admit it," she said sitting up.

I shook my head and quietly said, "I do not want you to go. What I want is for you to stay here."

"But I cannot," she said emphatically. "You will marry her, and I shall not stay to watch that happen."

I shut my eyes. The sensation of drowning came over me, eclipsing the bliss of a few minutes since. I remained silent.

"I am not trying to argue with you, Edward, or hurt you. But you have never denied that you will marry her. And," she paused, eyes aglow in firelight, "although I tell you that I love you, you say nothing."

"Jane," I whispered, reaching out to her. It was my law of action not to say what was in my heart, for to do that would also bring lies, and I wanted never to lie again to her about my awful truth.

"You do not feel for me what I feel for you," Jane said.

Her words wrenched my heart. So untrue!

"I am not angry," she went on. "It simply *is*, and I do believe I understand. How could *I* ever hope to compete with the matchless Miss Ingram? As is undoubtedly clear, Sir, I am not what she is. Not beautiful, I have no money, I have no family connections, you yourself consider me too young..."

My hands came to my face and I shook my head despondently. "Stop. Jane... please."

She sighed and softly said, "I suppose that tonight, here, I wanted to draw in as much of you as possible. The sight of you, taste, touch, the way you smell. I wanted your passion again, and I could not get enough." Our eyes locked again, and I wanted her badly. She looked down at her hands. "I will be gone when you wake in the morning."

I stared at her disbelieving. She may as well have slapped me. "Gone. What do you mean 'gone', Jane? Where?"

"A letter arrived from a woman I once knew. She wants me to visit as soon as I can come."

"What woman? Where is she and why must you go dashing off to her? Come on, out with it!"

"She is my deceased uncle's wife. I did mention her to you before, upon our initial interview."

"I recall. This is the woman who discarded you to a charity institution at the age of ten. And so?"

"Well, her name is Reed. Being quite ill, she has asked for me to come to her. Tomorrow I will meet the coach, and whilst there I shall seek another situa…"

"Jane!" I thundered, cutting her off in a rising flare of anger. "How long have you known this? And precisely when were you planning to tell me?"

"Before departing tomorrow morning, Sir. I would have left a note. I sent a letter off to Mrs. Reed's housekeeper only today and could not very well have broached my plans in the drawing room this evening seeing as your attentions were otherwise firmly occupied. And I came downstairs tonight hoping to find you in your study, but you did not go there. Waiting until the dead of night to rap upon your chamber door did not quite seem appropriate either, Sir."

I growled in frustration. "We are back to 'Sir' again are we? You are there before me in your underclothes, your entire being as yet aglow with our passion, and you will address me as 'Sir'? What's more, you will tell me calmly of this preposterous plan to leave me in a mere few hours?!"

She nodded. "I am going."

My mouth opened and shut once or twice. "It seems I have little choice in the matter, Jane. I've no right to forbid you from visiting family. For how long will you be gone?"

"A fortnight, possibly more. Perhaps permanently since I will seek a new position whilst there. If I advertise and receive a suitable response, there will be no need for me to return here. I will go directly from Gateshead to my new…"

"The Goddamned hell you will!" I shouted, becoming truly irate.

She smiled softly and crawled to me, gazing into my furious eyes. She kissed me and said, "I must go forth. This is not where I belong."

With that I placed an arm around her neck and brought her head to mine. 'Yes it is, Jane. Yes it is! You belong with me,' screamed my mute heart.

I grasped her jaw and said to her sharply, "You will come back, Jane. This is not a request but a command. Do not think of disobeying me. Should you stay away, I will come after you and find you."

She did not reply.

I needed to know that she would be in a safe and hospitable house. "Tell me of this aunt sending for you. Will she look after you? Will she see that you are lodged suitably and comfortably?"

"Her name is Mrs. Sarah Reed," Jane said with a sigh. "Her husband is dead since I was about four years of age. She remains mistress of Gateshead Hall, an estate some eighty miles northeast of here."

A moment was required to digest that. "Gateshead. I knew of a Reed of Gateshead. A magistrate."

"Yes. He was my mother's brother."

As the connection became clear, I gave a short laugh and looked at her teasingly. "You are gentry after all, Jane. Disconnected, but gentry nonetheless. I knew it to be true from the day we met."

"No, no Sir! I never presume upon the connection. There is no real connection as Mrs. Reed's letter is our first communication since I was sent away to school."

Questions came flooding my mind. "Then how did you wind up at a charitable institution such as Lowood?" I asked. "Surely this Sarah Reed was left with considerable means upon her husband's death. Did he not instruct his wife to ensure your proper education at an institution of his choosing?"

Playing with my fingers, she shook her head and said, "Whether he did or did not may only be known if I speak with my aunt once again. You see, Sir, my parents died when I was under a year old, and when Uncle Reed learned I was left orphaned, he took me into his home. He died after a brief illness but I resided at Gateshead with his wife and three children until I was ten. That winter she felt I would be better served at school. Mr. Brocklehurst, with whom you are familiar from the newspapers, interviewed Mrs. Reed and I at Gateshead, and the decision was made. I do not know if there were other schools considered, but I would doubt it."

"The decision for you to be packed off to school was as abrupt as that?" I could not help but doubt that a county magistrate and estate freeholder would fail to make provisions for the education of a beloved adopted niece.

Jane shrugged. "My aunt thought me burdensome, Mr. Rochester. She did not like me."

"Edward."

She smiled. "Edward."

"So what you tell me is that you would go traipsing off at great distance to the bedside of this contemptible aunt and expect me to grant ready permission to do so."

"She is dying. Perhaps she wishes to make amends. I cannot deny her that, nor can I deny myself a possible reconciliation."

I was roundly troubled by the unaccompanied journey and cool reception if not blatant hostility I foresaw awaiting her there. Jane was young and optimistic whereas in my more seasoned view of this surely lenient synopsis she gave, I fully expected Sara Reed to beget Jane further heartache and little more. "I do not like this," was my verbalised conclusion.

"No. But I must go."

Suddenly recalling my role as her employer as well as the party responsible for her welfare, I also realised she had received no salary as yet. "Then you will need money, Jane. If you are determined to stand vigil for this detestable woman's passing, I cannot forbid your will, but likewise I shall not have you travelling both alone and without money. You will spend your travel night at a respectable inn and ride only with reputable coachmen. See to it."

"Yes, Sir."

Now on my feet, I went to my jacket to extract my billfold. I removed from it a fifty-pound note and held it out to her. She recoiled in amused surprise.

"I will not accept cash from you at the moment, Sir! As you've pointed out, I am in my underclothes!" I laughed, too. If any situation would appear disreputable, it would be this one. She added, "Fifteen pounds is all you owe to me, and you can give it to me in the morning, Sir."

I placed my billfold into my jacket and returned to her. Kneeling before her, I gently pushed her down onto the rug and brought my weight onto her body, bringing her bare legs up around me.

"Not 'Sir'," I said, settling down on her and enjoying the regeneration of my arousal. "To you, I am Edward. And I will tell you what's more: you think I do not feel love for you, Miss Jane? You are wrong. You see it in me, you feel it in all I say and do. I know that you do. Come. Admit it."

She received my gentle thrusts with a faint nod and smile in reply.

I kissed her slowly and with all the loving passion for her that was in me, then looked into her eyes. "Tell me, young lady. What do you think now?"

Her fingertips stroked my cheek and she sighed. "I think that you are the only man I will ever want. I think that I love you to the depths of my soul. And I think being separated from you will be pure anguish."

I kissed her again. "You make my heart happy," I told her, smiling.

We lay on the rug talking and kissing softly as the fire burned lower. The clock in the entrance hall soon struck two.

"We should go up to bed," she eventually whispered.

I smiled. "Yours or mine?"

"Why Mr. Rochester, what an idea!"

"Miss Eyre, if you think I will see you go off to your own chamber now, after all of this and with you scheming to leave me indefinitely in a mere few hours, you are sorely mistaken."

She considered that. "All right then. Yours."

We stood from the floor and retrieved our scattered attire, myself into waistcoat and jacket whilst Jane gathered her clothes into a bundle and hairpins into her hand. Upon my insistence, I lifted her into my arms and carried her up the entryway stairs to my bedchamber. There, I deposited her clothes onto the sofa and removed my jacket, waistcoat, shirt and boots. Breeches I left on. We climbed under the thick covers and settled upon our sides facing one another, our four hands clasped before us.

"You know, I typically sleep naked as a babe," I told her.

"Do you now?" she replied, smiling. "I will remember that."

I stroked her hair away from her face. "Do not go, Jane. What will I do without you?"

She leaned in and kissed me sweetly. "Sleep now, my love," she whispered. "Give tomorrow not another thought."

My mouth kissed and nibbled her fingers as I closed my eyes. The thought of her leaving was agonising, but I reminded myself that it was I who had done the same a fortnight ago. Now I would know the pain she endured when I rode away from Thornfield for an indefinite expanse of time. I went away to find clarity and to steel my resolve against what must be done: to separate myself from Jane. And here we were, drifting off to sleep in my bed following an exhilarating episode of passion and a search of one another's souls. Hopeless.

As her breathing evened with sleep, I whispered to her, "Do not roam too far from me or for too long, Jane. I will be here waiting for you. You must have faith in me. For I do love you."

Chapter 18

A SINGLE CANDLE BURNED on the bedside table as Jane slept and I pondered. With eyes shut I listened to the sublime drone of rain falling in sheets against the casement and to Jane's fleeting sighs mingled with slumbered breaths. Tonight I was given me more than I ever could have hoped. After the hours spent thirsting for reassurance of her love, waiting for her, starving for her, fearing that I had lost her trust, I found her alone and willing to hear me. At first I drew on her love carefully. Then her love's floodgates opened. Her words, eyes, touch, every movement of her body, her kiss; they all consumed and permeated me so that now... now I knew. After years of self centred wandering, shielding my shattered spirit from further vain expectation, I knew what it was to be loved. Jane, my pure and innocent girl with blazing inherent passion; she loved me with such poignant intensity that I counted myself supremely blessed.

My hands went to her cheeks in the semi-darkness. Gingerly I kissed her lips as she slept, then lay back, thinking of our episode in the library tonight. At times she seemed to have a curious ability to use her reserve in passion itself; to artlessly draw from me my deepest, most vulnerable fervour. At other times, her own passive acceptance of my touch, or active pursuance of it, seemed driven by something beyond herself, leaving us both astounded. So sexually driven for a novice. She was my equal in this as in every way. How would married life be for us? Completely and utterly satisfying indeed. Of that I had no doubt.

I loved her response to me as it reverberated throughout her frame. I wanted to be the only man to every know this of my Jane; the only man to ever experience the wondrous capacity for love she possessed. 'You are the only man I will ever want,' she had said. My heart swelled, remembering the sincerity in her voice. I now kissed her lips again, could not help myself, but she continued sleeping soundly. I pulled her closer.

'It is night as yet,' I thought. Then I settled down and finally drifted off to sleep.

A dream met me without hesitation as I fell into slumber. My grassy field returned after keeping away for a week or more. But it was different now. A storm was blowing, and the once steady, golden sunlight was blazingly white one moment and deeply purple the next. Silvery leaves blew off distant trees, forming shimmering clouds travelling laterally before blowing apart. The grass alternately stood tall, then waved down flat. My angel was before me, her long hair blowing about us. My hands brushed it away from her face. I was compelled to kiss her and continually did so. Hungering for her purity, for her clean and honest love, I pulled her to me as the tempest strove to draw her away. Her eyes were frightened, and she reached for me. She slipped from my fingertips and was suddenly gone.

I woke with a start. Relief washed over me to find that Jane had not moved. In warm sleepiness she remained close alongside of me, but the dream disturbed me. The anxiety it reflected came from within, that much I knew, and although I settled down once again, a harassing combination of pleasure and pain surged from within and along my extremities.

Jane was here, her long chestnut hair on my pillow and her body next to mine. But as the clock chimed the half hour, my distress increased knowing that our time was short.

'Savour now, Edward. Do not ruin now. It is all you've got.' So I did. I settled down again, breathing in her lovely warmth.

"Love you, Jane," I whispered. Then sleep gradually returned.

But rest was not to be mine that night for I was soon inched back into consciousness by a warm, golden light nearby. Jane still had not moved and continued to lie facing me, breathing deep and steady. Suddenly vigilant, I opened my eyes and tensed. Candlelight floated above the foot of the bed. My heart lurched. I remained still and watchful as a figure turned, revealing the white material of a nightgown and long dark hair. She had returned to my chamber, again bringing a candle near to my bed.

"Bertha," I said low and severe.

Her aware, knowing and alert eyes were on mine. She approached my bedside and held the candle aloft, cocking her head as she studied Jane's sleeping face. I carefully extracted my hands from the bedclothes, at the ready and slowly rising.

"Your whore, Edward. Who is she?" she asked, her articulate voice unusually high and her posture growing aggressive.

As my heart bounded within my chest, a sudden concept flicked into my otherwise panicking mind that although she appeared to possess cognitive clarity and rational thinking, her psychosis was deeply rooted. I decided to play that hand.

"This woman is my wife," I answered, then calmly asked, "Why are you not with your husband at this late hour, Antoinetta?"

She was visibly startled. Her attention flicked to me. "My husband?" A quizzical expression crossed her features. Then a true, warm smile changed her expression entirely. The smile reflected happiness, transforming her flat countenance to one of loveliness. This smile she had never shown to me, not even in our earliest days, and I wondered at that.

As if suddenly remembering an important task, she said, "I must go to him."

Carefully slipping out of bed so as not to wake Jane, I took up my shirt and ushered Bertha to the door. "We must see you back to safety, Antoinetta," I told her. "This is not where you belong."

Taking a candle and reaching into the dresser for the north tower key, I followed Bertha along the path she had come. Walking a number of paces behind her, I remained at the ready should she turn to attack. She led the way upstairs to her stone prison and advanced into the final, hidden room to the fireplace where she stood before the sturdy fender with her back to me. I noted her keeper, asleep in a chair. Grace's head was tipped back against the wall as she snored fumes of hard spirits. No bottle or cup remained in sight. Checking my fury, I took the other chair and placed it directly before Grace. Bertha remained motionless before the flames.

I lifted a hand to Mrs. Poole's ear and loudly snapped my fingers. She woke with a start, bolting upright and blearily focusing on my face directly before hers. Finally she stiffened and set her eyes sidewise, saying nothing.

"Your charge visited me again in my chamber tonight, Mrs. Poole," I said, glaring at her. "The current location of your keys is where?"

She swung her surprised gaze to me and patted apron pockets, scanned the room's surfaces, then searched at her neck for a cord she often wore. Defeat was evident. "Sir, tonight I was terribly tired. She herself was sleeping soundly not an hour ago! Oh dear, this is most unfortunate. She must have...," but Grace stopped and wisely thought better of continuing explanations.

I looked to Bertha who was now rocking herself to and fro, wringing her hands.

"Find them," I commanded Grace.

She stood from her chair and said with a set jaw, "I shall, immediately, Mr. Rochester. Perhaps it is best that you leave us now so that I may... see to her," Grace said with an edge of severity.

Desolately I looked upon the two women, knowing that this longstanding arrangement was under rapid deterioration. Bertha's lucidity coupled with Grace's negligence had grown into a lethal partnership designed to effectuate tragic ends for not only both women, but for myself and for all of Thornfield's residents. Grace no longer felt entirely in command of her charge; a frustration she ameliorated with strong drink. Furthermore, Grace clearly was in the habit of employing tactics of behaviour modification that hinged on the abusive. A charge mired in demented stupor was surely far easier to subdue than an increasingly coherent and cunning one. But Grace would see to it that she maintained the upper hand. Of that I had no doubt.

I arose hastily to leave, not wishing to imagine the forthcoming scene. No sympathy could be mustered in me for Bertha, a woman who made attempts on my life and could tonight have harmed Jane as well. I simply must send Grace into comfortable retirement and replace her with another attendant. Yet breach of confidence was my ever-present fear. Considerable monetary compensation may ensure Grace's silence once far from Thornfield, or it may not.

I sighed wearily and retreated from the room. All north tower doors were locked behind me, futile as it was seeing that Grace's keys were unaccounted for, and I returned to my chamber. There I locked the door behind me and placed my candle on the bedside table. Without removing my shirt, I slipped into bed beside Jane, nestling close to her comforting warmth. She stirred and murmured, "Edward."

"I am here, love."

She opened her eyes and met mine, then encircled my hands in hers. Taken by a longing to pull her close, I turned onto my back and drew her on top of me. Her hair made a thick, warm curtain about our faces. She kissed me a sweet, lingering, stirring kiss. My arms went around her slender frame, hands into the back of her camisole, fingertips skimming lightly over silky skin. How was it that I could be thrust into wretchedness one moment and then lifted into such divine pleasure the next? My life craved the sanity and steadiness found with this lovely young woman. What could be closer to the heavenly and sanctified than this? Since knowing Jane, a deep sense of peace had descended upon me; a peace that long eluded me. Right now, with her in my arms, I knew that this was what my life should be.

'My God sanctions this,' I thought. 'He did not bring you to me for nothing, Jane. He did not create this bond only to let it die unfulfilled.'

"Stay with me," I whispered as she softly kissed my lips.

Her kiss moved to my roughened chin and to my neck. I closed my eyes against the candlelight, loving the feel of her lips and tongue on my skin. Such pain of separation mingled with the pleasure of her love.

"I cannot stay, Edward. You know that."

"I do," I responded with a shuddering sigh. "Jane, love me. Only me. Promise that."

"Geography will not change what I feel for you. But you will not promise the same to me. Will you?"

"I will. I do. You know my heart is yours."

"And what good is that if you are wed to someone else?" she asked.

For a moment I mistook her meaning and gave an involuntary start, then slowly moved her hair so the candlelight would show her eyes. Many times she had amazed me with her intuition, reading what was in my heart through my eyes. I searched hers. I saw nothing there to indicate she was conscious of my worst secret.

"Meaning ...," I began.

"Miss Ingram."

"Oh," I laughed. "Her."

Jane attempted to push away from me and fought my tightening embrace. "I must go! Let me go to my own room."

"No. Stay, Jane. You mustn't go yet."

She shook her head. "You hurt me with the secrets you keep. You have no faith that I can or will understand you. I feel it. You do not belong to me!"

"Stay, Jane," I repeated, looking up into her distressed eyes and restraining her from moving away from me. "I do not wish for my life to be the way that it is! I need you. You've pulled me back together into a feeling semblance of a man. You've resurrected me from years of walking death!" I paused, gratified with the pleasure these truths imparted and the joy of confession. "I know you must go as the coach will come for you this morning, but stay with me here for a while longer. Please." Presently she lay down beside me once again. "Jane, come. Kiss me," I whispered.

Her gaze was pensive but presently we kissed, soon with breathless depth and passion. Her resistance melted away and she returned my kisses as her hands swept over my face and hair.

The distant chimes of the entryway clock struck four times. Suddenly, each kiss seemed to be the last, but neither could allow it. I held her close and stroked her back. My hands wandered down to her hips and reached for her thighs, wanting them wrapped around me as she had done in the library earlier. I tried to bring them over my hips, but she tensed and pulled away, backing off a distance from me on the bed, kneeling there, looking down, biting her lip.

I came up and knelt before her, alarmed by her apprehension. "Jane, look at me."

She would not.

My fingers lifted her chin. "Jane." When her eyes met mine, I said, "Tell me you have no regrets for this night together. Or for anything we've shared. I could not bear it if you thought of me with regret."

She shook her head and smiled faintly, looking a bit embarrassed. "No. I have no regrets. Everything with you has felt right and natural. You do know that you are the only man I have ever kissed or touched in that way?"

My heart was bursting for her. "I know, Jane. You have a passionate nature, and your expression of it is indescribably beautiful to me. Truly. Your love is complete, earnest and unashamed. You, Jane, are beautiful. And you are always safe with me."

"Am I? With another episode as tonight, Edward, we would be irretrievable. We would be lovers."

I lifted her hands, my palms to hers and interlaced our fingers together. "We *are* lovers, Jane."

Her eyes glistened in the flickering candlelight.

"It is difficult for me to restrain myself with you," I admitted, "but you are of greater importance to me than any of my wants or needs." I listened to my own words and marvelled at how Jane had changed me. With her, I truly was a different and better man. Not self-centred. Not brutal and inconsiderate. She made me wish to give, to be honest and to love faithfully.

She sighed deeply. "I cannot live here and see you married. I will not stay to become nothing to you but a mistress."

My breath caught. "No, I do not want that either."

She lifted our locked hands and kissed my fingers. "The temptation when with you is too great. Our passion for one another too strong. I love you, Edward. Very much," she said, looking directly into my eyes, "But I want more." Her voice was breaking and tears stood in her eyes. "I want a family. I've never had one. Never have I had a home where I was loved and wanted." Her tears spilled fast.

"*I* want you, Jane. And I...," but I stopped myself.

"I want a husband and children. It will be impossible to find that here, and each day I remain takes me further from ever having that. If I give to you all that a husband deserves, I will have nothing more to share. Do you see my meaning?"

I did. "Yes," I said, my voice unsteady, tears claiming me also. My arms went around her shoulders, faces were buried in one another and we cried.

Presently she placed her hands to my shoulders to gently push me away. "I do hope you will find what it is that you want, Edward."

"*You* are what I want!" I insisted, tears breaking me down.

"But I am not good enough to be your wife."

I admired her strength to come forth with the crux of her fears. This grievous untruth was the sticking point of her understanding, and I could do nothing to explicate or assuage it. If I did, if I burst forth with the truth, I knew she would go away and never come back to me. At the very least, this way, I may yet see her again. That piteous aspiration was all I had.

"Not good enough to be my wife," I repeated. "Oh, Jane. You are so much more than good enough."

She looked about, shaking her head, apparently at a loss, then pulled away from me, came off the bed and stood up, wiping her tears away, and went to the sofa for her clothes. I watched her replace stockings, petticoats and boots, and helped her with the corset fastenings as well as buttoned her dress. Lastly, she pulled her hair back and tied its thick length in a knot. Then she sat quietly at the edge of my bed.

I came up behind her, kneeling, and placed a hand beneath her chin, tipping her head back, bringing my mouth to hers, kissing her with depth and wanting to reach right down into her where I could love all her; body, heart, mind and soul. Her hands came up over her head to my neck and pulled me down, returning my soulful kiss with energy. Many days and nights were to come in which I would long for this, when the sensation of drowning would come over me and this would be the breath my spirit demanded.

'Remember it, Edward. Every sensation, every minute detail.'

When we finally released one another, our eyes met and held, and we both reeled from our kiss with dizziness. We smiled at ourselves and each other. Soon she averted her gaze.

"I must go," she said, rubbing her face wearily. "I've more packing to do and must be ready to meet the coach at half past seven."

"The coach will come for you at the gates?"

"Yes. John made the arrangements in Millcote yesterday. Mrs. Reed's daughters sent the money for my travel expenses."

With this I was reminded. "Will you accept your salary now?" I asked, smiling at the image of her previous refusal.

She smiled, too. "Yes, all right."

So I went to my jacket, extracting the billfold. Amongst the notes I found the due fifteen pounds but only removed ten.

"Here you are," I said, handing it to her.

"Ten."

"Right."

"But now you owe me five."

I took her jaw in my grasp and brought our faces close. "Come back for it then," I said distinctly then stood back, watching the ignition of her fire that led to either sharp retorts or indignation. Admittedly I loved to challenge her and be challenged by her.

With wide-eyed innocence she pertly said, "Perhaps I will have you send it to me in the post."

"And perhaps you will wait for it until hell hath a Christmas frost."

"At least then I will have money for the holidays."

And we laughed. I took her hand and said, "Will you write to me?"

She looked up to me and shook her head. "No. I think it is best I do not." She saw the pain in my countenance and stroked my cheek once. "But I will write to Mrs. Fairfax when I know my plans better."

"You will return, Jane. Remember what I said. I can and will find you."

"No, Sir," she said. "Please, let it go."

"Let you go, you mean. I have a hard time with that, Jane. Self deprivation is not my strong point."

She smiled and played with my fingers. "At any rate, you will know where I am," she said. "I shall endeavour to find a suitable school for Adele whilst I am away and have the correspondence sent here."

I nodded. "Yes, all right."

She placed the ten-pound note in her dress pocket and moved toward the door. "Good bye, Edward. Sir." She laughed and her glistening eyes rose to the ceiling. "I do not know what to call you!"

I took her in my arms, rocking us gently side to side, then spoke aloud into her hair, "God, help me find the way. Lead me. And keep her safe. Please protect her." Softly I kissed her then released her. She squeezed my hand, turned and was gone from my chamber.

I looked at my vacant bed and sighed heavily, undressed and slipped under the covers. The bedclothes were as yet warm, and I smiled.

Through the remainder of the night, I never thought to sleep but rather lay there with eyes open and my mind touching on a myriad of points.

The truth of our separation's necessity repeatedly scorched me like a red-hot iron, but the clear conclusion was that Jane was far stronger than I. She could reach an understanding, forge her course and see it to fruition. I, you see, was capable of the first two measures but not the execution. My formerly steely resolve became a house of cards where Jane was concerned. Continually I was awed by her strength. Absolutely indomitable she could be when required. I knew she struggled no less than I as love and desire ruled her as well, but she was better equipped to check weakness. She would not allow passion and sentiment to burst away and compel the determination of her doom. I, conversely, could write volumes on the subject.

As daylight forced its first subtle glimmers between the drapes, I got out of bed and dressed, preferring to bathe and shave later. I washed my face, wet my hair, shook curls into place and glancing into the mirror, was dissatisfied with my reflection. Lack of sleep and a forlorn heart left my eyes drawn and vitality deteriorated.

"What on God's green earth does this girl see in me?" I asked my mirrored image. 'So beautiful' she had once said. "No, not this morning, Jane."

I wanted to watch as she met the coach at Thornfield's gates. The night's rain had ceased but the sky remained sodden and bleak. A long journey lay before her, and I hoped Leah would prepare for her a good breakfast before departing. Downstairs in my study, I left the door open, presenting an invitation for Jane to stop in before going. There I settled behind my desk and lifted the address of Henri Breault, the Spanish Town solicitor familiar with my marital history, and began to mentally formulate the request I intended to mandate.

Half past seven struck. I went out of the study to the dining room where windows looked out to the drive and gates. Jane stood at the end of Thornfield's drive, a box of belongings at her feet, shawl drawn tightly about her narrow shoulders, wearing a gray Lowood dress, straw bonnet and black leather gloves. Such a solitary little figure she made, and my entire being seized as I looked at her. I was most uncomfortable with this; with her going so far away alone. I was perfectly aware of the evil that men could do. But was she?

"She is a sensible girl," I told myself. "Independent and self-reliant."

Sentiments of protectiveness welled up in me again, strong and unshakable. How could I allow her to do this? Then as I considered walking down to the gates to forbid her leaving, possibly taking her box of belongings and returning with it to the house despite what protestations followed behind me, the coach came round the front of Thornfield and stopped at the gates. Her box was taken up onto the roof and secured. A coachman helped her into the carriage. I watched, feeling helpless as the horses proceeded on and she was gone.

Half past seven. Too early for a drink? I laughed sardonically. Hell yes, a drink! Why not? So I poured myself a generous brandy, returned to the study and there settled behind my desk in the antique chair. Diffused morning light poured through the diamond paned windows, but the brightness irritated me exponentially. The clock ticked in the hall, marking the expanding distance between Jane and I with each passing second. My nerves were strung taut.

There was a letter for me to write, and so a brief attempt was made, but something on my mind took precedence over all else. I threw the pen down.

'Not good enough to be your wife,' she said. Remembering this sent me fraught to the highest with wrath and resentment. My Goddamned blighted, detestable life! Damn this lying, loathsome existence that led someone as pure and good as Jane to believe such a heinous untruth! For her to believe that I considered her unworthy of me! Me, forsaken and wretched as I was.

'Edward,' inner voice calmly said. 'You must not sit there and numb your despair with drink. Instead, do something.'

I clenched fists and steadied myself, then opened the top desk drawer and removed a fresh sheet of paper.

'Do something,' urged the voice again.

Pen to ink. Ink scratched across paper:

Mr. H. Breault, Esq.:   18th May 1840

Perhaps you will recollect my name from a consultation circa summer 1825...

Chapter 19

I SIGNED THE LETTER with a flourished *E.F. Rochester*. Perhaps a brandy was inspiration enough for an increasingly flamboyant penmanship zeal, or it may have been the sharpening focus of long disordered and passed over ideas; of buried possibilities that should, and must, be exhumed. A previously frail flicker at the recesses of my mind, barely perceptible, evolved to a steadier and more tenacious glow.

The letter was read through once more. In doing so I became somewhat daunted by the sheer magnitude of the enterprise at hand. I of course intended to pay handsomely for a solicitor's investigation into Bertha's history and our marriage's origins, whatever the outcome may be, yet surely a comprehensive execution of the task would require a considerable allotment of time. Many months perhaps. Visits to archive locations, delving into musty, mouldy files, if the files as yet existed, would be undertaken. But most dispiriting of all was in knowing that Breault's task would require the cooperation of native inhabitants who may feel that an altered truth is truth enough, particularly for an affluent Englishman outsider such as I.

Indisputably, a good number of questions must be addressed. There were uncertainties I should have debated years ago, but at that time I naïvely trusted those involved, being far less acquainted then with the motivations and manoeuvres of blatant greed. I was so young, fresh and romantic in those days, but in short duration found myself devastated and lost. Suddenly I was mired in hopelessness, my sight (figuratively) blackened and spirit battered and bloodied; so much that I was unable to see beyond my despair and self loathing to the broad daylight of reality. For years I continued with this state of hate, desolation, and self-abandonment corroding my previously idealistic heart. I sought comfort in escapism, liquor, lust and squandering my fortune. I cared not a whit for myself or anyone else.

I looked down at my hands, then back to the morning light streaming through the windows. These hands. My hands. Touch. Women. Many women. Their skin, hair, eyes, bodies. Now, in the bright, silent sunlight I could again hear their cries of passion echoing in my brain. I could feel their fingernails digging into my skin. Perfume and wetness and satin. Their favours were mercenary, and I knew it as my body sweated over them. Recalling the sick feeling afterward of knowing I was merely another and wanting to get away, for nothing special did we share. It was my wealth they bedded. I was superfluous. Inconsequential. And so were they.

My life's path led me to that. 'God knows why,' I thought in dismay. I started out so good once; in the days before misfortune threw me down and kicked me incessantly.

The letter was tossed aside as tears came up to my eyes once again. Why so Goddamned close to tears all the time? I had not cried in years, many years, and now I found myself in such a state nearly every day. Hopelessness was long crushed and buried, or so I thought, along with the craving for loving touch and kiss. I had controlled it so well and blocked the threat of tender feelings breaking me down.

What did I say to Jane a few hours since? My words startled me as I heard myself speak them. "You've pulled me back together into a feeling semblance of a man." Christ, where did that come from? But it was only partially true. Yes, Jane was the reason I could again feel and be moved, but I was now more than a semblance of a man, I was all man. And with all of me, I wanted to be her man.

A deep shuddering sigh broke from me. "Jane. Oh Jane, you love me. You amaze me, you excite me. You've changed me. Stay with me. Do not go."

'Edward,' my inner voice spoke again calmly. 'Stop this. Finish your task.'

I dried my eyes and face against my sleeve then lifted the letter and read it a third time.

Following a detailed re-introduction of myself and the facts surrounding the deterioration of my marriage, I listed an extensive itemisation of documents I wished to see obtained and evaluated. These included various birth, marriage and death certificates, as well as the likely whereabouts of the personages' locations. Included was a list of Jamaican cities including Spanish Town, Kingston and Coulibri, and the names of all involved individuals with supposed correct spellings, dates of birth and last known whereabouts. An evaluation of the last will and testament of Jeremiah Mason was to be evaluated in reference to my affairs. Finally, I urged the solicitor to keep accurate records of billable hours and to regularly forward his list of accrued charges. An arrangement would be made with my banker and solicitor here in Millcote for correspondence involving payment of services. In closing, I urged absolute confidentiality, with final appraisals and recommendations to be forwarded directly to me. The letter was addressed and return correspondence provided with indelible ink. Then I set the letter aside.

There was a knock at the study door. "Come," I called.

The door swung open bringing Arthur Eshton, nattily dressed this morning and wearing his usual impish expression. "Edward, good morning to you, my friend!"

"Good morning, Eshton. I trust you slept well."

"I did," he said, studying me. "You, I can see, did not. Another all night bender?" he asked, lifting my glass to sniff the contents.

Unabashedly aware of my dreadful appearance, I asked, "Care to join me?"

"Before nine? Thank you, no. But you might ask me again at eleven." He surveyed me up and down with an amused grin, noting my bleary, reddened eyes, darkly shadowed morning beard and creased shirt. He made his recommendation.

"Coffee, Edward. That is what you need. Black and strong."

"And a smoke," I added, taking the tobacco pouch and papers from the desk.

Eshton went off to find a servant, returning presently to take a chair across the desk from mine. I rolled two cigarettes and handed one to him, then lighting up, we leaned back in our chairs and smoked thoughtfully.

"So, Edward. How goes the romance with your charming young governess? Freddie Lynn and I found her to be a most enchanting chess companion last evening."

"She's gone," I said heavily.

"Gone. Gone where?"

"Called away by family to attend the deathbed of an aged auntie. The Reeds of Gateshead Hall. Ever heard of them?"

He leaned forward and tapped ash into a black marble tray. "Actually, yes I have. I know of a John Reed; a true good-for-nothing reprobate, a drunk and a gambler with too much money for his own good and quite the following of bloodsuckers happy to relieve him of his fortune. Your Jane is related to that scoundrel?"

Suddenly I felt exceedingly unwell. I nodded and said, "Oh, dear God. I let her go." I wished with all of my might I had stopped her somehow.

"Never fear, Edward. The last I heard of John Reed, he was living 'round about London. White City, I think. When will she come back to Thornfield?"

"Maybe two weeks," I replied, shaking my head. "Maybe never."

His customary mischievous grin disappeared. "Edward, I am sorry. The two of you spent last night saying your good-byes then?"

"Yes. We did," I said and pulled deeply on my cigarette. I wondered if I looked as miserable as I felt.

His expression became all exasperation. "Edward, why can you not marry her? You love her! I do not understand why you allow this to tear you up. Call her back here and ask her to marry you! Or better yet, go after her. Get started. Go now!"

I blew a plume of smoke at the ceiling. "Extenuating circumstances, Arthur. Don't you recall my saying that? Nothing has changed."

"What circumstances? Some obstacle related to class or custom? She is related to the Reeds for God's sake, and they are affluent enough. Or is it the difference in your ages?"

He watched me shake my head in the negative.

"Then is it the Ingrams? Do you worry how they will react to you marrying your governess?" He smiled at that idea. "You know, Blanche is determined to obtain a proposal from you, and Lord Ingram asked only last night 'why in the bloody hell does Rochester not show his gumption and offer marriage' to that beastly daughter of his."

"I think you answered his question just then, Eshton," I said, tapping ash into the tray. "In my opinion, marrying for wealth and family connection is mere spitting distance from being a whore. How is it different? The act has nothing to do with love or compatibility or mutual sympathy. It's a business arrangement where the principals go to bed together and have children together, all without a shred of personal regard for one another. Worse than being a whore if you ask me."

"Look, Edward, I am the last one to push you toward a marriage of convenience. I want to see you marry your Jane. She's got fire, that girl. I can see you having a good life together."

I gave a short laugh, and with eyes closed, nodded. "Arthur, I want her so badly I am just on the verge of moving heaven and earth to get her."

A playful smile spread across his face. "It must have been some night together."

I glanced at him, then away to the recollections of my mind's eye. That last kiss. Her arms over her head, pulling me down to her mouth. "Lord have mercy, it was."

"You see, this is exactly why I am categorically unable to rally the enthusiasm to marry Louisa. I do not feel for her anything like what you feel for Jane. I see you, the way you are completely consumed by that girl, and do not know whether to pity you or envy you!" His sight turned inward. "No, I shall be honest. I envy you. I want to know that same fever from which you suffer."

"Then see that you do not offer Louisa marriage by acting on a misguided romantic whim."

"A drunken, lustful whim is more likely."

"One that will find a date set for you to wed your pretty Miss Dent."

John came to the open door bearing a tray and set it down on the end of my desk, glancing at me peculiarly. He placed a coffee before each of us and stood back. "Bath, Sir," he said; more a pronouncement than a suggestion.

"I will come upstairs shortly, John. Also, I plan to ride into Millcote this morning. Saddle Mesrour for me in an hour's time, would you?"

Eshton glanced up at me as he cautiously sipped his steaming mug. "Want some company?"

No, I really did not, but I needed to keep my thoughts light. Companionship was the most benign way of doing so. "Surely," I told him. "Give me time to clean up and we shall be off."

After extracting ourselves from the boisterous party sitting down to breakfast, Eshton and I escaped to the courtyard. Our horses were readied and my letter safely pocketed. We started off on the five miles to Millcote finding the morning weather turning out better than expected with the sky brightening considerably as patches of blue showed through dense clouds of slate. The world smelled fresh as a genial breeze rustled young, verdant leaves.

I hoped Jane's journey was progressing smoothly. A momentary pang revisited me as I again feared for her safety but also for what awaited her at the close of her travels; a contemptible aunt who rejected and discarded her as a ten-year-old child. Additionally there was the possible presence of a male cousin known to be a detestable miscreant. And what sort of women would the female cousins prove to be?

Jane did not deserve the lonesome lot she had been dealt, and for this my heart grieved. 'Come home to me, Jane,' I said to her in thought. 'I shall love you and hold you close to me. Let me be all the family you could ever want. Allow me to try.'

Upon arrival in Millcote, I went immediately to post my letter. The postmistress today was Olivia, the comely daughter of my land agent, Philip Bennett. After warm salutations she took my letter, noting its destination.

"How fortunate, Mr. Rochester! You brought this just in time as foreign mail will go out this afternoon. You will further be pleased to know that according to the Royal Post's weekly report, transatlantic correspondence has been uncommonly expeditious this season."

"Favourable trade winds," I commented, flipping through Millcote's directory on the counter.

"Is that so?"

"Yes, Miss Bennett. It is."

"Well then, your letter should arrive to Jamaica in two to three weeks," she said, all coquettish smiles. "I am additionally glad you came in as a letter arrived for you only yesterday." Our fingers touched as she handed it across the counter.

"Thank you," I said, turning to leave. "You will say hello to your father for me of course."

"Certainly, Mr. Rochester," she replied, eyeing me and drawing a finger across her shapely lips.

What was it about me lately? I was attracting the attention of women who never before looked at me twice. Upon exiting the post office I smiled thinking about that, about how I felt, how I perceived myself, and I was sure it was Jane. This *thing* that encompassed us, the strong sexual magnetism we shared; it heightened my masculinity and accentuated my virility, almost as if all were readying for exertion. For the labour of pleasing her. Of making love to her. It amused me that women in tune with their own sexuality could sense it. Also, I considered, perhaps being in love refined my features with its own beauty; my inner pleasure permeating externally.

Out on the street, for the first time I looked at the letter Olivia had given me. I flipped it over and read the return address finding there the effeminate curly-cue penmanship of Richard Mason, my dear brother-in-law, once again sending his obligatory periodic correspondence. Checking in he was, keeping a polished forefinger on the pulse of his investment: all that was mine. I stuffed the letter into my pocket and went to find Eshton in the bookshop across the street.

He was near the front of the shop, leaning against the floor-to-ceiling shelves, perusing a hefty volume on animal ethology. He looked up at me as I passed by and told him my destination.

"Poetry."

He nodded, and I disappeared down the aisle of verse and literature.

Absently skimming the titles and glad for a few moments' privacy, my mind continued on the topic started with the post-mistress's appreciative smile. Since that first night in the library, weeks ago, when I knelt before the fire and pulled Jane into my lap, something was ignited in my physicality as well as my heart. I could not say what it was. Call it a 'purpose'. Previously I was regretful of my broad chest and shoulders, my burly arms and thighs. But since that initial episode with Jane, and each escalating moment together thereafter, I felt that my body was made for her. It caused me to fairly quiver with urgency to exert my masculinity.

Again and again, erotic scenes played out in my mind. Our wedding day; returning from the church, kissing her, leading her to bed. I would make it last all day and into the night. I would please her repeatedly until she begged me to stop, give her all that I had and teach her everything that I knew. Touch and bodies and passionate cries and sweat.

If only it could be. I would be a good husband, faithful always, considerate, loving and thoughtful, until death parted us. But here we existed on this planet together, and we already were parted. It seemed to me a travesty, a mockery of love and a perversion of the divinely appointed bond we shared.

A fortnight more, she said; at the bedside of an ailing aunt with plenty of time to contrive her succeeding arrangements, to advertise for new employment and commit herself elsewhere. Would she come back at all? I had not yet gone into her room to find whether she left any belongings. She must have since she took a single box and nothing more. I would go there for a look upon returning to Thornfield.

"Find anything?" Eshton's voice approached from behind. "Perchance something I could present to Louisa? Our 'anniversary' is today. Three months, heaven help me."

I slapped the book shut. "The sharing of poetry with a young lady must be done advisedly, Arthur. Doing so has been known to bring the most unprecedented results. Believe me."

"Could it cause love to bloom where it was formerly absent?" he blithely asked, scanning the shelved titles. "Hm, here we are! A pamphlet of ribald limericks!"

"I tend to think not, my friend. The longer you keep this going with Louisa, the more likely it is that your liaison will end badly."

"She's been pressuring me to propose ever since the house party first gathered at Ingram Park. It's become a *competition* between she and Blanche for God's sake! The great race to the altar, like ancient Olympiads."

"Eshton," I chided. "You nearly sound embittered!"

"Not so! You must imagine them as I do. In loosely fitting robes with a circlet of olive twigs upon their flowing hair, running full belt in a fucking marathon for the entitlement to become our bed partners. Just think of it!"

I laughed. "Blanche will never win that race. Not with me as her prize."

Arthur looked at me seriously as we perused the dusty aisle. "You must tell her, Edward. Today. Lady Ingram has been making plans for your engagement celebration, did you know? I'd even wager they've begun arrangements for your wedding."

I groaned with aggravation. "One of them could consult me before charging ahead with this nonsense! Presumptuous, overbearing, rapacious fools. No!" I said, roused to absolute vexation. "No, let them go to all of that trouble and expense. Their embarrassment will be a well deserved lesson in humility."

He guffawed most enthusiastically. The shopkeeper peered down our aisle and placed a forefinger to his lips. Hushed, Arthur said, "We are a pair, are we not, Edward? Pursued by women both beautiful enough, but neither can be bothered with them. We are more interested in securing the ideal and unattainable. Where in the hell will it all end?"

"You said to me, Arthur, not a fortnight ago, 'You cannot lose hope. Without hope, we die.' It will end with bliss, if we make it so."

He sighed and looked distractedly at the shelves stuffed with books. "That is a most optimistic forecast, Edward, and entirely uncharacteristic for you. What fires this surge of hope?"

I shrugged my shoulders. "I am going to send a letter to Jane."

He brightened. "You plan to pour your heart out onto a sheet of paper and plead for her to come back?"

"Subtlety Eshton! Genius is not carved with a crude hand but rather one of surpassing delicacy. There is a single sentence I wish to say to her. And I should have said it last night."

He nodded, smiling. "Do it."

We rode toward Thornfield with a turbulent, mercurial sky above. Heavy rain clouds one moment were broken with piercing rays of sunlight the next, and finally rain came down as we rode amongst shadows and sharp golden rays. The breeze remained temperate and cordial. All was a seraphic display of God's brilliance.

I was overcome by a sudden inclination to seek His house, to be where I could speak quietly with Him. I could not recall the last time I had been in church, nor when I last brought my hands together and prayed. Never during my years of self-abandonment, that was certain. But recently, His patient and comforting steadiness seemed near, leading me to address Him again as I once did in my unpolluted youth. Riding toward home, His presence was intensely near in that solitary carriage lane under an awe-inspiring sky.

We came to a fork in the road where the left path continued on past Thornfield and the lane going off to the right led to the little village of Hay. I slowed Mesrour's canter and turned to Eshton coming up on my left.

"Arthur, I will go into Hay for a while. See you at the house."

"Right-o, Edward," he said, and we parted.

I rode on and came to the quiet, tiny hamlet that was Hay. It consisted of a bakery, a combination post office and bank, a church constructed of river-stone, timber and stained glass, a cottage housing Dr. Carter's surgery, a seamstress' shop and an apothecary. At the church steps I dismounted and tied Mesrour's reins to a post. The street was deserted except for a woman and small boy entering the bakery. I glanced round at the tidy graveyard surrounded by mature trees and bound by a low wall with weathered headstones standing scattered about. At the foot of the steps, I looked up to the bronze bell over the heavy oak door which today stood open revealing darkness within. I climbed the steps and entered.

The air was cool and dim inside, and I advanced quietly up the nave. The altar stood prepared for Sunday service. Coloured light dappled white cloth. A few rows from the front, I selected a pew and slid in, taking a seat. Presently, I felt my tensed shoulders and arms relax. I breathed deeply and soon felt at extraordinary peace. Surely, I was not alone. A benign presence was near, waiting. With eyes shut, my hands came together in my lap.

Softly I whispered, "You kindled in me a desire to save myself. I do not believe you wish to spurn me back onto a life of ruin and degeneracy. Lead me. Show me the way. Forgive me, please. I was a sinner and am sorry. Lend me your strength and wisdom. Help me to be a better man."

I tipped my head back, around and down. The silence and presence of my maker's comfort lulled my tumultuous heart. Tranquillity enshrouded me.

I continued my devotions. "You brought her to me for a reason. I love her with a pure heart and with all that I am. I pray that she will not be gone too far or for too long. Give her safety and comfort." A mystifying warmth rose within me. My head fell back again. "Lord, hear me. I appreciate the enormity of this. Our profound love is fettered by hopelessness. I cannot solve this alone. Be near me now."

For what length of time I remained there I do not know. Peace and serenity had enraptured me, and I felt undeniably that my existence yet held hope for a future of bliss. I opened my eyes and placed palms down at my sides becoming aware that a person was advancing toward me along a side aisle.

"It is good to see you here, Mr. Rochester," gently spoke a familiar voice. Mr. Wood, the young clergyman, was setting out hymnals for Sunday service.

"Good afternoon, Wood."

He stepped into the pew ahead of mine and sat down. "A good place for thinking, is it not?" he said, glancing around.

"Yes. I am finding that to be so."

"Is there something for which I could be of assistance?"

"Perhaps. It is my fervent wish that you will begin to see me regularly, and that you will preside over the momentous occasions I bring to you. But such is not my decision. It is that of our Lord, and I simply ask for Him to make it so."

He looked at me solemnly and said, "Mr. Rochester, would you not agree that the seeds of faith are always within us, and sometimes it takes a crisis to nourish and encourage their growth?"

I nodded. "I would."

"Then you came to the right place," he said. And rising from the pew he retreated back to the aisle. "Anytime you wish to talk or just come to 'think', please do so."

I watched him proceed with his task. "Thank you," I said.

I remained for a few minutes longer, then went out into the glaring daylight, mounted my horse and slowly wended my way home. The weather was too prodigious to disregard, and I relished every sight, scent, sound and sensation.

Once returned to Thornfield, I dismounted and led Mesrour into the lower gardens, leaving him to graze in the tender, young grass as I went to the river's edge. There I stood with hands thrust deep in pockets. Clear water burbled over multi-coloured stones, and rich, green vegetation swept along with the current. Everything was so beautiful. The natural world had always held a fascination for me, but today my vision was enhanced and nature's stimulus thrilled every nerve. I sighed and looked up at the massive stone hall.

Thornfield for me was always a reminder of Father and Rowland. It was theirs, and in life neither ever considered it mine. For years, simply looking at the place conjured burning resentment, and did still somewhat, being that it housed Bertha who represented their final treacherous legacy to me. But now it also held pleasant associations; evenings in my study by the fire, eyes meeting across a chess table, passion and kiss and that unforgettable 'Ohh, Edward, I love you' spoken last night.

'I could be happy here,' I thought as I roamed along the grassy bank. 'But not without you, Jane.'

Tonight I would write a letter. A very short one. Only one thing to say. And I was bursting to say it.

Chapter 20

Arriving home late that afternoon, I took Mesrour's reins and led him up the drive, through the courtyard, leaving him with a stable hand, then went into the house through the front entryway where voices of guests in the drawing room could be heard, talking animatedly amongst the click of billiard balls. With my rain-dampened jacket handed to John and a request taken for a glass of claret, I ascended the staircase with intent to change into suitable evening attire.

The second story was quiet other than the muffled chatter of Adele talking in French to Sophie behind the shut nursery door. Staying my step near the top of the stairway, I found myself at Jane's bedchamber door. No one was about. I went inside and shut the door behind me.

The hearth stood in deep shadow and drapes were half drawn, leaving the entire chamber silent, chilly and dim. I glanced around and was relieved to find Jane's paint box and easel tidily set aside in one corner. 'Thank heaven,' I thought, 'she is coming back.' I went to the wardrobe and opened it, smiling to find a grey Lowood frock hanging there neatly and a low stack of folded white underclothes lain upon the shelf. Pleased by their presence, I placed fingers to their cottony softness. With moving them slightly I heard a solid object move with them beneath. I raised the dainty undergarments and there found the pearls placed about her neck last night.

The sight of them pained me immediately. I lifted them, held them between my fingers and across my hand, grieved that she would leave them behind. I sat at the edge of her bed and gripped the pearls in my fist.

'Why would she do that? Had my gift meant nothing to her?'

On the bedside table were an extinguished candle and a folded white handkerchief. My hand went out to the drawer and I opened it, finding a small volume bound in black leather. Recognising it instantly, I lifted it out. *A Selection of English Poetry*, the book of verse I purchased in Millcote many weeks ago and since thought was left in my study. How strange to find it here in Jane's bedside table. I opened it to where a paper marker was left, and found the poem "The Passionate Shepherd to His Love". I smiled, remembering Jane reading it to me before the glowing hearth in my study; how we sat facing one another as she read; the way she placed the book in her lap upon finishing the verse and looked openly at me for the first time with love and desire in her eyes.

But now she was gone. "Many miles from me today," I whispered to the silence. Oh, how I wanted her painfully. I drummed fingers on the leather binding and sighed deeply. The folded slip of paper marking the page was blotted with indigo ink. I opened it and my heart leapt at the sight of Jane's own handwriting:

Edward Fairfax Rochester,
Come live with me. Be my love.
Jane Eyre.

I looked up and around the gloomy chamber, wondering how long ago she had written this. The slip of paper was held suspended in my fingers for a long time as I studied her penmanship, the way she wrote my name, particularly Rochester. God willing it would one day be her name if I were free to ask and she were inclined to accept.

Quite a riddle this created now, my gift of the necklace having been cast aside followed by the discovery of this private artefact; one I took as sure testimony of her love for me. I replaced the marker into the page and set the book on her bed. With the pearls entwined in my fingers, I considered unbuttoning my left sleeve and fastening the necklace again around my wrist but thought better of it. This was a gift given to her. If she wished to leave it behind and take no keepsake of me, then that was her choice to make.

At the wardrobe I replaced the pearls beneath her white under things and then taking the book with me, left everything else in its place. I listened at the chamber door before opening it, and hearing nothing for a number of seconds, silently vacated the room. But unobserved I was not. In closing Jane's door, a clearing of voice caused me to whirl around.

"Sir?" asked Mrs. Fairfax, just arriving at the top of the staircase. "Your... ah...your claret," she said, holding a filled goblet on a silver tray and looking quizzically from Jane's door to me. Her thin lips were drawn taught and eyes flashed flinty. I took the glass from the tray and returned her stony-faced gaze.

"Your guests await you, Sir. Miss Blanche especially," she said with emphasis on the name. "She knows you've come home and asked me to fetch you."

"She may expect me presently," I returned coldly.

Mrs. Fairfax shot a final condemnatory glance toward Jane's door, bobbed a curtsey and descended the stairs.

"Madam," I said and awaited her stayed step and attention. "I presume Miss Eyre supplied you with an address of her intended whereabouts prior to her departure?"

Her hesitance was perhaps a moment too long. "I believe so, Sir," she said flatly.

"You shall make a copy of the address and leave it on my desk. Tonight."

The matronly figure's reluctance was plain, and her lips were pulled so thin they disappeared. "I intend to post a letter to Miss Eyre after the first week of her absence, Sir. If you have a message that is not urgent, I would be pleased to convey it for you at that time."

Her interference and near insubordination nettled me thoroughly! "The address. On my desk, Mrs. Fairfax. See to it now."

She lifted her plump, increasingly florid face and with a, "Very well, Sir," continued downstairs.

Bloody hell! The absolute cheek! The Master of this estate was *who* exactly? I fumed all the way down the gallery to my chamber and shut myself in. Pacing the room, I tossed the volume of poetry onto the bed, muttering caustically. One lesson my father had taught me about privileged position was that 'we' *never, ever!* were answerable to servants. Their opinions were not only immaterial, they were nonexistent. In this case, Mrs. Fairfax, an otherwise staunch guardian of custom, seemed to think herself qualified to overstep that dictum.

As a Fairfax, she was a relation of my mother's through marriage, and since she had maintained the post of housekeeper for some twenty-five years or more, seemed on occasion to regard me as yet an adolescent. Beyond question, Mrs. Fairfax long sustained the aspiration that I would marry Miss Ingram, first instigated when the Lord and Lady visited Thornfield with their children at Christmas some years ago. It was Blanche's debutante year. Parents and daughter revelled in her season of societal introduction, the success of which was gauged in the number of besotted suitors left in her wake. Within hours of her presentation to Thornfield, executed with only slightly less fanfare than a Silver Jubilee, it was arranged that we sing together *dans son ensemble*. Beautifully, I might add.

Mrs. Fairfax fell in love with Blanche Ingram enough for us both. She considered it her duty to ensure Thornfield's maintenance of time honoured class order, and this meant seeing that like paired with like. Alice Fairfax meant to safeguard the post of Thornfield's mistress for only a wealthy personage of rank, and Blanche fit all requisites to a 'T'.

I was beginning to sense an army amassing around me; one hell-bent on attaining their end. I laughed to myself, knowing that as a counter-army of one, I alone held the final word.

Dinner that night was roast duck drizzled with an apricot sauce, and a delectable repast it was. Every guest was in a particularly ebullient humour, possibly owing to my pre-prandial word with John consisting of, "Wine. Lots of wine. Your staff is to keep their glasses filled. Understand?" For this, I earned his gap toothed grin and a snickering, "Yes, of course, Sir."

So, with all guests in high spirits and more than a mite tipsy, I rested back in my chair at the head of the table, confident that I had averted yet another day of nuptial entrapment. Henry and Frederick Lynn sat nearby, recounting for Eshton, Andy Ingram and myself a variety of anecdotes that had us splitting our sides with laughter. Lord and Lady Ingram meanwhile occupied another corner of the table, chatting animatedly with Lady Lynn. The young ladies giggled and gesticulated over their own conversation. Fine. Superficial exchange was about all I could tolerate tonight from this opulently attired, over-privileged flock, for my mind was far gone elsewhere. Glancing at the blackness beyond the windows, anxiety for Jane's safety sprang back keen and vigorous. Where was she now? I knew that all rest would be troubled until my eyes beheld her again.

A footman was filling my glass once more when I noticed Blanche rise from her seat and advance alongside the table in my direction. Was it the wine or did she actually look so inordinately beautiful tonight? Wearing a gown of sky blue silk with an off shoulder neckline, just enough bosom was revealed to ensnare the attention. Minimal jewellery adorned her neck. Her blonde hair was what kept my eyes on her however, as typically it was done up in elaborate configurations of plaits and ringlets, as frigid and untouchable as her austere heart, but tonight her hair was down in a mass of wheat-coloured, glossy, loose curls drawn softly back from her face and falling alluringly over her bare shoulders. She approached and looked over the other gentlemen momentarily before settling her attention on me.

Again, was it the wine? Her pale blue eyes emitted a depth and verve never before seen by me. She came close and rested a hand on my shoulder. Her scent was rosewater; subtle and arresting. "Rochester, join me for an evening cordial. Alone," she huskily murmured.

My male companions raised eyebrows in unison and sipped their wine amusedly. To refuse her would be ungentlemanly and besides, I enjoyed the sparks of envy darting from the eyes of the Lynn cousins and even from Arthur Eshton. His look, as always, was tempered with an impish grin that clearly bespoke, 'Here it is, Edward! Told you so!'

I stood from my chair and placed Blanche's hand to my forearm. "It would be my distinct pleasure to partake a liqueur in your exclusive companionship, Miss Ingram," I replied, hoping my slurred speech was mere imaginative invention. Standing before her, absorbing life and heart in her blue eyes through the haze of my own, my words were not entirely an untruth. We quitted the room amongst appreciative, hopeful gazes from the entire ensemble. Lord and Lady Ingram appeared as if about to weep; their breathing held and eyes glistening. I imagined hushed but animated chatter as well as wringing of hands and crossing of fingers once we were safely gone from sight and earshot.

Blanche led me away from the dining room and into the candlelit entryway. I expected her to take me to the drawing room, but instead we went along the darkened corridors to the library. There within, a fire blazed merrily in the hearth. No candles were lighted. My chair and another were set together intimately with a nearby end table bearing two snifters of cordial. So this had been planned and the assistance of my servants commandeered. No wonder Mrs. Fairfax looked so grave upon noting my interest in Miss Eyre's chamber. And no wonder John's grin. He knew the wine would be more to my benefit than anyone else's.

My hand slipped from Blanche's and I roamed away from her about the room. Images of my most recent visit here flashed in my brain. Erotic images. I glanced at the piano bench, then turned away from my current companion as a broad smile swept across my face. 'Oh, Blanche,' I thought. 'Did you ever choose the wrong place for this.'

She took the subsidiary seat beside my chair. With such a blatant invitation to join her, I walked around to the hearth intending to sit but noticed that Blanche's feet were set directly upon another place that caused recalled images to flash. Auditory recollections filled the silence... Jane's aroused and pleading words... 'Show me how to please you. Teach me, Edward. Please.' I drew a sharp breath, startled by the evoking clarity of her voice and by explicit memories of what happened next. I turned from

Blanche and rested a forearm on the mantel, aware that my eyes were wide and breathing stayed.

"Edward, won't you sit?" she asked.

"Not right now, Blanche."

She waited as I composed myself. 'Look at her, Edward!' an inner voice directed me. 'If you look at her and not around the room, you can manage this!' Presently, I turned to Blanche and found her studying me with curiosity. My smile became irrepressible, so taken I was with remembrances of last night and the futility of this assignation now. I held my breath and gave her my best expression of 'solemn in the face of hilarity.'

"What's on your mind, Blanche?"

She regarded me with some trepidation. Evidently, this was not going quite as she had envisioned. "The future, Edward. *Our* future is on my mind."

"Ah! Our future. Try being more specific."

She barely suppressed her exasperation. "Edward, please do your best to follow me in this," she said, taking my hand patronisingly in both of hers. "We must merge our fortunes. The Rochester name will become preeminent in this part of the country. An exceedingly influential *empire* will be born with us." She paused, awaiting a response.

I may have blinked once but gave nothing more. She became impatient.

"Furthermore, you must have an heir," she continued. "It is your duty to this estate to marry and produce an heir." There she paused again as I shifted my gaze to the fire. She pressed further. "You must take for your wife a beautiful and accomplished woman of nobility. There is no one better suited for you than…"

My eyes darted back to her and she silenced. I searched her countenance. Did she know about Jane? Blanche sat stiffly in her chair; her back straight and haughty chin raised. "Than…" I urged.

She was genuinely perturbed. "Edward. Ask me. I will not say 'no'."

I lifted my glass of cordial and threw it back in a single swallow, then surveyed her silently whilst my fingertips studied my dark evening-growth beard. She waited.

"Do you love me, Blanche?" I asked suddenly.

If she was taken aback, she recovered herself well. With posture straight and icy eyes on mine, the response was a staccato chirp. "Yes."

I nodded. "Tell me about that. Tell me how you love me."

"Tell you… Tell you what? I said I love you," she stated, unable to squelch her ire. "There is nothing more to say. Do you not believe me?"

"No, I do not. And if it matters to you at all, Blanche, whether I love you or not, allow me to quote Erasmus. You are familiar with Erasmus, are you not?"

"Who?"

"Hmm. Precisely. Desiderius Erasmus. The Dutch theologian? No? Well, he said, 'Love that has nothing but beauty to keep it in good health is short lived, and apt to have ague fits'." I surveyed her face, hair and shape. "I love your beauty, Blanche. That I'll not deny. But you," I said leaning forward and looking directly into her eyes, "You in there. You are not someone I can love. I can feel lust for you but never passion, never tenderness nor sympathy."

Tears began to glimmer in her eyes.

I continued, "You would be miserable, Blanche, if married to me. I have known a number of women, and I can tell you this with certainty: I am a heartless, unfeeling, brutal scoundrel with those who value me for no more than my name and wealth. Ask yourself, Blanche, does that describe you? Truthfully now."

Her posture gradually fell and she interlaced fingers in her lap. Her glossy, unbound hair obscured her face. Presently there came an erratic pattern to her breathing. She looked up. "Edward, no! That does not describe me!" she said with a broken, tearful voice. "I said I love you. This is me. This is how I love!"

For the first time since knowing Blanche Ingram, I felt sympathy for her. She was more human now than I had ever seen her before, and tears did nothing to diminish her beauty. Quite the contrary. She made a vision of such loveliness that I reached out to her, taking her hands in mine.

Her tears came down. "Edward, all of those people, my parents, the Lynns and Dents, our friends and neighbours! They all want us to marry! *I* want us to marry. Please, Edward." She was so soft and natural, her eyes so unearthly blue. Gone was her arrogance and haughtiness. Instead she was fresh and vulnerable, and I found the transformation beguiling. My hand touched her cheek, wetting my fingers in her hot tears as her soft, blonde hair drew me in.

We were so close. Her tears kept coming. I drew my wet fingers across her lips, gently grazing her teeth, brought my mouth closer and kissed her. I tasted the saltiness of her lips, and my hands went to the wetness over her face. She returned my kiss with more fervour than ever before. For me, it was our last good-bye. After years of skirting one another, each orbiting the other amongst our gentrified social circle, it was finally ended. There would be no more of the legendary courting pair of Mr. Edward Rochester and the Honourable Miss Blanche Ingram. The expectations and hopes of our friends and neighbours would be baffled, and we would detach our association to continue on entirely unrelated paths. I wished her happiness as I held her face to mine, softly kissing her mouth as tears fell and passion strengthened. Before long I released her and pulled away, licking the saltiness from my own lips. She knew. Her expression fell sorrowful but stoic.

I settled back in my chair and regarded her solemnly. "Never marry for wealth, Blanche, nor for family connections. Allow yourself to be happy." I held her hand in mine. "Allow yourself to love someone." She looked away, and I added, "You do not love me, Blanche. It is the idea of marrying, of meeting the expectations of others, particularly of your family, that you love."

She looked back at me, her softness perceptibly deteriorating.

"Blanche, you do not know me at all. And until tonight, I have never known you."

She levelled her clear blue eyes to mine. "I know you. Better than you think I do. You discard me because your heart is elsewhere," she said, leaning in to face me. "You think I haven't noticed? You cannot be serious, Edward. A governess?"

I bristled. It occurred to me that this had all been an elaborate ruse, right down to her choice of dress and arrangement of hair. How many feigned romances with insincere women, veritable actresses, could one man experience in his lifetime? My sympathy for her evaporated instantaneously. I saw her again for what I always knew her to be; callous, heartless and haughty. The sudden softness of her stone-cold heart and rain of lovelorn tears succeeded in dazzling me. That particularly was an impressive touch. My amused gaze was for myself, not her. 'I am simply too soft hearted,' I thought.

Blanche drew a deep breath and spoke. "So, seeing as you have no intention of asking me to join you in marriage," she said as her ice chip eyes raised to mine, "I will ask you. And consider your reply carefully, Edward. We are finished, absolutely finished, should you refuse me."

I leaned forward, meeting her ominous gaze. "Ask me," I said darkly.

She rallied her mettle. I watched as she recommenced softness; her vulnerability re-emerging. Leaning towards me, her enticing cleavage heaved gently, accentuated by a long corkscrew segment of glossy blonde hair nestling between her breasts. She caressed my hands, looked up at me with depth and presently wet her lips. Damn, she was good. She came in close beside me and caught an earlobe between her lips, sucking it gently. I shuddered. She whispered closely, her breath on my skin, "Marry me, Edward. I do love you. Make me your wife."

I faced her so that our lips grazed, and in the periphery of my thoughts, desire played traitor on me. My hands came up to her flawless face, and I saw a glimmer of triumph flicker in her eyes. I held the moment, savouring the thrill of standing upon this precipice. Which way to fall? But my blood was now seething on the boiling point of not lustiness but indignation. For the second time in my life, I was being lured toward an ill-advised union with a beautiful, heartless stranger. The first mistake continued to darken my every day, and here I was, presented with a nearly identical seduction some fifteen years later.

If I had never found love and was yet unmarried, would I accept Blanche? It was impossible to say. The years since falling into egregious error shaped me and changed me from a once fresh and romantic youth, and I was beyond recognition from that man. As Blanche nuzzled my cheek with hers, sighing alluringly whilst awaiting my acceptance, I promised myself this: I would never again in my life mistake physical beauty for purity of heart. If I could marry again, it would be for love. Nothing but love.

I held Blanche's face close to mine, delving deeply into her eyes, wanting to impress upon myself the look of a beautiful but barren soul; one entirely without the capacity to love truly. "Never," was my low but energetic reply to her proposal. "Never, never, never."

She pulled away from me, her face suddenly the picture of contempt.

Shaking my head in the negative, I affirmed my answer. "Never, Blanche."

She slowly stood, incensed. Within seconds she was fairly vibrating with fury. "How *dare* you?!" she demanded through gritted teeth. "You do not know the mistake you've made, Rochester. I shall see you ruined in our noble peerage, you mark my words! Go to your lowborn, proletarian governess. Your plain little trollop. Entirely suited for such a common mate, you are. I have always known you were never one of us! "

"Oh, belt the hell up, Blanche," I said hotly, rising from my chair. "Do yourself a favour and shut your mouth before it gets slapped."

"Yes, that would be just like you, Edward! Animal that you are! Come, why do you hold yourself back?"

Oh, how my palm trembled to strike her exquisite face and wipe that provoking smirk clean away. Instead I took a handful of her wheaten hair and glared into her glacial eyes. "You would love that, Blanche," I snarled fiercely. "There is no other passion to which you can respond. Nothing but a merciless, pitiless, inhuman bitch!" And I shoved her roughly toward the door.

A malevolent smile spread across her lips and she lifted a hand. With an extended forefinger, she stabbed at the air between us. "You mark my words!" She then turned her back, leaving the library and slamming the door behind her.

I exhaled heavily and fell back into my chair. 'I need this? And in my own home?' I shook my head, more than a little shaken by the sudden, vicious turn our conversation took, and having no doubt that Blanche would exert unparalleled spite to ensure my social ruin. The one gleam of hope came in knowing that all our society was wise to Blanche's tendency to malicious cattiness. Her slander may actually garner sympathy and precipitate my elevation to a higher standing.

'I need a drink,' I thought, 'and a smoke.' But for some time, I absently watched the hearth's leaping flames until my gaze fell to the rug at my feet and swept over its pattern. From my chair I went down on hands and knees, and bringing lips to the rug, repeatedly kissed it. "Not to worry, my love," I said. "She cannot touch us." There before the fire, I stroked the rug with an open hand. Remembering... abating the cut of Blanche's vindictive words by playing out the intensity of last night's scene in my mind. Still, my heart was heavily weighed with guilt for having kissed another. Jane would be hurt. I recalled her forlorn, dejected voice at the piano bench. '...you kiss that Blanche Ingram!'

Remorsefully I wondered why the kiss with Blanche happened tonight. "It meant nothing, Jane," I said softly, as if she could see and feel my contrition. "It is you I need. Only you. I am sorry, my love." And I ached for her all the more.

Finally I stood and turned to quit the library but noticed that Blanche never touched her cordial glass. So I swallowed the contents, then stormed from the library and in my haste to escape into fresher air, flew past the kitchen and nearly knocked the exiting John on his aged arse.

"Sir! Heavens," he exclaimed as I gripped his arm to steady him, "I am suddenly reminded of The Plough and Harrow on a Saturday night! Good times they were!" And we both laughed. "Young Mr. Rochester, there was a letter in your cloak pocket." He produced it and held it out to me.

I took it and reread the flowery script. "Ah yes, thank you. I will be in the gardens, John, should my guests seek me further tonight." From there I went to my study to pour a brandy and roll a cigarette, then taking my cache, went through the kitchen and out onto the path leading down to the orchards. A full moon shone above, accompanied by a diamond studded night sky. Young leaves of apple, cherry and pear trees rustled placidly on a warm, tranquil breeze. I approached a stone bench and took a seat, setting my tumbler of brandy beside me. Drawing on my cigarette, I held the letter up to the moonlight.

"All right. What does he want?" I asked aloud and opened the seal. It read:

11th May 1840

My dear friend Edward,

I do hope this letter finds you well. I arrived to England in March for the purpose of visiting a number of old acquaintances, and currently I am in Birmingham with plans to come to you at Thornfield next, arriving in one week if the weather remains amenable. I must speak with my sister on a matter of family concern. I am confident that she is in good health under your care. My stay at Thornfield shall not be long. One night is all.

With enthusiastic anticipation of seeing you again,

Richard

Speak with his sister? On a matter of family concern? What, had he forgotten she was completely and irrevocably insane? "Good luck with that, Richard," I chuckled. "Poor sod, you've grown as delusional as the rest of your mentally feeble family."

I noted the date of his letter. One week ago. He would be here any time. My guests would remain for another few days, except for the Ingrams whom I now fully expected to depart on the morrow, and now Richard Mason could be expected as well. My head fell back and I looked up at the night sky. "You are testing me, Lord. I do so love a divine sense of humour."

And there I remained in the orchard for perhaps another quarter of an hour, smoking and sipping, enjoying the silence and peace of nature's companionship, until my solitude seemed more like avoidance. I must face my guests and inform them that Blanche and I would not pursue an engagement, then offer cheer in the wake of their disappointment. This was my responsibility. Dispensing it must not be delayed.

"Yes, I am in charge!" I declared aloud to the lighted lower windows with great bonhomie. "I am the Master of this miasmic monument to marital mayhem! Thornfield Hall is mine now."

Sometimes, still, I must remind myself of that. After a deep swallow of brandy, I left behind the garden bench and wended my way back to the house along the orchard path.

Chapter 21

I ENTERED THROUGH THE kitchen door and passed amongst the bustling clatter of dessert clean-up where much scouring, rinsing, wiping and stacking were in progress. The abundance of provisional staff ceased their labours to grant me curtseys and bows as I strode between them, finally meeting overseer Mrs. Fairfax at the door leading to the front entryway. She drew a cambric square from her sleeve and wrung it mercilessly as she collected herself to speak. "Good evening, Sir," she offered in a quavering voice.

"Mrs. Fairfax," I stiffly returned.

"Ah. Yes. Leah and John wish to express their hope that the roast duck was enjoyed by all."

"It was."

"Then I shall inform them so. And Sir," she said, halting my resumed step. "The residence address of Gateshead Hall has been placed on your desk as requested." Her tone intimated penitence for our strained interaction of earlier this evening.

I softened slightly, resting a palm on her fluttering of hands. "Very well, Mrs. Fairfax." Then I continued away to find it.

"Mr. Rochester," she called after me with an eager smile. "Miss Ingram is just now waiting for you in your study."

That stopped me, and I whirled to face the housekeeper. "Is she now? And who invited her to await me there?"

"Oh, well, no one did, Sir. Miss Ingram quite acts as she sees fit."

Blanche's absolute impudence galled me. To think! Going into my study unaccompanied! To there I immediately went and stood in the darkness of the entryway watching through the door left ajar as she hovered at my desk, her fair features illuminated by nearby candlelight. She held in her hand a slip of paper, reading the contents before placing it down again on my desk. I knew what the words must read. Warily I entered the room, knowing that this beautiful woman was now my adversary and all interaction must see me on my guard. She looked up as I entered and her chilling gaze met me across the room. I shut the door and stood with my back to it.

"Edward," she said coming rapidly toward me. "You are not to speak of our conversation in the library tonight. Not a word of it to anyone."

"Oh? Why is that, Blanche?" I had not a shred of doubt that her motives were rife with artifice.

"I will not have you distressing Mother and Father, that is why! I will tell them of our parting once we have returned to Ingram Park. Do not shock them with the news. Let me see to it."

"Do you not think it is my duty to explain?"

Her ire sparked brighter. "No, I do not! Listen carefully, Edward, and it may be that you can understand this. You have misled a great many people; myself foremost and my parents close behind. For years you have been acting the part of my suitor. They, and I, were certain marriage was eminent." She turned her back to me and moved about the room. "Your treachery will cause great embarrassment for my family."

"Treachery! What treachery, Blanche? I never committed myself to you. And what of all the other suitors you've entertained during the past seven years? All of the other gents who have had their hands up your skirts and down the front of your gowns?"

She swung around to glare at me, speechless with outrage.

"Did you actually think your celebrated reputation had escaped my awareness?" I asked. "Word of a beautiful noblewoman with loose morals gets about almost as much as the subject herself."

Her glare was triple distilled hatred. "And you would have had nothing to do with that, would you, dear Edward? Reporting our details to your band of cronies were you?"

"No," I told her. "I never pass comment on trivialities."

She laughed ruefully. "Of course not. Which is why you will say nothing of our, oh, shall we call it… 'dissolved liaison'?" She came sidling toward me. My back remained to the door as she advanced closely. "'Tis difficult to believe that not one hour ago we shared an intimate kiss, is it not?"

I laughed. "No, since it meant absolutely nothing."

"Oh, come now! I know how hot you are for me, Edward. I have always known. Do you think you can merely shut that off?"

I nodded. "Done."

A cunning smile came across her face. "No. I refuse to believe that. Not you. For seven years I've been acquainted with your thumping core of lust, and intimately at that. So come, tell me, Edward. Are you as hot for your little governess? That homely child in grey sackcloth?"

Rage exploded in me as protectiveness of Jane shot straight up through my stratosphere. I placed a palm to Blanche's bare upper chest, and in one swift motion pushed her backward, around and roughly up against the study door. My blazing glare devoured her. "You will never, EVER! speak of my personal affairs again! Have you got that?" I seethed. "I want you out of my home, and if you dare ever in your evil, odious life meddle with me or mine, you will rue that Goddamned day, Blanche." Glaring at her murderously, I added through clenched teeth, "Bank on it!"

She was entirely unruffled, regarding me with both admiration and amusement. "Whether you wish to acknowledge this or not, Edward," she said, "you and I *are* perfectly matched." Then she took a handful of my jacket lapel, adding, "It is a shame you are not man enough to take me on."

"Get out," I said, shaking with fury.

"My family and I will stay through the end of the week as planned," she replied, smiling serenely. "I shall join them for cordials now." Then she kissed a forefinger and pressed it to my cheek.

Her nerve was simply unfathomable. Allowing her to pass, she brushed by me and vacated my study. I shut the door gently behind her, and turning toward my desk, could see nothing; could say nothing. Peace simply did not seem to be my fate. I shook my head in attempt to clear my thoughts. Walking past my desk I stopped to lift the slip of paper Blanche had perused, confirming my suspicion that it bore the address of Gateshead Hall. Fortunately Mrs. Fairfax did not also write Jane's name there, so in all likelihood the address meant nothing to Blanche, but still I could put nothing past her powers of duplicity. Tempests were brewing in that bitch's brain, and so I must act decisively. Cautiously. Must measure all words and actions carefully.

In the drawing room I found the party enjoying an evening of light conversation, reading and music. In a far corner, Eshton and Henry Lynn were absorbed in a game of chess. A number of expectant glances received me but I returned them with an expressionlessly benign smile that seemed to satisfy curiosity to some degree. The group understood that no engagement was secured, but at the very least status quo had been maintained. Blanche occupied another corner with the chatting Dent twins, laughing with great volume and repulsing me thoroughly with her inescapable voice. I remained subdued, making my rounds amongst the guests, sipping a glass of Bordeaux thoughtfully, but deep inside, my nerves jangled discordantly.

The last time I felt so unsettled, I was... where? Oh yes, I remembered where. I was in Jamaica, with a raving lunatic screaming obscenities at me from a bolted and padded adjacent room. Blanche and Bertha. How alike they were.

Singularly relieved I was when, as the hour grew late, guests began to drop off one by one to seek their bedchambers. With all candles extinguished I secured for myself a final glass of Bordeaux and ascended the staircase, sought my chamber and locked myself in. An uneasy feeling that predators were closing in was upon me, and although bolting my door against them was likely futile, it did lull me in some small measure.

A low fire burned in the hearth, diminishing the room's chill. I undressed and donned my dressing gown, went to the fire and lay reclined on the sofa, in deep thought. Threats of social ruin were worthless to me and so made for an entirely ineffectual ultimatum on Blanche's part. What did I care of society? For years I spent so little time in England anyhow, but surely Blanche must realise that. Was she cruel? Irretrievably. Obtuse? No.

What had been my grave mistake was to react so violently to her mention of Jane. I should have said was nothing or simply trivialised it. Now she knew how to hurt me for I unwittingly handed her the power to affect the only thing I truly cared about. If she dared to bring harm to Jane, dared to interfere, I could not be answerable for the wrath descended upon her.

The change in Mrs. Fairfax's manner today also held my attention. I fully expected her to say that she had lost Gateshead's address or give some other reason for delay. But she provided Jane's precise whereabouts, and with a smile.

'Blanche, you are behind this,' I thought. What might she have said and done whilst I was enjoying solitude in the orchard? Nothing to announce our discord to my guests; that was certain. Mrs. Fairfax as well appeared comfortable that my odyssey to the altar was squarely on track. 'Right journey, wrong woman, Mrs. F.,' I thought with a sigh, finishing the last of my Bordeaux. With the glass' contents having provided the desired soporific effect, I went to bed, lay on my back, arms thrown wide and closed my eyes.

"Jane. Jane, I miss you. Mmm, my bed smells of you. Holding you, kissing you here last night." Kissing...

Remorse descended upon me. I showed inexcusable weakness tonight by kissing Blanche. Was it too much wine? Yes, perhaps, but if I were to be faithful to Jane, then my vow must commence immediately. Fidelity does not begin on the wedding day. It begins with the declaration of love, and though I had not yet said the words to her, I did say them to myself and to my God. I resolved to be faithful henceforward yet was appalled at how quickly I faltered tonight. 'Not again will it happen, Jane. Never again.'

Kissing Blanche was senseless and surprisingly devoid of gratification. Intimate contact with a beautiful woman should by rule be thrilling, but it was not. Tonight's act proved markedly deficient compared to the rush that seized my body and mind when Jane kissed me. All interaction with Blanche, from the mediocre on down, reinforced the cherished gift of intimacy I shared with Jane. Acts of physicality alone could no longer slake my thirst for a woman. I shoved guilt away and settled down, allowing pleasant recollections of hushed, intimate conversation to envelop me, and soon I was asleep.

Somewhere in the night, dreams came to me; dreams born of my fears and longings. Most of them simply came and went, but one dream took precise shape.

Tall grass. The sky was dark; full moon and brilliant stars above. No golden sky or virulent sun to be found on this sojourn to my dream field. The air was windless. There, deep into the lonely field, my angel and I were in a desperately tight embrace down in the grass. My arms strained her slim, bare body close to mine. Her hands gripped my broad, naked back, pulling me down to her with all of her trembling strength. Her smooth thighs firmly clasped my hips. I made love to her; rocked us, forward and back, digging my toes into the earth for leverage. My mouth was at her soft cheek. "Love you, love you," I sobbed deeply and repeatedly into her skin. Her far higher-pitched, breathless "Edward!" vibrated in time with our rhythmic rocking. Pleasure and need. I cannot, will not, let it end.

Suddenly there came the scent of rose water. Never in my life had I dreamt a scent, but tonight it was there and unmistakable. In my dream, I clutched my angel tighter. Tremors wracked my arms and back, for I knew malevolence was near and we were vulnerable. "Don't!" I heard myself cry. Then the night sky transformed into pitched timber, taking on the coloured, dappled light of stained glass all around. I awoke with a start, sat up and placed my palms at my sides on the sheet. My heart raced as I glanced about the room. What had I been dreaming? Of the threatening presence of Blanche Ingram? While making love to Jane? In a church? I waited, listening. Nothing but the Hall's own disturbing brand of silence.

"I am absolutely losing my mind," I said aloud, and fell back onto my pillows. Quite some time passed before sleep returned, and meantime I lay awake recalling a letter intended for Jane, cursing myself for not writing it. Tomorrow. When finally I did sleep, the subsequent hours were mercifully dreamless.

The following days were marked by my own relentless trepidation but remained generally uneventful otherwise. I did place pen to paper, writing to Jane the sentence I wished to say, but it was that pearl necklace, my gift to her left behind in her wardrobe that inhibited my posting the words placed on paper. I had no certainty that my statement would be welcomed by her. 'Best to say it when you see her again, Edward. Be patient.'

Richard Mason's arrival was awaited not entirely with foreboding. There was no one, save for Grace Poole and Dr. Carter, with whom I could discuss Bertha's care and condition, and no one but Richard who actually harboured devotion for the wretched woman. True, he had wronged me all those years ago, grievously, but in our own peculiar way, a tie of kinship bound us. He must, however, be kept from Blanche's acquaintanceship for as crafty as she was, and dim-witted as he could be, I could not risk those two being left to private conversation. She would have my most closely guarded secrets out of him in no time. Days, however, went by with no sign or word from him.

One evening toward the close of the week, I noticed an interaction that suddenly turned the blood in my veins to ice. The party was in the drawing room, dinner and dessert long past, and everyone in mellow spirits as champagne and cordials flowed. I sat at the piano with Louisa Dent as she played a waltz, one for which I held a particular fondness. I looked up and noticed a pair sitting cosily in the window seat. Blanche and Arthur. She was leaning into him, giggling and fawning over him quite unreservedly. I turned and looked to Louisa sitting beside me, finding her eyes fixed on the same pair; her expression sober and wounded as she watched them, unblinking. I, too, was piqued, but not due to jealousy.

Arthur had been privy to my most guarded thoughts on a number of occasions, and so I did not relish the prospect of his alcohol loosened lips revealing any of it. As Blanche's icy eyes darted to mine, I was certain she was up to some chicanery with regards to me. One day more of her menacing presence was to be endured before being rid of her evermore.

Poor Louisa, however. She appeared so disconsolate, finding her more-or-less estranged lover enjoying intimate conversation with the beautiful Blanche. I nudged her shoulder and offered an encouraging smile.

"She certainly has an effect on men," Louisa commented while continuing a lazier version of the waltz.

"She is merely toying with him, my dear," I offered. "She wants something that he has. This is what our Blanche is all about."

Her eyes were filling. "I know. But it hurts so. I love him, Edward. He does not love me. It matters not what I say or the care I take with my appearance or even the attention I give him. All efforts fall flat with Arthur."

I took her soft, delicate hand and patted it. "A broken heart is essential for full appreciation of your true love when that person finally appears. Or so is my experience," I told her.

She rested her head on my shoulder. "Blanche is not your true love, then?"

I laughed. "Good Lord, no!"

She raised her head and looked at me, smiling. "I know who is."

Patting her cheek I replied, "And I am glad you do. But we shan't talk about that in present company."

Louisa whispered near my ear, "She is very sweet. And I like any girl who can whip Freddie Lynn at chess."

I smiled, enjoying the warm glow emitting from my heart. After recent days, happier feelings were more than welcomed. I kissed Louisa atop her dark curls. "Arthur needs to pull his nose out of the books and see what it is he's got," I told her.

She nodded, fingers moving over the piano keys. "If only he would," she said. Then, "Edward, I'd like to see you break with convention and marry only for love. Will you do that? Give us all hope that it can be done."

"It can be. And so I have your permission then, not to marry Blanche?"

"Heavens, I would grieve for you if you did," Louisa replied.

I lifted her hand and kissed it. "Good to know," I said, nudging her shoulder again.

The drawing room door opened and John entered, stepping quietly to my side. "Sir, a visitor has arrived. A gentleman. He claims you are expecting him."

"Yes. Thank you," I answered, then turning to Louisa, "You must excuse me, luv. Business often requires my attention at inopportune times. Are you all right? Shall I suggest Lady Lynn join you at the piano?"

"Oh no, Edward, I am far stronger than I look," she protested with a smile. We each cast a sidewise glance to the tittering couple at the window seat. "Go, Edward. See to your guest."

I gently squeezed her hand and followed John from the drawing room. In the entryway, he indicated to my study. "One Mr. Richard Mason, Sir."

I straightened my jacket and pulled a deep breath. "Quite. Have tea sent in, will you, John?"

"On the boil, Sir."

I opened the study door to find my brother-in-law standing at the fire's grate warming himself. Richard was a small and slender gentleman, always rather effete in my opinion, with dark hair and eyes set amongst a sallow, pale complexion. Tonight he wore a heavy overcoat and held a pair of gloves tucked beneath his tightly clenched arm. It was the latter half of May for heaven's sake, but he stood close to a blazing fire warming his hands as if it were Boxing Day. I entered and shut the door. He gave a start.

"Good to see you, Richard."

"Edward," he greeted me, finding his voice after a beat or two. "You are looking well."

"Thank you. I must say, Richard, you never change. You never age."

He laughed heartily. "Jamaican life is good for me. Warmth and an ocean breeze, Edward; I would not survive without them. Not for any length of time."

"Yes," I said, remembering quite well the heat of Jamaica. "John did offer to take your greatcoat and gloves, did he not?"

"Yes he did, but I cannot think of it, such blasted cold weather you have in this country. I've purchased eight jumpers since arriving and am wearing two now. The fire will set me right."

I urged him to sit, and our tea was brought in. For some minutes Richard detailed his current business dealings as a merchant in Kingston as well as his plans for travel this season. "The summers are dreadfully humid in Jamaica, as you will surely recall. And they are too cold in England!" He drew his chair closer to the fire.

Observing him as I sipped my tea, I wished to cut straight to the point of this visit. "Despite our frigid month of May, you ventured to northern England and to Thornfield specifically, Richard. You are here with a wish to speak to Bertha then?"

"Yes. I must," he said, setting his cup down with a tremulous clank. "Hopefully my presence will not unsettle my sister, but there is information of sorts I must share with her. Family related doings. Perhaps one time is better than another for speaking with her?"

Why the covert purpose? I looked him over and nodded in the affirmative, yet openly showed my distrust. "Perhaps there is. She has been quite lucid during the night-time hours as of late. I advise you not to try seeing her during day for you will find her as catatonic as a stump and that may prove upsetting to you, Dick. You should plan to stay for a night or two. You can visit with her once you are rested… tomorrow evening perhaps, and then I shall join you."

"No! No, that will not be necessary, Edward," he insisted, taking a shaky sip of his tea. "I must speak to her as soon as is feasible. You say she is best at night? Very well then, I shall see her tonight. My plans continue me to Leeds on the morrow as I am expected there at a house party, you see. No need for you to join me in seeing her. My visit will be brief. Please, I cannot delay." His desire to keep me ignorant of details was more than obvious.

"Richard, you intend to blow into my home and insist upon seeing your sister immediately? Foolhardy intention! You do recall of whom it is we are speaking, do you not? Or has so much time passed since last you saw her that you've forgotten what she is? Look at you! Exhausted from travel, cold, quavering like a leaf. Wait until you have rested and gained some strength."

"She will be pleased to see me!"

"She stands a full head above you, outweighs you by two stone and is even more unpredictable than you obviously recall. It is imperative that I join you in seeing her but cannot do so tonight. You arrive at a difficult time as I am entertaining guests."

He shook his head and dabbed at his lips with a handkerchief. "I cannot delay and will insist upon tonight. Furthermore, I must be permitted to speak with my sister in confidence."

I blinked at him slowly, annoyed as much with his illogic as his mincing style of obstinacy. Yet what irritated me most was his total misconception of the depth of Bertha's insanity; something I was reminded of regularly but from which he managed to remain far removed.

"Dick, at this yet early hour I will not desert my guests in favour of your request. Later tonight, after the house is quiet, we may visit her in the north tower together if you are to be so insistent. But still I must urge you to instead wait. Enjoy a restful night. I will alert Mrs. Poole of our intended visit and we will go upstairs together tomorrow evening."

He sighed and shifted in his chair. "I can manage her, Edward. Allow me to settle into a chamber for a short rest and to freshen my attire, then I must be permitted to go up to her."

How ignorant he was. I looked at his squared shoulders, straight back and pursed, colourless lips, reading mulish intent in a man whom I little liked and even less respected. Perhaps his fate should have been of more consequence to me if by no other motivation than mere human generosity, but such was not the case.

"Fine. Have it your way," I relented. "But not until all of my guests are long asleep. Not before one o'clock."

Soon thereafter, Mason was seen to a comfortably prepared chamber close to the north tower door. I preferred that he remain there, far from my other company, and he sensed that without dispute. The idea of being pressed to explain the basis of our kinship did not appeal to either of us. Richard appreciated the solitude of his chamber, a quiet meal there and a good fire after rigorous travels, so upon seeing him settled, I left him to himself.

"Wait until near one o'clock, Richard," I told him as we stood in the second story gallery. "And do not forget that she can become quite violent still. It would be wise to have me join you."

"No," he insisted. "No, you must let me go alone."

Dubiously, I set the north tower key on his dressing table and again looked over Richard's slender, frail frame, having no intention to seek my own bed until he was safely re-ensconced in his own chamber.

Late that night, after my guests had all repaired to their chambers and Thornfield fell swathed in night-time silence, I lay reclined on my sofa, waiting. The fire crackled and threw deep shadows as I sipped a glass of claret and noted every creak from above, below and all through the house. Fully dressed except for jacket, waistcoat and boots, I waited for one o'clock, listening for a single chime of the clock downstairs. The half hour had only just struck.

During the daytime hours, the distractions of my guests' spirited companionship, overseeing of hospitality details and silently battling a certain beautiful, ruthless opponent preoccupied me well, and melancholy could be kept largely at bay. It was the night that quite nearly reduced me to tears when loneliness and longing for Jane became almost intolerable. Alone in my chamber, I would think of our final hours together over there, on my bed, immersed in her love for me. I could no longer live without it. If I were not certain she would return to Thornfield, I would be off searching for her now, and search I would until I found her... tell her anything, give her anything, to make her come home. Bigamy? Illegitimacy of our children? These were ugly words that struck cold to my heart but they were mere words after all. Each held not a fraction of the power of reality, this reality, this pain, and their alternative of spending each night of my life as thus was unthinkable.

I sipped my claret and smiled, thinking of Louisa Dent's words, "I like any girl who can whip Freddie Lynn at chess." Yes, my quick-witted girl. I was so proud of her and would be pleased to call myself her husband. Louisa's acceptance of Jane should not matter to me at all, but it did. It added a welcomed note of justification, and besides, I did want Jane to be favourably received by my friends. Eshton already held her in the highest esteem. They all would find, as I had, that it was actually Jane who was too good for me. She was stronger than I, smarter than I, and purer of heart and motives than ever I was. From this day forward I would strive to match her in virtue and honesty, and earn the right to be hers.

The clock downstairs struck one. I listened for the click of door latches and locks unbolting, sipped quietly, waiting. Mason wished to go upstairs alone, but I could not have that. Thornfield was my house and Bertha my responsibility. I would follow him and be near in the likelihood of an incident.

Ten minutes went by and I listened, shifting uncomfortably on the sofa. Suddenly, there came a distant metallic 'clack'. I set my glass down and pulled on boots. Then I went to my chamber door, silently opened it and went out into the gallery. Along the matting my feet treaded his path by faintest starlight, finally approaching the north tower door. I found it left wide open.

"Careless, Richard," I said, shaking my head. Noiselessly I ascended the winding stairs and came to the next door, also left open. I entered the crimson bedchamber and advanced to the final portal.

"Sir?" came a whispered voice in the shadows causing my heart to leap. I spun around to find Grace Poole seated in a chair by the window. With a finger to my lips, I gave her a low "shhhh" then went to the door of the stone inner cell, also left ajar, leant against the wall and listened.

Richard's voice spoke low and equably. I imagined he and Bertha facing one another across the table in firelight. His hushed words strained my ability to hear so that very little of this one-sided conversation could be gathered. "... in Jamaica ... Father..." his voice dropped lower. " ...look so well ...must tell you ...Kerry... Antoinette." Voice became whisper, and I could make nothing of his words.

Then silence for a good minute.

"Antoinette... so sorry for you."

Silence again. I looked to Grace and she stood, brows pinched and shaking her head quizzically.

Bertha's voice came. "...tell me ...oh ...no" She escalated in pitch, "Why? Oh, my Kerry!" And her voice turned to sobbing.

Grace took steps forward. I held out a hand and mouthed, "Wait."

The sobbing was not soft any longer. Bertha was openly wailing, "Kerry! Oh no, no, my Kerry!"

Richard's voice: "Shhhh! Must be silent! Please, be calm!"

I looked to Grace as she advanced, her fingers hooked together and concern congesting her features. We waited, listening. A chair scraped across the stone floor and fell over. Wailing converted to ungovernable howling, and suddenly Richard's panicked voice filled the north tower as he attempted to hush his distraught companion. "Be quiet, Goddamn you! Your bawling will bring him!"

Grace was at my side, but I held a palm out to her and shook my head. "Not yet," I whispered.

Then, such a scream! "For God's sake!" Richard shrieked. "Help me! Rochester, come!"

With a great BANG! I swung the door open and flew into the room. Bertha had him pinned to the wall, one hand clutching his hair and her bared teeth sunk into his shoulder. Her other hand clawed brutally at his neck. Buttons of his shirt came away, bouncing across the stone floor, and her fingernails left bloody streaks from neck to chest. Richard screamed in horror, his eyes wide and his feeble arms incapable of pushing his far more strapping attacker away.

I locked an arm around Bertha's neck and pulled her off of him, driving her to the floor. Grace was at my side, lengths of rope in her fists, and with my knee and weight set into the lunatic's back, together we bound her wrists. Grace captured her kicking legs and secured them at the ankles.

Bertha continued her uninhibited wail, howling and crying, "No! Oh my Kerry!"

Grace and I lifted her and placed her in a chair, leaving Richard heaving with fright against the wall whilst we calmed Bertha, wiping her tear streaked, bloody face with a cloth. A dose of sedative regularly provided by Dr. Carter was administered. Soon she was quieter, crying softly, her hands bound behind her back.

I left Bertha's side and glared at Mason savagely. His wild stare left his sister and came to me. He had not moved from the wall but simply stood there, heaving and staring. I grasped him by the arm and fairly dragged him out of the stone cell and into the crimson bedchamber where I steered him toward the chair by the window and shoved him into it.

"What in Goddamned hell did you do, Richard?" I raged at him. "What did you say to her? And you'd better speak the truth. All of it! Or there will be hell to pay, I promise you!"

"Edward," he said, shaking with fear and retreating into the chair. "Please, it is better that I do not…"

"You will tell me now! I swear to Christ I can and will make your sister's attack look like a loving embrace if you fail to give me what I ask!"

He began to cry. "I had to tell her! She had the right to know."

"What?! What did she have a right to know?!"

He hesitated a moment too long, and my fury was wrought to uncontrolled violence. I lifted the end table beside him and threw it against a far wall. "NOW! You will tell me now!"

He trembled and cried. "Edward, I had to tell her of someone she once knew. It was a death you see," he tried to say soothingly. "The death of a close, ah, friend."

I came at him with fists clenched.

He burst out, "Her lover, Edward! A man before you. Kerry was his name. Kerry Collier. I was obliged to tell her that he was recently killed. He was once most important in her life you see, and she had a right to know."

"You are not telling me everything," I seethed. "I warn you Mason, I am just ready to tear you up!"

He shook and cried as I hovered threateningly over him with murder in my eyes.

"Richard, you tell me! Was she married to him?" I asked, trembling with rage. "She was! Why else would she have a right to know that he was killed?"

Mason sobbed and rocked himself. "Edward," he pleaded and looked at me with terror. "I do not know if they ever married. Honestly."

"Oh bloody hell, Mason! What in the name of all that is holy do you know of *honest*?! So she might have been wed to him then! Admit it!"

He scarcely whispered his trembling reply. "Well, possibly."

"You married me off to that woman knowing she was deteriorating into lunacy and all the while aware she might 'possibly' be wed to another?!"

"Edward, it was for the best!"

I clenched my fists and thundered a scream at the top of my voice, tearing my throat so it seemed.

A stern masculine voice suddenly called from the stairwell, "Is all well up there? Rochester, are you there? Rochester!"

Mason and I stared at one another. "I am not finished with you," I said, pointing at him. "Don't you move from that chair."

Down the winding stairs I went, bringing my wrath under control so to appear entirely calm before addressing my awakened household. In the gallery I found Lord Ingram standing in his dressing gown and slippers beside his son and the other younger gentlemen, all talking anxiously. Ladies peered from their chamber doors and squealed in relieved delight upon seeing me.

"Rochester!" said Lord Ingram, stepping forward. "What the deuce is happening in this house at such an ungodly hour? I demand an explanation!"

"Sir," I serenely replied and turned to all. "Gentlemen, ladies. A servant has had a nightmare; not an uncommon occurrence for him. Please, I must have you return to your chambers and be permitted to see to him."

"This servant must be most worthwhile for you to tolerate such hullaballoo in the dead of night!" Lord Ingram gruffed.

I put on a winning smile. "As masters of our respective estates, Sir, surely you would agree that tolerance for minor faults is a must when talent otherwise abounds? Recall your senior butler who partook the remaining muscatel at Christmas…"

Lord Ingram muttered, "Well yes, right you are, my boy."

"Yes, and I trust you enjoyed the roast duck this evening, Sir?" I heartily laughed, slapping his back. "This servant certainly is worth our efforts."

"Ah well, I do admire your attention to duty, young Rochester. Dinner was quite extraordinary," he conceded, shuffling under my direction toward his chamber door.

"Very well then, please, everyone!" I cheerfully called. "Return to your chambers so that I may effectively dispense the obligations of a munificent master. There you are, back to bed," and I ushered all to their rooms, nodding and smiling reassuringly. "Nothing to fear. Thank you. Apologies for your disturbed rest. Good night."

Eshton stood quietly beside his door, arms folded and watching me suspiciously. "Arthur," I said quietly to him. "All is well. Back to sleep."

"Need help?" he offered.

"No. All is well controlled. Please," I said and opened his chamber door for him. "To bed."

He nodded and disappeared, closing the door and locking it behind him.

Once I was alone in the gallery, I turned and hurried to the north tower stairway, taking steps two at a time. Back before Mason, I lighted a candle and looked him over. His shirt was blood soaked and his usual pallor was now ashen white, his lips blue. I would seek assistance for him but not before my questions were satisfied.

I leaned over him, freezing him with my bitter stare. "For the best, eh Richard?"

He did not meet my eyes. "Yes." It was all he would say.

"And why did she not remain with this man… this Kerry? Why was a marriage arranged with me?" I asked, my voice thick with embitterment.

His tears fell but he was now calm. "It was Father, Edward. He wanted only the best for Antoinette," he replied, looking up at me. "Kerry Collier was poor. You were not."

I sat down on the crimson bedside. Rage burbled in me still but was now tempered with inexplicable sorrow as I gazed at the sickening sight of this man before me. His body, his soul. They sickened me.

All of these years. My youth gone. Exploited at the will of two self-serving, avaricious old men. Bertha clearly suffered a grievous wrong as well. Richard, this pitiful, trembling fool dismissed by me as something of a half-wit these many years, had willingly served as accomplice to his father and mine in an arrangement that stripped me of happiness and liberty.

"Richard," I began, gazing around the crimson chamber. "Is Bertha actually your sister? And why do you call her Antoinette?"

He was silent, doubtlessly considering how much to say.

"You tell me!" I suddenly seethed through clenched teeth. "God help you, Richard, you've taken fifteen years of my life! You owe me that much!"

He cried softly and said, "She is my half sister, Edward. Father's child with, ah, another."

"Half," I repeated, piecing her history as it was told to me years ago. "Did you not once tell me that you and she are close in age; she being the elder?"

Richard wearily wiped his sweaty face with a handkerchief and gave a short laugh. "Elder. Well, yes, that statement would not be an untruth. We were born within two months of one another. Father was something of a rascal you see, Edward. Would it not be best to fetch the doctor now?"

"Oh, rally some mettle, man! You are in no grave danger with a scratch and a bite. I will fetch him once you've answered my questions."

"But I know nothing more! And there is a terrible amount of blood here. Look!"

"You know far more! And you will tell me all that I ask, advisably in a timely manner, for every minute you delay is another in which you go unattended. It is your choice, dear brother, to exsanguinate in that chair or not." The chair's loss would be of more consequence to me than his, but I held my tongue on that.

Richard mopped his face, cleared his voice and said, "Her mother was called Antoinette. She was an island girl, a Creole. I've no idea how they met but Father did love her, and although he was not discreet in this particular entanglement, he would never entertain the notion of marrying her. Knowing his inclination for pride, he surely thought her too lowly for such consideration. Her kin were boat crafters, fishermen, labourers, louts-about-town. Edward, could I please have a glass of water?"

"No. Proceed."

He drew a pained breath and continued. "Father wedded so as to take an appropriate lady to bear his children and make a proper home for him. This was my mother. At the same time, however, he brought his lover, this Antoinette I speak of, into the plantation as housekeeper. My half sister, Bertha Antoinetta, and I were born under the same roof during the same summer."

I nodded, finding little here to give explanation to my circumstances.

Richard's voice was trailing off to a weary slur. "You know that my mother was killed when I was yet an infant. The slave uprisings... a terrible time. She found herself away from home, in the wrong place."

"Your father did tell me something of it," I said more gently.

"She was too attentive a woman, my mother," he bluntly said and cleared his voice again. "Bertha and I were raised together once Mother was gone. We shared the plantation's nursery and were schooled together by governesses, quite as equals. Father accepted Bertha as his daughter but would not make a wife of Antoinette. She was Creole after all."

"And this excluded her from consideration?" I pressed. "It seems the question of marriage was academic at this point. His wife was dead, and with this woman established as keeper of his home, their daughter being raised alongside his son..."

"It was not simply that she was Creole, Rochester. She was not well," Richard exhaustedly said and tapped a finger to his head. "Most unstable in her emotions. Quite volatile. Given to excesses of gin and to consulting strange back-woods Creole sorcery, bringing into the house potions and chanting spells... frightening us all with her crazed remarks. Before Bertha and I were taking daily school lessons, Antoinette openly showed anger with old Jeremiah for not making her Lady of the Manor. Nor would he formally legitimise their daughter. She threatened to burn down the manor house. I even recall her holding a butcher knife point to her chest. One day we were told that she was found drowned in the sea, and there was no more talk of 'Miss Antoinette' from that day. Never did my sister cry for her mother."

For a time I digested his story, finally repeating my original question. "Instead of 'Bertha', you call her 'Antoinette'. Why?"

Richard's pasty lips spread to a repellent smile. "My sister used to be quite charming you know. She was talented, imaginative and engaging. She was a good friend to me when we were young, and in play she liked to be called not Bertha nor Antoinetta but her mother's name. She wanted to be called 'Antoinette'. Such is the only remembrance of her mother ever expressed by her, and so we all obliged. The habit continues."

He was sinking into the chair, looking colourless and fragile. Blood stained his shirt gruesomely, clotting in thick masses at his chest and shoulder. Help must be fetched.

"Richard, I shall go now for the doctor. Do not move. I will be back soon."

I went to the inner door and looked in, finding Bertha untied and put to bed where she slept quietly. A chair was at the bedside where Grace sat reading a book by candlelight. She looked up as I entered.

"She is all right, Grace?" I asked.

"I believe so, Sir. She's had a shock but will sleep now."

"Good. I am off to fetch Dr. Carter. Do you need anything of him?"

Grace considered for a moment before giving reply. "Yes, a touch of poppy and mugwort compound in absinthe suspension should keep her down for the night. And more Lithia crush. Your key is on the table, Sir."

I nodded wearily and took it with me, stopping to pour a tin cup of water for Richard on my way out. Then I was off, locking doors as I went down. Out through the kitchen I went to the stable with a lantern in hand, took saddle and bridle and set about tacking up Mesrour, placing the bit and fastening the girth mechanically.

Soon, I was riding through moonlight toward Hay. "Peace, Lord. Grant me some peace," I prayed as I went. Arriving in Hay, I summoned the doctor back to Thornfield.

Chapter 22

Dr. Carter followed me into the kitchen where I lighted a candle before setting off up the back staircase. We arrived on the second story adjacent to the bolted door leading to the north tower.

"She bit him, Carter," I said turning to him by light of the candle. "There are bites at his left shoulder and she clawed his neck and chest most severely. He's lost quite a lot of blood but his injuries are not fatal. Worst of all, he was frightened by her." I mentioned nothing of my raging fury that had, no doubt, added psychological trauma to the physical.

"And your wife? Was she injured?" the doctor asked.

I cringed. 'My wife.' I could not tolerate Bertha being referred as such. "None the worse, Carter. She was sedated and sleeping when I left her."

"Grace is with her then?"

"She is." I did not tell him of the shock Bertha suffered with Richard's disclosure. It seemed best to minimise all outside knowledge of details. Instead I added, "Mason will need to stay at your surgery until well enough to travel. I've a houseful of guests at the moment and cannot risk questions or discovery."

"Of course, Mr. Rochester. No trouble there."

We came to the final step and there I held the candle aloft, placing key to lock. But the door swung open with my slightest touch. My gut lurched.

"I locked this door," I told Carter. "And Grace has always adhered to strict orders."

We entered the crimson bedchamber. Richard remained in a chair by the window precisely where I had left him, in the same sunken posture and state. His colouring was sickly white, and he appeared to be asleep or unconscious. His shirt and chest were a grotesque sight of spattered black clots and fresh blood. All his attire clung to his skin, saturated with perspiration.

"Richard," I said, gently tapping his pasty cheek with my fingers. "Richard, wake now. The doctor is here."

He gave no response.

Carter handed to me an uncorked vial of volatile salts, and I wafted it beneath Mason's nose. Suddenly his head flew back and he looked up, wide-eyed, startled and coughing. He focused, staring at me in horror.

"Good morning, Richard! Had a pleasant rest did you?" I cheerfully said. Carter meanwhile was opening his shirt to examine the wounds.

"Edward," Mason sputtered anxiously. "Edward, what have you done with me?"

"Not I, my dear friend! Your *half-sister*. Surely you must recall your loving reunion tonight?"

"Oh. Yes," he said despondently. "I… I do."

"Sorry to leave you alone all this time, Richard, but you do seem to have fared all right."

"Alone?" he muttered deliriously. "I was not alone. She only just left me." Then he was taken with cries and whimpers as the doctor liberally applied antiseptic solution to his open wounds.

Anxiously I looked through the window at the greying sky. "Hurry, Carter. I must have him out of here before sunrise."

"Please, Mr. Rochester, you must allow me to finish dressing his wounds," the doctor said. "His flesh is torn at the shoulder and chest. There are fairly superficial excoriations at the neck, and I can see to those now, but these here! Gracious, they will require suturing. Best to see to it in my surgery where there is better light. All right, gather his belongings. We shall get him downstairs."

Within five minute's time, Mason's bedchamber was cleared of his belongings and he was safely installed in the doctor's awaiting carriage on the courtyard cobbles. The sky was brightening by the minute with the light of early dawn.

"Carter, keep him with you. He is not to depart from your surgery before I come to see him. We have much to discuss before he dashes off back to Jamaica."

"As you wish, Sir," the doctor said and went around the carriage to speak to his driver.

Richard leaned forward in his seat and grasped my arm through the carriage window. "Edward, you must try to forget what was discussed last night. It has no bearing on anything. Leave it all in the past and everyone will be better for it."

"As I said to you earlier, Richard, I am not finished with you. There is much to talk about."

"But I have nothing more to tell you!" he protested. "You know all that I do of her history, and besides, what good can it do now?"

"I cannot and shall not believe you, Mason. Your father and mine are now dead, which leaves you as the only living person who can recount the details of their deception to me. I am left responsible for *that*," I said, pointing to the north tower, "and as an accomplice to the plot I hold you accountable, Richard. You cast me down into a life of damnation. I want my life back!"

"You are her husband, Edward, and so she is your responsibility, not mine. There is nothing I can do to help you," he said and sat back in his seat.

The doctor opened the carriage door and climbed in beside him. Glaring at Richard, I said, "Tomorrow I will ride over to see him, Carter. See that he rests well."

"Not to worry for him, Mr. Rochester. He will be looked after and returned to good form. See you then."

I stepped back and watched the carriage roll away along the cobbles until it turned off the drive and onto the road. I then roamed about the courtyard in the chilly dawn air, considering all that had happened and was said last night.

What stupidity Richard exhibited, to come all this way with the intent of sharing distressing information with a mentally ruined woman, and then hope to escape without aftermath. Richard knew damned well what this Kerry Collier was to Bertha, and I was willing to bet my fortune that he was far more than a discarded lover from Bertha's youth. A hazy picture, one that painted a loathsome image of ruthless greed and deception, was sharpening into focus.

In terrorising Richard as I bore down on him brandishing clenched fists, I managed to wrest some crucial information from him, but not much as I observed in retrospect. He established that Bertha kept a lover before marrying me, but I had long suspected that. He also acknowledged the possibility of Bertha and this Kerry having married, but I recalled servant whisperings to that effect years ago. Richard dodged that interrogation quite successfully with his overdone act of infirmity.

What I now knew was that Bertha was the bastard daughter of a lowborn island Creole whose own sanity was of questionable merit. What flimsy lineage for a woman purported to be the offspring of a wealthy merchant as she was described to me! Maybe Jeremiah Mason actually was her father. Maybe not.

Clearly our marriage was achieved amidst carefully constructed deception designed to relieve both father and brother of her burden. On our wedding day, I signed my name to a certificate naming Bertha Antoinetta Mason as my bride, but in actuality, my understanding of her history was based upon little more than artfully composed fiction. Most importantly, Richard confessed that he and both our fathers were aware that she was succumbing to insanity at the time we married. But again, I already suspected that. And such knowledge could in no way help me now.

My early morning walk took me across the courtyard, down the drive and into the gardens. The single locale of Thornfield that could always charm me was the gardens. Nothing was formal there. The shrubbery and flowers grew haphazardly together creating brilliantly coloured palates and rich textures. I loved them in all seasons and as a child, my spring, summer and autumn days were spent communing with the beauty of our gardens and orchards. I grew as wild as they, and my youthful soul was at peace amongst natural things. They calmed me and hushed my unsettled heart as nothing else could. Particularly once mother was gone.

'Never did I ask for this,' I thought, gazing at the pink clouds of a sunrise sky. I only wanted to please. In those days, I thought that if I only did what he asked of me, he would love me. I wanted him to love me like he loved Rowland; his eldest and his best. My strolling came to a stop before a cluster of white foxglove. I crouched, touching the poisonous bell-shaped blooms, their throats splotched with luring crimson.

'Father. I let you sell my soul and my life. You sold me to Jeremiah Mason for the bargain price of twenty thousand pounds. No begging letters to be tolerated from Edward, no mean requests for money. In my youth and conceit, I quietly did all you asked of me and resolved to never disgrace you, hoping that if I toed your line, maybe then you might love me. How wrong I was.'

Straightening, I turned and wandered back the house. In through the kitchen, I ascended the back staircase and once on the second story, sought my chamber and closed myself in. There I undressed, drew the drapes and slipped into bed.

What a dreadful night. So weary. So achingly lonely. So in need of loving arms about me. Her deliciously warm body pressed to mine. Her soft whispers and kisses making me feel wanted, finally. What would I not give to have that? 'Be with me, Jane. Hold me tight and tell me you love me. Here in my bed, I will say I love you. I will say it and make you believe it. You are mine and I need you more than you can imagine. Safe and alone, the world will fall away… and we shall sleep.'

Alone, I slept.

Chapter 23

WHEN I WOKE again, broad daylight peered through the drapes, so I turned away and drew a pillow over my head. Voices could be heard in the gallery, and then a bustling clatter ensued, intensifying outside my chamber door. Soon, I was listening to instructions and chastisements volleyed between ladies' maids and servants as preparations for the Ingram family's departure commenced.

"They are leaving. Thank God!" I said aloud and rose quickly, throwing on my dressing gown. I went to the mirror and noted how exceedingly rough I appeared after a turbulent night, but not without a certain roguish allure I concluded with a smirk. A bath and shave would certainly be in order before going downstairs, but then, I rethought that. 'Hell with it, let them see me for what I am.' Perhaps my appearance would succeed in quenching that family's eagerness to partner me with their Blanche. I would wash my face, and that was the best they were going to have of me, damn them.

Drawing a towel across my jaw, I suddenly remembered the morning of my departure from Thornfield for Ingram Park, in Jane's bedchamber after carrying her there following the night here in mine. I visualised the scene so clearly. The way she looked as I lay her down on the white sheets of her bed, her hair all about the pillows. I recalled looking down on her, then lifting her lovely hands, bringing them across my face, over my blue-black morning beard. She smiled into my eyes as she touched me, taking pleasure in this unfamiliar sensation. We laughed. She reached and pulled me down, caressing the rough skin around my lips with hers, and kissed me in her remarkable way; the way that captured me inextricably, for her kiss could caress my wounded soul.

With some effort, I pulled my attention back to the here and now, and focused on dressing, soon examining my attire of charcoal trousers, white pleated morning shirt, burgundy waistcoat, tie and jacket. Having rendered myself reasonably presentable, I went out into the gallery and strode past the flock of kneeling maids preparing boxes and trunks to be brought down. Eyes were raised as I went past, and at the stairway I noted the appreciative glances that followed me. I smiled to myself. There was something about me lately. 'It's you, Jane. I know it.'

In the kitchen I found Leah and John scurrying amidst generalised chaos. All hands seemed to be both preparing and clearing breakfast items.

"It's gone nine o'clock, Sir! You have slept late today," Leah said as she hurried past me. "We will have breakfast up in half a tick. The Ingrams already have had their coffee, tea and scones. They refused a hot breakfast and wish to get a start on their journey."

"Can't argue with that, Leah," I replied heartily and poured myself a mug of coffee. Blanche was leaving and that ensured a superb start to my day. I took my coffee and went into the front entryway, finding the front door wide open and two carriages arriving into the courtyard. Footmen brought down the staircase an astonishing amount of luggage, and I stood aside watching them, hoping my glee was not too evident.

Within a half hour, all boxes and trunks were secured, and the carriages for transporting family and staff were at the ready. I remained in the entryway, second cup of coffee in hand, to watch the Ingrams descend the staircase. My additional guests were on hand to proffer wishes for a comfortable journey and to extend farewells. Quite a regal, showy group the family made as they gathered to stage their departure. Lady Ingram, dressed as always with opulent elegance, regarded me politely enough but glanced at my unshaven face with a measure of distaste. Lord Ingram and daughter Mary seemed embroiled in some petty dispute and so scarcely acknowledged their well-wishing friends. Blanche, dressed fetchingly in carmine silk, absorbed me with interest. She approached, pressed closely and drew two fingers across my bristly cheek.

"Love it, Edward," she breathed.

"Go home, Blanche," I said and sipped my coffee.

Her eyes surveyed me; my hair, face, clothes. She lifted my chin with an upturned forefinger and pursed her lips into an air kiss. In audacity she excelled, I had to give her that. Out in the courtyard, her parents and sister now stood chatting with my remaining guests about the favourable weather for their journey. Andrew appeared beside me, seeing his family off since he intended to stay at Thornfield and ride home on his own in a day or two.

Lord Ingram came to me in the courtyard and shook my hand earnestly. "A marvellous time had by all, Edward! We must do this again."

"So glad it was enjoyable for you, Sir." A feeble reply, yes, but it marked the greatest enthusiasm I could summon for such an idea.

He came closer and grasped my upper arm. "My wife and I have high hopes for you, Rochester. We understand that such decisions can not be made lightly." He furtively looked back at his wife and daughters. "I know she is a handful, Edward. An iron-willed, wicked little ball-breaker is my darling Blanche. Her mother is the same way, and I shall tell you, it has kept me enraptured for nearly thirty years," he said, grinning. "Blanche is beautiful, is she not?"

I nodded. "Undoubtedly, Sir."

His grin became downright lecherous. "There is nothing hotter than a beautiful hellion in your bed, young man. Take my word for it."

"Oh, Sir," I said with an amused chuckle. "I know of something infinitely better."

Lord Ingram looked at me quizzically and released my arm. I advanced to the carriage and kissed the hands of Mary and Lady Ingram, expressing wishes for a safe journey and helping them up to their cushioned seats.

"Rochester," Lady Ingram drawled, "we of course shall see you at Ingram Park in the near future?"

Blanche answered from behind me. "Of course we shall, Mother! You may be certain of that. He'll not stay away long." She remained on the cobbled drive, apparently waiting to have a word with me.

I turned from the carriage and went to her, standing with hands behind my back. Our eyes locked silently.

She stepped close and placed hands on my shoulders. "You must not resist me, Edward," she whispered against my shirt collar. "Despite our little tiff, I do love you. Still, now and always."

"Forget me, Blanche. I will do the same of you," I assured her.

She shook her head slowly, blonde ringlets flashing in the morning sun. "I want you. I always get precisely what I want."

"It is the chase and the kill you love, Blanche. Not me," I said deeply. "We are finished with one another." And not to be outdone by her in audacity, I punctuated my final remark by drawing my coarse chin across her soft cheek to which she gave an indignant squeal. Probably this was imprudent judging from her look of piqued interest, but despite my adolescent game, I knew that if I never again set eyes on Blanche Ingram, it would be a blessing nonpareil.

After having watched the carriages roll away down the drive, I returned to the house and joined my remaining guests in the dining room at breakfast. I took my place at the head of the table but had little appetite. I was exceedingly tired and my general quietude was wholly disturbed after such intense, ferocious scenes of last night. As soon as was socially acceptable, I retreated to my study but was not there five minutes before there came a tapping at the door left ajar.

Eshton looked in. "Want to be alone, Edward?"

"No, it's all right, Arthur. Come in. Sit."

"You've had some restless nights lately," he observed, taking a chair across the desk from mine.

I gave a short laugh. "Yes. Too many."

"And how is your servant? The one you were called to attend last night. Or was it the cook who had nightmares resulting in raging tantrums and the throwing of furniture?"

"I may consider telling you more on that but only under this condition. You must agree to reveal the nature of your conspiracy with Blanche in the window seat last evening."

"We were not conspiring!" he said defensively.

A serious gaze was levelled at him. "Do you have something to tell me?"

"Edward, what do you think? That I will reveal all of your secrets to your *intended* if she only smiles and jiggles her knockers at me? I did not mention Jane if that is what concerns you. What sort of friend would I be if I did that?"

"My 'intended'? Blanche?" I laughed heartily. "Is that what she told you?"

"That is what she's told everyone; that you two went off to discuss your upcoming engagement last evening but had a minor argument concerning details of date or wedding attire or some such nonsense."

"Oh sure, we argued over a 'detail'. Namely my emphatic refusal to marry her, ever!"

He laughed and regarded me with great amusement. "You refused, flat out, to marry her?"

"I believe my words, Arthur, were 'never, never, never'. Was I too vague do you think?"

"Edward, I knew it could not be true! I know that you love your Jane. But why Blanche's game? What is she up to?"

"Christ, I'm damned if I know. One minute she is threatening me with all manner of revenge for refusing her and the next she's telling me she still wants me. Unhinged, that girl is."

Eshton pondered that. "Do not be so sure. She is determined to have you," he said, taking the cigarette I offered, "because she's invested a tremendous amount of time and effort in you. All of society regards you as a pair and has done since her introduction, what, eight years ago?"

"Nearly," I said preparing a cigarette for myself. "It was time wasted, for both of us."

"Does Blanche know about Jane?" he asked.

"It seems everyone knows about Jane! Blanche included. Your Louisa shocked me last night by saying she knows the identity of my true love. How does everyone know?" I added accusingly, "Arthur…"

"Edward! It was not I. No one has to say it. Anyone who is remotely perceptive can clearly see the feeling between the two of you when near one another," he said, and I accepted that as being highly likely. We smoked without talking for a time, then he asked, "What more did you talk of with Louisa?"

"You. Well, she did the talking then actually."

"Me? What about me?" he asked. "Oh, permit me to guess! She told you, as she tells everyone, that she wants us to marry but I am far too much of a self-absorbed juvenile boor to focus my attention upon something so weighty."

"No, Arthur. She told me she loves you. And she knows you do not love her. Louisa is a sweet girl. I like her."

"And I like her too, but therein lies the problem. I feel nothing for her beyond 'like'. We have so little in common that conversation fizzles and becomes hard work! She has no interest in science, which you know is a consequential portion of my life. I need a woman with whom I can talk on a more cerebral basis than on next month's fancy dress ball or last season's bustle style. Louisa is kind and sweet, but I need more in a woman than that; if such a thing does exist. Think about it, Edward. What if Jane were flighty and superficial? Would you have given her, in your first interactions, anything akin to the regard you did? Would she have caught your interest with the same allure?"

I drew on my cigarette and replied decisively. "No. No, definitely not."

"Well then?"

I nodded. "I see your point, Arthur, though I am sorry to see Louisa hurt. She came to tears when Blanche was fawning over you last evening in the drawing room. So tell me; what were you two talking of then, giggling together in the window seat?"

He thought, recalling for a moment. "Nothing important. Mutual friends, society."

"Anyone in particular?"

"She talked mostly of the failed engagement of someone, ah.... an acquaintance of hers, a Georgiana something... yes, a Georgiana Reed." And in the next moment Arthur's expression fell flat.

I leaned forward, humourless and bristling. "Did you say anything to her, Eshton? Anything of the Reeds concerning what you and I recently discussed?"

"Edward, Christ, I told her...," and he thought for a moment while pulling deeply on his cigarette, "I said that I had heard of Georgiana's brother, John Reed, and that your governess is related to them. And that she recently had gone to visit Gateshead." He paused, staring at me wide-eyed. "Edward, I did not consider that Blanche might suspect your relationship with Jane."

I leaned back, drawing deep breaths in vain effort to control my anger.

Eshton asked, "You do not think that she will interfere, do you?"

"What, attempt to sabotage my relationship with another woman? Of course she will, Arthur! You grievously underestimate Blanche's capacity for vindictiveness."

With that I pushed back from the desk and went to the fireplace, pulled a final drag on my cigarette and flicked it into the ashes. "Excuse me, please," I said and vacated the study. A faintly existent but disturbing possibility was born in my mind. I went upstairs to fetch from my chamber the key to the north tower, then back out into the gallery, I went around corners, through the locked door, up the winding stairs, entered the crimson chamber and stepped to the final door. I knocked, and presently locks shot back. The door swung open revealing Grace before me, appearing exceedingly tired and serious.

"How is she today?" I asked.

"Come see her, Sir," Grace said and stepped aside.

There in the stone cell, I found Bertha seated at the table. Her head was lowered and her face obscured by long, stringy black hair. I stepped before her and crouched, moving her hair aside and peering at her closely but guardedly. She stared widely and blankly, quite in a state of catatonia, with an expression marked by ineffable suffering. She appeared as if to have been crying when her face suddenly froze.

"Has she been very long as such?" I asked backing away, unnerved by the sight.

Grace shrugged her shoulders. "I went into the chamber next," she said, nodding to the outer room, "to have a nap. And when I returned, she was sitting in this state, Sir. A little more than an hour she's been like this."

"Hmm. Grace, let me see your keys."

Her coarse, meaty hand produced a single skeleton key, not the usual ring containing keys to an apothecary chest and to cabinets of linens in the crimson chamber. "My apologies, Mr. Rochester. This is a spare. I have not yet found my ring of keys. She must have hidden them the night she escaped and visited your chamber. I have not had the opportunity to look for them."

I nodded, then stepped closer and asked, "Grace, tell me something. Last night, did you sit with Mr. Mason in the chamber next, after I had gone to fetch the doctor?"

Her hardened expression opened with surprise. "With Mr. Mason? No, Sir, I remained here. I was afraid missus would awaken in a distraught, perhaps violent state. It would not do to leave her."

"Yes," I said solemnly. "Commendable work last night."

"Yes, Sir. And thank you."

I threw a last look to Bertha, that pathetically damaged creature sitting mired in some unimaginable inner Hell before the leaping firelight, and quickly turned away the feeling of my own sanity wavering simply by being in her presence. I departed with my usual "lock up" orders and went downstairs, securing doors along the way.

My first stop was the chamber that had been occupied by Blanche Ingram. It was a prettily decorated room down a far corridor on the second story, and upon entering I found it quite tidy; the plush bedclothes smoothed and not an item in disarray. I stood in the centre of the flowery carpet, scanning all surfaces. In the wardrobe, I found only emptiness. In the drawers of the polished dressing table and desk, there was nothing. Heaving a great sigh I looked about the hazy room shrouded with bright morning light and my gaze fell on the bed. I strode directly to it and pulled the embroidered bedspread back, tossing the pillows aside. Again nothing. So I sat down on the bed and tapped fingers on the bedside table. I opened the top drawer and found within it a Bible. I closed the drawer again and sighed, looking around. My voice broke the silence. "I am overly suspicious."

Standing to leave, an impulse arrested my step. I returned to the bedside table, opened the drawer once more and removed the Bible. There, at the back of the drawer, were Grace's keys.

In my hand they jingled until my tightening fist silenced them. Images, possibilities and the weight of repercussions came flooding into my brain.

I retreated hastily from that perfumed and brightly illuminated, feminine boudoir, out into the gallery where I immediately found myself shaking in a cold sweat. Voices of my guests could be heard downstairs in the entryway, ascending the staircase. I turned and hurried to my bedchamber. Shutting the door heavily, I locked it and tossed the key ring onto the floor.

I was unsure of everything, myself included, questioning whether the years of vigilance in protecting my secret were skewing my perception of reality. All that I had striven to conceal, all of the anxiety and fear of exposure and all that I hoped to secure for the future; they suddenly seemed to teeter on the edge of a sheer drop. Could Blanche actually have gone upstairs last night whilst I was away fetching the doctor? Keys found in her bedside drawer could be a mere, unsettling coincidence, but if this were no coincidence, if she had gone upstairs and pried conversation from Richard in his delirious state, then I was clearly at the mercy of one without heart or pity. One who could look me in the eyes to say she loved me while drawing a dagger to sink to the hilt.

'You mark my words,' she had said.

"All right, Blanche, I am marking them."

Tomorrow I would ride into Hay and ask pointed questions of Richard. Upon finding this my sole option, I tried to settle myself. Realistically, what could she do with any awareness of my secrets? She wanted me for her own, did she not? 'Do not resist me ... I want you' were her parting words. Blanche would never jeopardise her own social standing, so if she actually wished to be my wife, then it would be to her benefit to remain entirely silent on any findings in the north tower. Unless she had discovered that I was already married. Certainly I would not care to have the details of my first marriage broadcast throughout local social circles, but as a romantic associate of mine for the past seven years, neither would she. Oh, the unfavourable gossip that would ensue!

Could Blanche use such information to wield power over me in another way? Possibly. Deeply jealous of Jane, she could attempt to drive the ravages of dishonesty and betrayal between us. Not much could sever us I thought, being most confident in the strength of our love, but broken trust and shattered confidence could chip away at our bond, eventually leaving it a worthless ruin.

I sensed the running of wolves. A number of players could conceivably attempt to devastate my hope for peace and happiness. Yet, I knew a counter strategy that could not fail, if done right. With that surety, I leaned back against the sofa and closed my eyes, presently feeling my tenseness fade away. Jane loved me. I was in love with her. Nothing else held relevance. I recalled the profound words of poet John Dryden: 'Love is not in our choice, but in our fate.'

"You, Jane, are my fate," I spoke aloud. "By loving you, I am a better person. I have once again sought God because of you. Being with you and taking you for my own is good and right. You are the only woman who can master me and are the one sweet, pure of heart, flesh and blood angel who can command my fate."

I knew what I must do, and that act must come soon.

She would be gone for another week. Suggestions came to me. I could ride to Gateshead and fetch her home before then. Then I thought, 'No. No, do not accost her. Let her be drawn back to her home and back to me. Of her own free will, let her stand before me again, and let me be strong enough and brave enough to challenge the world. To do what I know in my heart is right. To do what I feel that my God sanctions.' Exhaling heavily, I closed my eyes.

'Our night in the library, Jane. Kissing your neck and chest, gently, sensuously. Feeling your heart race against my cheek. Pulling you closer, feeling your thighs tighten about me. "Say it, Jane. Tell me." I drew it out of you, and you said it. You overflowed with it. You brought your mouth to mine and breathed it into me. It is in you, coursing through you, just as it is though me. I placed it there in you, this love. I meant to do it.'

Dreams of tall, waving grass awaited me. 'You cannot stop it now, Jane. You belong to me and I to you. Come home to me. Hear what I say to you and feel my love. Then say you will. Say yes.'

Chapter 24

ON THE FOLLOWING morning, I rode into Hay to call upon my injured and vigour depleted brother-in-law. Much of the night was spent in formulating questions and considering the most advisable manner of delivery so as not to create defensiveness. We would merely engage in a mellow exchange between two equable, self-possessed individuals. This would no doubt overextend my already exhausted thespian talents as what I really wished to do was throttle him, but I need not have wasted my time. When I arrived to Dr. Carter's surgery, Richard was gone.

"Please accept my sincerest apologies, Mr. Rochester," said the physician, noting my perturbed expression. "Mr. Mason was insistent upon going. I had no right to detain him."

"When did he leave?" I asked in astonished disbelief.

"Last evening, after dark. He was not nearly well enough to travel, but he said he would walk to Millcote if I refused to provide my driver and carriage, and seeing how obstinate he was, I do believe he would have."

I sighed with exasperation, muttering beneath my breath, "Underhanded, cowardly, mendacious, milquetoast of a..."

"Sir?" the doctor asked guardedly, noticing my rise of fury. "Are you feeling quite all right?"

"Oh just perfect, Carter," I spat then turned to leave. "Ah, yes. One other thing. The next time you are passing Thornfield, I would like for you to stop in to look at my... my wife."

"Certainly. Was she harmed during the altercation with her brother?"

"No, not as we have noticed. But you should be kept apprised," I said, "of her lucidity in the night hours. She spends the day in an immobile, unresponsive stupor but as the day becomes night she awakens to a notably contrasting alertness."

"Hmm," Dr. Carter puzzled. "I've read of this sort of thing. It is described as a circadian alteration in consciousness based upon the twenty-four hour waking cycle. How long has this been the case for her?"

"For about a month as Mrs. Poole recalls. Could be more."

He considered, taking a seat behind his desk. "And what is her age now? In her forties I presume?"

"Hell, I don't know, Carter. Her precise age would be anyone's guess."

"The change in her behaviour could be explained by hormonal flux," he thoughtfully postulated. "And this Mr. Mason? He is her brother I assume?" The doctor indicated for me to take the straight-backed leather chair nearby.

"Step-brother. And no, thank you. I shall not stay long."

Carter asked, "Mason arrived to the area for the purpose of seeing her?"

"Yes. To share tragic news with her."

"Tragic news?" he asked incredulously. "Of what sort?"

"He came to tell her of the death of a man with whom she once shared intimacy," I answered. "I was not present when Mason delivered the shock."

"Why in God's name did he come all this way to inform her of that? The woman is insane."

"Carter, I do not know why he felt compelled to do something so asinine at that. He felt that it was her right to be told, by him, that this man was dead."

"And how did she react to such information?"

"As you saw from the extent of Mason's injuries, she reacted rather badly," I told him. "Went from calm to hysterical in seconds. Crying and wailing, and then she attacked him."

"The man is a fool!" he said vehemently, shaking his head. "Obviously Mrs. Rochester is yet capable of remembering loved ones as well as comprehending the gravity and finality of death, but she is completely unable to withstand the impact of loss. She cannot cope with bereavement as a mentally intact person would. There are stages to managing grief, and your wife is entirely unable to meet such a process rationally or constructively. Her degeneration came to a plateau in recent years, but now, a significant shock paired with an unstable hormonal state... this worries me."

"Are you saying that her illness may deteriorate further? And because of Mason's visit to her?"

He nodded. "Possibly so. I will come by Thornfield if you wish, but as always, there is not much for medicine to offer. She needs protection from agitation and interference. If her own brother or step brother, whomever he is, cannot or will not protect her fragility, then the onus of her care falls entirely on you, Mr. Rochester."

Bitterly I said, "Since the day of our marriage, Carter, the onus has been mine."

He shrugged regretfully. "Such a tragic fate, Sir," he said, and I was not certain if he meant Bertha's or mine. With parting pleasantries and a handshake, I left Dr. Carter's surgery, mounted my horse and galloped homeward.

In a few days more, Lady Lynn and her sons Frederick and Henry returned to their estate. This left as my guests the Dent twins, Amy and Louisa, along with Andrew Ingram and Arthur Eshton. Now that all of the more senior and puritanical of my urbane visitors were departed, this younger assembly relaxed their stringent social standards considerably. We indulged in more wine and liqueurs than ever before, and everyone smoked round the dining room table following the dessert course; ladies included. Men removed ties and unbuttoned their collars. Amy and Louisa chatted to dining companions across the table, propped on elbows. We laughed frequently and raucously. Furthermore, the telling of ribald jokes became a competition of legendary proportions.

We played a game whilst lounging at the table called "Words to Live By" in which we each pronounced a favourite defining dictum. The group waxed philosophical one particular evening, as evidenced by Eshton's statement, "If you make money your god, it will plague you like the devil." But our collective jaws dropped when we came to the affable and darling Amy Dent who straightened in her chair and stated, "The harder they come, the more essential a firm mattress." Silence for some three seconds, then uproarious laughter echoed throughout the dining room. Incidentally, I noticed Andy Ingram studying a previously disregarded Amy Dent with new eyes.

The week continued as such, with our intimate group of five enjoying easy companionship, unfettered as we were after nearly a month of obligatory genteelness. By week's end, Andy and Amy were taking leave of the group for extended evening strolls in the garden, leaving me situated between Arthur and Louisa, both of whom often entered into a silence so strained that I was compelled to make polite excuses and take myself elsewhere. This elsewhere was typically the library, which had become my own sanctum; a place where I could distinctly feel the magical shroud of intimacy that enveloped Jane and I on a night that now seemed so long ago. I would remain alone, in my chair by a low fire, sipping whatever spirit chosen for that evening, waiting for her.

On one such night there came a tapping at the door. Mrs. Fairfax had sought me. "Are your guests enjoying themselves, Sir?" she opened politely.

"They are. Some more than others to be sure. What can I answer for you, Mrs. Fairfax?"

"A letter arrived for me from Miss Eyre today, Sir. I thought you would wish to know," she said, holding the correspondence in her hand.

Quickly I turned in my chair to look at her, and the letter. I wanted it in my hand and for her to go away. I stood; my fingers twitching as I advanced to her asking, "May I?"

"Well, yes, of course, Sir," Mrs. Fairfax flustered.

With great effort, I took it gently from her hand and said, "Thank you, Mrs. Fairfax. Good night."

"Oh. Well yes, good night, Sir," she said, her tone sinking with solemnity.

I waited until the door shut behind her, then went straight to the carpet before the fire and knelt down in the glowing firelight. I opened the folded paper to Jane's neat handwriting:

29th May 1840

Dear Mrs. Fairfax,

It is my hope that this letter finds you well. I write to apprise you of my current situation and plans for return to Thornfield Hall.

As you may recall, my Aunt Reed became direly unwell upon news of her son's recent death. I had opportunity to speak with her briefly upon my arrival to Gateshead, and she expired later that night. The funeral is now past and I am busied with assisting my cousins, Georgiana and Eliza, with their prospective arrangements. Gateshead, with all of its furnishings, is to be sold. In honour of my cousins' requests, I shall stay for perhaps another fortnight to help expedite their preparations for future.

Please inform Mr. Rochester that I intend to return to Thornfield in mid-June. You may also convey that I have sent enquiries to three schools appropriate for Adele's future education. The headmistress of each will write to him directly. As for myself, I have advertised for a new teaching situation.

More personally, I learned of an uncle in the hours before Mrs. Reed's death; a Mr. John Eyre who currently resides in Madeira. Some three years ago he attempted to locate me, but this did not materialise. I have now written to him and am eagerly awaiting his response. It is indeed comforting to know that I do have family.

That is all for the moment. My best to Leah, John and Adele. Regards to Mr. Rochester.

Yours Sincerely,

Jane Eyre

I dropped the letter to my thigh. It was dated five days ago. Her return could not be expected for another ten or more. The tone of her letter abounded with self-reliance and professional poise, and this indeed was fitting since the correspondence was addressed to Mrs. Fairfax, not I. Yet it was the 'Regards to Mr. Rochester' that ruffled me. I glanced to the piano and bench. Her breathless voice suddenly resonated in my head, 'Ohh, Edward...' My lips and tongue again tasted the feverish skin of her throat. All of the desperation to be close, the sexual energy that electrified us, words of love spoken in trembling voices; where was it now?

I exhaled a short laugh. "'Regards', Jane?"

Right here on this rug! What we had done together, or rather what *she* had done in her absolute bent to drive me to climax. Kissing softly afterward. Her voice, "I think I love you to the depths of my soul." Taking her to my bed where we whispered softly and kissed in the night, and finally, together, slept.

'Regards to Mr. Rochester.' Yes, quite.

Certain other points in her written tone disturbed me. Whilst at Gateshead she had advertised for a new teaching position, disregarding my direct order not to do so. But I knew upon her departure that she would, such an independent little thing she was, but I was angered that she would want to commit herself to other employment. Our personal relationship aside, I paid her salary for heaven's sake! I should have some voice in this scheme!

Earnest self-scrutiny was in order, and so mental interrogation of one ensued. Had I not recently considered exiling her to Ireland? And why? Answer: Yes, I did, as a means of removing temptation from my sight and grasp. Had I not left her the morning after our glorious first night together and run away to Ingram Park for the express purpose of rallying my strength to send her away? Why did I do that? Answer: Because I was seized with guilt and fear; guilt of deceiving her and fear of ensnaring her into a fraudulent union.

'Yes, Edward, so what has changed? You have achieved all you desired. She is gone and making plans to secure herself far away. So what's the trouble?' Answer: I cannot live without her; a certainty that is reinforced on a daily and nightly basis! Also, it could be that now I have hope.

'Hope of what?'

Answer: Hope that I am not married. Hope that I am a free man.

With a great sigh I acknowledged that my own indecisiveness damaged our love, and the sole blame for our current estrangement was mine. Jane's behaviour was ever sincere and consistent. She deserved better than I, and that hurt. Jealousy was also there amongst my broodings since Jane, my lonesome girl who once had no one, no family at all and no friends to care for her other than myself, now had cousins and an uncle. My confidence faltered. I loved her and wanted her more than ever, yet she suddenly seemed unattainable.

I re-read the letter. She seemed not mine but rather a cool acquaintance. Not at all my... (it was so hard to say it now) ...not at all my lover. I looked to the fire, to its crackling, enduring flames, and my soul spoke to hers.

'What is going on in your head, Jane? Talk to me. I will hear you and feel your words. Do you feel me loving you again? Kissing you? In leaving my lonely self at night, I desire with all of my strength to be with you, and then somehow I am. I will be the man you deserve. Finished with indecisiveness I am, and done with fear. My only fear is in losing you. Straight to hell with everything else! This relentless longing for you has cast me into fetters and chains of iron. Come home. Let me love you with the force of a frantic tempest!'

Her letter remained in my hand. It was my only link to her it seemed. My spiritual explorations presently led me down a path to where I glimpsed a certain blonde interloper and my sight came into focus. I began calculating dates and typical duration of post conveyance. Eshton and Blanche in the window seat. A letter sent. The timing was short but not impossible.

I considered going to my study and writing my own letter; a gushing profession of devotion, but that seemed pitifully trite. To write it onto paper and not be present to witness her reaction; to have no choice but to wait perhaps a week for return correspondence. No, I wanted to say it. I wanted to see her eyes when I said it. I wanted to bring my mouth to hers, taking handfuls of her hair as it came down. I wanted our delicious burst of passion to rage on and on. No, proclaiming my love in a letter would never do.

So I waited. Days passed in an anticipatory haze. I slept late every morning in a conscious effort to speed the time, but once up, my daily activities of entertaining guests whilst simultaneously conducting business kept me well occupied. Regrettably, I began drinking before noon yet managed to keep intoxication in check. It was a vain attempt at numbing an oppressive pain nothing could satisfy.

I watched my coupled companions with vague envy, particularly Andy and Amy who were fairly bursting with newfound romance, and I was pleased for them. They made a striking pair, well suited in character and disposition as well as externally. Arthur, I noticed, was purposefully cooling his courtship of Louisa by escaping into books or the gardens at every opportunity.

Louisa came to my study one afternoon to inform me that she had asked John to drive her into Millcote. She would meet a coach there and depart for home.

"Edward, I must thank you for a truly marvellous time here at Thornfield," she said taking the club chair I offered. "But you see it. Arthur and I… this is finished. I cannot be where he is."

We sat, and I took her hand across the desk. "I am so sorry, Louisa," I said. "You are a lovely girl. This is Arthur's loss."

She smiled softly, her heartbreak evident. "It is mine too," she mournfully replied. "I was quite prepared to marry him and devote myself to supporting his studies, despite his lack of wealth. But he gives nothing in return, and so I will likely be glad someday for a short spell of disappointment rather than a lifetime of misery."

I nodded my agreement.

"What was it Shakespeare said of heartbreak? 'The wound's invisible that love's keen arrows make.' Invisible maybe, but no less painful."

"I know what you are feeling, Louisa. Believe me when I say that I have been there too."

"Edward, I see that you have. Pain is evident in your features as well. Your young lady is gone, but you love her still."

With elbows on the desk, I folded my hands, my vision turning inward to the swirling storm in my heart. "Yes," was all I could give in reply.

"Does she love you?"

I shrugged. "I thought so."

"Then find her and make her yours, Edward," Louisa said, nodding encouragement.

I came around the desk as she arose to leave and embraced her. Then she was gone.

Within the next few days, Andrew and Amy departed Thornfield as well. Finally, Eshton announced that he must return to his family estate situated nearby to prepare for his return to Leiden University in Amsterdam. "I shan't sail for another three weeks, but my thesis requires attention at home amongst all of my books and clutter. May I return here to see you before I go?" he asked.

"Of course you may, Arthur. My home is always open to you," I said, then added smiling, "I hope you find your ideal woman at Leiden. Perhaps you will fall over one another in the library amongst the periodicals."

"One never knows," he said with his mischievous smile. "Jane is coming back soon, is she not?"

"If her recent letter to Mrs. Fairfax is to be believed, yes, she will be back in a few days more."

"Set everything right with her, Edward. About Blanche, you, all of it. Sit her down, speak from your heart and hold nothing back."

I laughed. "What makes you an expert on the subject? A certain young lady departed this house with her heart quite shattered thanks to you."

"Forget that, Edward. It was wrong with Louisa. I can feel for a woman, most passionately I can, but as I said, that intensity will never come if the romance lacks *substance*. I need meat and root vegetables; not baklava and pralines! I am tired of wasting my time, and I imagine you are as well."

"True enough, but what I am now is hungry," I observed.

"Hm. Me too. Just promise this before we abandon the topic. You will repair what you have with Jane."

"I only hope she will listen. She has every right not to after the way I've behaved."

He mulled that. "In my experience, a passionate kiss helps to capture most any girl's attention. Try it sometime."

Suddenly overtaken with a surge of longing for her, I sighed heavily. "Eshton, my friend, if that is the case then she doesn't stand a chance."

By late evening Thornfield was deserted of guests and had again fallen quiet. As the time neared nine, I went to the north tower to release Grace Poole from servitude, allowing her to join John, Leah and Mrs. Fairfax in the kitchen for tea and conversation. Grace was well overdue for a reprieve from her duties as evidenced by ever-deepening creases about her forehead and eyes. Her roughened features may also have been the result of daily consumption of strong drink; who was to say? I only knew that a replacement for her must be sought and a comfortable retirement guaranteed.

Unquestionably Grace Poole's length of servitude had earned self-indulgence and freedom in her waning years.

These evenings, if the weather accommodated I would take Bertha to the roof and allow her to walk ahead of me. I remained a few paces behind her, watching as she threw arms wide and breathed deeply, strolling ahead whilst humming unfamiliar tunes. She was cooperative in my charge and buoyant of spirit if not frequently talkative, but on one such night she surprised me by saying in her nearly forgotten musical voice, "You hear that, do you not, Edward?"

I listened. A whip-poor-will sang in the nearby wood. "You mean the calling bird?"

"No no. The voices. They call me and say it is time to come home."

I listened again. A bird, trees rustling, horses occasionally stamping in the stable; these were the only sounds I heard. "Who calls you, Antoinetta?"

"They all do. Richard, Father and Mother, Tessa. They ask where I've gotten to. But mostly it is his voice I hear." She silenced, glancing at me guardedly.

"It is a man you hear?" I asked confused, but likely it was her confusion making me feel that way. "Ah, you speak of friends and perhaps... lovers?"

She smiled and relaxed somewhat. "You do hear the voices! I especially hear his, everywhere I am. He still loves me these many years later," she said, giddily biting her thumbnail. "He has always loved me. Does that anger you, Edward?"

"No, Antoinetta. I am glad you've known love."

I so wanted to ask if in her youth she married her love, this Kerry Collier, but I heeded Dr. Carter's words that it was my duty to protect her from agitation. She was calm and the crying she had done in the days following Richard's deleterious revelation seemed to have ceased.

We were walking together tonight, talking quietly as we did in the early days of our marriage; during the hot days and nights in Jamaica when we strolled in our garden amongst the sweet aroma of night flowers. Even then I felt very little tenderness for her, and certainly no love. I was entirely unable to address my wife by her given name and could see from the start how that omission aggrieved her. She was always a stranger to me. Distant. And each day of our early marriage brought me no closer to knowing her or even wanting to. Antoinetta's heart, I now understood, was elsewhere, as was mine. Mine was with a woman I had yet to meet; some vaporous ideal. I would look at my wife in the moonlight as we ambled alongside the West Indies foliage, knowing with gut wrenching surety that I had made a terrible mistake.

"I will go home to him one day," she said, dashing my reverie. Her conversational voice was as yet an unnerving sound, having not heard it in so many years.

"Where is 'home' for you, Antoinetta?"

She smiled and her eyes became distant. "On the fishing beach by the pilings and thatched huts," she said, her thumbnail going back to her teeth. "That is where he loves me, all night, from sundown until sunrise."

I was happy that such a glorious memory yet lived in her mind and told her so, adding, "You will see him there again someday."

She smiled radiantly and brought her hands together before her, walking and gazing up at the moon and stars.

The following evening was spent in my study, reading. Eshton left behind with me his first copy dissertation on the migratory habits of barn swallows, and I sat with feet up on my desk, studying his findings with absorption. John came in and out of the room serving a brandy, lighting candles, tidying and such. I read on, pushing my brandy glass forward to be refilled, then retracting it. The door hinges creaked.

"Sir?" came a feminine voice.

I looked up. There she was, standing in the doorway. I may have gasped before abruptly standing. No words came to my suddenly vacant mind but a single one: 'Jane.' My eyes were riveted by her true physical image, such an absolutely arresting sight she made from head to toe. She wore a fashionably designed summer dress in sage green with lace at collar and sleeves, and pleats accentuating her tiny waist. Her hair was done up in a softer, more elegant style than ever I'd seen her wear. It became her exquisitely. But it was her face and form that made an irresistible sight, and when she removed her gloves, baring slender hands that weeks ago touched me so magnificently, my breath caught, tripped and stumbled. Inordinate strength was required to maintain composure.

I managed to offer a standard greeting. "Hello, Jane. Please, come in."

She stepped into the room but remained a sizable distance from me. "Mr. Rochester, I do hope you have been well," she offered. I looked for a tremor of her hands but there was none. I marvelled at her self-control.

"I've been quite well, Miss Eyre," I said, matching her in chilly civility. Then silence fell as we gazed at one another.

"Sir," she said finally, taking a deep breath, "I have returned to inform you that I must give two weeks notice. My employ here has been thoroughly appreciated, however it must end in order for me to take a teaching position at a school some distance away."

I sat back down. This formality nonsense had to stop. There was too much between us to play this ridiculous charade. "Jane..." I started softly.

She shook her head and raised a hand. "In addition, Sir," she continued, "I must request leave of you once again, to spend the day in Millcote tomorrow. My attendance at an essential appointment is required."

I for one began to cast decorum aside. "What appointment? With whom?"

"While I was away it was revealed to me that I have family. An uncle and three cousins. Two of my cousins are planning to meet me in Millcote tomorrow." With a shade of insolence she added, "I would wish to go if that is agreeable to you."

I stared at her. She was so changed, so cool. Her attitude held no warmth rendering her yet another beautiful stranger in my life. I shrugged my shoulders and said, "I haven't any interest in stopping you. But you could bring them here. You need not meet with them at The Black Swan or The George Inn. Return with them here and take the drawing room."

"Thank you. I may do that," she said and turned to leave.

'She cannot go! Think of something, Edward!' cried my mind. "Jane!" I said after her, "Ah, I...I still owe some salary to you."

She turned back to look at me. I took the billfold from my jacket, extracted a five-pound note and placed it on my desk. As she came forward I slid it toward her. She stood across the desk from me, surveying me with coolness.

"Is this all you require of me, Jane?" I asked, meeting her gaze directly.

"It is," she said, and our eyes fastened to one another's. She waited a few beats, then placed her palms on my desk and leaned toward me. "Mr. Rochester," she said, her gaze sweeping over my face, hair, and clothes. "I could reduce you to trembling and gasping right this minute if I wished to. You know that I could."

My heart lurched. "Then do it," I challenged, looking up into that sea of grey green as excitement rushed all through me.

She nodded, her eyes falling to my lips. "You would like that, wouldn't you? To take from me. To take it all," she whispered. Anger flared in her eyes. She crumpled the five-pound note in her fist and pushed away from my desk, turned and vacated my study, shutting the door behind her.

I sat back in my chair, stunned. "What in hell was that?!" I asked aloud.

That shut door drew me like iron ore to lodestone. "No. You are not going to escape me again, Jane. And I will not simply let this lie until you decide to come to me. You are mine. You love me. You said it, and I will not let you forget it."

I placed the brandy tumbler to my lips and advised myself silently. 'Work this through, Rochester. Be certain of what you will say and know what could happen if you go up to her chamber tonight. There is tremendous damage to undo. Try to see all from her viewpoint. Remember that it was you who left her when you went to Ingram Park. Remember that you never denied an intention to marry Blanche.' Her faith in me was lost, and that was my own damned fault.

I wanted so much to be honest with her but knew enough not to reveal any ruinous information. Yet I had no intention of lying to her either. I would simply avoid explanations and instead lay out the content of my heart.

Our nights in the library and my chamber... Her voice saying, "I love you to the depths of my soul." Passion I could not forget, keeping me tormented with longing for more. All of me raged to go to her. I went.

Chapter 25

Out of the study I strode, crossing the front entrance hall to bound my way up the staircase, when my progress was suddenly checked by an absolutely decadent aroma wafting from the kitchen. Knowing its source immediately and thinking along the lines of 'peace offering', I backed down the stairs. In the kitchen Mrs. Fairfax was preparing a tray of tea items at the servants' table. Leah stood at the massive black cast-iron stove, briskly stirring the contents of a large saucepan. I went to her and watched over her shoulder.

"Oh! Goodness, Sir! You frightened me," she laughed. "There are no secrets to be had from you! This was meant as a surprise, knowing how much you enjoy custard."

"Yes you do know that, Leah," I chuckled, reaching for a dishtowel so as to open the oven.

She tapped at my hand. "No you will not, Sir! I will not have you ruin that surprise as well. Good Lord, you are worse than a schoolboy…"

"Treacle tart! Bless you, dear woman!"

Cook turned and exchanged amusedly exasperated glances with housekeeper. "Mrs. Fairfax, have you ever in your career known a master to appear so informally and so often in the kitchen?"

"I daresay not, Leah," Mrs. Fairfax sighed. "His father never once saw this room as far as I can recall, nor his brother, Mr. Rowland…"

"Ahem! Ah, yes then, Mrs. Fairfax!" Leah exclaimed, silencing the old woman. "The less said on that point the better. Sir, the treacle tart shan't be finished for another quarter of an hour, and then it must cool. I will send John to fetch you when it is ready to serve, now please, be off with you!"

Comprehension came to Mrs. Fairfax only when I rapped with my knuckles on the planked kitchen table. She blushed and flustered, and I laughed at her reproachful look as I turned toward the door. Mrs. Fairfax lifted the tea tray to proceed in my direction as well.

"Where is that tea tray going, Mrs. Fairfax?" I asked.

"Oh, I mean to take it up to Miss Eyre, Sir. She is only just back from her journey you know. Did she not greet you in your study upon her arrival? I am afraid she endured the most exhausting travels complete with rain squalls, bad roads, slow drivers, and what's more, the poor dear comes back to us so terribly thin that I must wonder if Gateshead's cook fed her at all whilst she was..."

"I know she is here," I interrupted as an impulse took me. "And I wish to interview her concerning this jaunt to Gateshead that kept her truant from her duties at Thornfield for one entire month. She will be answerable for such negligent behaviour! Give the tray to me, Mrs. Fairfax. I will take it up to her and demand she provide an immediate debriefing."

Leah listened to that with a wry smile.

Mrs. Fairfax conversely took me in complete earnest and said, "Well, I suppose as master of the Hall your intent would be acceptably correct, but perhaps you will permit me a moment to prepare her. She will want to change out of her travelling clothes and smooth her hair. Allow her a cup of tea first!"

My hands closed on the tray and pulled.

"Sir, well, all right," she relented in her twittering way.

Leah continued to stir at the stove and looked at me with a suppressed smile, shaking her head.

I said to her, "Leah, expect me back in thirty minutes for tart and custard. Dressing down my hirelings always renders me ravenous!"

For a moment her eyes went heavenward. "Yes of course, Sir. If I am not here when you return, please do serve yourself. I shall be sure to leave a nice pitcher of custard warming on the stove and service for two on the table. Do try to be a lenient and forgiving master in the interim."

"Service for two?" asked a bewildered Mrs. Fairfax.

"Leah, your intimation astonishes," I said. "I am nothing if not beneficent to a fault." I left them both with a charmer of a smile.

The tea tray and I went up the staircase. In the gallery, Jane's sweet alto voice could be heard behind her shut door, singing softly to herself. With the tray set down on a buffet table situated between two windows, I went nearer to her door, leaned against the wall and listened. Now another impulse struck, and I went to my darkened chamber, straight to the writing desk where I removed *A Selection of English Poetry* with the scrap paper marker tucked in place and pocketed it. Back out into the gallery, I took up the tray and went to her chamber door.

My heart thumped and pulse raced as I stood outside Jane's room, listening to her tuneful humming and subtle noises of activity within. Warm firelight shone from beneath the door, mingling with star and moon light at the gallery's windows. 'All right, so she is in there. Think of Jane as you know her to be, Edward. Recall her words of love, her passion and kiss; that final kiss before she left for Gateshead! Recall the piano bench, her body, her breathless "I love you, love you…" Remember, remember…and have faith in her love's endurance.'

Oh yes, at the piano bench, her weight upon me and thighs around my body, then down on the rug, both her hands inside my unbuttoned breeches, sending my senses blurring with paroxysms of pleasure. My head reeled, and I was forced to banish all such recollection or else the tea tray would have been on the floor in seconds. 'Hell with it. Knock!' I commanded myself.

So I did. Immediately, her "come in" was called whereupon I balanced the tray on my forearm and opened the door. The chamber was very different from the last time I saw it, on the day the pearl necklace was found tucked beneath underclothes in her wardrobe. A cool night breeze stirred the June night air through an opened casement window, and the glow of a fire and candlelight brightened the room in hues of warm amber. Jane was at the far end of the chamber, half hidden by the bed and kneeling before the fireplace. She was emptying and arranging items taken from a travel box, humming a tune and working with her back to me.

I stepped forward into the room and set the tray down on a table, glad to be free of its precarious burden. My hands shook. I ordered myself to regain control immediately. Jane quietly continued her work, not looking back at her visitor as I quietly shut the door, then leaned with my back against it.

Straightening up and examining a white article of clothing, she asked, "Mrs. Fairfax, would you have a spool of white cotton for me to..?" and she turned around in mid-sentence. Upon seeing me, her slight body gave an instantaneous jolt, then she swiftly turned away, her back stiff, shoulders straight, head up. She had removed the jacket of her sage green suit, for a suit it was. A high-necked white blouse with lace trimmed collar and sleeves remained, and I found her enchanting in this soft, feminine white topping the sage skirt. Her thick chestnut hair, as I now viewed it from the back, was arranged in a plaited figure of eight with delicate tendrils falling about her neckline and narrow shoulders. I wondered at the change of hair and dress; the abandonment of grey Lowood frocks with hair pulled into a modest twisted knot. Not that I objected at all, so completely irresistible she was either way. My breathing quickened as I watched her from the door, but her prickly remoteness successfully kept my substantial thirst for her in check.

With her back to me she asked, "Is there a question I may answer for you, Mr. Rochester?"

I remained silent, gazing at her slim waist and slight shoulders shrouded in white. During her absence for what seemed like an eternity, I longed for her with every fibre of my being. Anguished hours were spent yearning for a moment such as this, consoling myself with memory and maintaining faith of her return. Now that she was within reach, I was filled with trepidation. She spurned me so coldly thus far. Fear of rejection must be placed aside so that I may untangle the knotted, mangled mess I alone created, bringing her back to loving, silken softness.

I left the door and went around the bed to where she was occupied in her task. Her straight back remained to me with her head turned slightly in listening. I sat down on the bed behind her. Urges and impulses rattled me, being so near her. Something about her hair lured my hands from my lap, and I envisioned bringing myself up behind her, running my hands up her bodice to her breasts, pulling pins from her hair...

She turned to face me, straightening her skirt as she knelt on the rug. Her face was expressionless and eyes fell on me unemotionally. "So?" she said. "Have you something to say, Sir?"

I merely nodded, not at all ready to say it.

She paused then said, "Congratulations are in order for you, I see! My cousin received a letter from your intended, Miss Blanche Ingram. It held an engagement announcement. It is my hope that you and she know only happiness together."

My heart sank: all fears confirmed. "Jane, please."

"Georgiana, my cousin, gave the announcement to me to see. Engraved, regal-looking stationary it was. But you already know that."

I closed my eyes and sighed. I knew that Blanche would not delay any opportunity for vindictiveness, and how right I was. How she managed to have a single false engagement announcement printed on stationery so quickly I could not say, but she must have paid a tidy sum for that trick. Hers was a truly staggering display of spiteful energy.

My eyes opened and I looked at Jane. 'Good God, what must she think of me?'

She remained kneeling on the rug, face turned up to me, awaiting a response. I had not the faintest idea where to begin. She helped me. Rising from the rug, she went to the wardrobe and opened it. Beneath the stack of underclothes there came the sound of her pearl necklace across wood. With it, she came to stand before me.

"Here," she said, holding the pearls out to me.

"What? What are you doing?" I asked, distressed.

"Take them. These were never for me. Give them to their rightful owner."

"Jane, they are for you. I gave them to you because I want you to have something so lovely."

She tossed the necklace onto the bed beside me. "Then you should not have bought them at all."

"Oh, is that right? And what about this?" I asked hotly, taking the volume of poetry from my coat pocket. "You seemed to have wanted to keep this in your possession."

She pulled a sharp breath. "You came in here and took that!"

"Yes. I did. And what about this, Jane?" I removed the slip of paper marking *The Passionate Shepherd to His Love*; the one reading in her handwriting:

Edward Fairfax Rochester,
Come live with me. Be my love.
Jane Eyre

I held it up in my fist. "Hmm? Tell me, Jane. Tell me what you mean by this!"

Life returned to her eyes and she blushed deeply red. She shook her head and looked away. "It is nothing. Nothing more than idle nonsense, Sir."

I shoved the paper back into the book and tossed it onto the nightstand. "I don't think so, Jane," I said, rising from the bed to stand before her.

Cornered, a simmering fury began to roil within her, replacing calm reserve. She stood there, her fists clenching and unclenching, shifting her weight, as I knew she did when anxious. She said, "I was terribly foolish to let this get away from me."

"To let what get away from you? Make some sense!"

"You! Me! God, how incredibly stupid I was to hope that you, Edward Fairfax Rochester, would want me over her! Go," she said, flinging a hand toward the door. "Leave me. Go and marry your beautiful, rich Blanche Ingram."

I shook my head vehemently. "No! I will not marry Blanche! Not now and not ever. Understand that."

"Oh, I know what you are doing," she said, her ire escalating and eyes blazing. "You thought you might come to my chamber and say, 'Jane, kiss me', knowing that with you I am weak. Well, I shan't be weak anymore. You do not want me. You have no love for me. I say to you *go*!"

"No, Jane! I will not go. Not until you and I have understood one another completely."

"Haven't you gotten enough from me? Or did you come here in hopes of taking the rest?"

"God damn blast it, Jane! Bull-headed little imp, you certainly..."

My consciousness suddenly whirled, vision blurred and a stinging pain inflamed my cheek. I stared at her. Did she strike me? She was so fast, I never saw her hand rise. I stood shocked and speechless in amazement as she stood her ground, features ferocious and hands at her sides in tight fists, bearing not a sign of remorse or tears. Lovely, petite, delicate thing, she was the picture of naked fury... and I liked it.

My first impulse was not violent reaction as it was the last time a woman struck me (Gia, for whom I felt little respect and no love.) It was real admiration for Jane's courage and spirit. I had led her into compromising circumstances and could easily have made a dishonest woman of her. I drew from her confessions of love and gave little in return, and now, as she understood my intentions, she was discarded in favour of a rich noblewoman. Far away from me at Gateshead these many weeks, she had time to seethe and allow doubts to break her.

"You," she said, trembling with rage. "You put me to this. I have nothing, and you took from me what you wished."

"No, Jane, you are wrong! That was never my..."

I saw her arm twitch but this time was ready for her. Her hand flew up to strike me a second time, but I caught it at the wrist. While arresting that one, her other hand flew up and I caught that one as well. She struggled against me. I gripped her wrists fast.

"You will not...," I said through clenched teeth, "...do that again!"

"Let go of me," she insisted, fighting to extricate her hands, but she was absolutely no match for me. Finding herself helpless, fury gave way and tears began to fill her eyes. "You are hurting me," she said, her voice breaking.

I released her wrists and instantly caught her upper arms, lifting her off the floor to fling her onto the bed. Before she could react I was on her. I captured her wrists again and held them both in my left hand above her head.

"What…? What are you doing?!" she protested, wriggling beneath me.

I was not entirely sure what I was doing but needed for her to listen to me, and that plainly demanded restraining her physically. Both purposes were now served.

"Mr. Rochester," she gasped. My weight was compressing her chest and she could not draw the breath to speak above a whisper. "Mr. Rochester, get off of me."

"No. Now be still and listen to me."

Presently, her hands relaxed their force against my grip and her arms went from tense to flaccid. I eased my weight off her chest and she drew a deep breath but remained silent. Tears spilled along the sides of her face to the bedspread and her lower lip quivered. Anger was spent, now giving way to grief. I was quiet, studying her face, watching her tears flow. She truly astonished me tonight with her inordinate fire and spirit. As yet I was amazed that she struck me, her master and estranged lover. If knowing a person created a picture, then key components clicked into place here tonight, and I understood this woman as I had not before. Her fury and resentment were born of anguished heartache, to which I was the focus. As she saw the situation, I overlooked her in favour of the beautiful Miss Ingram, reinforcing her insecurity of being beneath my consideration as a wife. She risked her valued autonomy by daring to share her most secret and guarded self, coming to want and need another, then was callously slapped down for giving so freely. So she slapped back.

As my Jane looked up at me through teary eyes, I reached and stroked her soft, creamy cheek. She allowed me to touch but remained guarded. Her beauty held me captivated. All of this woman whom I cried out for in the lonesome hours of night, I could not now have enough of her sight and feel. Quite beyond my conscious will, I drew my thumb lightly across her lips and wet my own, longing to kiss her.

'Not yet,' I told myself. 'She is not ready. Wait.'

"Jane," I began, "I've committed such wrong against you. I know that, and I am sorry." I then paused, considering my words carefully. This was not coming forth as easily as I had hoped.

She was patient as she lay there, her arms now free with hands above her head.

"Never did I ask Miss Ingram to marry me, nor would I. I do not love her or even like her. That announcement your cousin received and showed to you; it is nothing but a wicked device meant ultimately to trouble *me*. Blanche's behaviour towards you is inexcusable, but you must be assured that it is not you she aims to hurt. Upon the first evenings of her stay at

Thornfield, she could see the strong feelings I harbour for you and her jealousy was fierce. Anyone who observes us together can see what I feel for you."

My words earned a gentle smile.

My fingers stroked her cheek as I spoke, loving the feel of her. "Blanche learned from Arthur Eshton that you were gone to Gateshead, and as she is acquainted with your cousin Georgiana, she thought to carry off that engagement announcement trick. It was meant to damage us and make you despise me. Has she succeeded then? Hm?"

Jane shook her head slightly in the negative but said nothing.

"So, all talk of an engagement for Miss Ingram and I is pure rubbish. To be very honest, I hope to God I never see that woman again. Is this entirely clear with you?"

Jane nodded and continued to look at me seriously. She asked, "While I was away, and she was here with you, did you share private conversation? No, no, what I want to ask is this: did you and she meet privately? Intimately. Did you embrace her and... kiss her?"

My heartbeat staggered and I shut my eyes for a moment. Now it was I who was cornered. I swore to never lie to her, yet the temptation was so soon presented. She would know if I did and would then see in me a liar. I answered truthfully. "Yes. I did kiss her."

Jane's hands immediately fixed on my shoulders, pushing at me with all her might. Her attempts to push me away were nothing physically, but my heart ached for her as tears again spilled down the sides of her face.

"Please go!" she said, tears coming fast. Soon she ceased her futile efforts and covered her face with her hands. "My God, Edward, you are all pain to me. Please have some pity and release me." She was crying hard now.

I watched her for a time, whispering her name. Her chest heaved and shuddered but she cried quietly. Soon I lifted off of her and stood at the bedside, removed my jacket and waistcoat, and placed them on the back of a chair by the table. A handkerchief was found in my inner pocket, and I brought it to her.

"Jane, dry your tears. We must talk about this." She sat up and held the handkerchief over her eyes as she gently sobbed. I went to the table and found the teapot still reasonably hot, so I poured a cup with milk. "Sugar?" I asked.

Crying still, she gave me a 'sure, whatever' shrug, then weakly held up an index finger.

I stirred in a cube and brought the cup and saucer to her. "Come now, Jane," I said softly, sitting beside her on the bed. "Drink." With a shuddering exhalation that wracked her slight frame, she dried her face with the handkerchief and composed herself. She took the cup and saucer from my hands and drank, draining half. I turned to face her. She was the picture of a broken spirit; despondent countenance, red and tearful eyes, entirely fatigued.

"Finished now?" I asked.

"No," she whispered, shaking her head.

"Tell me. I want to know what hurts."

"Oh, why do you make me say it?" she said, her voice strained. "That night. The last time we were together. I said things to you. I did things! Then within no time you chose to be with her, as if our night together was nothing." Her tears began to fall afresh.

"Drink again," I said.

She sighed miserably and drained the remainder of the cup. I set it on the bedside table and turned again to her, taking her hand, but her defences were up and she rose from the bed. She went to the washbasin to pour from the ewer, splashed water over her face and dried with a towel, turning back to me with reddened, defeated eyes.

"Come here, Jane," I said from sitting at the bedside and held a hand out to her.

"No, Sir," she said in a firm, toneless voice. "I've had enough. I think you should leave my chamber now."

"I want you right here!" I directed, pointing to the floor before me. "Now."

Her hands smoothed her skirt and she walked slowly and cautiously to me, halting where I indicated.

I grasped her skirt on either side, allowing her the higher perspective, offering a perception of control. "Listen to me, Jane," I said softly to her. "Listen and believe what I tell you. What I did with Blanche was momentary, mindless nonsense. For me it was a parting and a gesture of finality; sort of an emphatic period on the end of a long-winded and interminably dull sentence. That kiss, as with our courtship altogether, was entirely devoid of any depth or meaning. She does not enchant me, does not excite me or interest me and for the most part never has."

"But she is beautiful."

"She has nothing above your beauty."

Jane sighed, "All men want to be partnered with Miss Blanche Ingram."

I tipped my head side to side, considering that. "Initially perhaps, I amongst them. She and I made a grand show for society, but our magic ended right there. If time with Blanche were a dance, then I paired with her expecting a thrilling tarantella, but what I found from day one is that she is capable of no better than a bumbling cancan. She is not the woman for me. Loneliness is capable of driving a person to all sorts of regrettable associations I am afraid to say."

Jane smiled and her posture loosened some, but she looked away, troubled still. I wanted her back, all of her, the way she was when I lay her down before the fire in the library, when she reached for me and had to have me.

"Jane, look at me," I said, my hands grasping her hips. "I desire only you. All the while you were gone was agony for me. I could not escape my loneliness for you. When you left my chamber the morning you went away, after our night in the library and in my bed, my heart desperately cried out for you. It did then, has done so since, and it does now." I paused as an exhilarating rush burst through me.

She noticed my surge and her eyes fixed on mine.

"I love you, Jane," I said, looking into her eyes. "Oh, how wonderful it feels to finally say it! I do love you. Every minute of the day and night, I love you... and no one else." I drew a sharp inhalation and smiled self-consciously. It was a poignant pleasure to splay out my most vulnerable sentiments to she who could master me so absolutely. "While you have me confessing my true heart I shall tell you something more, Miss Eyre. I've known I loved you since the day I met you."

Her tears spilled afresh. "When I felled your horse by the river."

"Yes. Then. I knew it then."

A smile spread across her lips, her hand rising to my shoulder, then to the high collar of my shirt and brushed my cheek. "Do you know that no one has ever said that to me in my life? You are the very first."

"I am sorry for the desolate life you knew before coming here. But know that as long as I am alive, Jane, you will be loved."

She was quiet for some moments, stroking my face, then said, "I love you, Edward. So much."

The words I longed to hear at last were said. I pulled her close to me. Here was my heaven.

She looked at me with concern. "Edward, may I ask this? What of Miss Ingram now? She continues to pursue you. Now that she has gone to considerable lengths to strike at you, will she not present herself in collection of her prize?"

I drew a deep breath. "Perhaps so. From what you tell me, she has a far differing interpretation than I of the word 'never.' However often it is repeated to her."

"Sorry?"

"She formally proposed that we marry. I answered 'never'. In fact I said it three or four times to my recollection." With my hands on Jane's hips, I pulled her close so that she stood between my feet and pressed my forehead to her. "Jealous thing."

Her fingers went through my hair. "If I kissed a handsome man, you would be jealous as well."

I nodded. Truer words were never before spoken. "If you kissed any man, I would be jealous," I replied, and she laughed at my hypocrisy. I shook her hips gently and said, "I love you. You are all I shall ever want in a woman. You must never doubt my love for you again."

She blushed. Her hand came up to my cheek and she asked, "Did I hurt you?"

To quote her from weeks past I replied, "I am tough. I could take it."

"Even while I was so heartbroken and furious, I missed you and thought of you constantly. I could not make myself stop."

I took her hand and drew her into my lap, wrapping my arms around her. My lips came to hers, lightly touching side to side, prolonging fulfilment. Then I kissed her. I cannot describe the pleasurable intensity of kissing her once again. Both her arms went around me firmly, and she returned my kiss with passionate energy. Having her back, all of her, I was once more rendered a complete entity; not the broken, yearning, anguished wretch of weeks past. I kissed her with depth, pulling her close, drawing her heat and breath into me. Like an enduring pain suddenly relieved, my fears sighed and groaned from deep within. This... this, was what I had awaited and wanted so badly.

I was ready and it was time. Nothing in my life ever felt as right as this. My arms held her close and gaze delved into hers. Kissing her lips, I said, "Jane. Marry me."

Her breathing was held and pupils dilated curiously. I smiled, knowing she was stunned considerably. A shiver came over her body. She was silent.

"Say you will marry me, Jane!" I entreated. "Say you will be my wife."

She pulled a deep breath and nearly spoke but then stopped. I continued looking into her eyes.

"Say something," I asked, becoming distressed.

"Ah... I do not quite know what to say."

"Do you doubt me?"

She nodded. "I believe that you love me, but I can not forget so easily what I've been feeling these past weeks. It was awful, the pain in my heart. I wanted to die."

"Please, Jane, forget what Blanche made you believe. It was meaningless, and so you must not waste time or energy on it."

"But I am all I have, Sir! I must protect myself."

"Edward," I corrected.

"Yes. Edward."

"My Jane, I will love you and protect you for as long as I live and be faithful to you always. I swear it. I must have you for my own! Please say that you will be mine."

She paused and I kissed her lips, cheek, neck; waiting, watching and listening to the fire crackle in the grate, loving to have her perched on my knee and my arms encircling her sweet body. She held me away and we looked at one another solemnly.

"Marry me, Jane," I again urged.

Smiles gradually brightened her face. "Yes," she said with a surprised laugh, and a shiver came over her again. "I will marry you, Edward. I will be your wife. If that is what you truly want."

My arms pulled her tightly to me. "Oh, God, Jane! It is! Oh, Christ in heaven, thank you," I said, my eyes stinging with tears. I kissed her lips, her face, again and again. "Jane, my God, Jane, I love you. I love you."

Her eyes were filling as well. We stared at each other in giddy amazement, wiping away tears. Both trembled in our smiling silence, taken with the sheer magnitude of our decision. Then I drew her mouth to mine and we kissed deeply, stirringly. After a time, our kisses became light and soft. We breathed, "I love you" again and again in our firm embrace.

"I will be a good husband to you, Jane. You will not be sorry."

"I know you will. But, you are sure of this?" she asked, releasing her embrace. She rose from my lap and stood before me. "I have nothing. I can bring nothing to our marriage. Only myself."

"It is all I want."

She paused. "I am eighteen."

"Yes, I know. Is that a problem?"

"Well, not if you see no trouble with it. But what of your friends? All of those guests you invited here? Whatever will they say?"

"Oh my love, I cannot imagine what petty, insular nonsense they already declare of me and the way in which I live, nor do I much care. I do know that Louisa Dent likes you. She actually encouraged me to propose marriage to you."

"Did she? Well, imagine that!"

"She did. Louisa said you are 'sweet' and was impressed that you bested Frederick Lynn at chess. And he, well, I did not care for his lascivious glances in your direction that night. And then there is Arthur Eshton. I think he is in love with you himself."

She smiled. "I like Mr. Eshton. He is a good friend to you."

"He is." Then I remembered something she said in my study earlier. "You say you've found cousins, and they want to visit with you tomorrow in Millcote. How did you come to contact one another?"

Jane settled down on my knee again, arms about my neck, and said, "On the night my aunt passed, her final words were to tell me of an uncle I never knew. His name is John Eyre, and he is my father's brother. Unmarried and childless, he lives in Madeira as the proprietor of a merchant enterprise. This John Eyre is apparently in possession of a modest fortune. He came to England in search of me some years ago, hoping to adopt me and make me his heir."

I mentally dissected that, imagining this man's age, whereabouts, wealth and solitary status. Did he have no friends or maybe an apprentice or a particular cause to name as beneficiary of his fortune? Must he travel to England to search for a niece he had never met? I supposed it was possible, yet my suspicion was piqued. My guess was that John Eyre had recently been informed of frail health and possibly was not long for this world.

"Go on," I urged.

"My uncle traced me as far as Gateshead where Aunt Reed told him that I was dead. She said I died of the typhus, during the outbreak at school when I was a child, and turned him away. He apparently left England greatly dejected."

"Good God how could she, this aunt of yours? To deny you a comfortable home and family? To instead leave you to God knows what fate, housed at a charity institution known widely for harsh treatment of its pupils? For what reason? Did she say?"

"My aunt disliked me and swore to never help me to prosperity."

"That is a rather pitiless judgment to hand down upon a child," I commented. "So with eternity before her, she suddenly became contrite?"

"It appears so. She provided my uncle's address and I wrote to him that very night, telling him of my whereabouts, schooling and employment. I did not expect to receive a response, not knowing whether he as yet resided in Madeira or if he was still alive for that matter. But a fortnight later, a letter in reply to mine arrived to Gateshead. John Eyre expressed his gratitude for my communication and informed me of three Eyre cousins here in England."

"Hang on," I said, catching a hitch in this information. "You have three cousins, and they are known to John Eyre. Why did he not come looking for them when he wanted an heir? Why did he go to such lengths to find you and then go away back to Madeira in disappointment?"

"That, Edward, is a question I hope to have answered in Millcote tomorrow. John Eyre it seems is on favourable enough terms with the three to notify each of my existence, but I would venture to say that there must be a negative twist to their kinship if he excluded them as possible heirs. A letter from a cousin soon followed. His name is St. John Rivers. His two sisters are called Mary and Diana."

Such a curious story this all made. "Intriguing, Jane. Tell me, where do your cousins currently reside?"

"West, near Preston. St. John is a vicar acquainted with our Mr. Wood here at Christ Church in Hay and is coming to visit him. He asked to meet with me. Diana, will accompany him."

I removed my look of dubiousness, took her hand and kissed it. "I am glad for you, Jane. An uncle and three cousins are a treasure indeed."

"Thank you, my love."

Marked protectiveness continued to congest my thoughts. Jane's cousins were senior to her and one of them was male; a mysterious vicar in a white neck-cloth. For unknown reasons I envisioned a wolf in sheep's clothing but of course said nothing to Jane. I lightly offered, "It would be my pleasure to accompany you in meeting with them."

"Oh, Edward," she gently protested. "I haven't much experience in making the acquaintance of strangers and so would prefer to go alone. I would do better unaccompanied for our initial meeting."

"As you wish," I conceded. Pressing the issue would seem suspicious to her and in all likelihood was entirely unnecessary. "And what of this St. John's school you mentioned tonight in the study? He offered to you a teaching position some distance from here did he?"

"Yes. St. John oversees a school for girls in his parish community. John Eyre mentioned to him my employment as a teacher, and so St. John volunteered in his letter to me that his pupils are in need of a schoolmistress. I was planning to apply for the situation when meeting with him tomorrow."

"Not any longer."

She smiled and blushed a little. "No. Not any longer."

I reached across the bed and lifted the pearl necklace. "I chose this for you. It hurt me that you left it behind."

She touched the pearls in my hand. "You looked around my bedchamber after I was gone."

"Indeed I did. I missed you and wanted to know that you were coming back. I wanted to be close to things that are yours, then found this."

"Leaving it behind was not an intentional slight, Edward. I did not feel this necklace was rightfully mine. Permanent separation from you seemed unavoidable, and it felt wrong to take it."

"Well. We must never be separated again, Jane. Never," I said, taking her hand and lacing our fingers together.

She looked at me seriously. "I know you felt it too; that it would be best if I left Thornfield. You said you must keep me from harm and wrong."

I sighed deeply. This conversation was veering into dangerous territory, so I employed a vigilantly practiced technique. I dissembled. "I said that because I considered myself unsuitable for you; too complicated for a fresh, young miss like yourself."

"And now?"

"Now I know I cannot live without you. Separation from you for a whole month obliterated any doubt of that. You love me and I love you. What else matters?"

She kissed me again. "There is much you have not told me of yourself, Edward. I know very little of your history."

"You need only know that I truly do love you. Listen only to me and to no one else. If you are told something that causes you to question me, then you must ask. I'll not lie to you."

She stood before me, studying my eyes, brushing raven curls away from my face. "All right," she agreed, then smiled archly. "I do have one question for you. You never told me, that night in the library, how old you are. Instead you skirted the question quite nimbly."

I sighed and scowled at her. "Will you change your mind about marrying me if I tell you?"

"Now that truly is ridiculous."

"All right. When is your birthday, Jane?"

"The twelfth of September."

"Then I am roughly nineteen and half years older than you. I will be thirty-nine in January. Satisfied?"

She smiled and bit her lower lip. "Satisfied? No, I am not. Not yet," she said, stepping closer to me, nudging my legs apart and standing between them.

My hands went to her skirt, around to her lower back, to the swell of her buttocks. "Jane. You promised that you would marry me and would be my wife. You understand what that means, do you not?"

"Tell me," she said. "Perhaps I do not."

"It means I am going to make love to you. After our wedding, that night, the next day... frequently."

"I know what it means," she said quietly. "I want you to take me to bed. I know you will make it wonderful."

"Oh, I will make you love it, Jane. Some men do not care whether their wives enjoy lovemaking, but I want you to desire it as much as I."

She lifted my face. Looking down at me, with her eyes the colour of her sage skirt, she was entrancingly beautiful; her hair, her clothes, her flawlessly creamy skin. In no way did I find her plain, and her beauty to me now was far from understated. "When you came into my study this evening," I said, "I thought you the loveliest, most desirable sight imaginable. I could not think. Almost could not breathe."

She gave me a self-satisfied smile. "This may be terribly prideful, Edward, but I made the decision not to appear before you again wearing a grey Lowood frock, with my hair pulled back in a twisted knot. To my understanding, you were betrothed to Miss Ingram. And after all you and I had said and done, I was angry, jealous and yearning for you still." She sighed and concluded, "A striking impression had to be made."

"Jane, I wanted you to come back to me. What you wore would not have mattered, but I do like this. You are so lovely, the desire of my eyes, and nice things suit you by nature."

"Edward," she said sensually. "Let me touch you. I've wanted to and have dreamed of it. Let me make it happen again."

"No. Not yet. You may as well know that you've agreed to marry a terribly selfish man, and there is something I must have from you first."

I reached down and lifted her skirts and petticoats, my hands on stockings behind her knees. I pressed my face to the material of her skirt and blouse as my fingers travelled upward. Her hands rested on my shoulders, then went into my hair as her breathing became audible, and my hands explored up her thighs to stocking tops where fingertips touched bare skin. She drew a sudden, convulsing breath and her hands became still. My fingers crept into her knickers and continued upward to bare hips, then cupped a firm buttock, grasping tightly and pulling her pelvis to my mouth.

"Edward..." she said, drawing short breaths.

"Jane. My Jane. I love you so," I whispered. "I need to touch you. Allow me."

Her hands became fists on my shoulders as I tightly gripped her smooth buttock while stroking the crease of her leg. She stiffened and gasped in anticipation as my fingers searched, touching soft hair.

"Relax, Jane. Do not tense."

Her breaths were drawn tight and stiff. I kissed the front of her skirt, fingers exploring soft skin of inner thigh, and I breathed deeply, inflamed by her stirring womanly scent through her clothes. My fingers turned upward to warmth, stroking hair. Had to have it, could wait no longer. I looked up at her as a single finger found hot, smooth wetness.

Her head flew back and she softly cried out, "Oh! Edward!" All of her body was taut as she swayed before me.

I removed my hands from her skirts and stood up, holding her trembling, slight body to mine and kissing her fervently. She had not the wherewithal to kiss me back. I lifted her in my arms and lay her on the bed. Unlacing her boots, I removed and placed them neatly on the floor, then climbed over her and kissed her. Her arms went tightly around my broad shoulders and she lifted up to me, licking and sucking my lips.

"Jane, I am so painfully hungry for you. I can hardly bear it."

With one hand, I reached down to her skirts and petticoats, battling the masses of material to get to her. She raised stockinged thighs around my legs as my fingers searched warmth beneath her knickers. I stopped kissing her and watched her eyes. They were on mine, her hands at my shoulders. Soft hair, heat, and then my fingers were right there. Her breathing was ragged and every muscle was strung taut.

"Relax, Jane. I will not hurt you. I love you."

She gave a short exhalation and her tension came down slightly. My middle finger lay into her wetness. Her back suddenly arched and fists gathered my shirt. She pulled in a sharp breath and held it.

"Breathe, Jane," I murmured softly. "Breathe through it and let the pleasure take you. Do not fight it."

Her back relaxed and hands loosened the material of my shirt. My fingers gently explored her. The sensation was driving me quite out of my mind, but her pleasure was my only objective.

"Edward. Oh. This is incredible."

I settled down at her side, my head propped in hand and watched her with fascination. The sight of her enduring my ministration was potently erotic; even more so, oddly, because she was fully dressed. Something about her high-necked blouse with lace collar, buttoned lace cuffs, the masses of skirting material and petticoats - all the while my fingers pleasuring her slick centre. I drank in her flushed skin and aroused eyes; the way she wet her lips and breathed unevenly. I wanted to feel more of her and inserted a finger. She gasped and arched consequentially, whereupon I met firm resistance.

"Mmm. My beautiful virgin bride," I spoke softly. "Do you like this, Jane?"

She smiled and raised her hands above her head, settling her arms back. She was much less tense now. "It is good, Edward," she breathed. "I love it. I love you."

"I could do this to you until morning," I told her. "Have you any idea how beautiful you are, Jane? You are entirely irresistible to me. I've missed you so very much and spent hours in the night, thinking about you and dreaming of doing this."

"Edward. Please. I cannot take much more of this."

I looked down on her fevered, suffused skin. "But you must. You are mine, Jane, and this is what I want of you."

Her hands began to wring together and warm wetness strained against my fingers, wanting more.

"Am I all pain to you? Hmm, Jane? You said I am all pain to you." And I glided a finger over her centre of pleasure.

"Oh!! Edward! Oh my God. Oh."

"Am I? Am I pain to you then?" I did it again, smiling down on her surges of pleasure that were as easy as a slight touch of expertise.

"No. You are not... You... you can pitch me down into depths of misery... Oh, my... But then... You love me like... Like I am sure it is a dream... Oh!! Yes!! Oh my God... Keep doing that," she breathed.

"I hate that I caused you misery. Does this make it better, love?"

"Oh!! Oh! yes! It does... And I care nothing for where you learned this but am so glad you did."

I laughed. "It was all in preparation to please you, my sweet young bride. Once we are married I shall to do this with my tongue."

For a moment she looked at me wide-eyed. "Oh, Edward. Oh, yes. More... please."

I read her excitement; her breathing, writhing and blushing skin. She was ready for me to release her. Catching her earlobe between my teeth I asked, "Shall I?"

"Edward, do it... make it happen... make me climax. I need it."

"Do you love me, Jane?" I asked, my finger lightly circling her most sensitive place. "Tell me you do."

"Yes, yes I do... from the first day... by the river... could never keep my eyes from you... oh, yes... so in love with you... playing chess... wanted you to kiss me so much... oh, Edward, oh my God... The poem... I could not hide my... oh, my desire for you."

"Ready for me?"

"Yes. Please..."

And I set about softly, rhythmically drawing her along the ascent. Her body tensed, every muscle straining. Arms above her head, her hands clenched into tight fists. Her head went back and breaths became miniscule gasps. Trembling ensued. I loved every second of watching her. Such a beautiful, natural sight, having the woman I loved in the throes of pleasure before me, mastered entirely by my touch. Such gifts we as humans are given. Simply awe-inspiring. When her tension was wrought to its peak, I held my own breath, knowing she was about to cross over, and then she did. Those exquisite first few seconds of climax quaked through her body, and I could feel delicious contractions in her wetness. I drew out her pleasure until all tension was gone.

She opened her eyes and gazed at me with amused adoration. "I really love you," she said smiling.

"Oh you only love me because I can do that."

"No, I love you for many reasons," she said, laughing, "but that is one of them. Umm, with your tongue?"

I took my fingers from her wetness, brought them to my mouth and licked them. "Yep."

She laughed. "Good Lord, what have I agreed to marry?"

"It is too late, love. You cannot refuse me now. This taste reminds me that there is something I must fetch for you from the kitchen. Are you hungry?"

"Yes," she said, stretching out on the bed. "I think I am."

"Good. Stay here. I shall be back shortly." Before leaving, I kissed her tenderly and added, "I love doing those things to you, you know. Once we are married, I cannot imagine that we will ever get out of bed."

"Mmm, nor can I," she said, reluctantly releasing me, then asked, "When do you want to....um, do it?"

Seconds later I caught her meaning. "When do I want our wedding to be?" I clarified, laughing effusively.

She laughed at herself. "Yes."

"What is today? Tuesday. How about Friday?"

"That soon?"

"Yes, that soon."

I thought of my answer as I descended the stairs. I did not want to delay for a number of reasons. There were plenty of individuals who posed a threat, and the sooner and quieter this was done the better. In all likelihood, I was luring Jane into a bigamous, defrauded union, but I had already grappled with that formidable quandary long and hard. I must have her, at all costs, and that was an end to it. There was a single glimmer of hope driving me; the hope of extricating myself from the bonds of my first marriage. Seeking to marry Jane was the path I chose, and I would give myself entirely unto it.

There was Blanche, who would no doubt commit any vicious act to disrupt my marriage to another. And there was Richard Mason who was still in the general area; Leeds he said was his destination after Thornfield, and his reappearance at an inopportune time could be disastrous. Then of course there was Bertha and Grace only just upstairs. Finally, I could not disregard Mrs. Fairfax who was abundantly clear in expressing her disapproval of my interest in Jane over Blanche.

No delays. This must be done posthaste. Then I would nervously wait to receive correspondence from solicitor Henri Breault in Spanish Town, Jamaica, and depending upon the findings of his investigation, Jane and I would either remain at Thornfield or bolt forthwith to the continent.

Three days until we wed. I must visit Mr. Wood at the church to make arrangements. Then a day in Millcote would be necessary to obtain the marriage license, our rings and, of course, a suitable dress for Jane. All other arrangements could wait. The wedding must be accomplished before the wolves came any closer and snatched my bride away.

'I am an army of one,' my mind declared. 'Just try to damage us! Try to take my Jane away from me. You will all see what a violent Goddamned son-of-a-bitch I can be!'

Silence prevailed in the entrance hall.

'Settle down, Edward,' Conscience advised. 'Let her love surround you like a shroud of tranquillity. She waits for you.'

Her voice wandered through my thoughts. "Let me touch you. I have wanted to and dreamed of it," she said.

To the kitchen for treacle tart and custard. Tonight, we would enjoy life's pleasures.

Chapter 26

In the kitchen I found Leah working by lamplight, quietly scouring a roasting pan at the sideboard. She looked over her shoulder as I entered and grinned.

"Ah, you are back, Sir. Did a nice cuppa help Miss Eyre endure your brutal chastisements then?"

Remembering the tray, I snapped my fingers. "Blazes. The tea set is yet upstairs."

"Oh, set it on the table in the gallery if you please, Mr. Rochester, and I will see to it. Is Miss Eyre feeling well enough after her tiresome journey?" she asked with her back to me. "Will she not come down to the kitchen for treacle and custard?"

I stepped near her and said, "No, I think she would prefer to wait for me upstairs in her chamber. I am happy to announce to you that Miss Eyre is shortly to become Mrs. Rochester. You are the first to know."

Leah whirled to face me, drying her hands on her apron. "Oh Sir! I knew it! Did I not tell John only yesterday that it was Miss Eyre you would have and not that hoity-toity Miss Ingram, if you will pardon my saying so, Sir." She shook my hand in both of hers. "Many congratulations to you both. I wish you great happiness!"

"Thank you, Leah. I predict great happiness. Now, about your treacle tart..."

"Yes of course. A celebratory pudding will it be?" she laughed. "I shall arrange a tray with a pitcher of custard and meantime you must select a bottle of champagne from the cellar."

This would make an odd combination for an engagement toast no doubt, but why not? Such a momentous occasion would be nothing without champagne. She took a candle down from a sconce above the draining board and handed it to me.

"There are two flutes waiting to be put away. I will arrange a fresh tray and just dash out for a small spray of lilac from the garden."

When I returned from the cellar all was prepared. Leah adjusted spoons and serviettes so they were arranged just so.

"Can you manage it all, Sir?"

"No trouble, Leah. I daresay you'd be surprised at what I can manage."

She eyed me suspiciously. "I must beg your pardon, Mr. Rochester."

"Nothing, never mind, " I said smirking and turned to the pantry door.

Leah followed. "Yes, well in any case, I am so pleased that Thornfield will become a family home once again. Miss Jane is a lovely girl and quite a befitting choice for you and for the Hall."

"Thank you. I could not agree more."

She went solemn suddenly. "Please, I must suggest you relate the news to Mrs. Fairfax gently, Sir. Her heart is set on Miss Ingram as your bride you see. It has been for years. She will accept your decision in time, have no fear of that, but I do often worry for her constitution. Alice is not entirely well."

I shook my head resignedly. "I know she is not. But as for her disappointment, I must say that Mrs. Fairfax's generation bewilders me. Their idea of marriage is more a partnership of financial affairs than sentiments of the heart. Father, you will recall, was the same way."

Leah was employed as a servant at Thornfield since I was a young man, first hired when Rowland inherited the estate some seventeen years ago. She and I occasionally fell into familiar conversation on staff come and gone, local gossip and occasionally on Father or Rowland, though a respectful deference was always maintained.

"Your father was ever taken with matters of finance to be sure, Sir, and your brother as well. Demonstrative, soft-hearted men they were not," she reflected.

"And look at where it got them. I strive to learn from observed mistakes as well as my own," I said resting the tray on the table. This table...

"Well, Alice feels a personal duty to maintenance of class order and becomes starry-eyed imagining a regal, socialite mistress for Thornfield Hall. I cannot imagine why she does, since her good friend, Mrs. Boone at Ingram

Park, is quite possibly the most harassed and discontented housekeeper in all of Yorkshire."

"Yes, I can imagine the time Blanche and Lady Ingram must give their staff," I said. "My concept of a wife is altogether different from what one might expect. Never have I been won over by showy displays of arrogance and wealth. And so Miss Ingram and I have proven, time and again, to manifest characters incapable of existing in combination."

Leah smiled. "Yes, Mr. Rochester. And this is why I am confident that Miss Eyre will bring you the happiness you deserve."

"She already does," I replied quietly.

Leah caught her breath and beamed with shimmering eyes. "Well, here we are," she said, clearing her throat and lifting the heavily laden tray. "Go. Share this magnificent feast with your lovely bride-to-be."

"I will," I said and left Leah with a conspiratorial grin.

Climbing the staircase, I returned with my cache upstairs. Jane opened the door for me. She was in the process of brushing her long, chestnut hair, and I stopped in the doorway to stare at her hip-length glossy tresses, admiring their smooth waviness after having been done up in plaits. Still with the pain of her absence fresh in my mind, I absorbed her reality with a longing that verged on delirium. I glanced at her bed; my fingers, her silken wetness; her head back, the tendons of her neck straining as pleasure took her. Whether brushing her hair was intended to be a seductive act I could not say for her, but the dazzling simplicity of it resumed my arousal like a combustive burst.

Innocently looking over the tray items, she smiled eagerly and asked, "What is all this you've brought?"

"Provisions, my love," I said, my mind playing out images involving protracted hours of passion that were anything but innocent.

She smiled playfully and came near to kiss me. "The man I love has brought me treacle tart and custard. Can life be any better?" She collected the tea set, leaving the table cleared.

I set the dessert tray down and encircled her waist, taking her in my arms. "It does get better. Every day of our lives together will be better than the one before. I will make it so for you, Jane. I promise you that." She kissed me with such depth that my knees nearly buckled. When she released me, I held her shoulders to steady myself. "Thank you for saying yes," I whispered.

Her arms were around my shoulders and she softly kissed my lips. "What would you have done if I refused your proposal?" she asked.

"Never would happen," I murmured, a hand wandering down her thigh. "I can be most persuasive. And persistent."

She smiled. "Yes, so I've found."

"You know, I cannot tell you how gorgeous this is," I said, lifting her thick hair. I held her close and lay light kisses on her cheek, my breath near her ear. "My lovely young bride."

Her fingers went to my throat to undo the buttons of my shirt collar.

"Wait," I said. "Wait just a moment. Let me take this tea set out. Leah will be expecting it." I opened the chamber door and went out into the gallery, setting the tea tray on the buffet table.

In turning back to Jane's door, I heard another door unclose far down the gallery. It shut again and then came the metallic sound of a bolt locking into place. Lantern light glowed at the far end of the gallery, flickering and moving amongst the deepest shadows. I glanced back to Jane's chamber with hunger to return to her, but my ear caught the sound, far along the gallery, of a deep and onerous sigh. Duty seemed to require attendance, so I reluctantly set off toward it down the gallery.

Standing against the wall near the entrance to the back stairs was Grace Poole, wearing a singularly weary and dejected expression.

I approached out of the shadows and asked low and edgy, "Grace, is everything all right?"

"Sir. We are having a terrible time tonight. Missus has quite driven me to the end of my rope," she replied, her voice and posture fraught with dejection. Grace was never one to complain. She offered nothing further until asked.

"Well? What is she doing up there then?"

"She insists upon 'going home' as she calls it. She knows that her brother was here and wants him to take her back to Jamaica. She cries almost constantly in the night, Sir, and I quite simply need a rest from it. She goes on vehemently and constantly through all night, then by morning she is like the living dead once again."

I sighed wearily, recalling Dr. Carter's prediction for Bertha's decline. "She was doing so well."

"Lately, when out on the roof walking at night, she has been quiet. She smiles and seems to be listening to, I don't know, **something**. God knows what. At such times she can be remarkably clear minded. But inside her room these last few wet and chilly nights," she said, shaking her head in exasperation, "she cries and pleads with me to open the door and help her. To get a letter off to this Richard or send a messenger after him so that he can take her home. During the day she is tolerable, either somnolent or entirely unresponsive. The differences are quite dramatic."

I glanced at the door to the north tower and remembered Carter's parting words, 'The onus for her care falls entirely on you, Mr. Rochester.' This was truly the very last bloody thing I wished to contend with at the moment, considering the assortment of pleasures awaiting me nearby, but I was under hard-line obligation, and Grace did look entirely at the end of her rope.

"Shall I go up to sit with her awhile?" I sombrely asked.

"No, Mr. Rochester," she replied firmly. "She's been swearing and ranting fiercely about you all evening. She says you keep her imprisoned here, you stole her from this Kerry person she speaks of, other things... pure venom. No. I urge you not to go up there, Sir."

"Is she locked inside her room?"

"Oh, yes. She may harm herself but nothing else. I am sorry, but I needed to get away."

"You were quite right, Grace. You need respite. I've considered giving you an extended leave from your duties and bringing in a replacement for a time," I said sighing heavily. "I will send out a request to the Grimsby Retreat tomorrow morning."

"Thank you, Sir. What I need at the moment is a...," she started and despondently looked away, shaking her head.

"A drink," I finished for her. "Go, Grace. Go unwind and have some time to yourself. Only be sure to lock up when you return to the north tower tonight."

"Certainly, Sir," she said exhaustedly and turned to descend the back staircase.

I remained there some time, hands deep in pockets, sensing my euphoria of minutes ago vanishing by the second. I looked at the ancient oak door knowing that Bertha was up there, stalking about and hating me savagely in her maniacal state. I leaned forward and brought my hands to my knees, staring at the matting beneath my boots, my mind clawing for the answer to extrication. How was I to live here with my bride, waiting for that damned letter to arrive from Jamaica and watching this situation with Grace and Bertha spin out of control? I could not have this! I could not subject Jane to the proximity of such danger any longer. And I could not hope to build a marriage under that malignant presence hovering only a stone's throw away. What to do about Bertha?

Ferndean. Yes, she must be relocated. The next question was when to do it. I exhaled loudly, thinking. When could I move Bertha out of Thornfield without raising suspicion? Also, Ferndean needed work and at the very least a few days of preparation before it could be inhabitable. Arrangements must begin straight away. Christ, another assignment to be tackled on the morrow.

My mood had plummeted from sweet exhilaration down to the abysmal. A twisting, warping tempest was whipping up, brewing remotely within me. It whirled and spiralled, intermingling with a much pleasanter but equally persistent storm. The latter was more an ache in the pit of my stomach, one that began in my study, with grey green eyes consuming me and daring me across my desk. All surged into being, ebbed and flowed quietly, then raged undeniably, backing away but ever-present and unshakable. My body screamed for release, my heart wailing for that ultimate intimacy.

My lusty appetite for one woman was now soured by enmity towards another. Aggressiveness had seeped into my core and quaked deep within so that sharing further intimacy with my lovely Jane may now be conspicuously bereft of the gentleness and tender touch she deserved. Therefore it simply was out of the question. Intuitive as Jane was with me, she would sense my altered mind immediately. Best that I join her for our champagne dessert, bid her a good night and then return to my chamber where my lust and I could go it alone. I pulled myself upright and clambered to take on a facade of blissful contentment; something that had come so naturally not twenty minutes ago. Jane was waiting.

"Come on, Edward," I said to myself. "This is the happiest time of your life. She said yes!"

An inner voice echoed from within my heart's tempest, 'Oh, sure she said yes. You are a better thespian than even you expected; defrauded, lying, selfish wretch!'

"Oh, God, what am I doing to her?" I asked the gallery's darkness. My certainty in deciding to marry Jane slipped. I fought doubt, barring it obstinately. Simultaneously I crushed back sexual aggression and turned toward Jane's chamber.

I entered the room and found her sitting at the bedside, perusing the little volume *A Selection of English Poetry*. Our feast was spread on the table with two places set facing one another. Unaware of my polluted transfiguration, Jane came to me with a contented smile, taking my hands. I returned her smile but something in it was clearly amiss causing hers to promptly fade away.

"Come," I said, ignoring her sudden gravity and led her to the table where I uncorked champagne and poured. She quietly took the flute set before her. Frustrated with myself, I crashed the bottle down on the table. I could not have this! Not after all that was said and done here tonight. In a matter of hours, we had come such a long way together and this separation of minds was unacceptable.

"No, Jane," I said and held out a hand to her. "Please, come here."

She came and stood before me. I patted my thigh whereby she gathered her skirts to sit across my lap.

"No," I said again, regarding her with hard-set features.

She knew what I wanted. She reached and touched my cheek, then smoothed my furrowed brow, presently hitching her skirts to throw a leg over mine, straddling my thighs. I fluffed her petticoats so that nothing separated us but knickers and trousers. Underneath all of that material, I grasped her bottom and pulled her close. All was done without a word. She leant over to retrieve her serving of treacle tart and a champagne flute. She tasted from the spoon but then set it down decidedly, her hands coming up to my neck. Her thumbs stroked my jaw.

"Are you all right?" she asked.

I nodded, hardly trusting myself to speak.

"You left this room one man and came back quite another."

I lifted my serving of tart and poured a generous helping of custard over it. Jane took the bowl from me and set it on the table. I released a petulant sigh.

"Tell me what is wrong," she said.

Still I remained silent.

"Remember that I can read you, Edward. Something happened out there in the gallery. Something about...," she said, her eyes narrowing, "...mmm, not something new. Something that has troubled you for some time. Am I wrong?"

I looked up into her eyes and silently asked, 'You will leave me. Won't you?' And I felt my eyes fill as both my hands went under her warm hair behind her neck, fingers interlacing, and I brought her forehead to mine. Her hair fell around her shoulders, and her sweet soap and water scent filled me to intoxication. It was some time before I dared speak.

Finally I whispered, "Jane, please. Tell me you love me," with desperation thick in my voice. "Promise you will not leave me. I need you more than you know."

She looked at me seriously, wary of my evasiveness yet touched by my dependence. As was her wont, she set aside questioning and chose to comfort. Her hands lifted my face and she kissed over my eyes, forehead and cheeks. I asked myself how I had existed for so many lonely years without such loving touch. She whispered, "I love you" softly and repeatedly. Her words and touch healed me.

She leaned back and looked at me. "Better now?"

"Yes. Much better." I took a champagne flute and handed it to her. "Let us toast our engagement. To love and a life of peaceful happiness," I said.

Jane assented with a single nod. We clinked glasses and sipped. She set her glass down on the table and took her bowl, licking the spoon.

"I simply love custard," she said. "At Lowood, we were allowed it once each year on Christmas Day. The few girls who remained at school during holidays anticipated it all year. There were only about twenty pupils and teachers who stayed behind while all others went to relatives or friends for the holiday. After becoming a teacher myself, I was admitted into their Christmas custard secret."

I smiled at her innocence. "Oh? And what is your secret, Jane?"

"Well," she said, tasting custard and tart, "all Lowood students and staff were forbidden sweets. Mr. Brocklehurst as yet held much influence over the school's treasurer, and subsequently cook's foodstuff allotments, keeping careful watch over our meals and servings. He felt it his responsibility to mortify our bodies to save our souls, you see. But on Christmas Day, once church services were dismissed and he went home for a grand supper with his wife and daughters, Lowood's typical rations were prepared. But in Miss Temple's rooms however, milk, eggs and sugar for custard were brought out of hiding. She managed to smuggle them in herself and in ample quantities during the preceding days. Teachers and older girls helped measure and stir as the little ones watched. Better than presents it was; both enjoying our custard and foiling Brocklehurst's dogmatic rule if only in one small way."

I watched her relish this simple pleasure, not wishing to say that I was given custard with most every Sunday dinner as a child. I smiled, thinking of the life of ease and indulgence that lay ahead for her following years of little more than struggle and deprivation.

We conversed for the next hour or more, on family mostly. She told me of her cousins at Gateshead; the societal debutante Georgiana and the convent-destined Eliza, and also of cousin John Reed's death (a suicide as it turned out) after leading his mother into near financial ruin. She related the little of what she could remember of her Uncle Reed and shared what sparse details she knew of her parents.

"My mother was a Reed," Jane said, sipping her champagne. "I am told the Reeds were a considerably well-to-do family some years ago. But when my mother married a poor clergyman, her family disowned her, all except for her brother who was most fond of her. After both my parents died, he took me in, and his wife was most displeased. She did not like me from infancy."

"Surely she did not tell you that herself?"

Jane nodded. "Oh yes, she did. She said I was 'a whining, pining little thing' and was angered that her husband lavished more attention on me than he did his own children. Servants at Gateshead who knew my mother say that Sarah Reed was always jealous of her husband's close kinship with his sister."

I smiled, thinking of where I was and what I was doing whilst this was happening. Twenty-ish? Those were good days, but they were verging upon disaster.

As the clock downstairs struck another hour, I told Jane of my family, or rather the complete lack thereof. All were now dead, including aunts and uncles on both sides. Some cousins existed, or so I assumed, but their precise names and whereabouts were unknown to me.

I shared with her my recollections of my mother, who existed radiantly in my memory as a female version of myself with the same jetty, wavy hair and same colour eyes. I inherited her love of nature and remembered her as a loving, vibrant, patient woman who laughed frequently and hugged me often. Rowland was ever distant with our mother and would resist her embraces, which hurt her I knew.

"What happened to your mother?" Jane asked.

"My mother died when I was a child. She expected a baby for the third time when I was five years old, but the long anticipated Rochester daughter was stillborn. Then a fourth came almost directly afterwards; another boy. He lay breach, and the doctor could not turn him. For many hours my mother struggled, lost considerable blood, became exhausted and could try no more. Then it was finished. Both died in childbirth," I said flatly. "Those details were not told to me until many years later, when I was quite a grown man."

"Oh. I am sorry, Edward. Do you remember much of that time?"

I sighed, thinking back. "Some, yes. Only that she was there one day and gone the next. Our servants cried and hugged me often as I recollect. Father left Thornfield for several months following the funerals, travelling to the continent I suppose, trying to ease his own pain. I was left behind and very lonely for her. She loved me." I recalled my mother's lilting voice as she spoke to me and her skipping step as we walked in the gardens and meadows together. "Her laughter made Thornfield a home, Jane. This place was so changed after she was gone. It went lifeless, cold and dreary. The place had no heart without her." I lifted Jane's hands and kissed them. "Until you came."

She smiled, rosiness brightening her cheeks. "Tell me about your brother," she asked. "You've mentioned him to me as a rather haughty, pontifical man. Mrs. Fairfax said that he is deceased nearly ten years."

"Correct," I said, sipping champagne. "Rowland makes for an interesting story. You see, Father handed Thornfield over to him when he came of age, though Father of course remained in residence as overseer of the estate. Rowland had in no way proven his reliability nor, shall we say, his *sobriety* for such an enterprise. I was away from home at this point."

"Sobriety? Rowland was a..." and her voice lowered to a whisper, "he was a drunkard?"

"No, Jane. Wine and spirits were only the beginning for my brother. His tastes preferred the more exotic. As far back as I can remember, Rowland represented the epitome of self-indulgent behaviour and felt that it was his right to help himself to all of the world's pleasures. This is what comes of being raised entirely without discipline."

"Why was he never disciplined? Where was your father's regulation of his behaviour?"

"My love, as the sole heir to a considerable family fortune, Father saw leniency as befitting for his first-born. He was far tougher on me, and I subsequently learned an appreciation of right from wrong; better than my brother anyway. Rowland was all recklessness and conceit as a young man with no ability to foresee consequence. He drank heavily from adolescence, and I know for a fact that he smoked opium fairly regularly by the time he was twenty. Then he sustained a riding injury in his early twenties resulting in chronic shoulder pain, and the local physician supplied him with indiscriminate supplies of morphine for years afterward."

Shocked she asked, "And what did your father say of this?"

"Nothing. Ian was blind and deaf to Rowland's faults. Always was."

Jane considered that. "Your brother never married?"

"He was set to marry the daughter of a German viscount, but as the wedding day approached, she instead chose to abscond with a lover; her ladies' maid as rumour had it."

Jane stared at me. "You are making that up!" she said and licked her spoon, riveted.

"I am not. God's honest truth," I said and drained my champagne, then refilled. "So, here we had Rowland, humiliated upon great expense incurred and gentry over the entire county invited to a wedding that never happened. What did he do? He took himself a lover as well; someone he would never deign to actually marry but who assuaged his wounded pride well enough."

"Oh my. Who?"

"The kitchen maid."

"What? Here? His servant?" she asked, utterly taken aback.

I nodded. "The lowest of the low. I never saw her myself but by all accounts she was very beautiful. And very young."

Jane cringed. "How young?"

"Fourteen."

Her jaw dropped. "Stop it!"

I shook my head. "I only tell you all of this since as a Rochester you should know our family background beyond the dull stories behind portraits in the gallery and on the drawing room walls. So to continue, my dear brother at age thirty-three was enjoying a not-so-discreet liaison with his young servant girl who understandably became completely besotted with her master. It lasted for many months so I am told, as she had him thoroughly beguiled with her favours. Unfortunately the silly child hoped for a marriage proposal."

"Oh, I see disaster coming..." Jane said, taking a sip of champagne.

"It did," I nodded. "She foolishly imposed a very weak ultimatum to which he responded by sacking her and ordering her off the premises. But knowing his habits, she reappeared one evening after his customary three or four post-prandial whiskies accompanied by doses of narcotics strong enough to drop a horse. She interested him in a little love-making for old time's sake, and in the middle of it his heart seized."

"My God!" she said, staring at me. "Dead?"

"As a post."

After a few moments she asked, "How did your father take this?"

"It killed him. Rowland was his favourite and his best. Father suffered a stroke that left him all but paralysed and he was dead within a month."

"Oh. My," Jane said with a gulp. "Poor Mrs. Fairfax. She was present at Thornfield during that time. I can only imagine her fits of anxiety."

"Leah and John were here as well. The Hall had a much larger staff in those days, and they were a good group, much like family. Together they coped until I was called home by Father's solicitor, Alistair Blakely."

"Where were you during all of this?"

"Travelling. I believe I was in the West Indies at the time," I vaguely replied. "I was not in attendance for either funeral. Both were done quickly and quietly with little fuss and no public mention. Mrs. Fairfax was given the task of sending out cards to friends and business associates announcing both Ian's and Rowland's passing as well as my return to the estate."

"How completely tragic," Jane reflected. And we were silent, listening to nothing but the Hall's occasional creaks. Then she smiled faintly. "Your brother died in the middle of it?"

"That is what the constable told Father," I replied matter-of-factly.

She tried to contain her mirth. "Rowland Rochester, the Master of Thornfield Hall, this pompous and imperious, holier-than-thou individual you've described to me, in actuality died drunk and drugged while bedding his fourteen year old kitchen maid mistress?"

I shook my head. "No. There was no bed involved. They did it in on the kitchen table."

She burst into riotous laughter. I smiled as well. It **was** funny. I had laughed about it countless times myself.

"So that is the story of how you came to inherit all of this," she said, glancing about the room.

"Extraordinary, is it not?"

Jane nodded. "It is. But tell me, Edward, what would have become of you had your brother lived? If Thornfield remained his?"

I sighed, knowing where my home would be; in Jamaica, leaving Bertha behind in that hilltop house with an attendant while I travelled the world in search of comfort as I had done these past eleven years. But instead I said, "Oh who can say, Jane? Perhaps I would have gone into the priesthood."

A second burst of laughter echoed in the room, and her hands flew up to her mouth. "I do so enjoy absurdity!" she giggled.

My arms went around her. "Are you put off on marrying a Rochester after hearing that tale?"

"No," she said, giggling still. "As long as you have no story more outlandish than that one."

I made no reply to that.

She ran a finger along the rim of her bowl and brought sticky sweetness to her lips. "Tell me something, Edward. Men take lovers, mistresses, whatever they wish to call them. How is it that a baby does not result more often?"

"It does if both are not careful. There are ways of avoiding it."

"And I am guessing that you are well versed in such methods," she said, gazing at me knowingly. "You have made love to a number of women?"

"Some," I replied cautiously.

"Does it hurt?"

"What? Hurt? Hurt whom?" I asked, feigning innocence. "Why would anyone do it if it hurt?"

"You know what I mean, Edward. Will it hurt for me? In the beginning?"

"I hope not," I said, wrapping my arms around her tightly. "I cannot say to be entirely honest. I am told it can be painful the first time but have no experience from which to speak. No woman has ever had me as her first."

Jane smiled. "Well, then. This is something we shall discover together." She laid her hands on my shoulders and kissed me, her thighs tightening around mine. My arms closed around her and she slowly kneaded her soft warmth against me.

"Jane," I said, grasping her hips to stop her. "Come now. It is late and I must leave you."

"Why must you?"

"This is no place for me at the moment. Besides, I have work to finish tonight. Now off!"

"Edward," she said, looking at me intently. "Stop withholding from me. If you do want me for your wife as you say, then you must learn to share all of yourself with me."

I inhaled deeply. "You really must listen to me now, Jane! It is best that I go. I am feeling very little tenderness and do not wish to frighten you. Rather aggressive to be honest. It would be best if I went to my own chamber, so please, stop that!"

She did not. "What for? Tell me."

"Jane!" I barked with exasperation. "My excitement is painful! I will leave you now to go where I can release my tension alone, without fear of saying or doing something to frighten you. Is that direct enough for you?"

Comprehension dawned on her features. "Edward. Please. Let me watch you."

I released a stifled laugh. "No!"

She became serious. "There is nothing about you that could be distasteful to me. You need not fear driving me away. If it is you and is honest, then I want it. This is not a battle between us!" she said insistently. "Teach me, and I will accept what you teach. That is what you fear, is it not? You fear my rejection. What a fine way to begin a marriage."

"Jane, my true self is not always as attractive as you seem to think."

"Then show me, because all of what I see is beautiful. Not everything is your responsibility, Edward. If I am your love and your best earthly companion, then hand over decisions to me for a time. Let go of restraint." She glanced to the bed. "I did it for you not long ago."

I regarded her nervously. The last time I knew total acceptance was our night in the library when she asked that I show her the way to touch me. My excitement surged again upon the very thought. A release so powerful had not happened for me since... since possibly ever! Mistresses and self-gratification are about equivocal as years taught me. They relieve the ache, but the emptiness and hunger remains.

I said, "True passion coupled with loving touch has no substitute , so I find with you, Jane. I am afraid of sullying that."

"You cannot," she said.

"Would you like to take a wager on that?"

"What? You want your five pounds back? Not a chance," she said and purposefully squirmed down against me, sending a shock wave through my body. An involuntary cry of profanity escaped my lips. I was appalled with myself.

"Jane. I did not mean to say that. Accept my apology."

"Tell me what it means," she asked, her skin becoming flushed with arousal.

"So curious you are! If you must know, it is a coarse term for 'making love'. Do not use it."

"Oh. I see," she said, smiling interestedly. "Edward, you are going to stay here. I did not resist you tonight, and you are obliged to give the same to me. I want the debt repaid now."

"No," I said firmly. "Now get off."

She continued to roll her hips against me, breathing hotly about my ear and unbuttoning my shirt. "I want to know all of you, Edward. Show more to me. Give it now."

My resistance was falling to pieces. 'I can manage this,' I thought hazily. 'Swear no more and remain gentle with her.' I breathed deeply, taking in the erotic pleasure of her body working mine as she unbuttoned slowly and deliberately. Her hands came to the dark hair of my chest, fingertips exploring and becoming lost in tactile sensation. Taking a more passive attitude, I brought an arm up and put my hand down the back of my shirt, eyes shut, sipping champagne, sighing and groaning as Jane gently and sensuously teased me along.

When I reopened my eyes, I found her watching me, captivated by my arousal. She came forward and kissed me deeply, her hands into my hair, pulling my mouth to hers. She turned to the table and took the pitcher of custard, sank her fingers deep and brought them dripping to my lips. I licked and sucked them greedily. She watched, her face all lustiness, and licked drips of custard from my chest.

All of this was rather more than I could tolerate. I strove to maintain gentleness and passivity, really I did. But the night already held too much. My loneliness with waiting for her, elation upon her sudden appearance, poignant arousal, pain of her spurning me, exhilaration and promises of love, the thrill of proposing to her, and then, the dashing of my euphoria as dismal reality crashed in. Now this. My mood had been swinging wildly, and rationality was now cast into the dust. As passion rushed, her restrictive clothing irritated me exponentially.

Lust fought for full sway. 'She wants it all? Give it to her then!'

"Fucking corset! Take this off!" I snarled.

Now firmly beyond control, I grasped her hair, pulling her head back and heaved my breath into her neck, biting and sucking her skin. I had warned her. This was not my fault now. All my body shook as she obediently unbuttoned her blouse. My fingers went to the buttons to speed her progress but were useless with trembling. The blouse came away and I tossed it away to the empty chair. My hands went to her back to undo corset hooks, eyes and laces. It came free and was tossed aside as well. Her filmy white camisole remained; the swell of her breasts and rigid nipples beneath. My hands went around to her back, beneath the material, frantically absorbing her smooth skin, the feel of her spine, ribs, and scapula, maddeningly fighting to keep myself from letting go completely. I brought my lips to her neck and roughly kissed and licked, feeling shivers come over her body.

My arms went tightly around her, kissing her mouth hungrily. I took the hem of her camisole and lifted it over her breasts, needing at very least to look if not caress and squeeze. We heaved and groaned, delighting in the sensation of our unclothed chests, arms, shoulders; the intoxicating feel of touching so much bare skin. Again our mouths came together, kissing so deeply, tongues exploring as guttural groans rumbled in our throats. I lay her back on my thighs, camisole lifted high and back arched. Beautiful. Light-headedness brought my perception to reel. In her youthful suppleness, my bride-to-be was an unbelievably gorgeous sight, and I could no longer restrain my touch. My hand supported her back while fingertips travelled up the centre of her chest to her throat, then down to her breasts. Her thighs tightened around me. I squeezed and kneaded and teased her nipples as she drew sharp breaths; brought my mouth to the rigid pinkness to lick, nibble and suck voraciously.

Her voice... "Edward. Oh, please. Oh, oh, Edward!"

I heaved and gasped over a breast, sucking rhythmically. My hand went to the other and worked that one as well. Must get her there. As her body tightened, she ground her pelvis down on mine. Within seconds, her crescendo came forcefully, spasms jolting her slight frame and shuddering through her. From beginning to end she pleaded "Edward! My Edward!" in rapid succession. I held her tightly and whispered softly as she pitched and swayed in her unravelling languor.

Now I would go to my chamber. My own excruciating need demanded attention, and I could scarcely wait to get to it, but once recovered, my Jane was energised, sprang upright and took firm control of this escapade. She kissed me wantonly as her hands went down to the buttons of my trousers. I grew quite near to restraint's edge as my excitement was wrought as far as it could go. Away it broke.

I stood and lifted her with me. Her arms wrapped around my shoulders, legs tightly about my hips. I carried her across the room, grabbing the towel by the washbasin on the way and set her down on the bed. She knelt before me to complete the removal of my shirt and unbuttoning of my trousers. My breath came in violent gasps and heaves, and although I managed to remain silent, I was dangerously close to slipping out of control. Images and desires flashed through my fevered brain. I kept them suppressed until... until her hands went to the sides of my trousers and yanked them right down my hips.

Exposed to her now in all my intensely sensitive, throbbing hardness, I completely lost my grip on self-restraint. Hands went into the bed-hangings and grasped the canopy frame tightly. She knelt before me; her smooth, warm touch perfectly mastering every sensation. I writhed and heaved, quelling cries struggling for release. Her mouth trailed wet kisses from my neck to chest to swelling, straining biceps. She licked over my ribs into the axillae and growled something about loving the way I smell. The pace of her hands quickened.

What happened then was shocking even to me. As she heightened my pleasure, her mouth went to my nipple where she remained, sucking and teasing it, igniting a final desperate groan of pleasure, but then... then, intermingled with my cries came a conscious stream of sexually explicit filth that continued on for what seemed like ages. She smiled against my nipple as rapid, profane descriptions of every carnal, lascivious sexual act was forcefully emitted from somewhere within me. Words and possibilities she had surely never heard in her life were rained down on her. And not generally spoken. This part of me made it clear that I wanted to do these things with her.

Undaunted, she never slowed, never pulled away. I could feel her lips smile against my skin and was spurred on only further.

Soon a shocking numbness erupted in the crest of my spine and flashed downward. I verged on slipping into climax but somehow could not. Deep and husky, my own voice came to me as a shock. "Aaaarrrrgh!!! Fucking finish me off!" I demanded.

She did.

All thinking, speaking and breathing ceased as waves of orgasm overpowered my mind, and I gasped in ecstasy with each repeated paralysing spasm. My knees buckled as final convulsions emptied me, and fists tightly gripped the canopy frame or else I would have gone down.

Drained and wrung out, I hesitantly lowered my hands and found that I could stand. Bringing my trousers up, I turned and collapsed onto the bed. My exhalations were heavy and my heart thudded like a barrelling combustion engine. I shut my eyes.

'Oh, my God,' I thought. 'What I said! I could not stop it! What will she think of me? She will never marry me now.'

Jane lay nestled to me. Slowly I opened my eyes, dreading the forthcoming scene. Coldness and distance would replace her love. 'Before we marry, I will need time to think' or some other such nonsense she would say. I braced myself for the worst and turned to look at her.

She was on her side, looking at me brightly. Her lips curled in a most delicious, naughty smile as her eyes gazed upon me with enthusiasm. I brought fingers to her face and touched her cheek.

"Told you so," I hoarsely said. "You should listen to me."

"Edward, no. I have no regrets, nor should you. Not ever," she replied. "Oh my love, you are so beautiful! Everything about you and all of what you gave to me here… I loved it."

"Nothing frightened you?"

Surprised, she said, "No. Why? Absolutely not! You will have to explain to me some of what you said, but I am not frightened."

Tears came up to my eyes. "Jane. You came here months ago so innocent. Look at what I've done to you."

"Nonsense, Edward. What have you done to me? Nothing that would cause either you or I to repent. What have we done together really? We've touched and kissed, but nothing more. You've taught me ways to show you my love and have shown me what rapture you feel upon receiving it. Is that wicked? I think not."

I gave a short laugh.

She added, "And if I did respond to your mind and body with disgust, would I make for you a suitable wife?"

All of the rejection meted out by previous lovers who simply did not *fit* with me came rushing back. Their deprecatory looks, hasty exits, their myriad of excuses.

"No," I said and took her in my arms. "No, you would not make for me a suitable wife then. Oh Jane, I am so thankful for you."

"And I for you. There is no cause to feel shame. I would only do these things with you, for you are mine," she said, her hand going up into my hair then sweeping down my body. "All of this is mine, and I love everything you are, Edward. So you see, I am comfortable sharing anything with you."

I turned on my side toward her. Those eyes. My God, they could look right inside me. My fingertips came up to trace her lips, nose and cheeks.

"I love you. Tell me you know that," I said.

"I think so. You only just told me tonight that you love me, after all."

"Well I do," I said, taking her hands in mine. "I love you. Jane, come live with me and be my love… and subject yourself to the filthy, sexual cesspool that is my mind, on a fairly regular basis."

"My!" she gasped dramatically. "What girl could refuse an offer such as that?"

"Not you thankfully, my lovely Jane."

Candles and firelight burned low. We kissed and whispered. Then slept.

Chapter 27

I N THE VERY early hours, I awoke chilled by a cool breeze wafting through the open casement of Jane's bedchamber. Shirtless, I lay with her atop the bedspread, holding her hand pressed to my heart. I shivered and tried to resume sleep but could not. Instead, I dozed fitfully for a time but finally abandoned further attempts at slumber, turned to look at Jane and raised a hand to caress her bare arm and shoulder. She slept curled on her side, as yet in camisole and skirt. By light of the night sky I could clearly see every curve of her serene features, the slope of her little nose and the arc of her full and sensuous lips that lured my own and caused my heart to alter pace.

She loved me and would be my wife. Thank God. This seemed a gift I scarcely deserved, and if it were a true offering, then lifelong gratitude would be my debt to repay. This could also be divine punishment, for if she were to be taken from me, the depths of my misery would surpass any I knew thus far.

No. This was right and good. My maker loved me despite my many faults, and there was no doubt in my mind that He Himself selected her to be brought to me. The corrupt secrets of my heart were well known to my God, but the purity and goodness there was not overlooked either. So like Adam, provided to me was a perfectly designed helpmeet so that I would no longer live alone. It was if the Lord found a tiny diamond amongst acres of rubble and lifted it out of my bleak surroundings to place in my empty hand; a test to find what care I would take with it.

"I'll not disappoint you again, Lord," was my whispered prayer. My thankfulness in gazing at her sleeping face by moonlight was both profoundly consuming and deeply humbling. Watching her motionless figure beside me in the chilly semi-darkness, I became quite lonely for her, but to wake her would be a selfish act, and behaving as such must come to an end. I would go now to my own room. As a regretful farewell, I raised her hand from my chest and brought her fingertips to my lips, kissed their softness and surrounded each soft rise with my teeth.

'Go Edward. Go to your own bed and sleep these last few hours before dawn. Then rise early and begin preparations to wed this woman you love.' No reproachful conscience spoke to me now.

I got up from the bed and found my shirt, slipping into it and buttoning to my chest. At the bed I gently leant down over her, lowered my face and kissed her. I found this a delicious sensation, softly kissing and nibbling her warm lips as she slept. She slowly turned her face up to me and responded in her sleep. A deep exhalation came, arms slowly raised, hands met my broad shoulders and travelled around to my back. Self-denial would forever present a struggle for me.

"Jane, I must leave you now," I whispered.

"Oh, no. Do not go," she responded, eyes opening.

"I must. And you should get into your nightgown. Your skirt will look a wreck if you sleep in it all night."

She acknowledged my words with a sighing "mmm" while her hands came down my thick upper arms and squeezed lightly. She kissed me; her plush lips capturing mine with exquisite gentleness, making my arms quiver as they supported my weight.

"Enough now, Jane," I whispered, wishing more for her to continue than stop. But I was yet uneasy with what I allowed to occur here tonight following my proposal of marriage and her acceptance. I could not help but feel that I had sullied the purity of our momentous decision and felt it best to remove myself immediately.

I said, "Once I return from Hay this morning, we will go into Millcote together for the license and afterward to take you to be measured for a dress. Then you can meet your cousins at noon."

With a final kiss, I pushed off the bed and stood, offering my hand to help her stand as well. In her stocking feet she was considerably shorter than I, and I delightedly pulled her slight frame into my arms, resting my cheek atop her head. I was awed by the happiness and pleasure we could bring one another, as well as by the pain and damage that could be inflicted. Along with a dull ache of shame left by my tirade, her words of earlier left an additional scar as they echoed in my brain: 'My God, Edward, you are all pain to me. Have some pity...' Incredible it was to me that she spoke the words 'I really love you' not an hour later. We are capable of amazing feats of forgiveness and reconciliation as humans, are we not? Some of us more than others, to be certain.

Forgiveness of myself proved evasive as I could not banish thoughts of my conduct. The memory filled me distressingly, and so I released her from my embrace, acutely repentant for having drastically overstepped myself. She backed away, looking up at me, her eyes reading and searching mine in the silvery glow of night. Presently she went around her bed to the wardrobe and removed her white nightgown from within. Her hands went around the back of her skirt to unbutton. I turned away, for to watch, I now felt, would be unseemly. She had come to me as an innocent, and I could not help but feel remorse for having led her astray despite her willingness to follow.

'Yes, Jane, everything is my responsibility. At near twenty years your senior, I am more experienced and am already a damaged soul. I harbour a violent protectiveness for you, and that should and must extend to protecting you from myself.'

I listened to the shifting of fabric being removed and placed, then her wardrobe door shutting. The rustling sound of her long nightgown approached, and I turned. She stood before me well covered with nightgown buttoned to the neck. White cotton glowed brilliantly in the light from the moon. She was my own angel, the same from my dreams, who held me and kissed me and made love to me in our grassy field with a fiery, bloody sunset above, knowing my heart as well as I or my God.

Choked with emotion, I said, "I dream of you at times."

It was all I could manage to say before the familiar stinging rose quickly into my eyes. My love for her contrasted sharply with the singe of fear and remorse. It was all too much to shoulder and came down on me hard. I dropped to my knees before her and wrapped my arms about her sweet, soft body, turned my face and nestled my cheek between the sharp rise of her hips. Her hands held my head close to her, fingers deep in my hair and caressing. I whispered incoherently. Some was prayer and some was inner monologue running wild.

After unknown time spent engulfed in her comfort, my hands went subconsciously to her spine, then down over the rise of her bottom. Suddenly aware of my actions, I stood and backed away. She looked up at me, so patient, so aware of my unsettled and erratic heart. I looked away. No more tonight, I thought. It is best to go. I led her to the bed and turned down the covers, indicating with a weary sweep of my hand for her to lie down. She smiled and obeyed, gathering her hair and lying back, her head resting on the pillow. I covered her with the bedclothes and sitting beside her, lay a single kiss on her lips.

She said, "You are uncomfortable with tonight. With what we did. What you said...during."

"I am uncomfortable with who I have been, Jane." I lifted her hand to my lips. "Tonight, I allowed an old association to contaminate my time with you."

She smiled. "I know that you have had lovers, Edward, and you need not tell me of them if you are distressed by their memory."

"No, I know that I need not talk of them, but you should know that there was never any love in it then, during those years before you. I would be rough, hostile and inconsiderate with women, and I felt no remorse for it. I cared little for what they thought of me afterward because, you see, nothing I said or did could extinguish what feeling was not there to begin with. Greed was their reason to share themselves with me. Knowing that to be the truth, time and again; it damaged me."

"That is all finished now."

"Yes, but I brought it to life before you tonight, and that was wrong. Anger and aggression play no part in my feelings for you. I love you. And I trust that you love me."

"I do. Edward, even in your urgency you are ever considerate. You must not disregard that."

Finally, I began to feel more at ease. "I like who I am with you," I said. Then I was silent, thinking of other apprehensions clouding my mind. "Why, upon our first night together in my chamber, did you let me touch you and kiss you, Jane? You are a novice. Why did you not rebuff me?"

She smiled. "Even a novice can feel desire, my love. We shook hands per your invitation, but in the manner to which you refer, it was I who touched first."

"But what do you know of men? Very little. I think we've established that."

She lay looking at the ceiling. "I do not know much, Edward; only what you've taught me. And before coming here, I suppose my soul was asleep. Then being near to you each evening in your study, our eye contact...it was almost physical. Did you not think so?"

"I did."

"I knew I loved you and even then wanted to love you with my body. I thought about it, dreamt of it, imagining the details and the possibilities. And then you let me take that first step. You made all of it safe because you loved me as well."

"But I failed to say it until tonight."

"Did you not love me until now?"

"Silly girl, of course I did. As I told you, from the first day, in the rain by the river, and since then I have known it like I know my own name."

"Well then. It comes through every time you look at me and speak to me," she said, reaching up to touch my rough cheek. "And so I may be a novice, but I have no fear of you, not any longer. You must feel no shame for what you are now or what you have been. I love it. Do you understand that? All is you, and I would have you no other way."

I leant over her, my arms slipping around her and drew her up to me in tight embrace. "I thank God for you," I said, kissing her lips and pressing her body to mine.

What more could I share with her about myself in hopes of acceptance? Anything? Everything? For years I bore the burden of my disastrous first marriage alone. Not once in fifteen years had I conversed openly with another person about Bertha, never was shown another's viewpoint or was given encouragement that life yet held hope for me. Like a prisoner locked away and abandoned, I endured misery and hopelessness entirely alone. But here was my angel before me now. Would she listen patiently and without judgment to my worst secret and love me still? Would she come with me to church to stand before God, promising herself to me for life although I was yet bound by man's law to another?

I lowered her onto the bed and looked at her in the moonlight. 'No,' I thought. The risk was far too great. If I were wrong, the loss of her would kill me. I simply could not do it. So I gazed at her seriously and said, "I want you for my wife."

If Jane had anticipated a revelation, and I believe she had, then she was disappointed. She turned onto her side and closed her eyes. "Then make it so," she said.

Cool breezes swirled about the room, stirring the air and gently fluttering the bed-hangings. I kissed her cheek. The backs of her fingers absently stroked my coarse, shadowy chin.

"Good night, my love," I whispered.

"Mmm, 'night,'" she murmured, and was asleep.

"I know," I whispered to her. "So tired. You've travelled so very far to come home to me. Bless your lovely heart for doing so."

At the table I took my jacket and waistcoat from the back of a chair, not forgetting the champagne bottle and a glass, and with a final gaze at Jane's sleeping form, left her chamber to seek my own. Once there, I opened the casement windows letting in the freshening breeze and moonlight. I went to the sofa before a darkened fireplace and sipped champagne until daylight, considering the tactics of my next move.

At sunrise John was summoned. Bath and shave were arranged, then I dressed per my usual sartorial elegance which today included midnight black jacket and trousers, pearl grey shirt, black cravat and silver blue silk waistcoat if you must know and I assume you must. When satisfied with my appearance I went to the kitchen to down a mug of coffee laced with chicory and sent an order for John to prepare Mesrour for my ride to Hay. News of my engagement was imparted to no one else, desiring to accomplish my first task of the day forthwith and avoid the delay polite pre-nuptial prattling would bring.

The morning continued bright and clear. A crisp current of wind rustled amongst verdant trees and waved the tall grass of Thornfield's meadows. I took the road toward Millcote, turning off after some minutes down the river path that led eventually to Hay. The water flowing beside me sparkled serenely and the valley hillsides all about were dotted white with grazing sheep. It was a perfect day. My pleasant journey closed as the steeple of Hay's little church rose up above a canopy of willow trees. I brought Mesrour to a halt besides the stone building and secured him there, glad to see Mr. Wood's bay horse grazing in a small adjacent meadow. I climbed the front steps and entered through the open door into dim, chill darkness. Advancing up the centre aisle, I looked about for the clergyman. He found me before I did him.

"Mr. Rochester," he said approaching along the aisle. He smiled and extended a warm hand to be clasped. "It is good to have you come back. Out visiting today?"

"No, Wood. I have a request to make of you."

"Well then, sit. Please," he said, indicating to a pew. "How may I be of service?"

I came straight to the point. "You can perform my wedding ceremony. Day after tomorrow," I said, all abruptness.

He nodded pensively and said, "Congratulations."

"Will you do it?"

"Of course. And your intended? I assume you have taken the time to choose a bride for yourself," Wood said, a gentle reproof of my impetuosity. He glanced to the doors and aisles, apparently in search of my said intended.

"She will be here."

"You will need a license you know. It can take a day or two to secure."

"Yes, I know about the license and will have it today."

"Friday," he repeated. "What time?"

"Early."

He thought for a moment. "Nine?"

"Good enough."

He took a deep breath and looked at me circumspectly. "Why the haste, Mr. Rochester? I should like to meet your bride-to-be prior to the happy occasion. To know her name at very least."

"Her name is Jane," I said, distractedly glancing about at the stained glass windows depicting various biblical scenes. They drew from me words I might not otherwise have spoken.

"Ever have a devil chasing you, Wood?"

"Have I? Yes, I did once. Years ago. Mine's name was Rachel."

We sat in silence, nodding philosophically at one another.

I stood and stalked to the bright rectangle of daylight glinting at the open door. "Friday. Nine o'clock," I called back to him.

From there I galloped Mesrour back to Thornfield where I went in through the kitchen and found Leah stacking dishes at the draining board; all items from last evening's tart and custard feast. Seeing the pitcher caused me to start, remembering fingers plunged into its sticky sweet depths and... what happened afterward.

Leah turned and addressed me over her shoulder. "Good morning, Sir!"

I helped myself to a blueberry scone from her morning's baking and took a bite. My reply was a saucy, muffled, "'morning, Leah."

"And how was your champagne dessert of last evening, Sir?"

"Divine," I answered, smirking.

She raised her eyebrows and looked away, sighing dreamily.

Mrs. Fairfax then bustled into the kitchen, reading some scrap from the post and rapping out orders, "...breakfast is to be served upstairs in my rooms. Yes, that will be for Adele, Miss Eyre and myself. And please, Leah, provide an extra helping of... Oh! Good morning, Sir. My, you are looking rather dashing today... yes, Leah, an extra helping of butter and please be sure..."

I cut into her babble. "Yes, Leah, and whilst you are taking all of this down, please be sure to arrange a special meal for Friday around mid-day. Settings for two. For my bride and myself."

Leah stiffened and swung around to face away at sideboard, her back to Mrs. Fairfax and myself.

"Your bride?" asked a shocked Mrs. Fairfax. Her pince-nez glasses fell from her nose to dangle by a fine chain pinned to her hefty bosom.

"Mmm, that is correct, Madam," I said, finishing my scone. I surveyed her whilst chewing, attempting vainly to keep my grin concealed. "This Friday I shall marry Miss Eyre. Nine that morning should not be too early. What do you think, Leah?"

Leah glared at me.

"No opinion to voice, Leah? How about you, Mrs. Fairfax? Nine o'clock is a perfect time for a wedding, would you not agree?"

The old housekeeper's hands fluttered the letter she held and her complexion came up rosy as peeled beets. "Dear me, Mr. Rochester, I nearly thought you said Miss Eyre is to be your bride! I do have such spells. Perhaps I should sit."

"My bride *is* to be Miss Eyre," I confirmed and stopped to swoop before her face. "*Not* Miss Ingram." I kissed her plushy cheek and left the kitchen.

From there I went into the entrance hall and climbed the staircase. On the topmost step I called to Jane's shut door. "What keeps you, Jane? Are you not yet ready to go into Millcote?"

Her muffled voice came from inside. "Just finishing my hair! Allow me two minutes!"

I sat down on a carpeted step and timed her with my pocket watch. As I was about to call out a second time, her door unclosed and she came forth. Her hair was done up in a style similar to that of last evening, with a flattering softness that bespoke maturity and vulnerability both. Her cream hued pleated blouse was somewhat more severe than the white lace collar and cuffs but still very attractive. Her sage suit had been brushed and smoothed to perfection.

I arose to my feet. "May I say you are looking most fetching this morning, Miss Eyre?"

"You may, Mr. Rochester. And you are quite debonair, despite having stayed up all night drinking champagne."

I took her hand and pulled her close. "Does anything get past you, witch?"

"Not much," she said and gave me a quick peck on my lips.

"Shall we go?" I urged.

"Edward, I must have some breakfast. I took nothing yesterday but our little picnic and am feeling a bit giddy with hunger."

"Well then for heaven's sakes, my love, let us see you fed!"

Minutes later we were seated at the kitchen table enjoying a light morning repast of tea and buttered blueberry scones. Jane lifted her teacup but checked it at her lips, smiling over the surface before us.

"This table?" she asked, running a hand over the time-smoothed planks.

"This very one," I replied. And we chuckled to one another over the pretty china cups raised to our lips.

I reached and took her hand in mine. "Are you nervous?"

My question caught her in mid-sip. "Hmm?"

"About meeting your cousins today."

She swallowed and smiled. "Oh. Umm, not really. St. John seemed quite respectable and well educated by his letter."

I set my cup down on a saucer. "What did you think I meant, when I asked if you were nervous?"

Her blush gave her away. "Nothing. Never mind."

I leant forward, searching those eyes, her face, the way she held herself. "You are," I said.

She was silent, considering how to respond, then she relented. "Well yes, of course. Aren't you?"

"No," I said decidedly and kissed her hand, knowing that some situations call for absolute confidence. "Has all not been pleasurable for you thus far, Jane?"

She looked about us to be sure no one was near. We were alone. "Yes. You are very careful with me, Edward. But will you always be this way?"

"Always."

"Some of what you said last night did not sound so gentle," she said teasingly.

"It would never give me pleasure to hurt you. I only want to love you, protect you, live my life with you and take you to bed whenever we wish. I want to give you all that I am and ever have been, and then I want you to look at me like you do and say you love me. Those, Jane, are the deepest wishes of my heart."

She caressed my fingers with hers and gently intertwined them. "When will you do that? When will you tell me everything?"

I had felt disclosure nearing for some time; closer each day. My fear was not what it once was because I trusted her. "Soon, Jane. Very soon."

I left her to obtain enough cash from the safe in my study to cover today's expenses. Upon returning to the kitchen, I found her placing gloves and ready to depart. I led her out to the courtyard where John stood beside the coach awaiting us, helped Jane inside, and then turned to John.

Speaking low I said to him, "I will need Ferndean prepared for habitation. See to it as quickly as can be arranged."

He looked at me with astonishment. "You will take your bride to live *there*, Mr. Rochester?"

"No. It is the inhabitants of Thornfield's third story who are to live there. Understand?"

"Ah. Yes, Sir. But Ferndean needs a terrible lot of work; likely even more since the last time I was there to see it. The caretaker tells me of holes in the roof, damaged eaves and broken windows allowing rainwater inside. He says the floorboards are warped, the drapes are mouldy, not to mention the attic being a bat's haunt…"

"You will hire a crew and get at it, John. Make arrangements in town today to have all of it done. Can I trust you with that?"

"Of course, Sir! Men will surely be found at The Black Swan around midday today. I may have to pay handsomely for them to forfeit other jobs."

"Then do it," I said and climbed into the coach, taking my place beside Jane.

It was a pleasant journey to town on that warm and sunny June morning. I held her hand as she hummed melodiously beside me whilst the carriage rumbled past green meadows and low stone walls. Together we identified the calls of various birds and talked of places, people, studied subjects, wishes and dreams. We delighted in our easy companionship, laughed often and found again and again that our psyches fit together to the completion of both. I caught her eyes on me in a sidewise, secretive glance. Smiling, I returned her gaze, drew her mouth to mine and kissed her. My eyes lingered on her, recalling last night. I cleared my throat and growled deeply, turning my eyes from her to the window.

Knowingly she nudged my arm and leant in to kiss my cheek. She whispered, "I know your thoughts, Mr. Rochester."

"You start these things you do, little witch," I teased, wondering whether John would know if I undressed her down to camisole and knickers right here. Our journey unfortunately was too short for such shenanigans, so I went for mental stimulation instead.

"So Jane," I asked in mild interrogation, "I want to know more on a topic broached by you before I departed your chamber last night. In your words, you've been 'imagining it, dreaming about it'. Would you care to elaborate?"

I watched her look away smiling and draw a sharp intake of breath. She looked so prim in her tailored suit, hands folded in her lap; quite a paradox to the images circulating in her mind.

"My imaginings in those days, Sir? When we spent evenings together in your study as master and governess? This is the instance to which you refer, I assume."

I nodded, grinning at her.

"I was attracted to everything about you. Your eyes, hair, lips..." her gaze swept over me. "Your shoulders, so broad and powerful. But most of all it was your hands. I was mad for your hands."

I laughed deeply. "My hands?"

"Yes," she said, her cheeks flushing. "And then with the poem you asked me to read, I knew you felt for me what I did for you, and so it was safe. Touching you would be honest and right." She paused a few moments. "Our first night together, the night of the fire in your chamber, your hand inside my nightgown, touching me! What sent me over the edge was knowing your lovely hand was there, as much as feeling it there."

I smiled at her, taking that in. I loved her so; every animated expression, each change of accent or voice inflection, the language of her body speaking so beautifully to mine. Never in my life did I believe I could love someone so completely. It thrilled me and comforted me, and yes, sometimes frightened me. She read my expressions now as only she could do and lifted my hand. She was humming a tune and closed her eyes, kissing my fingers. I rested my head back against the richly upholstered seat cushions and looked at her beside me.

"Cannot wait to marry you," I whispered.

Her smile spread over her lips and through her heart.

We arrived in Millcote with nearly two hours to spare before Jane was to meet her cousins. I immediately took her to the magistrate where we stood in the reception office at separate podiums to complete the various forms in application of a marriage license. Once the papers were signed, stamped and reviewed, I steered Jane toward the door and slipped pound notes to the young and suitably impressed clerk, along with a stern glare.

"Today," I commanded him.

Out in the street, I grasped Jane's hand and pulled her along to the textile warehouse. Within seconds of entering she was whisked away by the resident seamstress for measuring whilst I meantime perused the finest bolts of fabric in everything from silks to brocades. Capturing the arm of a passing young seamstress, I decided to pose a challenge.

"For my young bride," I surreptitiously said to the wide-eyed miss. "She needs underclothes. Something more, shall we say 'appealing?' than white cotton knickers and camisoles. What have you to suggest?"

The girl pressed a slender forefinger to her cheek, taking on my request with all the weighty solemnity of a high court judge. Moments later she looked up at me, eyes sparking suggestively. "Yes, Sir. I know just the things. You leave it to me."

"I will do that. Add it to my bill," was my covert response, noticing Jane re-emerge from the fitting room.

Finally we were shown a selection of white bridal gowns in various stages of completion. I backed away, leaving Jane full reign of choice in wedding attire. A dress was chosen, remanded to the seamstress' care, and we again went out into the street. The time was a quarter to twelve.

Jane and I leisurely sauntered along the street bustling with mid-day commerce toward the end of the road and The George Inn. Suddenly finding that we were directly outside the door of a jewellery shop, I halted us both.

"Confound it! Wait!" I exclaimed and pulled her abruptly to the door. "Good Lord, I nearly forgot that we must choose our rings!"

"Edward," she said, tripping along behind me, "I feel compelled to tell you that there are times when your impetuosity verges on the manic."

"I haven't any idea what you are talking about," I said, gripping her hand and drawing her inside to a glass display case. "Now look at these wedding bands."

"It is nearly noon, and my cousins will be waiting for me! I shall leave you here to make the selection." She attempted to extract her hand from my grip.

"Stop trying to escape me! You at least must have your ring finger measured."

She grumbled, "Oh, you are going to make me late!"

"Stop your grousing. Now listen, Jane, I will be in the book shop after two o'clock and will wait there for you."

"All right, fine."

In another two minutes she was measured and with a kiss to my cheek was bolting away. Opening the door, she stopped to point at me. "Choose something simple. Nothing pretentious."

"Overbearing, dictatorial little pixie, off with you!" I ordered.

She threw me an engaging smile, mouthed the words "love you", turned and was gone. My heart fluttered. I immediately went to the doorstep to seek her slight form hurrying toward the end of the road and watched her safely cross between carriages and riders to The George Inn. Then I spent the next hour choosing our wedding bands. My choice was not ostentatious, nor plain, but rather they were perfect for us.

Afterward I found my way to the bookshop as the two o'clock hour approached and located an unoccupied table near the back of Life and Physical Sciences. With a volume on comparative anatomy selected, I settled down for a bit of heavy scholarly immersion. For three quarters of an hour I diligently studied but then broke my concentration, realising Jane had not yet arrived. I glanced up to see Arthur Eshton enter the bookshop, looking about vaguely. I raised a hand and he came forward to take a chair opposite mine.

"Edward," he whispered, shaking my hand heartily. "How very good to see you."

"And you as well, Eshton. What brings you to Millcote?"

"Boredom. Waiting to depart for Leiden in a fortnight. What are you reading?"

I showed the book. "Actually I am killing time waiting for Jane. She was to meet cousins at The George Inn and should arrive here any time."

He swung around to look at the door. "Excellent! I'd like to see her again," he said and added with that impish grin, "All is well with you two?"

I smiled. "Jane and I are marrying. Day after tomorrow."

Eshton suddenly blazed with jubilance. "Edward!" he said, slapping my arm. "Good man! And a marvellous girl you've chosen. I wish all the best for you."

"Thank you," I warmly replied.

"But what, ah... what of your 'extenuating circumstances'?"

I tapped fingertips on the table, considering my reply. "I shall answer that with a quote, my friend. It was Byron who said, 'The walls we build about us to keep sorrow at bay, also do well to fend off joy.' I feel it is time to allow myself to experience joy. She makes me happy, Arthur. Very."

"I've not heard a better reason for marrying than that," he said grinning, but then his expression abruptly fell.

Gently I asked, "And Louisa? Have you spoken since being at Thornfield together? A letter exchanged or an invitation to dine?"

"No. Not a word. "

I nodded and gave him a sympathetic smile. Always I had been somewhat envious of Eshton seeing as he was blessed with an irrepressible spirit and was never down for long.

After permitting himself some seconds of melancholy he said, "I had a letter from Andy Ingram a week since! It seems that he and Amy are going strong and attended an Italian *opera buffa* with his parents and hers in York since we saw them last. How unjust that a rascal such as Andy can find love, but a tremendous catch like me, me!, all chivalry and intellect and attentiveness, cannot. Blimey, is there any justice?"

"Careful not to forget the good looks," I added.

"Well that goes without saying."

"Eshton, my boy, you will find your girl. As I said, she will likely fall over you in the library at Leiden, her nose in a book, the same as yours. So tell me. What more did Andy have to say for himself?"

"He mentioned Blanche. Do you want to hear about it?"

"Probably not," I said but then reconsidered. "Well, better the devil you know than the devil you don't. Go on."

"From what he says, I think you have no need to worry about her any longer, Edward. Our Blanche has a new love interest! Andy says she is perfectly besotted with this new beau she's been dragging about by the cuff, poor bastard."

"Good for her," I replied, immeasurably relieved to know her attention was now occupied elsewhere. "She's been seen on this dupe's arm at all the fashionable 'dos' of late?"

"Oh yes. Andy said she is away from Ingram Park just now having followed her new suitor to a house party in Leeds."

"Leeds. A house party," I repeated and my gut lurched. "You are certain about this?"

"Yes. It seems Blanche and her dandy admirer claim a mutual acquaintanceship with the hosts. Why do you ask?"

"Arthur," I said, attempting to quell a rising dread. "Andrew did not happen to mention the name of this new man of hers, did he? Or perhaps where his home is located?"

"Yes, he did," he said, considering. "He is foreign apparently; owner of a merchant enterprise in the West Indies. Why? Edward, what's wrong? You are suddenly rather pale!"

I felt utterly sick. "Mason. The man's name is Mason."

"Yes, that is exactly right! How did you know?"

I stood unsteadily and lay damp palms flat to the tabletop. Good God. The room turned a snowy white before my eyes and sweat came up fast along my back.

'Heaven help... help me. Blanche. You with your icy eyes and glacial heart. Why do you hate me so? Or love me so? Or are they one and the same to you?'

Although it was a warm June day and rather stuffy in the bookshop, I was suddenly chilled to the bone. I looked about; desperate for help, an answer, extrication.

Eshton's hand took hold of my arm. "Edward! Sit, please. Sit down before you fall down. I am sorry to distress you. I had no idea you would react in this way to news of Blanche with another man. Do you know this Mason? I thought you would be pleased."

My knees bent and I came heavily down into the chair. My mouth was parched and my head empty.

Glancing to the door, I vaguely noticed an attractive unknown woman enter the shop, and my perception snapped into focus a few seconds later as my own lovely Jane followed directly behind her. Escorting them both was a tall, blonde gentleman whose looks diverted all wretched thoughts of Blanche for he reminded me immediately of a falcon; handsome and cold with piercing, heartless eyes and an almost predatory surveillance of his surroundings.

"Ah," I said, mustering some spirit. "Here is Jane. And with her must be cousins St. John and Diana."

Eshton and I rose to our feet whereby Jane found us and beckoned her companions to follow to our remote table. The group approached, and somehow I made an acceptable endeavour at gentlemanly introductions but can recall little of it. I shook hands with St. John and Diana Rivers and introduced Arthur Eshton to them both. In a rather intangible way I watched as Eshton gathered my Jane into his arms and kissed her cheek, congratulating her on our engagement. My hand lay upon his shoulder as a silent, 'that's quite enough.'

Mr. Rivers made cursory pleasantries before wandering off to peruse Theology texts an aisle or two over, and Arthur stood before the stuffed bookshelves of the Life Sciences section speaking with Diana Rivers. Meanwhile, Jane slowly lowered into the chair vacated by Eshton, taking my frigid hands in hers.

"Are you unwell, Edward?" she asked, searching my face with anxiety.

"Yes, quite unwell, Jane." I piercingly felt not only hunted but the hopelessness and futility of flight. Wolves were circling and bearing down.

With loving comfort and a strengthening smile she said, "Come. Let us take you home and see you to bed."

I nodded, vastly soothed my her steadfast devotion and made the excuse, "Unfortunately, Jane, I am not eighteen years old any longer. I cannot stay up drinking wine all night and hope to function well the following day." I was dissembling again. Best to remain quiet.

"No, you cannot. And as a married man, you must plan to spend your nights with me, engaged in far better pursuits," she said, warming my chilled hands.

"That will do well."

She looked about the bookshop. "Shall I have Diana and St. John come along to Thornfield?"

"By all means invite them."

She glanced beyond my shoulder and grinned. "Look," she said with a nod.

I turned to see Diana, who was quite vivacious and pretty, speaking animatedly to Arthur whilst pressing a forefinger to the binding of a shelved volume. His eyes sparkled as they met hers, seemingly delighted with his newfound companion and their common interest. Jane went to talk with the conversing couple, and I turned to see them reply with enthusiastic nods and exchange of warm glances. Jane then disappeared to the find St. John. Heartened somewhat, I went to replace the comparative anatomy book. Eshton was soon at my side.

"Edward! She is beautiful, is she not?" He was scarcely able to restrain in his enthusiasm. Giving me no time to reply, he continued, "You will not believe this! I scarcely can. Did you know she studies ornithology! Good God, she has read Buskirk's dissertation on courtship plumage of the male chimney swift! She can quote statistics!"

"Oh how nice," I replied, making no effort to conceal an amused grin. "But you must settle down, Arthur, and try to exhibit a measure of composure. You do not want to scare her off."

"Oh. Right. No, of course not," he said, clearing the smile from his face.

"You must come to Thornfield tonight for dinner," I said in invitation. "I think we can all do with a few bottles of the Hall's finest, a bit of Leah and John's culinary inventiveness and the entertainment of new friends."

"Yes, thank you. I will be there."

Our group gathered once again, agreeing to meet at my home for dinner at seven. St. John expressed interest in taking the next coach to Hay for a visit with Mr. Wood at the church. Arthur offered to escort Diana on a late afternoon expedition through Millcote's shops, and minutes later I was infinitely relieved to have Jane to myself, secluded once again in the privacy of the coach for the five mile journey homeward. We sat together as before, side by side, her hand in mine, travelling in comfortable silence.

With her head reposed on my shoulder and my cheek resting atop, she asked, "Feeling any better, Edward?"

So much was beyond my control. But my intentions were good, my heart was pure (mostly), and I felt that my God was with me. Best of all, I had Jane's love.

Lifting her chin to kiss her lips, I replied, "You are here. And so I am better."

Chapter 28

THE CARRIAGE ROLLED into Thornfield's courtyard and was met by the figure of a mightily aggrieved little Adele. Upon our alighting, she was immediately before us, scowling and scolding at having been left behind; the only solution being for Miss Eyre to immediately come play with her in the gardens. Patient and good-natured as Jane was, she assented. I smiled, watching as she was forcibly pulled away in the direction of the orchards. Poor Jane had endured quite a lot of that today.

With my mind squarely on tonight's supper, I went into the house and directly to the kitchen to find Leah ferociously punching down risen bread dough, her sleeves rolled to the elbows and skin chalky white with flour. The sublime aroma of loaves baking filled the room. I took a place at the table and watched her activity; weighing the rudeness of helping myself unbidden at the oven's cooling racks.

"Leah," I said. "Yours must be a mightily therapeutic occupation, pummelling so much dough. Something similar to a lively public house brawl on a Saturday night I imagine."

"You will never catch me ruffled, Sir, and now you know why!" she said breathlessly.

"Possibly I can ruffle you, after all. What would you think of arranging a semi-formal dinner for five tonight? At oh, around eight o'clock?"

"What's the time now?" she impassively asked, continuing to work.

I checked my pocket watch. "Ten past four."

She paused and raised her eyes to the ceiling; floured fists permitted a moment's rest. After short consideration, she brought down her verdict.

"Start with wild mushroom, marjoram and Madeira sherry soup. Follow with the nice rabbit-thyme casserole cooking at the moment and add to it cheddar parsley dumplings. Slices of the lovely crusty whole meal bread you see over there," she said nodding to the sideboard, "with herbed butter, of course. Finish with a wild strawberry syllabub. Will that suffice?"

Heavens! Would it suffice?! "Before I drool on your bread dough, Leah, I shall take my leave," I said and got up from the bench.

"Are you hungry, Sir?"

"Quite. Blueberry scones and tea only go so far."

"Well then," she said and was at the sideboard preparing a thick slice of crusty bread slathered with butter. "This should hold you over. As you are here, may I ask whether preparations for your wedding proceed without trouble? Is there something I can do to help?"

"No, everything is well organised," I replied. Then simply from curiosity, I asked a question to which I always expected a dull negative and so never broached. "Pardon the saucy enquiry, Leah, but how is it that you never married, lively and talented as you are?"

She grinned and resumed kneading, eyes on her work. "Thank you, Sir, but I was married, briefly, when I was very young. We were sixteen, the both of us. Then one year later he joined up for the American Wars and was amongst the first deployed. The letter came not long after... 'His Majesty's Royal Navy regrets to inform you...' It came shortly after my eighteenth birthday."

In all the years Leah was employed at Thornfield Hall, it was always my assumption that she opted for a sheltered life in service over marriage and family. Her answer surprised me to speechlessness. She stepped back from the table, her lip quivering, then cleared her throat and seemed to shake her grief away. Stalwart woman. She came back to the table and punched down the dough with noticeably more muscle than before.

"Leah, I am so sorry," I said softly and, I hoped, sympathetically. "I did not intend to conjure painful memories."

"No, Sir, of course not," she replied with a faint smile. "It does not disturb me to talk of him. Quite the opposite. But I am amazed that no matter how much time passes, it is a wound which never begin to heal. But," she said, punching down bread dough, "as with all disappointments, we go on because we must."

I watched her exertions for a few more moments before asking, "You will stay on at Thornfield, will you not? After I am married, you do plan to stay."

She looked up at me, bewildered. "Yes, Sir. Where else should I go?"

"Nowhere, I hope. Mrs. Fairfax however may opt for a change."

Leah smiled and swatted a floury hand through the air. "Oh, Alice will adjust, Sir. Her foremost wish is to see you happy. And she wants little ones! Give her some babies to love and she will be a happy old bird once more."

I chuckled softly, taking a bite of bread. I would be avoiding *that* for a while. "Thanks for the chat, Leah," I said. Then I went in search of a pitcher and some good, dark beer from the cellar.

In another half hour, I wearily climbed the staircase and went straight to my chamber. There I drew the drapes and lay down on my bed, exhaling deeply, my arms thrown wide and my eyes shut. Reflections focused on the image and motivations of Blanche Ingram.

Could I be mistaken in her threat of treachery, and a connection between she and Richard Mason exist only in my own mind? Or was there a connection that merely represented some extraordinary coincidence? Possibly her suitor was not him at all but rather some other West Indian owner a merchant business, currently in Leeds, with a name that sounded like 'Mason'...

Hah! No. There could be no doubt about it. It was Richard.

How could it be though? Again, I tried the possibility of coincidence. Perhaps she had met him out in society somewhere; at a social event or charitable function. She and her mother were known to attend philanthropic affairs, as consistent with fashionable aristocratic diversion. It was possible for their introduction to have occurred in this manner since he had been in the country for some time visiting acquaintances. She could find him attractive, I supposed. He was likely what most women would define as pleasing; effete and delicate in my opinion but handsome just the same and not without the financial means to offer every impression of wealth.

I considered the notion of Blanche having found Grace's keys at the back of her bedside table drawer and taking them up to the north tower the night Richard was attacked. Did she watch as I left the Hall and rode away into the night to fetch the doctor? What would she have seen and done whilst in the north tower? Would she have approached a strange man, lying motionless in a chair in the darkness? And if so, would she have had the nerve to speak to him? Especially as his condition was so gruesome and frightful? I simply did not know. Blanche had no shortage of audacity, that was certain, but would she actually have approached a stranger lying prostrated in such a ghastly state and engaged him in conversation? This would require feats of temerity unfathomable for any woman. But Blanche was not just any woman. I was sorry I had ever won her attention to begin with.

If only Blanche would... vanish.

Thoughts of Blanche Ingram did not disturb me much longer, secure as I was in Jane's love and constancy. Jane and I could overcome anything and be stronger for it. Reckless as I had become with her acceptance of my marriage proposal, I truly believed this now.

Without further ado, I dropped off for a most restorative nap.

The sweetest part of my lie-down was in awakening. A gentle weight came over the length of my body, hands slid beneath my shoulders, and kisses under my chin tipped my head back. The lowering sun of evening shone through a gap in the drapes. My eyes opened to see chestnut brown hair and grey-green eyes looking up to mine. I smiled and inhaled her sweet scent deeply.

"'Tis time to wake, my love," was whispered at my neck.

I stretched luxuriously and brought open palms to her back; down, down over her lovely, rounded bottom as I raised a thigh around her and pressed her pelvis to mine.

"To hell with dinner. Let's stay here," I murmured as she kissed me.

"No, indeed. You will need your strength," she replied, "for at least the next few days. Then you can rest for a while."

Vexed, I dropped my hands to the bed. "Why ever should I want to 'rest for a while'? We are marrying! I have no plans to rest!"

"Come downstairs where we can discuss it over dinner, Edward. I've directed Diana and St. John to the drawing room. I hope that was right."

"This is your house as well as mine now, Jane, or will be in another two days. You were right to see them into drawing room. Now off you go whilst I make myself presentable."

I washed my face and changed clothes, replacing my shirt with one of crisp white and adding a knotted silk jacquard tie. With my unruly black curls arranged, I surveyed the entire picture in the mirror. Stylish, elegant and slightly devilish. Perfection.

I arrived to the entrance hall in time to see Arthur Eshton hand away to John his overcoat and hat, then stiffly take his place on the matting, awaiting welcome.

"Glad you could come, Arthur!" I called, approaching him. His evident nervousness amused me mightily.

"Would not have missed it," he said, straightening his clothes and smoothing his hair. I could not help but laugh aloud. "Edward, compose yourself! This is difficult for me," he hissed, glancing around to be sure he was unheard. "I think, um... oh hell, I think I am in love with Diana!"

I laughed until my sides ached. "I have never seen you so nervous! Relax, Arthur. She is merely a pleasant young lady. You only met her today!"

"Oh? And how long did it take for you to know that you loved Jane? Hmm?"

He was right. "Yes, you have me there, my friend," I nodded. "I knew straight away. Come, let us reunite you two lovebirds. Birds! Now is that not perfectly appropriate?" I laughed again.

He regarded me peevishly. "Your mind is slipping, Rochester."

Our group gathered in the drawing room where pleasant conversation ensued, including congratulations and best wishes from all on the upcoming nuptials of Jane and I.

Diana, as it turned out, was employed as a governess as well, and she had us laughing about her most recent assignment tutoring a twelve-year-old boy who was expelled from school when tobacco and drawings 'of a suggestive nature' were found amongst his personal articles. Arthur and I exchanged knowing grins at that, recalling our own similarly guilty behaviour at school. How inapt for the boy's parents to choose a beauty like Diana to reform him!

Looking at her, I guessed Diana's age between twenty-two and twenty-five years, and conversation soon confirmed that she was the youngest of the three siblings. She had yet to be married and no suitor was mentioned. Arthur appeared near bursting with glee.

St. John and Diana's sister, Mary Rivers, also was currently serving as a governess. Mary had been unable to join her siblings' excursion to Millcote as her employment would keep her in Harrogate where she attended the education of a wealthy family's three daughters. She would not be free to leave her situation until the following week.

St. John, the eldest of the three, talked of his incumbency as vicar of Morton's parish church. Morton was a tiny farming village near Preston, and although he continued to reside at the family home situated nearby, he was preparing for travel to India as a missionary with departure projected in six months time. I must admit that St. John was a strikingly handsome fellow, possessed of imposing height, blonde hair, penetrating blue eyes, and a faultless bone structure. Yet, severe and staid he was, dressed in an exquisitely tailored, parsonical costume and wearing an unsmiling expression. I observed that this was a man after my father's own heart.

St. John declined an aperitif whilst others partook, claiming in his low monotone to have found Christian fulfilment as a 'teetotaller'. As all present with the exception of Diana were unfamiliar with the term, St. John took opportunity to educate our imbibing group on the sermons of Richard Turner, a clergyman known to him personally in Preston who preached the merits of total abstinence from all alcohol, not only spirits. Once his tongue was permitted rest, St. John regarded us with a pious, wintry smile and may actually have expected us to toss our wine into the nearest planter, but if so, then he was disappointed. I studied him keenly. St. John reminded me of someone, and for a time I could not place whom that might be. I sipped and searched my brain.

It came to me. Yes, of course! St. John was very much like my brother, Rowland! Regarding him dubiously, I wondered if he too led an existence of secreted hypocrisy. Time would tell.

Dinner was announced, and as we moved into the dining room, Eshton came close beside me. "A thousand laughs that bloke, inn'e?" he whispered.

"Be nice, Arthur," I warned in reply. "St. John may someday become your brother-in-law."

Eshton's eyes settled on Diana, and he gazed at her adoringly whilst muttering something incomprehensible. He was clearly beyond help.

Leah's impromptu culinary challenge proved quite a sensation that evening, and our delectable meal was further complemented by light and engaging conversation. Upon Leah and John clearing away the dinner plates, the evening's mood took an unanticipated turn when St. John broached the subject of his and Diana's plans for the upcoming days. He hushed the group and turned to me, opening in a decidedly nettlesome tone.

"If I may, Mr. Rochester…"

"Please, Mr. Rivers, call me Edward."

He gave a single, slow nod. "And 'St. John', if you will."

"Of course."

A pinched smile preceded this address: "Diana and I are to travel to York over the upcoming days to meet with a certain solicitor, one Mr. Reger, who has requested our presence in his offices next week. We will stop at Harrogate to collect Mary on the way. It is imperative that Jane join us for this audience with Mr. Reger."

I glanced at Jane seated to my right. She met my eyes but remained silent.

I said, "St. John, you are aware that Jane and I are marrying on Friday morning?"

"To be certain, I am," he said. "However, this is a matter of vital importance, Edward. I had the unfortunate assignment of informing Jane today that our uncle, John Eyre, suffers from a protracted and likely terminal illness. His solicitor in Madeira has delegated the task of obtaining an audience with his heirs," he said with a hand to his chest and nodding to Diana and Jane, "to a brother attorney here in England; this being Mr. Reger. The meeting is requested for early Tuesday morning."

Jane turned to me and took my hand. "I am sorry to interrupt our plans, Edward. Should we not wait to marry? For a week or perhaps two?"

"No!" I resolutely replied. "We are marrying on Friday morning. You may attend the conference, Jane, seeing that it is 'imperative'. That much I will allow at this time. We shall discuss privately the details of timing and travel." Rising from the table, I went to refill my wine glass at the sideboard, quite aware of my stern voice and countenance. Jane watched me solemnly.

Eshton broke the uncomfortable silence that followed, diverting the group as he carefully segued the conversation toward the city of York's sights, dining and shopping.

Diana was properly impressed and said, "My goodness, Mr. Eshton! You certainly seem to have a comprehensive appreciation of all the city has to offer. Would it not be pleasing to explore York in collaboration, as we did Millcote today?"

"Miss Rivers," he said. "Nothing, and I truly mean *nothing*, would please me more."

"Oh? 'Nothing' Mr. Eshton?" she saucily replied.

As amusing as their flirtation was to observe, I felt myself suddenly mired down in weightier topics. "If you will all excuse my absence," I said rather petulantly and went out of the dining room.

Directly into my study I went, leaving the door open and slowly paced about, sipping wine and examining this change of events carefully. I had no intention of leaving Thornfield at this time. Bertha was to be moved to Ferndean within the next few days, and so I must be present for this to proceed without difficulty. So for that reason, Jane's absence would be fortuitous.

Also, there was now the additional threat of Blanche scheming who-knows-what which left a sense of foreboding that blighted any consideration of venturing away. Furthermore, routine business required my attention, as well as discussions with my solicitor and banker on payment for Breault's investigation. Thus far, only one letter had come from Jamaica and that was sent by the attorney's clerk who merely acknowledged receipt of my request. Since then, nothing.

There was a tapping at the door. Jane stood in the doorway, studying me hesitantly. "May I come in?"

"You need not ask, Jane."

She advanced a few steps. "I am sorry to request leave of you at this time," she said quietly. "The timing is unfortunate and not of my choice."

I went to the door and closed it, placed my wine glass on an end table and took her in my arms. "I am not angry with you. I am disappointed," I said. "How will I watch you leave me once we are married? And after this upcoming weekend?" I held her closely and kissed her, my hand lowering to her firm bottom. "Hm, Jane? Tell me."

She smiled up at me gently. "You will not join me in York?"

I shook my head. "I cannot, my love. Obligations require my attention here."

"So we shall have a romantic weekend before I go. And I should only be gone three days." Then she asked, "Will we never have a honeymoon? One in which we travel together?"

"We will Jane. I will take you anywhere in the world you wish to go. And when we are exhausted from travelling, we shall retire to our secluded villa on the edge of the Mediterranean Sea."

"*Our* villa?"

"Yes. Ours. What's mine is yours. Do you think you would like to go there?" I gently kissed her cheek and down her neck, drawing her tightly to me.

"Secluded. On the edge of the Mediterranean? Just you and I?"

"Alone."

"Mmm. Edward. Why are we not going sooner? Take me there," she said and kissed me, softly at first, then deeply.

Becoming excited far too quickly, I brought my hands to her shoulders and held her away from me. "Jane. We marry the day after tomorrow. We must not become carried away before then."

"A little bit carried away, Edward?" she said, grinning and reaching for me. "You think about last night as much as I do. How it all took us away. Come, you must admit it."

"Yes, but I do not want to touch you again until you are my wife. I cannot trust myself, nor do I trust you to stop me."

She stood still and brought her hands down. "I would."

"No, Jane. I know how to send you right out of yourself, and believe me, if you give me half the chance, I will do it."

My words registered with her, and her expression went solemn. The pressure at her shoulders lessened and presently my hands dropped away. She backed further off and hesitantly began, "About my leaving on Monday…"

"What of it?"

"I've travelled alone before, and it is not so far. Here is an idea. Perhaps Diana will stay to attend the wedding and travel with me on Monday to York. St. John can collect Mary without her."

"It is not *the* wedding, it is *our* wedding. And I think asking her to stay would be a sensible option."

"Yes, Edward," she said and went to the door. "I took the liberty of directing Leah to prepare rooms for St. John and Diana. He will be leaving early tomorrow."

Peevishly I replied, "You took no 'liberty', Jane. Again, you did right."

"Thank you, Sir." With that, she returned to the dining room.

I went to my desk and settled into the antique chair. It did not occur to me until some minutes later that she had addressed me as 'Sir'. Our interaction had taken an abrupt and strained turn.

Is it not odd how our most sequestered and unspoken struggles have a way of roiling turbulently to the surface, unbidden by conscious thought? After a few minutes of heavy rumination and a smoke, I knew what my trouble had been. It was fear. What bridegroom does not approach his wedding day with some degree of anxiety? And it was true that I did not trust myself with her. Each intimate encounter we enjoyed thus far had escalated significantly and my thirst for her was ever present. I never thought judgmentally of her for allowing my kiss and touch and for giving of herself to me. Everything, from laying her hand over my heart on our first night in my chamber, to pleasuring me last evening; all were done from nothing but pure love for me. Love like I had never known in my life.

Yet, two nights remained before we were to wed, and I was determined to keep them chaste with no regrets or guilt of overstepping myself. Already there was enough fear and guilt with which to contend, and so when I woke on the morning of our wedding, I wanted to consider myself as blameless as could be. I would take her to church, a place where I felt God's presence with infallible conviction, and would make the most solemn promise of my life. No matter what a sheet of paper a half a world away claimed, this woman, this Jane Eyre, would become my wife. And never, ever would I look back with shame for my actions or doubt. If securing a clear conscience meant keeping Jane at arms length until I was invited by Mr. Wood to kiss my bride, then so be it. When called upon to do so, I could be the veritable model of self-restraint; a paradigm of virtue and abstinence. I could, really!

You do not believe me, do you?

Thoughts dutifully shifted back to my stratagem for the upcoming days. It seemed our plans would now be altered slightly, but these revisions appeared to be to everyone's ultimate benefit. St. John would depart the next morning for Harrogate to meet his sister Mary and continue on with her to York. I had hoped for our wedding to be a solitary event, with only Mr. Wood and his clerk present, but now Diana would stay to attend, and Arthur appeared so eager to be included that an invitation must be extended to him as well. Most fortuitously of all, when I ventured to move Bertha to Ferndean early next week, Jane would be conveniently absent. And all of this would occur with our wedding ceremony taking place precisely at the time I had staunchly dictated it would.

The remainder of the evening passed in the enjoyable society of my soon-to-be bride and our guests. Jane and Diana alternately played piano and sang while St. John shared details with Arthur and I on his plans for missionary work. An interesting and odd man he was. He may have been described as personable had he not been so priggish. As he spoke I wondered at his capacity to connect with another soul, and if so, what sort of soul?

Piano silenced, and as the hour was late, quiet reflection ensued. Feeling rather in my cups, I decided to prod the good vicar. "No wife for you, St. John?" I asked.

He drew a sharp breath, apparently finding my question impertinent, and diverted his eyes. "No."

Diana piped up from the piano bench. "St. John was in love, Edward, but he lost her. She tired of waiting for him to propose marriage."

"That is enough, Diana!" St. John said, his predacious eyes glittering at her.

"Why, dear brother? It is all true and unfortunately ancient history now. You see, Edward, St. John was in love with a wealthy young woman named Rosamond. And she adored him. But Rosamond was admittedly rather prissy and delicate, so since my brother insists upon pursuing life as a missionary, he felt this young woman to be an unsuitable choice despite his hopeless love for her. St. John delayed her, and the next news of Rosamond was of her marriage to another."

"Thank you, Diana, for that accurate if insensitive synopsis," St. John said and abruptly stood. "I am going to bed. Good night all. Edward, your hospitality has been most appreciated." Then he stalked out.

"He is very touchy about Rosamond," Diana commented once he was gone. "It is terribly regrettable that his taste in women does not meet with his grand plans of self-sacrifice as a missionary. But he may find his ideal match yet. There is someone for everyone I do believe. Not so?"

"Certainly, Diana," I said. "Arthur, was it not you who once said something dreadfully poetic of hope? That without hope, we die?"

"You are quite correct, Edward," he replied peaceably. I was pleased to see his eyes meet Diana's in exchange of a gaze resplendent with hope.

It was not long before the remaining party dispersed. Eshton had before him a journey of three miles to Stoneleigh Park, which should be a pleasant one as the weather remained favourable and the moon shone brightly. Diana bid him a heartfelt 'good night' as they enjoyed a slow handshake that continued for a full two minutes. Being a warm and demonstrative young lady, she then kissed Jane and I on either cheek, expressing her thanks for a lovely evening and found her way upstairs to settle into the room most recently occupied by Blanche Ingram. Eshton watched until she was out of sight, sighed, and departed with words of thanks for a marvellous evening.

Jane came past me in the entrance hall, and with a quiet "good night, Sir," began to climb the stairs. I grasped her hand to stop her. She turned and we stood eye to eye.

"Is that all?" I asked. "No more than a 'good night'? And what is this 'Sir' all about?"

"You said you do not trust me," she said, looking at her shoes. "I must admit that stings a bit. And you seem to wish for some distance and formality, so… I am giving it."

I brought a hand to her cheek, fingers into her hair. Eyes locked. "Jane, do not go yet. Stay."

She came forward and kissed me. Her hands she remained fixed at her sides, but good God, how her kiss could melt me, sending all conscious thought far, far away. All resolve could be replaced in an instant by my body and mind's single demand of 'More!, Give me more!'. I forced myself to think while her mouth kissed mine; my lips and tongue savouring the pleasure of tasting hers. This was precisely how our interludes became so increasingly passionate. Each touch and caress fit us together perfectly and lured us as if under a magic spell toward that final, ultimate act. Amazing it was to me, kissing her now, that we had not yet succumbed. Hell, I was stronger than I gave myself credit!

Her hands came tentatively up to my chest.

"Keep your hands down, Jane," I murmured.

She smiled and dropped them to her sides. She moved closer, her toes off the step, her body swaying against mine. "I feel you," she said, smiling and kissing.

"Do you?" I asked and gave the quote, "'Beware the fury of a patient man'."

"Mmm. Who said that?"

"Dryden."

"Well, Edward, 'A reserved lover, it is said, always makes a suspicious husband.' That was Goldsmith. See? I know something about men."

I smiled. "Stop talking and kiss me."

Soon, I had come to the end of my tether with this pleasurable diversion and stopped her. We stood before one another, conversing quietly and bestowing the occasional kiss.

"Go to bed," I finally told her. "Tomorrow will be hectic, and you need your sleep."

She nodded. "I must teach Adele for at least the morning hours. In the afternoon, I will go with Diana to Millcote for my wedding dress."

"Yes. The seamstress will have a second package for you besides your dress. You must not leave it behind."

She looked at me sceptically. "All right."

"Afterwards, go to the magistrate's office to obtain the certified copy of our marriage license."

"Yes, Edward."

"Then be sure John goes to The Black Swan for a case of claret I've ordered. The innkeeper will be expecting him."

"Claret? Who is that for?"

"You, us."

"Me?"

"Yes. Do you never read Geoffrey Chaucer?"

"Apparently not closely enough," she said with a fretful expression.

I laughed and grasped her shoulders, turning her away from me. "Go, my love. Off to bed." I would tell her the reason for the claret later. Maybe.

I watched her enchanting posterior form ascend the stairs, then turned myself toward the kitchen where Leah and John stood at the sideboard, wiping dishes and stacking them. I conveyed my appreciation for our remarkable and memorable meal tonight, then turned to the room's third occupant. Sitting at the table was Grace Poole, looking as weary and dejected as she had last night when I found her at the north tower door. She was drinking what appeared to be a cup of tea. With her, however, one could never be certain.

"Good evening, Sir," she said and stood from the table. She remained there, seemingly in want of a private audience with me.

"Grace, seeing as my guests have either departed for home or gone to bed, shall you and I have a word? In the study?"

She followed me there, and I set about lighting candles. "So, Grace. How did she behave today?"

"Oh, no trouble to speak of. Missus was quiet. Tonight she is bright and alert; on a rant about writing a letter to her brother, asking him to come take her away. It is the same thing every night."

I gave a short laugh. "She wants to write the letter does she? Does Bertha even remember how to read or write?"

"I do not know," Grace said thoughtfully. "She is not allowed sharp objects such as pencils and has never before written anything for me; only some scrawl with chalk or ash on the walls."

I waited. Grace had fallen silent. "And so, Mrs. Poole, is there something more you wish to discuss?"

I had not offered her a chair, hoping to keep our discourse brief. I wished to go to bed.

"Sir. It has come to my attention that you plan to marry in the near future." She paused, her hard-featured face set, unsmiling and unflinching.

'Oh, here it is,' I thought. Grace knew full well what Bertha was to me. This supposedly equable and respectful conversation might very well come down to a bottom line. "And what of it?" I answered carefully.

She glanced about the room for a few moments, then slowly swung her eyes back to me. "It seems to me, Sir, that your 'situation' must change."

My eyes narrowed. What in hell was she getting at? "Change?"

Grace nodded.

"It will. Ferndean is to be prepared for habitation."

"Habitation? By whom? She and I?"

"Yes. Precisely."

"Alone? Without a caretaker? And no cook?"

"I will provide what you deem necessary, Grace., as I've always done. If you want a servant and assistant in the house with you, I will provide it."

She drew a deep breath and considered that. "I see."

"I also have every intention of securing a temporary replacement for you as we discussed last night. You may take as much time as you need to get away, to see family or to have a holiday of your choosing."

She straightened to her full height, her shoulders set and facial features hard as if hewn in stone. "Well then. I thank you for your consideration of my future and… hers. May I extend to you my congratulations on your upcoming wedding, Sir?"

I responded with a nod.

And with a "good night, Mr. Rochester" she was gone.

I poured for myself a liberal dose of brandy and opened the diamond casement windows looking out onto the gardens, settled into the antique chair and brought boots up onto the scarred, time-worn desk's surface.

"Bloody hell," I said aloud and laughed. Even to me my laughter approached hysteria. I did not seem to have enough hands to hold back the walls crumbling about me.

'Damn it, let them fall. I am too tired to fight anymore!'

And with a smile on my lips, I gazed at the moon while sipping a marvellous vintage brandy.

I thought of Jane; of tonight on the stairs and last night in her chamber. The fire she ignited in me each time we kissed, the frenzy that rioted through me with her touch! She was my love, my future and my life. For too long I had been denied regular gratification, but with our wedding that would change. Alone now and relaxing, I wanted her intensely. Why should we be set apart when we were so much better together?

My boots went back onto the floor. I swallowed the remainder of my brandy down and closed the casements. Extinguishing candles on my way through the room, I went out of my study and up the stairs, onto the second story and along the darkened gallery where I came to Jane's door. I stood there for some minutes, thinking, listening and allowing that sweet pain of anticipation to wend its way through me. No sound came from within. My fingertips touched her door and brushed along the wood's grain, down to the cool brass door-handle. My hand closed around it and turned. The door opened.

Moonlit room. Casement window widely open. No fire, no candles. She lay prone in her bed, hands raised beneath her pillow, face turned away. She wore a white nightgown with hair smoothly brushed about her. I shut the door and walked around the bed. Knelt down beside her. So peaceful, no tension in her face and body. My hand went up, fingers smoothing her hair from her face. Soft skin. She made me touch her simply by being. Her lips parted and she inhaled a breath, then slowly turned onto her back, hands above her head. I loved to watch her.

Waking, she said, "Edward?" Her eyes opened and she gently reached for me.

"I am here, sweet love."

"Do not go. I will behave if you want me to. Only do not leave."

I smiled but my heart was stormy. "I will stay if you wish. Jane, I hurt you tonight and am sorry. I do trust you. You are stronger and more determined than I could ever be. I turned my own self-doubts around and made them your failings. They are not. Forgive me."

She softly stroked my face. Her hand went down to my silk jacquard tie. "I like this," she said, running the silk through her fingers.

"Do you?" I said, and reached up, pulling the knot undone. I removed it from my neck and nestled it against her cheek. "Then it is yours."

She brought it over her cheeks, lips, and forehead. Her eyes on mine, she unbuttoned her nightgown to mid chest. "What is yours is mine?" she asked and brought the silk tie down her neck and over her bare skin.

"Yes. Exactly."

"Am I yours?"

"Forevermore."

"Would you like to remove your jacket, Edward?"

I did. And waistcoat and shirt and boots. I climbed into bed with her. Nothing lusty, nothing frenetic. Just sweet, pure bliss.

Go ahead and be smug. You were right.

Chapter 29

I AWOKE THE NEXT morning in my own bed. A brilliant rising sun gleamed through gaps between the heavy velour drapes leaving a fiery rail of light across the bedclothes and myself. Nesting finches twittered noisily outside my casement, and Pilot barked from somewhere off in distant fields. I stretched, knowing I must rise and begin a structured day but groaned wistfully, wishing far more to resume sleep, for there I could luxuriate in remembrances of last night and in the extraordinary pleasures found during intimate hours with my Jane. Roused to wakefulness, I lay in bed thinking only of her. My heart's pace quickened and hands went up to block light from my eyes, wanting to see her in memory and feel her in recollection.

'My God, Jane. I said you are a witch. Your power over me is unearthly. Your love, enrapturing.'

My waking dreams took me to her again, in moonlit darkness as cool breezes and night sounds reached us from the casement. She drew me into her bed. Her kiss was passionate, her hands travelling over my bare chest and up over my shoulders. Fingernails grazed across my back. She lay me down. Like the ethereal angel of my dreams, beautiful and virginal in white, she kissed my mouth, slowly, sweetly and stirringly. Her fingers went into my hair. I felt a falling away of time and tension, truth and reason. She meant to give my body pleasure and to take it for her own. Her warm hands grasped my wrists and pressed them to the bed. She would not permit me to touch her.

Jane's purposeful, methodical love was all gently flowing sensation, touch and kiss. Her lips brushed my face and across my forehead as I breathed deeply of her fresh, warm, youthful skin. Eventually she released my wrists, and her mouth and fingers moved down my body, lingering for a while before slowly moving on. Her body was pressed atop mine, and she worked unhurriedly. Deliberately. Vulnerable and controlled, I was restrained by the spell she wove. Her hair swept over my bare neck, chest, abdomen, and oh, what a delicious sensation. Tactile sense narrowed, focusing on the precise nerves enduring her ministrations at that moment. Her tongue and lips drew excitement from my skin. Teeth would gently but firmly clasp; pain exquisitely intermingled with pleasure. She brought me to tremble and softly cry her name. My breathing was laboured. A voice came from someplace; mine, imploring her to stop. I cried out again, begging her never to stop.

Her hands at no time wandered where they had the previous night although it was not long before I found myself pleading for it. Her answer was a soft 'no, my love', single-minded as she was in her purpose. I knew from her own rapid breathing that an escalation of need raged through her as well. But my earlier words 'we must not become carried away' must have kept her closely in check for reserve and control remained well intact throughout.

Gently her lips kissed over my quivering bare abdomen to the waist of my trousers, her soft cheeks nudging the material down. Oh, I wanted it so badly.

With my fists together at my forehead, I sobbed and pleaded and growled, "Jane, please. Release me."

She worked her way up my body and licked my chest, her sweet torment nearly bringing me to tears. Her tongue lingered, searching and sucking. Fingers crept into the black hair beneath my arms, and sensation leapt to convulsion.

Side to side I turned my head. "Cruel... witch... oh, Jane. Love you so."

After an unknown time, her kisses lightened, scarcely touching my skin as she eased me back to myself. "Turn over," she breathed.

I brought a hand down to her face, brushing hair from her eyes. I would do anything she asked. "Jane. My sweet Jane."

She kissed my hand. "Turn over, Edward."

I obeyed, turning and raising my hands between pillow and my face. My eyes closed, focusing on her touch as she explored my bare back. I groaned deeply with content.

"Your back, Edward, is so strong and powerful," she said, caressing over rise of muscle and down the valley of my spine. "Your body is beautiful."

Gradually I calmed, knowing that her pleasures would be mine for the taking with only two days left to wait. I breathed deeply, following every motion of her fingers. Thus content, I felt assured enough in her acceptance to disclose a little known facet of myself. She would inevitably discover it anyway.

"Shall I tell you a secret, Jane?" I murmured.

I could feel her lips smile against my skin. Her hands came to the hair under my arms and caressed downward. "Yes. Tell me."

"Well, Jane, for many years, since adolescence I suppose, I've gone out into Thornfield's meadows during late summertime and helped with the haymaking."

Her kiss and touch came to a stop. "You have?"

"Mm hm. A man cannot keep a muscular body merely by conducting business or lazing about. And I like haymaking. There is something poetic about the work, cutting a wide swath of grass with a scythe." I lifted onto elbows to look back at her.

Jane's eyes met mine with a grinning expression of charmed interest. She bit her lip and brought fingertips to my shoulder, delineating each hard, sinewy detail.

"I would watch the farm labourers, working the fields near Lowood in the summertime. Some of the girls who remained all year at school would watch them, staying well out of view, of course. The men stripped to the waist and cut hay for hours in the blazing sun. They were quite fascinating to watch really."

I smiled at her over my shoulder, then lay down again. So this was the way my Jane's innate sexuality was first stirred.

"Tell me what you mean by the work being 'poetic', Edward. I want to imagine you at work making hay."

I drew a deep breath and considered. "Well Jane, it is an almost metronome-like rhythm of moving, rotating the body and twisting at the waist... step, swing, step, swing.[1] It is all efficiency of motion combined with strength. There is pride in the way tall grass is sliced and how it falls in straight, even rows, and then collecting it with hayforks into smaller heaps later to be raised with poles into great solid haystacks. True, it is hot work out in the sun during July and August, but I feel so powerful and vigorous and become as brown as an Indian after two months of manual labour that

---

[1] The Haymakers by Steven R. Hoffbeck, Minnesota Historical Society Press, 2000

I am quite sorry when we are finished for the year. All of this work must be interspersed with the continual management of estate finances of course."

She lay kisses down to the base of my spine. "Tell me then, why did you, the privileged son of a wealthy landowner, begin to help with haymaking?"

"I was never groomed as an heir, you must remember, Jane. I was a mischievous boy, bored during the summertime at Thornfield on holiday from school. I watched the labourers work and wanted to have a go. So they invited me to try. Father had little concern for the manner in which I spent my days and was glad to keep me occupied and free from trouble. He actually encouraged me to go out to the meadows each morning."

As I spoke, I visualized the sweeping waves of tall grass and listened to the rustling sound it makes in the breeze; blue skies above, birds calling, pheasants and grouse rising as I approached.

"I have always loved being out-of-doors, Jane. The sweet smell of cut hay, the beauty of nature, singing and working under the sun. Man can be no closer to God than right there."

She sighed contentedly, and I knew she understood as no other woman ever could. She asked, "Does no one pass comment on the Master of Thornfield Hall making hay alongside his farm labourers?" She now was slowly and deeply kneading the muscles of my low back with her thumbs.

"Only a few know who I really am. I keep to my work and never squander time in talking."

Her fingers beautifully loosened my tension.

"So, Jane. Does this revelation disturb you? Do you think such physical labour unbefitting of Thornfield's master and your husband?" I knew the answer, but reassurance was never wasted on me.

Her hands came under my chest as she laid her breasts to my back and nestled her cheek between my shoulders. "The truth?" she asked.

"Of course."

"It excites me to no end, Edward," she said and her hand roamed down over the curve of my buttocks.

I smiled with absolute content.

Our time together that night was more intimate and sensual than sexual; was simultaneously stimulating and relaxing. The hours spent in her bed proved relatively chaste as she was determined to remain consistent with my wishes expressed earlier. Soon we settled into a sleepy embrace. Her eyes closed and she no longer answered when I spoke to her. I held her to my bare chest for a while longer. Sometime after the entryway clock struck three, I disengaged myself carefully from her nightgown and bedclothes, and regrettably left her to seek my own bed. Once in my chamber, I undressed completely, slipped under the covers and with a smile on my lips, welcomed sleep.

So upon waking, the magic of last night was broken by daylight. I lay in bed and marvelled at the freshness Jane's love breathed into me since she first entrusted me with it. She and I together, our intimacy and sharing of our inner selves, created a physical experience unlike any other known in my life. In general, I considered myself experienced with the methods of giving and receiving physical pleasure, but adding love to physicality changed the entire landscape of my expertise. This was different. On so many planes was this different.

I smiled, knowing that last night it was I who had been led through unknown territory. My novice bride-to-be directed every step of a powerfully sensorial and intimate experience, and I simply lay within her mastery and submitted. The irony amused me mightily and I smiled broadly, allowing myself a final, luxurious stretch. I could not wait to return the favour.

'Well, Edward. Tis time you were out of bed,' I thought. A busy day lay ahead before I could be married the next morning, so I leapt up to commence my day.

I will not recount every tedious detail of that Thursday; only the more noteworthy. I cannot have you becoming exasperated with my compulsive attention to detail, and so for you, dear reader, I will attempt to abridge.

Alone I breakfasted in the dining room as I was accustomed to do and afterward received my stodgy agent, Phillip Bennett, in the study. A day of mind-numbing tedium commenced, replete with thorough assessment of the books, balancing of accounts, evaluation of current stock and share quotes, and the attempted deciphering of land contracts enshrouded in scarcely legible legal jargon. Philip and I found it best to save the last for my solicitor, Alistair Blakely, whom I was to meet in the following week for discussion of payment for Breault's Jamaican-based investigation.

I had a dreadful time maintaining concentration through all of this donkeywork. Magnificent strength was required to wrench my mind away from Jane and the sorcery of her love last night. The way she captivated and manipulated me, enticing sensation as she...

But once again I digress. Continually I strove to redirect my attention back to the dryness of standard business.

The post arrived in late morning as with every Monday and Thursday. Today it included only banking and investment statements along with the third expected letter from schools queried by Jane in reference to Adele's future education. I placed all three mailings together for Jane to review later in the day. I sighed with disappointment and frustration since this was the final opportunity for a letter to arrive from Jamaica before my wedding, and continually I cherished a feeble fantasy that correspondence would arrive, bearing at minimum some shred of hope that I was a free man.

'It does not matter,' I thought, flinging the letters down on my desk. 'I am not married! But tomorrow, I shall be. Tomorrow I will marry the only woman I have ever sincerely loved. I've waited long enough for her to come to me. Let nothing stop me now.'

Bennett and I broke for mid-day luncheon at one o'clock. I directed him to the dining room and welcomed him to begin his meal unaccompanied whilst I went in search of Mrs. Fairfax to whom I wished to impart a request. She was found exiting her rooms on the second story, and she turned from her door as I advanced, offering a quick, deferential curtsey.

"Mrs. Fairfax," I returned with a nod.

She charged ahead with exchange, issuing the following formulation. "Leah assures me, Sir, that you are in earnest concerning plans to marry tomorrow. Please accept my sincere wishes for a lifetime of happiness and prosperity together."

"Thank you, Ma'am. I do appreciate your saying so. Have you seen Miss Eyre today?"

"Oh, yes, Sir. She is with Miss Rivers, beginning preparations for the wedding. I believe they are now together in the gardens," she lowered her voice to a whisper, "but when I left Miss Eyre, she was washing her hair."

I attempted to conceal a smirk. "Yes, I imagine her hair presents quite an undertaking. Do you think, Mrs. Fairfax," I asked, diminishing my voice to identical hushed tones, "that she will allow me to assist with washing her hair once we are married?" I held an eager and sincere expression. Why did this old biddy transform me into a cheeky adolescent at every turn?

"Sir," she began, obviously scandalised. Her complexion went from florid to crimson. "I, ah, well, I am sure she can manage without..."

"Never mind that now, Mrs. Fairfax. I have a request to ask of you. I want you to replace the linens in my bedchamber once Miss Eyre and I have departed for the church tomorrow morning. Sheets," I said, stressing the word. "I want crisp, fresh sheets. Pristine white would be best. And pillows, Mrs. Fairfax. Lots of pillows. Towels and such." My gaze became more intense as her rheumy eyes widened. "And bring all of her clothes to place into the wardrobe. Her... **under things**, stockings especially. I want them, Mrs. Fairfax. Do you understand?"

The housekeeper's mittened hands came up, fingers fluttering about her quivering mouth. "Yes, Sir," she managed to squeak out.

"Good. That is very good," I muttered, putting on a nefarious smile and turning slowly away. I nearly bust a gut holding my laughter until well out of earshot. Part of me is perpetually fifteen years old. I confess it.

I went to a deserted bedchamber on the second story, one boasting the best views of Thornfield's gardens. From the window there, I could see my Jane clearly, talking with her cousin at the edge of a haphazardly arranged and brilliantly coloured perennial bed. She was attired in a grey Lowood frock and sat perched on a fence rail, swinging her black leather ankle boots forward and back. Her hair was thoroughly wet, dark and heavy as it hung down her back, and Diana was brushing through it, spreading its lengths over Jane's back to dry in the mid-day sun. Though I could hear nothing of their talk, Diana chatted away gaily while Jane listened with little interruption.

Diana was a pretty young woman, and I imagined that Arthur Eshton would find the loquacious, effusive manner of his new love interest entirely charming. But my eyes and thoughts were constantly on Jane. Even now, as she thought herself unobserved, she radiated an otherworldly quality that held me spellbound. She made me need her urgently, love her intensely, admire her completely, lust her a lot and even fear her a little.

Fear. Yes. It never escaped my consciousness that she was strong, self-reliant, stubborn and unafraid of denying herself for the sake of preserving dignity. If this love we shared were considered by her to be wrong, illicit or dishonest, then her love for me would surely extinguish like a flame in a rainsquall. Although it might try to live, it would eventually succumb and die. I knew this like I knew her.

She already had shown this to me once; upon returning to Thornfield from Gateshead, believing me to be engaged to Blanche Ingram. Eyes that could impart all that her loving soul had to offer became lifeless and cold at will. Her body that delighted in giving and receiving pleasure became all prickly stiffness. She could shut herself off and away. So yes, I did fear that side of her.

With a final glance to the pair in the garden, I vacated the bedchamber and proceeded to the dining room where I rejoined my agent. We consumed a fine bottle of muscatel with our enjoyable luncheon (especially good were Leah's treacle and ginger buttermilk scones) and conversed over coffee on the corrupt state of local politics. Now provided with sustenance for further hours of high finance enslavement, Bennett and I staunchly repaired again to my study and set about balancing the foreign accounts.

In mid afternoon, Adele's piping voice could be heard in the entryway. I excused myself from Bennett and went to speak to the child. Shutting the study door behind me, I greeted Adele with a teasing, "What is all this raucous noise about, *ma petite amie*?"

"Ah, Monsieur Rochester! Did you know Miss Eyre and Miss Rivers will take me with them to Millcote?"

"Will they now? All right then Adele, I have an assignment for you. Tell Miss Eyre that she must, and I mean absolutely must, order dresses for herself whilst at the textile warehouse for her wedding gown. They are to be pretty every-day dresses so that she will cease wearing those drab, gray things... do not tell her I said that. You understand me, Adele?"

"*Mais oui,* Monsieur! Dresses for Miss Eyre! I do not like the grey ones she wears either. She is so pretty and they are so plain."

"Adele, your perspicacity exceeds your age."

The child frowned. "Monsieur?"

"Your vision, your perceptiveness, Adele! Now go!"

Returning to the study and settling back before my duties, I heard distantly the sound of their carriage setting off.

After another hour of columns, numbers and mathematical equations, I had endured about enough of this fiscal affliction for one day. Bennett stayed for tea but departed shortly thereafter, and I was left alone. I reclined on the sofa in my study to doze for an hour, then went outdoors for a stroll in the gardens. I returned to the house, read a portion of Sterne's *Tristram Shandy* through which I had been slogging for over a week and spent an inordinate amount of time fidgeting impatiently. As the clock in the entrance hall chimed once again, my overwrought mind relentlessly drew all thought back to Jane. I wanted her here with me, securely by my side. This was a dangerous time for us, and it was best to retain her close. Wolves were circling in the shadows.

The dinner hour came and went. I took a companionless supper in the dining room; something done a multitude of times in the past but never received with welcome. I thought of last evening, here in this room with Jane and her cousins, reflecting that it was the first formal meal she and I ever took together and the first entertaining of guests conducted as a couple. But although she would become mine absolutely in mere hours, she would again leave me to lone meals and a solitary bed at the start of next week when she went off to York.

'She will be gone for only three days, Edward,' I thought. But I ached for her already.

As the sun descended to the horizon on this day approaching the solstice, I was immensely pleased to hear the rattle of a carriage entering the courtyard. In a few moments more, Adele's chatter was heard imparting with thoroughness the details of her Millcote sojourn to the staff. John's voice and then Mrs. Fairfax's twitter could be heard appointing tasks and imparting instructions, and amongst the commotion came the crackle of wrapping-paper. I stepped forth from my study to see brown paper parcels being dispatched up the staircase by Leah, Mrs. Fairfax and Adele. John remained in the entryway to greet me.

"Quite a pleasant afternoon we had in Millcote, Mr. Rochester," he said. "The claret was packaged and waiting at The Black Swan as you requested. It's in the carriage still."

"Good. I will bring it in."

"As you wish, Sir. I also confirmed that a team of men have begun improvements at Ferndean Manor."

"Excellent. So, where have Miss Eyre and Miss Rivers gone off to?" I asked, looking through the open front door to the courtyard.

"The ladies chose not to come back with me, Sir," he said with a confounded expression. "They wished to stay in Millcote for supper and then walk back to the Hall alone this evening. They went away to the book shop before I could raise objection."

I stared at him in astonished silence, then nodding resignedly turned on my heel toward the front door. In a decidedly downcast frame of mind, I went out to the carriage and retrieved the wooden box of wine, hauled it onto my shoulder and into the kitchen. I set it down and knelt beside it, absently prying off the top and placing bottles in the expansive pantry. The kitchen door swung open and Leah entered.

"Good evening, Sir. Oh my, you should let John do that!"

I sat back on my heels and wearily replied, "Wine is ultimately the charge of lord and master. And a single case of claret will do no harm to my back."

She accepted that with a shrug. "I was thinking this afternoon, Sir, of the mid-day meal requested to follow your wedding tomorrow, and I have an idea for both food and setting that may pique your amorous interest."

Enlivened by her creative devotion to the task, I said, "All right, dazzle me with your ideas, Leah."

"Well Sir, anticipating gorgeous weather similar to that we enjoyed today, what would you think of taking your bride on a picnic?" She followed with suggestive images. "Romantic, secluded, excellent food and a vintage wine. A blanket spread over the grass?"

As she spoke, pictures snapped sharply into my brain, and I was immediately certain that there could be no other way. "Leah," I laughed, standing and embracing her. "You are a genius. A picnic is just the thing!"

"I think she will like it, Sir."

I took her hand and patted it, thoroughly unable to clear the smile from my face. We nodded and smiled clandestinely at one another. With sincere thanks I left her and adjourned to my study where I poured brandy with a liberal hand. Taking both tumbler and *Tristram Shandy*, I went upstairs to my chamber, opened the casement widely and stood sipping, admiring the sky's last colourful streaks after a well-set sun. It was a warm night, and a gentle breeze swirled into the room. Momentarily I considered going upstairs to look in on the third story occupants, but the idea was discarded almost immediately. To look upon Bertha now, on the eve of my wedding, would be a desecration. Her face would defile my joyous anticipation and destroy the belief to which I clung of a blameless and virtuous quest for a true wife. Bertha could only rob me of the peace for which I prayed. So I dithered.

After removing jacket, tie, waistcoat and boots, I opened a few buttons of my shirt and went about the room lighting candles. With book in hand, I reclined on the sofa. It was quite a long while before I heard the first tones of talking and giggling that caused me to raise my head and listen carefully. Through the open casement, the sounds came closer and finally were in the courtyard just beneath my window. The creak of the front door followed, then silence, and that silence continued for a long while.

Eventually I grew drowsy and considered going to bed. But no. I wanted to see her. She had kept away from me all day; her attentions monopolised by a new companionship.

Was I jealous? Yes, I was! Jane was mine first. For a time I was her sole society. She came to me with no friends and no one to love her or protect her; certainly with no one to concern themselves at all for her well-being. I became her foundation, and slowly from the ground up, grew to be her comfort and shelter until I alone was her home. I knew of her longing for family and was genuinely pleased that she found kindred, but still, it grieved me to share her time and attention.

My book was set down and I arose from the sofa. I blew out candles, approached my bed and brought hands to my shirt to undress, but just then a soft tapping came at my chamber door. My heart leapt and I grinned. I wanted her in my arms, to lift her off the floor and carry her into my chamber. To lay her down - bed, sofa, floor - it mattered not. To feel her body and hear my name whispered.

Then I halted my step. 'We must not become carried away,' echoed a voice from some distant place within.

I went to my door and opened it. There was Jane, slowly pacing the matting amongst the shadows, dressed in her nightgown, with feet bare, and long hair brushed smooth. The moon shone through the gallery window casting its glowing luminescence upon us. I exited my chamber and shut the door behind me, leaning with my back against it, waiting for her to speak.

"Are you angry with me?" she finally asked.

"No."

She came near and looked up at me, reading, searching. "Your business conducted today? I trust it went well."

"It did."

She exhaled sharply. "Do not be angry with me, Edward. I enjoyed my time in Millcote with Diana."

I gave no reply.

"She lives so far away! I only want to know her a little before we go our separate ways. And this is such a beautiful night. I thought it would be pleasant to walk home to Thornfield."

"Was it?"

"Yes. It was."

"You returned more than an hour ago. What have you been doing?"

Jane sighed. "When we returned, I took Diana into the library to play songs for her on the piano."

Now I was becoming outraged. "You took her to the library so she could hear your songs? The songs that you wrote for me?"

"Was that wrong?"

"No, Jane. Go to bed. Mrs. Fairfax will wake you early," I said, turning away.

"Edward, stop this! You are behaving as if you are jealous."

There was no point speaking an untruth. "I *am* jealous!"

"Of Diana?"

I adopted one of my better commanding tones. Not my best, mind you, since I reserve that one for the most special of occasions. "Go to bed, Jane," I ordered.

"No! We shall discuss this now," she said obstinately, standing straight before me. In her white nightgown buttoned to the throat and her bare feet, she tried but did not exactly succeed in embodying an authoritarian presence. I cracked a smirk. When her hands went to her hips, my laughter came out unchecked.

She stepped close to me. "I am angry with you as well. I awoke during the night and you were gone."

I smiled down at her. "I could not stay in your bed, Jane. You know that. Besides, I do not sleep well in clothes."

She gazed at me mischievously. "Will um... will you require the same of me? To undress for bed?"

"It would be appreciated."

She grinned, lacing her fingers and bringing them to her lips. She stepped back and wandered about the matting.

"Did you bring the marriage license back with you?" I asked.

"You will find it on your desk," she replied.

Of course. Silly question. "And your gown. Are you pleased with it?"

"Very much so. I think you will like it," she said, continuing to walk in the moonlight.

"Jane," I said.

She stopped and looked at me.

"Come here," I said, pointing to the floor directly before me.

She came close again, her toes touching mine. "Yes?"

"My jealousy flares because I am accustomed to having you to myself. I can not endure sharing you."

She looked me over, and I could see in her eyes to where her thoughts had turned. "Do you think, Edward, that you will be sharing me at this time tomorrow night?"

My arms went around her, pulling her slight frame close. "By the time I am finished with you this weekend, Jane, you will not be fit to think straight, let alone hold a socially acceptable conversation."

She smiled, considering that. Her hands went up to my shoulders and around my neck. "Edward, I could not stop thinking of you today. I *am* yours. All of me," she said, taking my hand. "Heart," bringing my fingers over her left breast. "Body," directing my other hand over her flat abdomen. "And soul," lifting on her toes to kiss my lips.

Smouldering passion flared and I entwined her in my arms, kissing her full and forceful. Her hands came to my face, taking my mouth with identical feverish intensity.

She suddenly stopped, breathless. "Come with me, Edward," she said, taking my hands and drawing me toward her chamber. "For an hour, possibly two."

"No, love," I said, kissing her again. "We must keep to our own chambers tonight. Go now. Go to sleep quickly and tomorrow will come sooner."

She released my hands reluctantly and took steps toward her chamber, then stopped and turned to me. She said in pensive wonder, "We, Mr. Rochester, will go to church together tomorrow morning, and there we will marry."

"Yes, Jane. We will." I waited, watching her. "Are you becoming frightened?"

She shook her head 'no' and looked toward the casement into the moonlit night. With solid conviction she turned to me and said, "I would do it right now."

I stepped to her and took her again in my arms, smoothing her hair away from her face. White moonlight reflected brilliantly in her eyes as she looked to mine. No doubts between us. Never a moment of uncertainty. This, our marriage, is what must be.

I whispered, "My love. So would I."

Chapter 30

As is my frequently self-contradictory wont, I suspended my own order and detained Jane there on the matting, kissing her.

"Good night, my love," I whispered, unable to let her go though I knew I must. The warmth and wet of her sweetly pliable lips held me against my ever weakening will. With a hand to her cheek and fingers in her hair, I wrapped a husky arm around her willowy frame and strained her close. All strength was required if I wished to comply with my own decree. We must sleep apart tonight to keep from finding ourselves overtaken with passion, although both were consumed with desire. I felt it in her kiss. She was without fear or hesitation. She trusted me entirely and was prepared in every way to place her fate in my hands.

I broke our kiss and looked to her chamber door then back to mine. Leaning down I wrapped both arms around her middle, lifting her effortlessly off the floor. My heart raced and I breathed laboriously, resisting the impulse to take her to one chamber or the other. She was my love. It was only right to want her as I did; to desire the act of taking her to bed and making love to her. I almost could not endure the anticipation. All of me was crying out for her to be entirely mine.

My face turned up to hers as I held her high against the gallery wall, and I kissed and licked her mouth hungrily. "Oh, Jane. Love you. Make you my wife."

"Edward," she whispered with forearms on my shoulders and fingers into my hair. "It would not be wrong. No one will know but us. I do not want to stop and be without you tonight." Her thighs came to clasp my hips tightly.

"Shhh, Jane, do not tempt me," I breathed. "Your love. You make me weak. Tomorrow. We must wait until tomorrow."

With infinite softness she kissed me and gradually eased our passion down. Her body trembled against mine as my arms held her to me. "Edward. I love you so. Keep me with you always."

I set her feet on the floor and we stood for some minutes in tight embrace. "Jane. Promise me now. Promise you will never leave me. No matter what I might have done, you will always believe in me and will know that my love for you is true."

We stood there in the gallery, on the matting and in the moonlight, palms together and fingers interlaced.

"I will, Edward. And you must promise that your love will never change; that you will never regret marrying me, never think me too young, too disconnected..."

"Hush, Jane. Do not say such things."

"Promise you will never desire someone else," she said, and looked away with a precise individual crossing her consciousness.

I smiled and stroked her lovely cheek. "I promise you that, Jane. I never will."

Our deepest fears were spoken and nullified. Both felt the importance of this moment.

"I am glad you came to me tonight, Jane. How is it that you always know the way to strengthen us?"

She placed a hand over mine and kissed my wrist. "It is you. My love for you leads me there. No thought is necessary."

I smiled. "How very blessed I am to have found you. Or really it was you who found me."

We listened as the clock downstairs struck eleven times. Once silence resumed, I stepped away from her and said, "Off to bed with you now. I want you well rested for tomorrow."

She smiled and nodded. I watched her withdraw into the darkness and listened as her chamber door gently closed.

Returning to my room, I undressed and slipped into my dressing gown, then sat at the edge of my bed. Having no desire to sleep, I paced about, trying to keep my mind vacant.

Amidst the exhilaration of the hours preceding my wedding, there came the distinct re-emersion of an inner voice, one I'd been diligently working to keep at bay. In suffering Jane's absence from Thornfield these many weeks, I managed to silence the warnings once foisted upon me by logical and sober Conscience. Prior to her departure, the voice was quite at the ready, quick to point out every flaw in my designs and to warn of repercussions. Fears at one time consumed me. Doubts asserted that my love for Jane could only bring her harm and wrong. That feeling was once so unshakable that it drove me from Thornfield in hopes of finding clarity and resolve enough to release her. Pathetically vain was that misguided hope.

Our love soon proved to be forged of far stronger materials than mere human determination, but rather drove us together and moulded us like so much clay into a single vessel. Loving her felt entirely right and therefore could never be wrong. She knew me better than any woman ever had in my life and witnessed aspects of my nature and temperament sure to drive a lesser woman away. She accepted and loved all of me. The truth was now what I wanted it to be, and I would shape the future to my precise specifications.

I paced about some more before going to my open casement to lean upon the sill, breathing deeply of cool air and enjoying the silence of night. Distant, muffled voices came on the breeze, and I looked up across the courtyard to see a light, a lantern it was, moving between the battlements. The solitary glow reflected against billowing white material and long black hair. Grace Poole was slowly walking, holding the lantern aloft; her charge a pace or two ahead. Their words were lost to me but the tone was not. The two women were bickering irascibly; Bertha gesturing with peevish energy as her arms occasionally flung about and Grace answering with sharp retaliation. I watched them as they walked the length of the roof and turned back.

'Damn it, I meant to write to The Grimsby Retreat today, requesting Grace's replacement.' With all of the business drudgery at hand and my mind preoccupied with Jane and our wedding, that business was entirely forgotten. Well no matter, I would get a letter into the post on Monday after Jane departed for York. Then Grace and I would transfer a hopefully tranquil Bertha to Ferndean Manor where the change of surroundings might ameliorate her agitation and improve Grace's despondency.

The pair disappeared from view toward the roof's trap door and silence once again resumed across the courtyard.

No more weighty rumination or intricate arrangements to consider. Bed. Sleep. 'You must be in prime form for your bride tomorrow,' I told myself.

With my dressing gown thrown off, I slid beneath the covers, extending an arm to caress the vacant sheet beside me. This would soon become *our* bed, not only mine. "Our bed," I whispered and drifted off.

Every hour I awoke, listening to the distant chiming of the hall clock. Too soon the twittering of nesting finches in early morning darkness heralded a summer solstice sunrise. Restorative sleep must have come eventually for I next opened my eyes to a blazing sun at the ungodly hour of five. Despite a fitful night of little rest, I awoke full of audacious energy, lolling amongst the white cotton sheets and smiling contentedly as I imagined this time tomorrow morning.

My Jane would wake with me here in our bed. I would turn to her and delight in her unclothed beauty, revealed for me, her husband, in the fresh morning light. I would kiss and caress, touch and excite. Playing her along masterfully, I would ready her to receive me, and would again make love to her. I writhed with serene anticipation, closing my eyes and imagining such a scintillating scene.

With a rumbling growl I bounded out of bed, eager to commence this most anticipated of days. Today, I would make Jane my wife.

Quickly I donned temporary togs of khaki breeches and a coarse white winter undershirt. I chose to remain barefoot on this warm summer morning. 'Good enough until I've had a bath and shave,' I thought.

All bedding was torn away from the mattress and left in a heap at the foot of the bed. At my wardrobe I carefully selected wedding attire consisting of midnight black jacket and trousers, a crisp, white, high collared linen shirt and white silk waistcoat with matching jacquard tie. Diamond cufflinks. She would like this strikingly handsome, sophisticated costume. I held the ensemble together and grinned with vain satisfaction.

For another half hour I futzed about my bedchamber, tidying the writing desk and clearing space in the wardrobe for Jane's clothing. As I worked, a door somewhere down the gallery unclosed. Light-hearted female chatter commenced, moving quickly about between rooms and occasionally fading away to the first floor. John and Mrs. Fairfax's voices were amongst them, apparently arranging a bath for Jane in her chamber. Normally all baths except mine were taken in the annex off the kitchen, but today Jane would be introduced to the luxury of bathing in her bedchamber. I was abundantly pleased that Thornfield's servants had thought to extend this fond gesture of regard on our wedding day. She would become the Hall's mistress, and they undoubtedly were enthusiastic to see this long-vacant status once again occupied. Pacing the floor of my chamber, I enjoyed my own rising exhilaration. Finally, I could rein myself back no longer. It was time to venture out.

On my way to the staircase in a rather preoccupied state, I found myself outside Jane's door. There I remained transfixed, listening to water in motion, pouring and splashing. I smiled, allowing temptation to lure me. Should I?

Conscientious adherence to self-imposed law denied me a splendid episode in her bed last night, but, as you know, abstemiousness never was my strong point. So I moved toward her door, my hand reaching.

It suddenly opened placing Diana Rivers directly before me. She brightened and giggled, shutting the door behind her. "Good morning, Edward! Such a lovely day for your wedding, wouldn't you agree?"

"Good morning, Diana. Yes, the weather does appear to be in our favour." This impromptu charade that I had not been about to join my bride for her bath suited me just fine. "Jane is having her bath at the moment I presume?"

"Yes, she has only just begun," Diana whispered with a wink, then hurried off down the gallery toward her chamber calling back to me, "Sophie and I must press clothes! If you will excuse me!"

Listening for Diana's door to shut, my reply came as a low and rumbling, "Yes, off you go, Diana." I went directly to Jane's door and soundlessly entered.

Her bath had been arranged before a low fire in front of the hearth, and in its steamy depths my bride was reclined, submerged to her chest with her hair piled high and pinned atop her head. Dreamily scrubbing her neck, she sang softly to herself and did not immediately notice me. I gave an "ahem."

"Edward!" she yelped. Her arms came across breasts, knees rising out of the water, and she turned away laughing before looking up at me with a pleasing smile.

I went to the tub and knelt down on the floor behind her. "Good morning, Miss Eyre," I said, bringing a hand under her chin and tipping her head back.

"Good morning to you, Mr. Rochester," she replied as my mouth came down and closed upon hers. My impassioned kiss soon relaxed her modesty. Dripping hands went over her head to my neck, pulling me close. I drew my cuffs to the elbows and submerged both hands into the bath where they grasped her slim waist, moving up her slick body. Fingers lingered at side swells of her breasts and continued up, my hands wrapping around her raised arms. I gradually released our kiss.

"Mmm, good morning indeed," she said. Her arms came down, covering her breasts again. I smiled, wondering at her sudden shyness. "You should be having a bath for yourself," she gently chided and stroked my face. "And a shave?"

"Plenty of time for that. I want to have a look at the marriage license and get some breakfast first. Be sure you have something to eat as well. We mustn't have you fainting at the altar."

"Oh not me. I am too excited to faint." Her eyes sparkled gloriously at me.

"Good," I said and took the flannel to soap her back but stopped upon looking at it more closely. "What is this?" I asked, holding up the thin, grey square.

She turned to see. "It is a Lowood standard issue flannel, Edward. You dislike it?"

Noticing also a sparse grey towel that lay folded upon a nearby chair, I was horrified at the poor quality of her customary toileting items. "Threadbare things! You may instead wash and dry with scraps of lace! Get rid of all of them! Good Lord, I must take you shopping." Moving long wisps of wet hair from her shoulders I asked, "Despite necessity to involve this tattered bit of cloth, may I have the honour of assisting your bath, Madam?"

She laughed. "You may, but only for a moment. Diana will be back shortly."

So I gently washed her shoulders, neck and back with a soapy flannel. The beauty of her delicate body, particularly the narrowness of her feminine shoulders and the softness of her graceful neck, rendered me breathless.

"You are lovely, Jane. If I've never said it to you before, then I say it now." Wet to the elbows and kneeling behind her, one hand slowly washed whilst the other held her shoulder in a pliant grip. I suddenly became quite conscious of how small she was in comparison to my breadth and bulk. I lay a nibbling kiss on her shoulder and gently asked, "Are you nervous at all, Jane?"

She met my eyes and nodded. "I am."

"The wedding?"

"No, not so much the wedding. It is everything really; a new life, new name, expectations. You must know where my fears lie in particular. I rely upon you to teach me what I need to know, Edward. Do not assume I know anything because I probably do not."

I moved to the side of the tub and delved my gaze into her eyes. "Are we talking of the same thing?"

She bit her lip and nodded. "I believe we are."

"You are nervous to receive me tonight."

She blushed and drew knees tight to her chest. "Yes."

"Jane, I feel in your kiss that you want me the way I want you. Follow that need and trust me. Will you do that?" My fingers touched her knee exposed above the water's surface and slowly moved down her thigh until my hand was quite submerged. "Feel no uneasiness with me. You never have."

She eased, looking at me with trust and love.

Bathwater wet my sleeve to the elbow as fingers parted her modest thighs and brushed their aim. "I will escort your initiation with the utmost gentleness, my love. Today brings my task of taking you to soaring heights. Trust that I will."

She relaxed her arms across her peaked breasts, reclined and let knees touch bath sides.

"Yes. That's the way, Jane."

She sighed. "I do trust you. I only want you to be pleased."

I smiled at the blush over her chest. "If you are pleased, my sweet love, then I am as well."

Hearing a distant bustling clatter from downstairs, my fingers reluctantly abandoned Jane's silken smoothness, and she drew arms across her breasts.

"Enjoy your bath," I said, kissed her and went to the door. There I added, "I liked your song. Will you sing it for me later today?"

"If you like." And she continued to wash.

Downstairs in the kitchen, I secured from Leah a large mug of imported coffee selected for this distinctive occasion. In a sprightly humour, she handed to me a plate of toast with grapefruit marmalade and assured me that an informal breakfast would be on the kitchen table straight away. I leaned against the sideboard and polished off my toast whilst sipping from a steaming mug, reflecting that this was shaping up to be the best of all possible wedding days. Mrs. Fairfax entered, gabbling orders to Leah about preparing enough breakfast for Miss Rivers and Mr. Eshton as well, should he so desire to partake upon arrival. My housekeeper cast a tense glance and strained smile in my direction. I returned with a broad grin, sure she had discovered my visit to Jane's chamber this morning and disapproved of my taking liberties.

Going past Leah, I affably nudged her shoulder, raised my mug with a wink and a 'thanks', and went directly to my study to get a look at the marriage license.

Behind my desk, I opened the diamond casement windows overlooking the gardens. The picturesque scene drew from me awed admiration as it seemed that even the weather chose to smile serendipitously on my behalf. A gorgeous azure sky provided contrasting backdrop to the vibrantly coloured perennial gardens and to Thornfield's grey stone battlements. Clouds of puffed cottony white remained motionless in the blue heavens as the quiet of early day accompanied this pristine image. And so I took my place behind the antiquated desk of my study with a heart assured that my best days lay ahead and all motives exemplified none but sterling righteousness.

Sipping my fine coffee, I engaged in a customary informal manner of prayer and gave thanks to God. As evidenced by the incomparably beautiful day provided for my vows to be spoken to Him and to the woman I loved, not to disregard a rather sweet start to that day, I believed that He not only sanctioned my actions but encouraged them. I loved Jane so entirely, so unreservedly. She was brought to me by chance and accident; the only woman with whom I could find the love and acceptance denied me all these years.

"I am so very blessed, Lord," were my words. "Give to me the strength and constancy to be the best husband to her that I can be."

I sighed meditatively and enjoyed a damned good cup of coffee.

Alone and reflective, I recalled a humid, overcast morning in Jamaica long, long ago, in which a young and fresh-faced Edward Rochester anxiously awaited the arrival of his wedding hour. I could clearly see that youthful version of myself, resplendent in bridegroom attire, standing before a mirror. A fine cup of coffee was in my hand on that pre-wedding occasion as well, but it likely contained something more to the tune of three parts coffee to one part whisky. Conceitedly I admired my reflection then, actually believing that the beauty of my bride and myself were all the prerequisites necessary for a successful marriage.

Bertha Antoinetta Mason, my bride, was undeniably beautiful and engaging, yet was in every respect a stranger to me. Our limited interaction thus far had failed to prove one iota of affinity between us. Beneath my machinations to appear self-assured to the point of arrogance that morning, I prayed to my God then as I did now, but my devotions did not pour forth with gratitude from a committed and certain heart. They were a plea for assurance that I was not about to commit the most grievous mistake of my life.

No assurance came. What did arrive was a frantic Richard Mason. He burst into the room quite on the verge of tears and wailed, "She won't go through with it!"

I could see him in recollection, standing in my chamber, disconsolately informing me that Bertha refused to dress and absolutely would not marry me. My immediate sense was total relief. But after some seconds of silent reflection, I became more concerned with my pride and the certain humiliation this turn of events would bring me. So I left my rooms and sought hers, approaching my bride attentively, kneeling beside her chair to take her hand and speak gently.

I asked, "What have I done to displease you, Antoinetta?"

Her pretty face was clouded with anxiety. "You've done nothing. I simply feel afraid."

"When you are my wife, there will never be reason to feel afraid," I softly replied.

She covered her face with hands and sobbed. "Yesterday, when we were having tea, Richard came in. You went away to the windows together, and you laughed! I do not like the way you laugh. Your laugh frightens me!"

I held her hand, recalling the scene of which she spoke, but found no consequence in a brief, jovial conversation with Richard. I fabricated an explanation.

"But I was only laughing at myself, Antoinetta. You see, my dear, since coming to Jamaica, having spent so many of those first weeks sick in bed with the ague, I have lost such a terrible lot of weight. Greater than one stone! Here, look at the way my best suit hangs on me so poorly!"

She thought for some moments, then shook her head despondently. "You know nothing about me. Why do you see in me a wife? I am not your wife."

Caressing my bride's hand and kneeling before her, I reassured her as compellingly as I could. "Not yet, my dear. But you will be." Such words were spoken by me that morning, at that precise moment and then an hour or so later; words I since wished an immeasurable number of times to rescind. "I will trust you if you will trust me," I said, searching her dark eyes.

She was silent for a time, then she relented. And we married.

A nearby blackbird cawed loudly, returning me to Thornfield Hall, fifteen years after that day. I shook my head with habitual self-contempt.

"Forget that, Edward," I whispered. "You made a mistake. The Lord asks us to forgive, and that includes forgiving yourself. It is time to move on." I sipped my coffee and gazed admiringly at the morning sky as it deepened to a richer blue. The clock in the entrance hall struck seven times.

The study door creaked and Mrs. Fairfax peered in. "Sir?"

I began to rise from behind my desk with breakfast in mind. "All is ready?"

"No, ah, Sir, not quite. I hoped to have a word with you this morning, if you please."

I sat. "Yes, of course." I could not help but smirk, foreseeing opportunity to fluster the old lady with more sophomoric cheekiness. Brides and bathtubs for a topic, Mrs. F?

Clearly lacking her usual bustling punctiliousness, she came forward before the desk. The elderly housekeeper was uncommonly troubled. I ceased to smirk.

"Is there a problem, Mrs. Fairfax?" I solicitously asked.

"I do hope not, Sir," she began and then paused. I waited patiently and soon she found her voice. "Sir, may I ask your plans for permanent residence once you are married? Can we expect you to remain at Thornfield Hall? Or will you take Miss Eyre abroad for a honeymoon of indefinite length?"

Having not come to any decisions for long-range plans, I shrugged with uncertainty. So much hinged upon Breault's anticipated précis. "I imagine we shall remain here until mid autumn, Ma'am, then likely pass the winter months at the villa in Narbonne. I will keep you apprised, fear not."

"No, Sir, it is not on my behalf nor the staff's for which I am concerned. We are all quite accustomed to your unexpected departures and reappearances." Her fingers fidgeted before her starched white apron.

"And so...?" I urged.

Her eyes met mine and lips pursed colourlessly. "I thought it may be advantageous for you to take your wife away from Thornfield, sooner than the autumn, if I may express an opinion. Sir."

I leaned forward and looked up at her seriously. "Take her away? Before autumn? Why is that?"

Mrs. Fairfax shifted anxiously and cleared her throat. "I fear for your continued happiness, Mr. Rochester, and for that of Miss Eyre. She is very young, and I fear that she is without the worldliness to effectively shoulder adversity. Having become quite fond of her since she first came to us in November, you see, I merely encourage you to insulate her from...," she searched the ceiling for the right word, "...from distress."

"Distress?" I repeated hotly. "Jane and I are marrying! And you will come to me hours before our wedding and accuse me, your master, of bringing 'distress' upon my bride?"

She shook her head. "No, Sir. Not you. Not intentionally," She paused again and heaved a deep sigh.

My blood was beginning to seethe. "Make your point, Mrs. Fairfax!"

Her colour was crimson and her thin lips quivered. "I brought the post to you yesterday, as you will recall."

"Yes. It is here still," I said, nodding to the stack of unopened letters.

"Well, Sir, an additional letter arrived. One that I did not bring to you. It appears to be intended for Miss Eyre. I placed it in my pocket, meaning to give it to her straightaway but did not see her and forgot about it until late in the afternoon when she was out. Then I looked at it more closely. I think you should see it." The housekeeper removed a square of heavy grade ivory paper from her apron pocket and passed it to me.

The letter was directed to a 'Miss J. Aire c/o Mrs. A. Fairfax' with Thornfield's address to follow. There was no return address offered but the postage mark was stamped 'Huddersfield'. I turned the letter over. A ridiculously ornate seal in red wax secured it closed, pressed with an emblem that I had most recently seen upon an invitation to a house party. Foreboding crept in and coiled about my gut.

"Sir," Mrs. Fairfax asked quietly, "I realise my eyes are not what they were and my spectacles are of little help, but does that seal bear the initials B.I.?"

I abstractedly nodded. "Your eyes are better than you think, Mrs. Fairfax," I said, just discerning a B.I. amongst the flowery filigree.

"And so I am correct in assuming that this letter was sent by... ah, that it was sent from Ingram Park? And is intended for Miss Eyre?"

"Appears to be, Ma'am."

"I have no wish to trouble you on your wedding morning, Sir. Perhaps you will think me gossiping and meddlesome for saying so, but I do suspect malice is afoot. The severance of your association with Miss Ingram some weeks ago was not apparently to her satisfaction. Some servants do talk, Sir."

I looked up at her, predicting what would come next. It did.

"As with this and perhaps other issues," she said with a pointed glance, "you cannot buy discretion."

Piqued, I asked, "Do you, Mrs. Fairfax, believe yourself fully apprised of the details to which you allude? Details concerning Thornfield's third story occupant?"

"No, I do not consider myself entirely apprised, Sir, but John did impart your intention of readying Ferndean Manor for habitation."

I nodded vehemently. "Then allow me to assure you that shortly there will be no cause to trouble yourself in broaching *that* topic again. Do you follow me?"

Chastised, she softly replied,"Yes. I do, Mr. Rochester."

"Good. Now, if you will excuse me," I said with a nod to the door.

Mrs. Fairfax retreated, then turned. "I do hope the letter's contents will prove innocuous, Sir."

"As do I. Shut the door, please, as you go out."

I looked at the letter. Huddersfield. The town in which I purchased Jane's string of pearls during a visit to Ingram Park.

"Blanche," I laughed derisively. "Malicious bitch that you are." She took a stab at Jane's name and came up wrong, then attempted to cover her tracks by leaving no return address. Why then did she place her seal? I tore the letter open, my heart thumping loudly, and read the following:

> 10th June 1840
> Miss Aire,
>
> This missive is written in anonymity to protect your interests and mine. Please do not suspect that the following disclosures are designed to grieve you. With profound wretchedness in my heart, I ask that you devote careful contemplation to the truth and give faithful consideration to your own inexorable uncertainties.

I snarled aloud, "Oh, blow it out your arse, Blanche!"

> Let it be known to you that Edward Fairfax Rochester is a married man. It can be proven through inquiry to the Central Magistrate of Spanish Town, Jamaica that an authentic marriage certificate (number 4822) undeniably exists and is entirely irrevocable.
>
> Mr. Rochester was married in 1825 to Bertha A. Mason in Spanish Town. Mrs. Rochester is estranged from her husband but does currently reside in England.

My hand and the letter dropped to the desk. 'Good God, Mason. The details she was able to extract from your feeble mind!' Revulsion for them both led nausea to rise within me. I hesitantly continued.

> It pains and distresses me, though surprises me little, to learn that Mr. Rochester has entered into a romantic liaison with one so exceptionally young and inexperienced as yourself. One scarcely out of girlhood.
>
> You should be made aware that this profligate is no gentleman. He boasts an extensive history of brutish and lustful treatment of women toward his own licentious interests. A seemingly passionate nature belies the selfish and merciless heart within. Do not allow yourself, Miss Aire, to be deceived so callously and so perversely debased.
>
> I urge you to flee Mr. Rochester's treacherous presence immediately. My sincerest prayers are with you.
>
> A Friend

I flung the letter across my desk, watching with potent vexation as it caught air and ended up on the floor some yards away. My trembling hand

Rochester   323

dropped the coffee mug to the desk, spilling its contents over my wrist and miscellaneous banking papers. Irritation and wrath rioted through me.

"Damn you, Blanche! God damn you!"

Elbows went onto the desk and my head into my hands, this perfect day having suddenly turned to dreary murk and my joyfulness to despondency. Furious with Blanche, Mason, myself, God, anyone and everyone, I released my anger aloud.

"You'll not shake me! Blanche, I'll not give you the power to thieve my happiness and devastate this day for me. I will prevail over this and somehow, some way, bring you to suffering you can scarcely imagine!"

Expletives flowed and whirled, centralised around Blanche's name and image. What in hell was wrong with that evil vindictive bitch? She knew! Damn her, she knew! She knew with factual certainty that I was married!

Ever since the day in the bookshop when Arthur Eshton inadvertently revealed a connection between Blanche and Richard, I was certain she was plotting something. I could sense a menace associated with her very thought but held fast to slim hope that their link was mere coincidence or that her attentions were drawn elsewhere and away from me.

The goings-on in Blanche's viper's nest of a brain were clear. Since there was no way she could have me, then no one else should have me, and for her trouble she was bent on my eternal misery. She was absolutely irate that I had, as she saw it, strung her along these past seven years, wasting her efforts with the impression that I was eligible to offer an advantageous marriage. She was not going to let that transgression go without whipping me soundly for it.

'Oh God, to whom else had this information been passed?'

Dizziness took my mind as I envisioned a form letter disseminated to gentry over this and surrounding counties. Her words came back to me, and I remembered the glint in her ice chip eyes as she shook with fury saying, 'I will see you ruined in our noble peerage, you mark my words!' As she stormed off that night, I had no doubt that she would exert unparalleled spite to ensure my social ruin. She now had the artillery to do just that.

But such a *threat* really did not matter at the moment. What did matter was that Blanche's letter had been intercepted. Had it reached Jane, the outcome for this day would have been disastrous. Jane would have brought it to me, faithfulness in her loving heart, and she would have asked what that horrible Blanche was up to with such nonsense. Our plans to marry today would then be demolished. I would have brought her here, into my study, shut the door, sat her down and taken her hands. With unfathomable wretchedness shaking my voice and contorting my features, I would have told her everything. Temptation to lie, or at least dissemble, would have been formidable, but when faced blatantly with guilty accusation, I could not lie to her. Many times she had amazed me with her intuition, reading what was in my heart through my eyes. She would look into me and know.

Being despised by her as a liar would be worse than any other repercussion. I knew that the truth must someday come forth, there was no escaping that, but I wanted it to come from me, when I was ready.

"Not today. No. Today is for us and is sacred."

I ran hands through my hair, reminding myself that I as yet needed a bath.

'Sometime in the future, Jane, when we have been married, oh, a year and a day at least, then I will tell you everything. Once you have settled into existence as my wife and reasonable time has passed, then perhaps I will not fear losing you as I do now. Perhaps then you will choose to stay with me and love me despite my misfortunes and mistakes. As for now, I fear you would go. I am sure that you would, and my ensuing pain, our pain, would be unendurable.'

I went around the desk to lift the letter off the floor and stood with it beside the sofa, studying the seal. If Blanche so eagerly wanted anonymity, then why the deuce would she place her seal? Then it came to me. She did not place it. She left the letter in the hands of another, her ladies' maid perhaps, to post. It was this person who conducted the routine task of sealing a letter and sending it off.

'Is it too lowly a duty to post your own damned letter, Blanche? Your haughtiness, dearie, has tripped you up this time!'

This confrontation of Jane was really a rather inept attempt at injuring me. I read Blanche's letter a second time, counting her mistakes. She had Jane's surname wrong. It bore both her personal seal and her local post office stamp. And she was missing a number of truths that rendered my story infinitely more scandalous.

Richard was obviously careful in what he revealed, for how embarrassing it would be for him to tell a beautiful young lady the whole truth! That he calls a violently insane woman 'sister', and she currently lives imprisoned by her resentful husband; a circumstance he himself helped to orchestrate! Richard wisely chose to omit those particulars.

Blanche knew the year of my marriage but not the month or day. And what actually caused me to smirk was that the certificate number was off by two digits.

'Intentional, Richard? Or are you really so irretrievably obtuse?'

The last paragraph I thought priceless. 'A selfish and merciless heart', she wrote.

'Well yes, I am selfish, Blanche, I will give you that, but any mercilessness is reserved only for you, dear heart.'

And what else? 'Brutish and lustful treatment of women'. I supposed there was some truth to that as well. Women who valued me only for my wealth and station did inspire an eruption of my worst behaviour.

'Actually, Blanche, I am more the rough and ready type, and my soon-to-be wife *really* prefers me that way.'

My first urge was to tear the letter to shreds and throw the remains into the nearest fire.

'No,' Instinct advised me. 'Keep it. Lock it away, but do not obliterate it from existence, nor from your memory.'

I opened the desk's lower drawer to remove the locked box holding artefacts of my life in Jamaica, including the pair of briefly worn gold wedding bands. There I placed Blanche's letter, amongst all of the other caustic evidence of my reckless mistakes.

A tapping at the door caused me to start. The door creaked open. "Sir, your breakfast is on the table," said a bubbly spirited Leah. "And John has prepared your bath."

I looked up at her. "Thank you, Leah. I will be along momentarily."

A jovial, masculine voice could be heard in the courtyard, then in the entrance hall. Leah happily announced, "Ah, Mr. Eshton has arrived, Sir!" She went to him, offering a warm welcome, breakfast and coffee.

I shook away all adverse, fatalistic thoughts. Within a few moments a newly ignited purposeful and determined fire raged in my heart. Nothing was going to stop me today. No more years of emptiness, despair and heartache. My life thus far had been a wasteland of lonely bleakness, but today, today I would take for myself the woman with whom I was absolutely in love and would make her my wife.

I glared about at invisible enemies. 'Try to stop me. Just try it!'

In the centre of my study floor I went down on one knee and prayed, "God pardon me and man meddle not with me. I have her and will hold her." I looked up and considered my physical reaction to such a statement, deciding that I felt marvellous. God was with me, my bride was readying herself for me, and our closest associations were pleased on our behalf. With a little luck, this just may come off without a hitch.

The time was drawing near.

With a smile on my lips, I strode out of the study toward the kitchen in search of breakfast and a second splendid cup of coffee.

Our story continues with part two of three,

Rochester:
Consummation

By J. L. Niemann
Coming soon

Printed in Great Britain
by Amazon.co.uk, Ltd.,
Marston Gate.